W9-AEM-160

# IN THE COMPANY
# OF OTHERS

This book belongs to

Virginia M. Absher
110 Comfort Way
Washington, IL 61571

# MITFORD BOOKS BY JAN KARON

*At Home in Mitford*
*A Light in the Window*
*These High, Green Hills*
*Out to Canaan*
*A New Song*
*A Common Life: The Wedding Story*
*In this Mountain*
*Shepherds Abiding*
*Light from Heaven*
*The Mitford Bedside Companion*
*Jan Karon's Mitford Cookbook & Kitchen Reader*
*Patches of Godlight*
*A Continual Feast*
*The Mitford Snowmen*
*Esther's Gift*

## THE FATHER TIM NOVELS

*Home to Holly Springs*

## CHILDREN'S BOOKS

*Miss Fannie's Hat*
*Jeremy: The Tale of an Honest Bunny*

## ALL AGES

*The Trellis and the Seed*

## JAN KARON PRESENTS

*Violet Comes to Stay*
*Story by Melanie Cecka · Pictures by Emily Arnold McCully*
*Violet Goes to the Country*
*Story by Melanie Cecka · Pictures by Emily Arnold McCully*

*A Father Tim Novel*

# IN THE
# COMPANY
# OF OTHERS

JAN KARON

VIKING

VIKING
Published by the Penguin Group
Penguin Group (USA) Inc., 375 Hudson Street,
New York, New York 10014, U.S.A.
Penguin Group (Canada), 90 Eglinton Avenue East, Suite 700, Toronto,
Ontario, Canada M4P 2Y3 (a division of Pearson Penguin Canada Inc.)
Penguin Books Ltd, 80 Strand, London WC2R 0RL, England
Penguin Ireland, 25 St. Stephen's Green, Dublin 2, Ireland
(a division of Penguin Books Ltd)
Penguin Books Australia Ltd, 250 Camberwell Road, Camberwell,
Victoria 3124, Australia (a division of Pearson Australia Group Pty Ltd)
Penguin Books India Pvt Ltd, 11 Community Centre,
Panchsheel Park, New Delhi – 110 017, India
Penguin Group (NZ), 67 Apollo Drive, Rosedale, North Shore 0632,
New Zealand (a division of Pearson New Zealand Ltd)
Penguin Books (South Africa) (Pty) Ltd, 24 Sturdee Avenue,
Rosebank, Johannesburg 2196, South Africa

Penguin Books Ltd, Registered Offices: 80 Strand, London WC2R 0RL, England

First published in 2010 by Viking Penguin, a member of Penguin Group (USA) Inc.

1   3   5   7   9   10   8   6   4   2

Copyright © Jan Karon, 2010
All rights reserved

Excerpt from "My Butterfly" from *The Poetry of Robert Frost,* edited by Edward Connery Lathem. Copyright 1934, 1969 by Henry Holt and Company. Copyright 1962 by Robert Frost. Reprinted by arrangement with Henry Holt and Company, LLC.

Publisher's Note: This is a work of fiction. Names, characters, places, and incidents either are the product of the author's imagination or are used fictitiously, and any resemblance to actual persons, living or dead, business establishments, events, or locales is entirely coincidental.

LIBRARY OF CONGRESS CATALOGING IN PUBLICATION DATA
Karon, Jan.
In the company of others : a Father Tim novel / Jan Karon.
p. cm.—(The Father Tim series)
ISBN: 978-0-670-02233-5
ISBN 978-0-670-02212-0 (trade edition)
1. Clergy—Fiction. 2. Americans—Ireland—Fiction. I. Title.
PS3561.A678I44 2010
813'.54—dc22
2010024268

Printed in the United States of America
Set in Bembo

Without limiting the rights under copyright reserved above, no part of this publication may be reproduced, stored in or introduced into a retrieval system, or transmitted, in any form or by any means (electronic, mechanical, photocopying, recording or otherwise), without the prior written permission of both the copyright owner and the above publisher of this book.

The scanning, uploading, and distribution of this book via the Internet or via any other means without the permission of the publisher is illegal and punishable by law. Please purchase only authorized electronic editions and do not participate in or encourage electronic piracy of copyrightable materials. Your support of the author's rights is appreciated.

*To readers of this work,*
*I dedicate these words*
*from the Kavanagh family crest:*

# SÍOCHÁIN AGUS FARISINGE

*Peace and plenty*

# IN THE COMPANY
# OF OTHERS

# One

The beams of their hired car scarcely penetrated a summer twilight grown dark as pitch in the downpour.

His wife's fear of being hemmed in was only slightly greater than his own. As the road narrowed to a lane the width of a sheep track, he took Cynthia's hand and peered out to sullen hedges pressing on either side. He was peevish at being crammed into a rain-hammered Volvo with a testy driver and a box of books, which for some bizarre reason they had thought they couldn't live without.

He closed his eyes, then thought it best to keep them open. He was a lousy traveler. Indeed, the aggravation of getting from Atlanta to Dublin had exceeded his worst expectations. Following a delay of seven hours due to storms in the Atlanta area, the trip across the Pond had been an unnerving piece of business which shortened his temper and swelled his feet to ridiculous proportions. Then, onto a commuter flight to Sligo Airport at Strandhill, where— and this was the final straw, or so he hoped— they met the antiquated vehicle that would take them to the lodge on Lough Arrow. When he located an online Sligo car service a month back and figured how to dial the country code, hadn't he plainly said this trip would celebrate his wife's birthday as well as her first time in Ireland? Hadn't he specified a *nice* car?

In any case, they'd be getting no consolation from the driver, a small, wiry fellow so hunkered over the wheel that little more was visible than his headgear—a mashed and hapless affair of uncertain purpose, possibly a hat.

He had visited County Sligo as a bachelor ten years ago, with his attorney cousin, Walter, and Walter's wife, Katherine; they had driven to and from the fishing lodge on this same road. In any weather, it was no place to meet oncoming vehicles.

He unbuckled the seat belt and leaned forward.

'Aengus, I think we should pull off.'

'What's that?'

'I think we should pull off,' he shouted above the din of rain and wipers.

'No place to pull off.'

'Ask him how he can possibly see anything,' said Cynthia.

'How can you possibly . . . ?'

'I see th' wall on m' right an' keep to it.'

'Doesn't appear to be any cars coming, why don't we stop and wait it out?' Torrential. Second only to the hurricane he'd driven through in Whitecap.

'I'll get round th' bend there an' see what's ahead.' Aengus muttered, shook his head. 'Bleedin' rain, an' fog t' bleedin' boot.'

'It's what keeps you green,' shouted his wife, opting for the upbeat.

'That's what they all say. M'self, I'm after goin' on holiday to Ibiza.'

He sat back and tried to stuff his right foot into the shoe he'd removed on entering the car.

'Timothy,' said his wife, 'if there's no place to pull off, what happens when people meet another vehicle?'

'Someone has to back up. I never quite understood how that gets decided. Anyway, there'll be a pull-off along here somewhere; they seem to appear at very providential places.'

'When he said he keeps to the wall, I realized those aren't hedges. There's stone under all those vines.'

He thought she looked mildly accusing, as if he'd neglected to pass along this wisdom.

'Walls!' reiterated Aengus. 'Landlord walls.'

He had promised her this trip for years, and for one reason or another, it had been often deferred, twice rescheduled, and even now there was a glitch. Last week, Walter and Katherine had been forced to postpone tomorrow's planned arrival in Sligo until four days hence. Walter's apologies were profuse; after months of red tape and head scratching, he said, the date for meeting with a big client had come out of the blue. His cousin hated the inconvenience it would cause; after all, Katherine was the only one among them with guts to drive the Irish roadways. She was a regular Stirling Moss—fearless, focused, fast. Too fast, the cousins had long agreed, but what could they do? They were both cowards, unfit for the job.

Until Walter and Katherine arrived at the

lodge with wheels, he and Cynthia would be stuck like moss on a log. 'How will you manage?' Walter had asked.

'Very well, indeed,' he said. In truth, Walter and Katherine's delay was the best of news. He and Cynthia were badly in need of four uneventful days, having been thrashed by the affairs of recent months.

Soon after she fractured her ankle and lapsed, unwilling, into what she called her Long and Unlovely Confinement, he learned he had a half-brother in Mississippi. There had been a few shocks in his seventy years, most of them occurring during forty-plus years as a priest, but never anything like this.

As a kid, he'd once pulled that nearly impossible stunt of St. Paul's and prayed without ceasing—for a brother. It didn't work. Then, sixty years later, there was Henry Winchester. Henry, with acute myelogenous leukemia, needing stem cells from a close relative.

He had quartered in Memphis with Cynthia for weeks, giving over his stem cells through apheresis, standing watch at Henry's bedside and feeling in an odd and confusing way that he was fighting for his own life. His long road trip in a vintage Mustang hadn't helped, of course.

Then, playing out the proverb of 'when it rains it pours,' came the sudden flare-up of his diabetes only days ago.

'There's no way we're not going,' he told his wife, whose recent sixty-fourth birthday had gone largely uncelebrated.

'There's no way we're not going,' he told his doctor, who had seen him through two diabetic comas and was as hidebound as they come. Hoppy Harper had preached him the lipids sermon followed by the exercise sermon, pulled a stern face to ram the points home, then caved. 'So, go,' he said, popping a jelly bean.

Four days. To walk the shores of Lough Arrow. To row to an island in the middle of the lake and picnic with Cynthia. To sit and stare— gaping, if need be—at nothing or everything.

It would be roughly in the spirit of their honeymoon by the lake in Maine, where their grandest amenity was a kerosene lamp. It had rained then, too. He remembered the sound of it on the tin roof of the camp, and the first sight of her in the white nightgown, her hair damp from the shower, and her eyes lit by an inner fire that was at once deeply familiar and strangely new. He hadn't really known until then why he'd never before loved profoundly.

Cynthia nudged him with her elbow. 'We're around the bend.'

He leaned forward and shouted, 'We're around the bend. You were going to stop.'

'There's nothin' so bad it couldn't be worse—another bend comin' up.'

He sank back in the seat. 'That's the way of bends. They keep coming up.'

'What am I t' call you?' shouted Aengus. 'Are ye th' father or th' rev'rend?'

'Reverend,' he said. 'I'm the Father back home, but in your country only Catholic priests are addressed as Father.'

'Here for th' fishin', you an' th' missus?'

'No fishing.'

''t is th' fishin' capital of th' west, you should have a go at it.'

'We could reach out and touch those walls,' she said. 'It looks like we're going to rip the side mirrors off their hinges.'

He made another feckless go at shoeing his right foot. 'Always looks that way.' His earlier foray here had earned him rights to play the old head. 'Never happens.'

Aengus gave him a shout. 'I've been thinkin', Rev'rend.'

'What's that?'

'There's seven or eight them Kav'na families in Easkey.'

'Good. Wonderful.'

She foraged in her handbag, which did double duty as mobile library and snack hamper. 'Here,' she said. 'Eat this. It's been four hours.'

Raisins. He ate a handful with a kind of simple shame, recalling chocolate with macadamias.

She leaned close, her breath warm in his ear. 'Do you think he does this for a living? He isn't wearing a uniform or anything.'

'Ask him,' he said. He was sick of yelling.

She unbuckled her seat belt and leaned forward to the hat. 'Mr. Malone, do you do this for a living?'

'What's that?'

'Drive tourists. Is it what you do . . . all the time?'

''t is the only time. 't is m' brother's oul' clunker. I mow verges for th' Council at Sligo.'

She sat back and rebuckled. 'He mows verges,' she said, looking straight ahead. 'It's the only time he's done this.'

There was no point in pursuing that line of thought. 'The sides of the road where weeds grow,' he said, in case she didn't know from verges.

Rain drummed the roof. The fan in the dash spewed air smelling of aftershave. They moved at a crawl.

'Mother of God!' shouted Aengus.

The sudden slam of brakes jolted them forward. A blinding light . . . on top of them. His heart pounded into his throat.

Aengus flashed the Volvo's high beams, scraped the gears in reverse, and squinted into the rearview mirror.

'Bloody lorry,' he snapped. 'We'll be backin' up.'

# Two

The walls ended; the rain slackened; parting clouds liberated scraps of pale light. The hedges now were merely tumbled stones and August bloom twined with ivy, foxglove, scarlet creeper.

Aengus Malone had learned a certain dexterity on his mower; his skill at locating and backing into the previously overlooked pull-off had been brilliant. The lorry driver had given three blasts of his horn as a thumbs-up.

'That was some scrape you bailed us out of,' he said to Aengus. 'Well done.'

'It's m' lucky hat that done it.' Aengus reached up and patted the thing. 'Me oul' mum give it to me.'

'If it weren't so dark,' said Cynthia, 'we might see a rainbow.'

'There's some as see rainbows at night, but those would be fairies.'

'You believe in fairies?'

'Ah, no, not a bit. But they're there noneth'less.'

'You've never seen one, then?'

'If it's fairies ye're after, they're said to be very numerous in Mayo.'

On a slope in a grove of ancient beeches, the dusky, formless shape of the lodge appeared, its windows luminous against a starless night.

His wife drew in her breath.

Broughadoon.

'That would be candles burnin',' said Aengus. The Volvo rattled over a cattle grate. 'Looks like th' rain's shut down your power.'

'Stop,' said Cynthia. 'Please.'

Aengus braked; the motor idled.

'It's the most beautiful sight I've ever seen.'

She sat for a moment, bound in one of her spells, then opened the door. A pure and solemn air spilled in; his right foot slipped into his loafer.

She got out of the car and stood looking along the slope to the fishing lodge, at fog drifting among the cloistered beeches. 'Listen,' she said.

They listened.

'Nothin' much t' hear,' said Aengus.

Rain dripped from the shadowed trees, pattered on the roof of the car; a breeze stirred.

He watched as she got back in the car and closed the door and looked at him and smiled. Then she leaned to him and kissed him. Her faint scent of wisteria mingled with the Sligo air. He had never been so happy in his life.

As they drew up to the lodge, figures appeared on the stoop, silhouetted against the light from the open front door. Three barking dogs bounded onto the gravel and squared off with the Volvo.

There was a considerable shaking of hands with innkeepers Liam and Anna Conor, as the dogs ganged a-glee about their feet—two Labradors, and a Jack Russell dancing on its hind legs.

Anna, the striking-looking woman he'd known a decade earlier, gave him a hand-wringing that jimmied his teeth. He admired all over again her tousle of copper-colored hair and, without meaning to, blurted the sentiment aloud.

They were joined by a white-haired old man wearing a tie and cardigan and brandishing a walking stick. In the gabble of greetings, he decried their weather as 'foul and infernal.'

Somewhere, thanks be to God, something

was cooking. 'Lamb,' he said to his wife. He could devour a table leg.

He recognized the feeling he experienced on his wedding day nearly eight years ago—as if he'd lost the proper sense of things and stepped outside his body. He was a cannonball fired directly from the quiet desperation of a hired car into a domestic muddle of energy and good cheer.

They were herded through an entrance hall, its walls fairly crammed with fish mounted in glass cases, and into a sitting room lit by candles and an open fire. A half-finished jigsaw puzzle was spread on a table among a loose aggregation of sofas and wing chairs.

He felt at once the keen pleasure of the room: its book-lined walls and good pictures, the impression of ease.

In a corner, three men murmured over a card game by the light of a candle. A distinguished-looking fellow sat reading a newspaper by the firelight and stroking his white mustache; upon seeing them, he stood at once and buttoned his jacket.

'Heads up, gentlemen . . .' Anna lifted a small bell from the sofa table and pealed it. 'Reverend Timothy Kav'na and Mrs. Kav'na of North Carolina, meet our anglers—Tom Snyder of Toronto, Hugh Finnegan of Maryland,

and there's Pete O'Malley. Pete's a Dub who lived many years in Texas.'

'O'Malley here.' O'Malley stood, saluted. 'Welcome.' The other two pushed back their chairs, stood, raised a hand.

'They're with us every August since 1997,' said Anna. 'They're after catching our dinner tomorrow.'

He gave the trio a thumbs-up. 'Go, Terps,' he said to Hugh Finnegan.

'And there's Seamus Doyle from up the hill at Catharmore, who visits most evenings with the Labs. Seamus is our master of assorted entertainments, chiefly checkers and jigsaw puzzles.'

Seamus of the white mustache crossed to them for another round of hand-shaking. 'How long will you be in Ireland, Reverend?'

'A couple of weeks.'

'They say a couple of weeks makes a habit.'

'We wouldn't be against it. Not a bit.'

'I spent a lot of years in the States. Always good to see someone from the oul' country, as I call it.'

He surveyed the room and those in it—a whole universe of life and pluck at the end of a narrow road in the middle of nowhere.

Somehow, the two three-suiters, the umbrella, and the glasses case he'd left on the back-seat got toted in by Liam. Then came Aengus, tailed by the two Labs, schlepping the carton of books, their carry-ons, a flashlight, and the box of raisins. Off they went across a sitting room carpet worn to the lining, and along a hall, where the lot of them vanished into the gloom. A young woman with a nose ring and cheek tattoo offered hot towels; the Jack Russell sat at his feet, looking up, a chewed shoe clenched in its jaws.

It was all a dazzle. After years of talking, planning, and idle speculation, they were here. He wanted to sprawl before the open fire like a lizard and lose consciousness.

Cynthia had stepped away to look at a painting he remembered—of men in curraghs spearing basking whales in the treacherous seas off Arranmore.

'It's good to have you back,' said Anna. There was an honest country style about her garb of shirt, skirt, apron, and clogs.

'It's great to be back. The trip is my wife's birthday present.'

''t is no surprise your wife is beautiful.'

'Yes,' he said. 'Inside and out.' He wasn't likely to get over his pride in showing her off. That they were married at all still waked an astonishment in him. 'We're both needing a few days to unwind. There's no better place to do it than here.' The most excitement he could recall from his first visit was a wandering cow in the kitchen garden.

He wiped his hands with the towel and replaced it on the tray. 'Many thanks,' he said to the server, who cast a cool glance beyond his.

'We're so sorry about the power being out, but it happens often with the big rains.' Anna turned and spoke to Cynthia. 'I hope you don't greatly mind candle power, Mrs. Kav'na.'

Cynthia came to them and slid her arm in his. 'Not in the least. I love candle power.'

'Such dreadful weather, it's been raining for three weeks. I do apologize.'

'Please call me Cynthia, and you needn't apologize for anything at all. I love rain.'

The old man stumped up with his cane. 'A villainous rain!' he declared in a loud voice.

'Meet my father, William Donavan, he's our keeper of the fire at Broughadoon. The Kav'nas are from the States, Da. North Carolina.'

'Rev'rend, missus, good evenin' to you. We're destroyed by th' rain entirely.' William removed a handkerchief from his vest pocket and gave his nose a fierce blowing.

He reckoned William a handsome man,

even with a once-broken nose that had been badly set. The rope of an old scar crossed his left temple.

'Now, now, Da, not entirely. But no one goes hungry,' she assured them, 'our Aga is fired by oil and there's a lovely rack of lamb roasting for your dinner.'

'I'm desperate with th' hunger,' said the old man.

'Our own lamb,' she said. 'We hope you'll approve. The dining room in thirty minutes, then, straight down the hall and to the right. Flashlights and chamber sticks on the book table.'

'Chamber stick,' said Cynthia, not knowing the term.

Anna laughed. 'Something to stick a candle in and light the way to your bedchamber. Oh, and when you're ready to retire, we'll bring buckets of hot water so you can have a wash.'

A good-looking woman brimful of energy, just as he remembered. Ten years ago, she appeared to run the place virtually single-handed. He didn't remember meeting William before, or Liam.

'And what may I get you in the meanwhile?' asked Anna. 'Whiskey? Glass of wine? Cup of tea?'

'A cup of tea,' said his wife. 'I'll just find the powder room first.'

'Ditto,' he said.

'Straight across there, next to the sheep painting. And behind the sofa there's the honesty bar and a box for outgoing mail.'

Aengus arrived at his elbow. Something looked very different about their driver, though he couldn't say what. A brown fellow, wrinkled as a dried apple.

'Bang-up, Aengus. Thank you.'

'Ah, well, we didn' get drownded, so.'

Owing to the criminal diminution of the dollar, this would be no mean gratuity; he dug into his pocket and pressed more than a few euros into Aengus's hand. He was in turn handed a business card troubled by age and a series of phone numbers crossed through in pencil.

'You'll have no vehicle a'tall 'til th' cousins come. Best give us a shout if there's need.'

'What if you're mowing?'

'We'll send a cousin of our own, we've thirty-odd, m' brother an' me.'

'Thank you, Mr. Malone,' said Cynthia. 'Be safe out there. Not too much backin' up, if you please.'

Aengus grinned, a sudden and remarkable sight, and hurried out.

'You first.' She nudged him toward the sheep painting.

'Ladies first.'

'What's that smell?'

'Turf. They're burning turf. Takes some getting used to.' He remembered how much he'd learned to like the pungent odor.

Liam bounded up. 'Everything is in your room, Reverend. I hope you'll be happy with us. Welcome again to Broughadoon.'

'Thank you, we're thrilled to be here.'

A lean, handsome Irish face, he thought, with intense blue eyes and hair graying at the temples. 'I don't believe we met when I visited a few years ago.'

'I was helping rebuild the west wing of the oul' place, and keepin' my head down. There's still work going on, I hope it won't disturb you. Anyway, you'll see more of me this trip, I'll be givin' a hand with dinner and cookin' your breakfast.'

'The full Irish breakfast I so fondly remember?'

'And skip the blood pudding, Anna says.'

'Correct. My wife, however, is eager for the blood pudding!'

Liam laughed. 'Is she Irish?'

'Her maternal double-great-grandmother

was from Connemara, but we know nothing
about her except she was very cheerful-looking
and played the fife.'

'I expect you met the lorry coming in.'

'I'll say.'

'Sorry about that. It was my wine whole-
saler, he was held up by the storm and finally
had to run for it. By the way, the delay of your
cousin and his wife opened up the room they
requested. Always the silver lining.'

'Always,' he agreed. 'The books. I don't recall
seeing so many books last time, or paintings.'

'My father's library passed to me years ago;
we finally got the shelves built last spring.'

'Beautiful millwork on the shelves.'

'Thanks.'

'You did it?'

'My da was a builder, I grew up with a hammer an' saw. I wanted his books to have a good
show. A few good pictures also passed to me,
including a Barret you'll see in the dining
room—it's a beauty in afternoon light. Anyway, books and pictures for me, and the house
up the hill for my older brother, Paddy, thanks
to God.'

'Thanks to God!' Sitting nearby with Seamus, William thumped his cane on the floor.

'Refresh my memory. What's the meaning of the name Broughadoon?'

'From the Irish, *both an dún*—hut of the fort.'

'This being the hut, and the fort being . . . ?'

'Catharmore—on th' hill above.'

'So. It's a pleasure to see an open fire.'

'Ireland's gone modern, I'm afraid, though Anna and I try to keep some of the oul' ways. Speakin' of oul' ways, sorry about the power, 't is usually back on in no time.'

Through the open window, he glimpsed the taillights of the Volvo disappearing along the road. And there, on the antlers of a mounted deer head, hung Aengus's hat, as shapeless off as it had been on.

'Aengus Malone forgot his hat,' he told Liam. He felt oddly remorseful.

'So he did. We'll leave it just there 'til he comes again.'

They had no plans for Aengus to come again, as they'd be traveling with Stirling Moss in the future. 'A pity he left it,' he said, 'his old mum gave it to him.'

'Aengus Malone forgot his hat,' William announced to Seamus. 'Leave it just there 'til he comes again.'

Seamus was filling his pipe. 'Aye,' he said, looking up and smiling. 'Will do.'

On going in to dinner, he spied a large, well-thumbed book lying open on a table by the dining room door. Names lined the pages.

'Want to sign the guest book?' he asked Cynthia.

'I'll do it tomorrow; I'm famished.'

He couldn't resist. Squinting in the dusky light of the candle sconces, he picked up the pen and made the inscription.

*Timothy A. Kavanagh, Mitford, North Carolina.*

There. His Irish name in an Irish book, on the heels of an Irish rainstorm. It was official.

# Three

They found extra blankets, and piled covers on until the pair of them were pressed flat as hoecakes. It's the way he'd slept as a boy in Mississippi, beneath the heavy homemade quilts of his Grandpa Howard's country house bed.

'Wonderful dinner,' she murmured. 'Lovely people. Great pillows.'

'Happy?' he asked.

'Happy.'

They lay facing each other in the light from a candle in the chamber stick.

'You're trembling,' he said. 'Shall I close the window?'

'No, I'm just excited by it all. I'm glad it took so many years for us to get here.'

'You're glad?'

'That it was long delayed and hoped for makes it all more precious. I love Broughadoon, it's just right for us.'

He felt the blood beating in his temples; blood removed to America by his ancestors in 1858, and now returned. 'What would you like to have from this trip?'

'Time to enjoy being in my skin. There's something by Thomas à Kempis: "Everywhere I have sought rest and not found it, except sitting in a corner by myself with a book." I want to sleep in tomorrow—sit in that lovely old chair in the corner and read, and listen to the sounds of this place, and speculate.'

He was not keen on her speculations; they led to rearranging rooms, writing and illustrating books, painting kitchens and hallways, having fifteen yards of topsoil hauled in.

In the distance, the bleating of a sheep. Rain rustled in the downspouts.

'One of the poems is coming,' she said.

One of the Yeats poems she had worked for weeks to memorize and which he hadn't yet heard.

'It must be recited,' she said, 'or it might go away.'

'You don't want to wait for a bench in the garden or a stroll along the lough?'

'Are you too worn to hear it?'

'Never. Count me never too worn.'

> I went out to the hazel wood,
> Because a fire was in my head,
> And cut and peeled a hazel wand,
> And hooked a berry to a thread,
> And when white moths were on the wing,
> And moth-like stars were flickering out,
> I dropped the berry in a stream
> And caught a little silver trout.

He lay looking at her in the sheen of candle-light, realizing again that he was fond of the lines at the corners of her mouth.

'Moth-like stars,' he said. 'Yes, go on.'

> When I had laid it on the floor
> I turned to blow the fire aflame,
> But something rustled on the floor,
> And some one called me by my name.
> It had become a glimmering girl
> With apple blossom in her hair

Who called me by my name and ran
And faded through the brightening air.

She had worked hard to memorize poems by
the Dublin-born poet besotted with Sligo, had
used them as a litmus test for the memory that
sometimes failed and left her anxious. 'We all
lose thoughts and words,' he told her. 'I can
never remember romaine when I'm thinking
of lettuce.' It was a paltry confession; she deserved better. Did he often think of lettuce? she
had asked.

Though I am old with wandering
Through hollow lands and hilly lands,
I will find out where she has gone,
And kiss her lips and take her hands,
And walk among long dappled grass,
And pluck till time and times are done
The silver apples of the moon,
The golden apples of the sun.

He lay quiet for a time, moved by the words
and the way she delivered them, as if she lived
in them and had opened a door and invited
him in.

The trembling was running out of her like a
tide.

'Glimmering girl,' he said, brushing her cheek with his fingers. 'Brightening air. Thank you. Well done.'

He kissed her.

'Very well done.'

'He wrote it for a woman he was mad about, but she married someone else.'

He recalled the briefest image of the tall, polished Andrew Gregory on Cynthia's porch, ringing the doorbell like a schoolboy lover. He had thought Tim Kavanagh's number was up— but no, she had preferred the short and balding country parson.

Again, the distant bleating. He got up and closed the window, snuffed the candle flame with his fingers, and got back into bed.

'So amazing,' she said. 'Open windows with no screens.'

'No bugs.' They were pretty buggy back in Carolina. 'Coffee or tea in the morning?' Liam said the first pot would be brewed at seven; breakfast from eight 'til ten.

'Coffee. Thank you. I love you.'

'I love you back,' he said, quoting the thrown-away boy he'd been blessed to raise from age eleven. 'And I don't want to hear another word about your memory going south.'

'What's a Dub?' she asked.

'Someone from Dublin.'

'What's a Terp?'

'The Terps are the University of Maryland's football team.'

'I'm destroyed by these pillows entirely,' she crooned. She turned away, then, and backed up to him, assuming what his grandmother called 'the spooning position.' 'I'll just be backin' oop.'

She would try on the Irish accent 'til kingdom come. He buried his face in her hair, in the smell of it. 'I have a poem.'

'You're the sly one.'

'This is something we've both known for a long time. To you before the close of day . . .'

'Yes. Good.'

'Creator of the world, we pray . . . '

She recited with him the verses of the old hymn, the one they sometimes prayed together at night:

> From all ill dreams defend our sight,
> From fears and terrors of the night . . .

Her slight, whiffling snore, then, and the faint chiming of a clock somewhere down the hall.

He lay unmoving, sensing fields rolling be-

yond the window like a green sea, opening out
to his memory of Ben Bulben's shadowed hulk,
the ragged etch of Classiebawn against a lowering sky, the road winding along the coast of
Connemara.

The Hunger Road, they called it; he wanted
more than anything to show it to her. The sight
of the road itself, however, had not been as gal-
vanizing as the photograph on a postcard among
the papers in his father's locked desk.

As a boy, he'd been careful to know when
the lock was off, and had gone at once to the
photographs, to read the faces and try to imagine something of the line down which his blood
flowed.

The shot of the road had been taken roughly
a century after the 1840s when emigration numbers were at their highest. The road was empty
of people or cars, curving along a bleak winter
coastline where mountains jutted abruptly from
the sea. Tens of thousands had walked this road
to ships they believed would carry them from a
hell of loss and betrayal to America and Canada
and Australia and freedom. For many, that was
true. For nearly as many, the vessels became
known as coffin ships in which countless numbers of Irish perished in the crossing or sank
with their boats while scarcely out of view from

shore. And the worst wasn't over—in ports where officials refused to allow debarkation, typhoid took its toll in 'many a foul steerage.' A labored paragraph on the back of the postcard had told him this.

There was no one whom he could ask why, or how it had happened; his father never mentioned his Irish heritage, nor did his grandfather, who, to his death, expressed a strange and often embarrassing inflection in his southern speech. Ireland was off limits, big time; Tim Kavanagh's lineage was a myth not to be examined.

At some point, he stopped looking at the picture on the card, and looked only at the images of strangers wearing odd clothing—one fellow with his trousers rolled above his knees, standing proudly with a cow outside a thatched cottage; another wearing a rough-cut suit in front of a limestone church and cemetery; two boys playing in a walled garden, and a cat curled on a crooked bench; a woman with dark hair and sorrowful eyes, very beautiful; a man with a large mustache overlooked by a large nose.

He took his watch from the night table and squinted at the illuminated face. Ten-thirty. It was five-thirty in the afternoon in Mitford. He ran the figures in his head—an hour to the Hickory airport in Puny's station wagon, with their luggage and her double set of twins; an hour's wait with a two-day-old copy of *The Charlotte Observer*; roughly a two-hour flight to Atlanta in a plane the size of his carry-on; in Atlanta, a two-hour wait and a seven-hour delay; then seven and a half hours to Dublin with a two-hour wait before boarding an hour's hop to Sligo, followed by a half-hour in baggage claim and the dicey trek with Aengus Malone.

Roughly twenty-five hours in motion, and no sleep to speak of. He was wrecked, but not ruined—with a few good hours tonight, he could easily get in sync with the time difference.

He was not a man to part easily from home, from his dog, from his now legally adopted son, Dooley, who was twenty-one going on forty-five. Such things need watchful tending, like a cook fire. One mustn't go long away from connections lest something fragile die out. One could not fetch that particular fire from neighbors.

He'd noticed that she was carrying a couple of sketchbooks in the red handbag as big as a Buick. Why was he surprised? She was an artist, he should expect her to carry sketchbooks. While rummaging for a granola bar in the depths of that mess kit, she had set the watercolor box on the seat beside her, innocent of his stares.

So. Sketchbooks and watercolors. Just in case, of course.

Last week, she showed him the e-mail from her editor, James, in which she was exhorted to 'get a book out of Ireland.'

She hit reply. 'James—the only thing I intend to get out of Ireland is pleasure. Your devoted author.' She handed over the printed declaration. 'There, darling,' she said, 'remove that worried look from your face.'

Such intentions were all well and good, but books had a tendency to pop out of her like a jack from a box. He had never liked jacks-in-the-box.

Out of the blue, the mania would take hold, and for months following she would be cut in twain: half for him, half for the book. She gave it all the tenderness and passion of a mother toward a child, and at times all the brooding of a woman toward a lover. She would be there and not there, all at once—the way he had been, perhaps, during so many seasons of his priesthood. There and not there, all at once.

'Fire and ice,' someone had said of him in the days when he was searching for God and trying to make up the emptiness. And even when, into his forties, he had at last been found of God, it was the very same, except then he was absorbed utterly in the telling of the truth and sparing nothing, least of all himself.

He didn't want her committing her soul to another book, not now. He didn't want to be on this trip alone, though at her side daily. After more than sixty years of bachelorhood, he had discovered a terrible truth:

Without her, he was beached.

He scooped her closer to his chest and belly and into the curve of his bent knees.

Silver apples of the moon, golden apples of the sun.

Together with the sound of her light snore, the rain dripping from the leaves was his cradle song.

# Four

He opened his eyes at five o'clock sharp, just as he did at home, just as he'd done for more than forty years as a priest. No international time clock could trump four decades of habit.

Still no power. He took the first of two daily insulin shots and read the Morning Office by the uncertain beam of a flashlight. Then he prayed for Dooley and Henry and Peggy and all the rest who made up his world, deciding at the end to include the smaller realm of this sleeping household.

He removed a sweater, a shirt, and pants from the massive armoire, and shucked out of his pajamas. Roughly an hour until the coffeepot would appear on the sideboard. He couldn't say he felt exhausted or even mildly disoriented; he had slept well and felt fine, which wasn't bad for the seventy years he celebrated only weeks ago—or was it seventy-one? He kept forgetting. He zipped his pants, buckled his belt. It was tomorrow when he'd be a rambling wreck.

There was a stinging chill in the air, like early October might feel at home in Mitford. He looked out to a shroud of fog over the slope to the lake, the three fishermen trooping down the shadowed path in their Wellingtons. As a limestone lake, Lough Arrow had no silt to be stirred by last night's heavy rains—the fishing today would likely be good.

He went to the bed and pulled the covers around Cynthia's shoulders, and stood looking at her, bemused. Six decades of living alone couldn't trump eight years of marriage—he marveled still at the sight of her sleeping in his bed. Or was it he who slept in hers?

He fastened his tab collar, put the notebook under his arm. In the hall, he was pleasured by the primal incense of burning turf.

For all the sound made by his passage down the stone stairs, he might have been weightless, a sylph. On the landing, he stopped and buttoned the brown cardigan and turned to look beyond the windows. In the gray murk of early light, a fenced garden. A spade thrust upright into black loam. A blue wheelbarrow; the fire of ripe tomatoes on the vine. He was starting down when he saw a dim figure moving along the path by the garden wall. He adjusted his bifocals. The girl who had brought around the hot towels, riding a bicycle with a large parcel in the basket.

Firelight shimmered over the dusky walls of the sitting room; chunks of hand-cut turf blazed on the grate. Unlike the resinous logs back home, there was no snap and crackle from de-cayed masses of plant material; turf burned with nary a murmur. He gazed into the color and heat of the fire, stretching his hands toward the flame in gratitude.

It was good to be away, after all. Even with the long haul to get here, he felt an ease in his shoulders as if he'd let go some large wen. He turned his back to the blaze, looking about the room at walls glazed with years of turf smoke, and shelf after shelf of books which he might search for hours without guilt over time taken from the lawn mower or the weed patrol or his almost-daily visit to Mitford Hospital. And there, hanging on either side of the door to the dining hall, a display of early sepia photographs he hadn't noticed last night. Groups of men in rough coats and trousers, formal in the act of holding aloft silvered fish; knock-kneed boys displaying their own prize catches—a way of life he'd never known, given a father who believed fishing promoted sloth. Sloth—right now, he'd like a double shot of it, straight up.

The clock ticked, the fire simmered; he was rooted to the spot in an agreeable coma.

An odd sound, then, something like a sneeze.

He peered around. In a corner, the Jack Russell sat motionless in a wing chair.

'Bless you,' he said, keeping his voice low.

The dog cocked its head to one side and looked at him. It was a steady look, conversational in feeling. He'd read somewhere that dogs don't make eye contact. Baloney.

He sat facing the fire and marking the lingering scent of last evening's pipe smoke. His grandfather, firing his pipe and flicking the match into the smoldering Mississippi night . . .

He put his feet on the footstool, if only to see how it felt to lean back, let go, breathe. The aroma of brewed coffee drifted up the hall. *Yes.*

The dog hadn't moved.

'Bolted any rabbits lately?'

One ear cocked.

'I have a dog—a Bouvier mix named Barnabas. A hundred and ten pounds. The Old Gentleman, we call him; likes nineteenth-century poetry.'

Two ears cocked.

'You, on the other hand, have the look of a nonfiction man. The history of the American West, I'd say. Cowboys, Indians, that sort of thing.'

He'd never seen a Jack Russell sit still. A mite long in the tooth, perhaps, though last night's tango on hind legs had been impressive.

'It's said you were named after a parson; a John Russell, I believe, who did a little breeding with his fox terriers, and voilà, here you are.'

The dog suddenly leaped off the cushion, dashed from the room, and returned with the chewed shoe, which was deposited with a certain delicacy by the footstool.

'No way. Don't even think about it.'

The dog sat his ground—head slightly lowered, brown eyes gazing up.

Toss a shoe once, you're engaged. Toss a shoe twice, you're married. He concentrated on the fire.

The dog made a sound, something like a politician clearing his throat before a filibuster.

He stared at the ceiling.

The throat-clearing again.

He grabbed the notebook and was down the hall in a shot.

The dining room by candlelight had been handsome; it was less so in a morning light breaking palely through overcast.

Above the sideboard, a large painting of low mountains and a lake at sunrise. On the water, a lone fisherman casting a net from a boat, a white swan in the rushes. On the painted hill of the far shore, a cottage with a single lighted window and a plume of smoke from the chimney.

The George Barret. And a big George Barret, into the bargain. He leaned over the sideboard and squinted at the signature. The senior or the junior Barret? He couldn't tell.

The coffee had been set out ahead of schedule, kept warm on a heated tile; a wheeled cart by the kitchen door gave evidence of an early breakfast for the fishermen.

He poured a mug of coffee and took it to what they'd already claimed as their table, and sat facing the triple windows. In the way women were loath to travel with good jewelry, he had pondered whether to carry his Waterman. Carry it, said his wife. *Vita brevis!*

He removed the cap from the pen she had given him years ago, and opened the notebook

to a blank page. He felt no haste. How seldom
he'd sat without some pressing inclination,
watching mist steam off a lake, sunlight coloring
a far shore. Through a door open to the garden,
the sound of a rooster crowing . . .

He warmed his hands on the mug and inhaled the oily, slightly sweet scent of dark roast.
It was nearly impossible to trump a blank page,
a good pen, strong coffee.

*Dear Henry,*

*We are happy to be at Broughadoon and, as
promised, I'll share our experience as faithfully as
I'm able.*

*To quote a fellow guest from Dublin, there's
'a monstrous good view' from where I sit in the
dining room of the lodge, c. 1860s. After the heavy
downpour of yesterday evening, the morning appears
to be fairing off, as we say in Mississippi, and the
view reveals itself with shy satisfaction. Outside the
windows, flower borders of considerable ambition,
with a deal of old buddleia or butterfly bush, and
three enormous beeches beyond. We were told last
night at dinner that the beech grove consists of eleven
such specimens roughly a thousand years old.*

*Further along on a gradual slope from the lodge,
a wide sward on which I see something moving—a
herd of deer, knee-deep in ground fog—thrilling to*

*behold. Then the tree line of a darkly green patch of forest descending to the pewter sheen of Lough Arrow with its several small, uninhabited islands. Beyond are hills with a house or two, and low mountains lit now by the sun.*

*One finds certain useful words worn to a nubbin—which, as a poet, is a fact you well understand. I refrain, then, from using 'magical,' though that would definitely work. (When I was here ten years ago, we scarcely had time to look at the view, being out and about like chickens with their heads cut off, so there's a sense in which it all feels new.)*

*Have brought and am reading St. Patrick's Confession and the collected poems of Yeats, while Cynthia has a go at Patrick Kavanagh, the poet and novelist—no kin as far as I know. I wonder whether all you've been through in recent months has wrung any verse from you. If suffering wrings it, then you have much to say to us.*

Sounds of movement in the kitchen adjoining the dining room. The smell of cooking. Good smells.

A door slammed somewhere.

*Walter and Katherine delayed four days, so no immediate visit to the ruin of the fortified Kavanagh*

*house (not a castle, though we like to call it one),
or the cemetery where my—and also your—
great-great-great-grandparents are buried. When W
and K arrive with wheels, I'll tell you more. But be
advised even at this early stage that the land of
saints and scholars is greener than can be imagined.
Which reminds me—Cynthia says she will put
something on paper to send your way, a watercolor
or two.*

He stared out the window, searching the few houses on the opposite shore, thoughtful.

*It is among the oddest experiences of my life to
find now that someone shares my heritage, my very
blood. You must tell me how it's going with you—
this adjustment to having a brother. As for me, I
like it very much, yet I shake my head often as if to
clear it.*

'There you are, have you seen her?'
'Ní fhaca, ar chor ar bith.'
Loud voices in the kitchen. Anna. Liam.
'Is scríos mór i—scríos agús míchlú,' said Anna. 'I am broken by such willfulness.'
'Is é an grá a caithfidh si a fháil tar éis an rud go léir.'

'*Caithimid go léir an grá a fháil ach ní tagaimid tríd an gáitéar ag lorg é?*'

'*Tá Bella ag pleidhcíocht linn.*'

'*Tá Bella ag iarraidh muid a bhriseadh.*'

'*Níl*, Anna, we mustn't be broken . . . *ansin ní bheidh éinne aici chun tacaíocht a thabhairt di.*'

The sound of a pan or pot crashing to the floor.

'Now look what I've done. All that lovely rhubarb . . .'

Anna weeping.

Liam spoke in a low voice, then said in English, 'For God's sake, I hope no guests are about.'

The kitchen door pushed open to the dining room; he met Liam's startled gaze. Liam moved to close the door, his face ashen. There was an awkward pause. 'Ready for breakfast, then?' Liam asked.

'I know I'm early. No hurry at all.' He felt a flame of embarrassment. 'Thank you.'

He tucked the letter into the notebook and adjusted his glasses and stared for a long time at the view, unseeing—at a small island forested with trees, at a yellow boat moored on its narrow shoreline. He got up and tried looking again at the Barret, but moving clouds obscured the light.

Liam entered with a tray, averting his eyes. He set a warmed plate on the white cloth, then a French press, a cup and saucer. The cup rattled in the saucer. 'I'm completely undone, Reverend. Please forgive us.'

'Not at all. I hardly understood a word you said.'

Liam removed the empty coffee mug. 'But you heard the boil in it.'

'Language barriers can't disguise feeling, that's true. But it's forgotten entirely.'

'Thanks. I think it's the first time we've blurted our business in the ear of a guest. It won't happen again.'

'Gone from my mind.' Not gone yet; he felt mildly rattled.

He stared with wonder at his breakfast. A pair of eggs with yolks the color of a Florida orange, surrounded by sausages, bacon, new potatoes roasted in their skins, a broiled tomato, thick slices of brown soda bread.

'A pot of raspberry conserve there, and that would be blackberry jam. The berries weren't so sweet this year. The rain.'

'Wonderful. Thank you.' He felt the tension in the air, wanted to dilute it somehow, but could not.

'Anna remembered you like rhubarb; we'll have it tomorrow morning. Did you rest, please God?'

'I did,' he said. 'Feel good, actually. The lag won't hit 'til tomorrow.'

Liam held the empty tray like a breastplate. 'I see you're writing a letter, we've stamps.'

'Thanks, I'll be using a few.'

'Do you fish?'

'Never got the hang of it, I'm afraid.'

'It's comin' on to a grand, soft day. If you need anything at all, there's a bell on the sideboard. We're after usin' bells here.'

'You may not see my wife until dinner. She'll be happy enough with the view and the work of one of your good poets. I'll take her breakfast up, if I may.'

'The full Irish, you said.'

'Correct.'

'I apologize again for the power being off. We usually get quicker service.' Liam paused. 'There's a good deal to apologize for this morning.'

'It's quite all right. Really. We're very happy.' He poured the steaming coffee into his cup. 'How do you make blood pudding, anyway? I always wondered.'

'You begin with a couple liters of blood—'

'Of course. Sorry I asked.' He managed a credible laugh.

The Jack Russell sat at the open dining room door, the shoe clenched in his jaws.

'What's the little guy's name?'

'Pud.'

'As in pudding?'

'Just so. Some call them puddin' dogs. He's the fourth breed off the early Jack Russell. Shorter legs, longer body. He's a pest, he is, no manners like the old Labs, but good about stayin' out of the dining room. Any bother to you?'

'None at all. We have a dog the size of your sofa.'

'There's a law says hostelries can't have dogs about.' Liam cleared jam dishes from the fishermen's table. 'We've always had dogs about. They may haul us to the guillotine for 't, but they'll have to catch us first.'

He hammered down on the eggs, sopped bread in the yolks. 'Was it Irish you were speaking?'

''t was. As a child wanderin' these regions, I heard it often. My mother spoke Irish; my father loved hearing her speak it, except when she was angry; 't would tear th' head off a billy goat.'

Liam carried the tray to the kitchen door. 'Anna is fluent, did a devil of study in it. The last great remnant of our culture, some say.'

'A very different sound to it, I hope you'll teach us a phrase or two while we're here.'

Liam nodded, hesitated, then pushed open the door with his shoulder.

This was the first of only three such breakfasts he would allot himself in Ireland. He savored it to the final crumb.

*P.S. I have just had the most satisfactory breakfast since boyhood, when the sausage was new-made in the fall and your mother fried up a panful.*

*The light is changing over the lake—no pewter now, but platinum tinted with crimson. Something moving out there, I like to think it's the three fellows who*

Liam came into the room, rolling his sleeves down, buttoning the cuffs. 'I'll just be goin' to Riverstown in a bit. Post office, victualler, butcher, that sort of thing. It's my day off . . .'

'Doesn't sound like a day off.'

'A day away from th' oul' grindstone. I wonder . . . with no vehicle . . .' Liam was tentative. 'I'd be happy to fetch something for you.'

'Thank you, very kind, can't think of anything.'

'Would you . . . be after comin' with me?'

He was surprised, but pleased. 'Why, yes. I'd like that.' Something in the air was released. 'What time?'

'I'll just get your wife's fry out to you, and we can muddle along in the old Rover in a half hour or so.'

Muddling along in an old Rover was precisely what he'd like to do.

He felt a certain satisfaction toting the tray upstairs. Even as a child, the act of being useful had pleased him.

He balanced the heavy tray along his left arm, turned the knob, eased the door open. 'Room service,' he announced, pushing the door shut behind him.

She turned from the window and smiled. She looked happy; it was his favorite of her looks.

He wasn't surprised to see her in the ancient robe that nobody in their right mind would schlep across the Pond. Chenille. In tatters. Hanging together by threads.

They had been married only a few months when she brought it out of its rightful concealment, and paraded in the thing. He thought it was a joke and roared with laughter—not a good idea. He noticed a spring in her step whenever she wore it; she called it her Darling Robe.

Not that he needed some filmy lace business; no, please, he was an odd duck who thought flannel sexy if his wife wore it, this was another story altogether. Hadn't Peggy preached him a blizzard of sermons on 'goin' ragged'? Hadn't that been among the worst of sins in those days, to go ragged even if there had been a crucifying Depression and another horrific war and the cotton crops failing?

She was beaming at him. He forgave the robe and set the tray on the footstool by the green chair.

'Why didn't you tell me?' she said.

'Tell you . . . ?'

'How beautiful it is here.' She sat in the chair and pulled the robe about her ankles.

'I tried. But Ireland requires another language.'

'I was remembering the trip to Hawaii with my parents, I was nine years old. I wanted to stay inside for long hours. The beauty was so intense and unrelenting, it woke a pain in me.'

'Let's don't be waking any pains here.'

'I read a poem once—The beauty of the

world hath made me sad, This beauty that will pass . . .'

'Now, now,' he said in his pulpit voice.

She looked up, laughing. 'I think the poem may have been written by an Irishman.'

'That figures.' He removed the plate cover with a flourish.

'How amazing,' she said. 'The yolks are the exact color of my favorite crayon in first grade. Thank you, sweetheart.'

'In the absence of your morning *Observer*, I bring a report from the outer realms.

'It's fairing off to a grand, soft day.

'The Barret is a beauty.

'The eggs are laid on-site.

'The sausage is from a local farm, ditto the butter. And there was a big row in the kitchen.'

'Who?'

'Liam and Anna.'

'About what?' She thrust down the plunger of the French press.

'I don't know. It was all in Irish.'

'I wish I could have heard it. What does it sound like?'

'That's a hard one. Maybe like burning turf smells—strange, powerful, from the gut of pre-history. I understood only one word. Bella.'

'Italian for beautiful,' she said, pouring the coffee, 'and a perfectly good word for this breakfast. I'm in heaven. Which is the blood pudding?'

'There,' he said, pointing.

She peered at it. 'I wonder how it's made.'

'First, take two liters of blood.'

She burst into laughter. 'You can't scare me.'

'Don't I know it,' he said.

'What sort of blood?'

'Curiosity killed the cat.'

'Do you mind if I stay in the room 'til dinner?'

'Not at all, I thought you would.'

'Will you be bereft without me?'

'Ha! I've already received an invitation.'

'To go fishing?'

'My dear girl, in a few minutes' time, I'll be muddling along in a Rover possibly as old as the megaliths. Off to Riverstown with Liam, back after lunch. Need anything?'

She forked a sausage, waved it in the air. 'I have it all. Go and be as the butterfly.'

It was their old mantra; he relished hearing it.

In the bathroom mirror, he examined the scruff on his face. Nothing much he could do about it until the power came on. He stood back and ran his hand over the stubble, unable to remember going a day without shaving. Well, maybe once or twice when he had the flu.

He realized he was whistling as he went down the stairs.

# Five

'None but Seamus will be stirrin', poor divil. He's th' butler at Catharmore—always up at th' crack, cooking, polishing, laying fires. God above, th' man's a saint.'

'Fires in August—that's usual?'

'We keep a bit of fire burnin' year-round, th' Conors.'

They were having a shout over the rattle which filled the Rover from front to rear; the scent of last night's rain poured through the open windows.

'We'll do a quick shot around the drive, then be off.'

The road was steep, rutted, strewn in places

by blossoms of wild fuchsia loosed by the downpour. Fallen trees decayed among brambles at the wood's edge.

'Most of the house is on th' ruin—still an' all, it looks out to one of the finest prospects in th' west of Ireland.'

They rounded a curve overhung by rhododendron. The house appeared on a treeless prominence, engraved against a billow of clouds.

He was unaccustomed to limestone houses. In his rustic view, limestone was the material of stoical municipal buildings with their crust of soot and pigeon droppings.

'The Conor cabin,' Liam said, ironic.

He sensed that he was to think Catharmore handsome. He did not.

'Built by an Irishman in the early 1860s, name of O'Donnell. Thanks to a rich uncle, O'Donnell emigrated to Philadelphia as a lad— medical school, a successful practice, everything a Sligo boy could dream of. Came home to Lough Arrow with his wife in 1859. The hunger years had put th' passion in him for helpin' th' poor at home.'

'The lintels, the keystones—very striking,' he said. His mother and Peggy had raised him to look for the positive in every common thing. 'A splendid portico.' It was the best he could do.

'Father bought it when he was fifty-two; moved out from Sligo, where he owned a sizable building operation. Came with an invalid wife who was after havin' th' country air. Then his wife died, and he married her nursemaid.'

Liam braked for the view down the slope.

At the foot of the hill, the blade of blue water, slicing through green; the clouds—cumulus, immense, on the move. He instinctively crossed himself. 'Glorious,' he said, genuinely touched. 'A privilege to see it.'

'The red roof showin' among the trees, that's us at Broughadoon. The specks on the water might be our lads. I put our order in for five bric and a nice pike—this afternoon, there'll be four American women on us.'

'Whoa.'

'A book club, they told Anna, that turned off to a poker club.'

They laughed.

'But lately 't is a travel club.'

'Flexibility, that's the ticket.'

The Rover rattled along the grass circle at the front of the house.

'The nursemaid was my mother, Evelyn McGuiness. Twenty-some years of age and a ravin' beauty, they say; one of seven raised in a one-room cabin a few kilometers from here. Fierce an' ravishing, my father called her. Th' lord of th' manor made a mighty case for himself, but she says 't was th' fine Irish house she married.'

Five bays. Windows on the second and third floors blind with interior shutters, as if hiding the rooms from bird and hawk; vines protruding from copper guttering. As they approached the portico, three Labs raced down the steps.

'That's Roddy th' yellow, Kevin th' chocolate—you met them at th' lodge—and the oul' black fellow's Cuchulain.' Liam braked and dug biscuits from the pocket of his windbreaker. 'Show y'r manners, ye lazy cods. Ah, Cuch, ye're a good by, yes ye are. Roddy, ye're latherin' up m' arm, get a grip on y'rself.' He flung a handful of biscuits across the grass. 'Run for it, lads, ye're too fat altogether.

'There was a garden wall ten feet high,' Liam said as they drove down the hill. 'My brother, Paddy, pulled it down. He can have the place and all th' nuisance of it. I'm happy with my books and my Barret.'

'There's a senior Barret and a junior, I believe.' He had read a little about Irish art; the senior was definitely the bigger ticket.

'This is th' senior. Paddy's after me to sell it, or give it to Trinity College—as if he ever gave two quid to th' place.'

'You're a Trinity man?'

'Read Latin and botany at Trinity. Barely half a year was all I could take of it. Too confinin'. When Father died at th' middle of term, I made off for Lough Arrow an' never looked back. Truth is, I grew up wild as bog cotton; took my degree in th' woods and fields.'

He'd taken a degree of his own in the woods and fields. The sweltering summers of his Mississippi youth had been his favored university.

'I learned off a few poems as a lad, but a bit of something by Synge is all that comes to mind these days—*I knew the stars, the flowers and the birds, the grey and wintry sides of many glens, and did but half remember human words, in converse with the mountains, moors and fens.*

'I excused myself from bein' raised, you might say. I liked bein' in th' open, studying flowers and weeds and bushes and bugs. I was brought up by th' people, really—snagged hares, took 'em to a cottage door for my supper. Was wild as a hare myself—a wonderful childhood. The upbringin' I lacked from my mother, I got from twenty others. I never felt so happy as when sittin' by the open fire of a cottage, listenin' to a story or a fiddle or talkin' to the old people about home cures. Ah, they'd go on about pus and gangrene and bile and deformities of all kinds—

people risin' up from their coffins at a wake, birthin' infants with two heads. Fascinating.

'I like to think I wasn't a completely bad fellow, for all that. Didn't drown any cats or cut th' tails off dogs, though I did scare th' daylights out of a teacher I tangled with more than once. I pulled a bedsheet over m'self when she was walkin' home at dark, jumped out of th' hedge, and yelled at th' top of m' voice, May th' divil put warts on y'r oul' nose! She was easier on me after that, and I was easier with her—'t was an unspoken pact we had; I think she knew who was under the sheet.

'But see here?' Liam tapped the right side of his nose. 'A wart. Came there some time later, but made me wonder, nonetheless.'

They laughed, comfortable.

'Is primogeniture still practiced here?'

'Outlawed in the sixties. Ever since he was a kid, Paddy was fierce to have th' house. When Father died, there was no chance of Mother sellin' th' place, though God knows, there was hardly two bob left to maintain it—he was eighty-some when he passed.

'I did my bit to help—worked as a finish carpenter around th' villages and townlands; at weekends, came home and tried to keep th' place standing. Paddy had graduated Trinity a few years before, joined forces with an ad agency in Dublin and tricked himself out as an art director. Our mother was proud enough—though she was after havin' a doctor in th' family. Then off to London Paddy went, where he became somethin' of a star in the ad business.

'He lived in London a few years, married twice, divorced twice, made a name for himself. Then off to New York an' puts together his own outfit an' marries again. 't was a smash, th' business, but a bust, th' marriage.

'When he came home a few years back, he'd just sold his company to some Madison Avenue bucko. He was what any man in Sligo would call rich—but here's where th' cheese gets bindin'. 't was his dream to turn Catharmore into a country house hotel. 't is th' fashion, you know, turning our country houses into hotels.'

'Helps keep the roof over your head.'

'Th' place had run down altogether; we thought he'd gone simple.'

'Catharmore is competition for Broughadoon, then?'

'Ah, no. He never finished th' job. Mother wanted the ground floor done up first, for a good impression to the guests; and of course th' kitchen had to be done up if you're to feed a mouth in these parts. He cobbled that together with a crew from Dublin, and what's done is grand, I'll give him that, but th' cost was three times th' bloody estimate, an' no place yet for a guest to lay his head.

'His money was gone, th' wind was whippin' th' tiles off th' roof, and th' drink took over completely. 't was a right cod.'

The Rover splashing through pools along the lane; in the hedges, rain-washed light on scarlet fuchsia.

'Broughadoon—is it part of Catharmore?'

''t was. Th' lodge would have passed to me, but Mother sold it off after Father died. Maybe a hundred acres in terms of your American real estate. Anna's father bought it.'

'William.'

'Aye. He deeded it to Anna when we were married; he has life estate.'

They were silent for a time.

Along the verges, a colony of bizarre vegetation—leaves the size of small umbrellas, fruit similar to a pineapple. Scary stuff.

'*Gunnera tinctoria*. Th' blasted wild rhubarb. 't is takin' us over.'

Even the Irish had their kudzu.

'Meant to tell you I saw deer this morning,' he said. 'A breathtaking sight in the ground fog.'

'We farm deer for Sligo and Dublin restaurants, and our own tables at Broughadoon. Around forty head these days.'

'That's roughly the number up to destroying my rosebushes back home.'

'We get a bit of that, too, th' buggers, but the herd you saw is fenced. I'm also runnin' around eighty head of sheep on land leased from a neighbor, and of course there's th' chickens—some for eggs, most for meat. A patch of bog gives turf for th' hearth, I cut it m'self when I can.'

'Well done.'

'In this business, have to paddle like a son of a gun to keep the oul' head above water. Anna makes our preserves, does most of th' cooking, keeps th' gardens, books th' guests, runs th' lodge altogether.'

Liam glanced at him, suddenly shy. 'A grand woman, Anna—I'm mad for her. I'll never forget the day she threw herself at me, as she says. I thought she loved me, but she wouldn't marry me, for all that. She said no, but there was th' look of yes on her face. 't was like she was boltin' th' door with a boiled carrot.'

He laughed.

''t was a desperate time, I felt I might lose

her. Then one day I was walkin' along the oul'
cart road an' she was standin' on th' bank, so,
and suddenly she just leaps off th' bank, I saw
it in slow motion. Just surrenders herself to the
air, to me, an' lands in my arms, nearly knockin'
me over. An' that was that.

'She got herself a finer education than my
own. Her da sent her to Mount Anville in South
Dublin, where th' sisters took a great likin' to
her. She has the gift for French and Italian, and
a fine way of speakin' her feelings.'

'We married above ourselves,' he said. 'How
many guest rooms?'

'When I'm done down th' hall, a total of
nine. Looks like I'll have to do th' finish work
m'self. Nobody wants a day's honest labor anymore. Gave th' boot to a bloody Englishman last
week; he had th' skills of an angel an' th' soul of
a devil. Could cope to stone like nothin' you
ever saw, but couldn't keep his mitts off th'
dope.'

Fields interlaced by crumbling walls. A cow
barn with a single blue shutter. 'Ireland is more
beautiful than I remember,' he said.

'*By suffering worn and weary,* your Mr. Longfellow wrote, *but beautiful as some fair angel yet.*'

'You know Longfellow!'

'No, no. 't was a line my father liked to quote. When he wasn't fishin', he had his nose in a book.'

'You love his books.'

'Maybe because I loved him. He was a very fine class of a man. Very devout. We fasted, we confessed, we walked the Mass path. He loved us, though there was none of that touchy-feely stuff the young get nowadays. You knew you were loved and that was enough, you never wanted more. He set me on his lap occasionally, which was closer than I ever got to my mother. I remember being uneasy up there where his whiskers seemed to have a life of their own.'

They turned out of the lane to the highway.

'God above,' said Liam, 'I've gnawed your ear off.'

'Not a bit. I happen to like stories of other people's lives.'

'My mouth is a terror, Reverend, and that's a fact.'

He laughed. 'Listening is one of my job requirements.'

'My father was a grand listener, I could tell him bits I couldn't tell anyone else. There's something about you that reminds me of him.'

When they arrived at Broughadoon after

two o'clock, he found his barefoot wife enthroned in the green chair, wearing jeans and a sweater.

'Tell me everything,' she said. 'Then I'll tell you everything.'

Even in a locked room, she would have something to report.

'Made the rounds,' he said. 'Saw Catharmore, the big house on the hill. Went to the butcher, the baker, the candlestick maker. The butcher was a fellow named Cavanagh spelled with a *C*, who knows nothing about us poor goats with a *K*. Twenty-foive yares agoo, he said, there ware foor of us in th' village. There'd be soom of 'em yet if 't weren't for th' big chains coomin' in.'

''t is stirrin' th' Irish in ye,' she said, pleased.

Actually, he had felt a stirring—some sense of home or consolation that he hadn't expected.

'Let's see. We bought stamps. Saw a castle in the distance—Liam says castles are a dime a dozen, one on every corner like the American drugstore. Then we had lunch—a turkey sandwich with lettuce and tomato on whole wheat. Drank a pint.'

'A pint of what?'

'A pint of what everyone else was drinking.' She laughed. 'In Rome.'

He sat on the foot of the bed, exhausted. 'Okay,' he said, 'your turn. I guess you know the power's still out. They can't send workmen 'til tomorrow, and Liam's fit to be tied. The landlines are down, too, of course, and their computer. Not good for business.'

'I'm in need of a real bath, but I love the power being out.'

'You would,' he said.

'When you left, I . . .' She sneezed.

'Bless you.'

'I sketched the view from the window. Want to see?'

'Is the pope a Catholic?'

She had always been tentative about showing her work to him. She gave over the sketchbook as a child might—abashed, hopeful.

'Yes, yes,' he said, gawking. A flame of pride shot up in him. 'You're a wonder.'

'Do you mean it?'

'I absolutely mean it.'

'Would Henry like it?'

'He'd be thrilled. I'll finish up his letter tonight, we can send it off tomorrow.'

'And this is the dear lady who'll be doing our laundry.'

Bad teeth, radiant smile, thinning hair. The face of suffering, the face of courage.

'Maureen McKenna. She helped Anna work on putting this place back together. Born with a deformed leg. Can cook, iron, clean, and sing. She's the sunshine of Broughadoon, Anna says.'

He turned the page.

The girl who had brought the hot towels around. Scornful. Beautiful in a menancing sort of way.

'Bella,' she said. 'Bella Flaherty. Anna's daughter by a first marriage. Plays the fiddle—a trad musician.'

'Trad?'

Traditional. Plays the old tunes.'

He was strangely unsettled by the portrait. 'You've been busy.' He stooped to kiss her forehead. 'How did you learn all this?'

'It's a very talkative household.'

'You can say that again.'

'Broughadoon is the perfect place at the perfect time, sweetheart. I love being here.'

'Ah, Kavanagh, what don't you love?' It was another of their mantras.

'The spelling of Jane Austen's surname with an *i*. Cold showers. Fake orchids.'

How she came up with this stuff without a moment's hesitation was as unfathomable to him as how to extract nickels from someone's ear.

'How's your ankle?'

'Hurts. But I took something for pain; it'll be fine.'

He dumped stamps and pocket change on the dresser. 'It was all that sitting for so many hours.'

She sneezed.

'Bless you.'

While in the Rover, he'd thought of calling Robin, the Irish distant cousin who gave the tea party those years ago. He'd entered her number into his cell phone, not sure whether the number would even be current. And Dooley—he should call Dooley. His cell phone . . . where was it? Maybe in his blue jacket. He should probably look for the charger and the connector thing, and get some juice in it when the power came back.

She took a handkerchief from her jeans pocket and sneezed.

'What's with the sneezing?'

'When you left, I was dying to go back to bed. But I couldn't. After I sketched the view, I felt compelled to get dressed. Thought I'd visit the beech grove, and watch the chickens pecking at their kitchen scraps.'

She liked her birthday present; he relished seeing the pleasure in her.

'But I got no further than the library, which

is where I found this—beneath a stack of books in the corner. It spoke to me, somehow.'

She reached to the table beside the chair and hauled a large volume into her lap—it was a whopper. 'Being the private journals of Cormac Padraigin Fintan O'Donnell, MD, Lough Arrow, County Sligo,' she read from the flyleaf. 'And be warned—the dust of the ages is gathered here.'

She had a pretty volatile allergy to the dust of old books. 'Should you be doing this?' he asked.

'I have to do this,' she said.

She put on her glasses, opened the leatherbound book, and read to him.

14 March 1860
Freezing winds off the Lough
    A late Spring of blistering cold yet Caitlin & I are besotted with comfort in our rude Cabin near the Lough—Thick walls, an agreeable hearth & a dirt Floor warmed by Uncle's Turkey rugs have made it more than hospitable.
    No draft can seek us out in our alcove bed—my Books line the walls on racks I joined myself & are a fine insulation into

the bargain. For a Surgery, God in his mercy has given us a Turf Shed attached to the Cabin, a scantling of a room—it serves well enough though difficult to heat in frigid weather.

We have been spoiled these many years by the comfort of Uncle's grand Residence in Philadelphia to which we repaired at his urging from our wedding sojurn in Italy. He spent such little time in his well-furnished Home that we had it nearly to ourselves & four servants into the bargain. C eventually assumed the running of his Household for which he esteemed her very highly. Uncle did not discuss where he often lodged—we assumed it was with someone rumoured to be his mistress, of whom he never spoke—at least to myself. We did not learn the surprising truth until his death.

C & I wonder yet why he declined to marry—surely it would have been socially beneficial to his many Enterprises. As well, we wondered at his refusal to attend Mass though we exhorted him on many occasions to come with us to Old St. Joseph's. I confess that we never fully

understood Uncle but had a profound
affection for him as did countless others.
For all the resentment of Irish in that city,
he was admired & respected by Catholic
& Protestant alike.

Working by Lantern to complete
the Drawings—careful to restrain any
impulse to vainglory though this in no
way owing to Balfour's summon to
modesty. Such a consuming task could
not be carried forth without Uncle's rare
& valuable books on architecture—
Palladio and Inigo Jones being the masters
who inspired the design of his fine house
in the township of Philadelphia. Thanks
to God for many felicitous hours spent
with him as he labored over the
drawings—often seeking my opinions and
observations though they issued from rude
instinct only.

Must amputate Danny Moore's
gangrenous leg on the morrow—he is but
eighteen & the provider for his Mother,
Grandmother, & four Sisters. Caitlin and I
will travel horseback to their cabin for the
surgery taking a basket of food,
chloroform & a flask of Whiskey—what

thin comfort can be offered at such a
grievous time.

A desperate Circumstance—Heaven
help this decent son of Ireland.


'Here's the backstory,' she said. 'Fintan
O'Donnell was the bright, devout son of a poor
tenant family who lived near Lough Arrow.'

'Liam gave me a quick bit on O'Donnell.
But keep going.'

'Turns out he had what we've all dreamed of
at one time or another—a rich uncle. So the
uncle, who lived in Philadelphia and was busy
making a fortune in shipping, said he would
sponsor the brightest boy of his sister's four.
The family proposed Fintan, and off he went at
age seventeen, frightened out of his wits. I was
sorry for the brothers, how it must feel to be
the unchosen, but they absolutely didn't want
any part of it and practically shoved him onto
the boat.

'He trained as a physician, had a very successful practice, and married a nurse whose
family had immigrated from Roscommon. But
he mourned the hunger years in Ireland and
the evictions and the fevers and all the rest—he
said he could sometimes audibly hear the toll-

ing of the death bell and the lamentations of his people.

'He wrote this in the frontispiece:

> I hereby stand with the venerable William Stokes who said when elected President of the College of Physicians: Loving my unhappy Country with a Love so intense as to be a Pain, its miseries & downward Progress have lacerated my very heart.

'When he was fifty years old, he came home to Lough Arrow with his wife, Caitlin, to devote himself to the poor. His uncle had died some time before and the estate passed to Dr. O'Donnell. In light of that and the money he'd earned in his practice, he had deep pockets to fund a free clinic.

'Timothy? Are you all right or shall I stop?'

'Don't stop; I'm with you.' He moved to the wing chair; he would just rest his eyes . . .

'The doctor and his wife were looking for land in these parts and made the acquaintance of Lord Balfour, an Englishman who'd built a big pile up the road from Broughadoon. Good timing, or maybe not, Fintan saved the life of the lord's ten-year-old daughter, and made some headway with the old boy's dysentery. So Balfour gave the doctor roughly two hundred acres of his own immense property, but with the caveat—get this—that O'Donnell wouldn't put on airs in the architecture of his house. O'Donnell thought it would be grand to accept the land.' She sneezed. 'Want me to stop?'

'No, no. Go on.'

17 May

S. O'Connor came with his wife last night at a late hour—having no pony, S. walked the four miles in the traces of his cart, pulling her along—her abdomen swollen & tender, much vomiting.

Attempted to remove Appendix but too late—expired ten minutes past midnight, S. distraught, keening, alarming the dogs—Caitlin managed to hold the poor man down as I dosed him with Laudanum—he slept warm in Surgery beneath one of the Turkey rugs.

S. returns the corpse home after noon this day—the putrid smell from the rupture pervades the Surgery & cannot be kept from the Cabin though the windows be thrown open.

A cruel cold rain at seven this
morning—we pray heaven would stanch
it for the cart to pass home dry.

Moira O'Connor, mother of four living
& two deceased. May God rest her Soul.

She turned pages, searching passages.

20 September 1860

The people of these Parts take great
pride in the building of the House.
Caitlin & I recently met a lad down the
shore who held his hat over his heart as
we passed—twas not ourselves he saluted,
but the Irish house that rises in his view.

As we went by Canoe yesterday to
O'Leary the Shoemaker, Keegan & I
looked up and saw the bold silhouette
against the mackerel sky—as Months have
passed since I viewed it from such a
vantage point I was surprised to find the
new Garden walls giving the look of a
Fortification. Even in its yet skeletal form,
the house appears defensible & mighty on
its high prominence & gives the People a
sense of being protected by their own. I
admit that seeing it thus has warmed me
with pleasure.

Though the worst years of Famine have recently passed, we are Haunted yet by the devastation which appears to have no end. Mark this. It is not merely a well-made house by the Lough, but a Proclamation to the Irish people that it is an Irish house built by Irish resolve—on Irish soil sanctified by Irish blood.

May it proclaim that day when our Bonds be thrown off & our people free to govern our Destinies.

'You're fading, sweetheart. Get in bed; we'll do this later.'

He hauled himself up and undressed and did as he was told, eager for the consolation of the pillow. 'Get in with me,' he said, patting the blanket.

'I'm right behind you.'

She sneezed, blew her nose, pulled off her sweater.

'Very sad to think of those times, though heaven knows, what had passed and what was coming was fearful in the extreme. Anna says Liam read a few pages when Paddy's work crew found it; it was stashed behind a wall.'

'It belongs to Catharmore, then?'

'Anna says Paddy had no patience for it and

turned it over to Liam for the library. She's never read it, the ink is too faded. Of course, the doctor's handwriting isn't the best, either, but now that I've got the hang of it, it's flying along.'

She stepped out of her jeans. 'What does his house look like, Timothy? Is it beautiful?'

He heard the hope in her voice.

She slipped in beside him, and he turned to her and touched her cheek.

'In its own way,' he said. 'In its own way.'

# Six

Dinner progressed with several toasts to the anglers' skill and good fortune. *Slainte,* meaning good health and pronounced slawn-cha, sounded in the room more than a few times.

'By the way,' Cynthia said to Bella Flaherty, who was taking dessert orders, 'who cleaned all those fish? I cleaned a fish once, it was a terrible job.'

'I cleaned the fish. Fileted them as well. 't is nothing. There are two desserts this evening: Moroccan figs poached in a syrup of ginger and honey, with Anna's lemon verbena ice cream—'

'I love figs,' said Cynthia. 'I'll have the figs, thank you.'

'You haven't heard the option.'

He liked it when his wife raised one eyebrow.

'Anna's rhubarb tart with raspberry purée and crème fraîche.'

'I'll have the figs,' said Cynthia.

While he'd lodged here with Walter and Katherine, Anna had sent them off on a day trip with a rhubarb tart, still warm in its swaddle of white napkin. The fragrance of brandied fruit and baked crust had filled the car, touching him with a grave longing for something he couldn't name.

They'd driven as far as the highway when Katherine braked the car, turned to the back-seat, and snatched up the basket which rode next to him. No one spoke as she unwrapped the tart, broke it into three pieces, passed out their portions, ate her own in roughly two enormous bites, wiped her mouth on the hem of her skirt, and declared: 'There. That's the way I want to live for the rest of my life.'

Hooting with laughter, they were truant children on the run from authority.

Speaking above the throb of the generator, he gave Bella his order. 'I'll have the tart, please.' Then, hopeful, 'Is it served warm?'

She looked at him with hooded eyes. 'Anna's tarts are always served warm.'

The kitchen door swung shut. 'Who does Bella remind you of?'

'I was just thinking that,' he said. The thrown-away boy at age eleven, when he landed on the doorstep of the rectory—their adopted son, Dooley.

In the library before dinner, he and Cynthia had exchanged introductions with the Atlanta contingent, who were seated now at the next table.

'We hear you're a travel club,' said his wife.

'We started as a book club,' said Moira. 'But we never got around to discussin' books.'

'We drank wine and talked about *men*,' said Debbie.

Laughter at the club table.

'I still cannot believe,' said Lisa, 'that I took th' trouble to read *War and Peace* cover to cover, even the epilogue, and never once got a chance to discuss it.'

'That's when I was havin' work done,' said Moira. 'I did not feel like readin' a book that weighed more than my firstborn.'

'So, anyway,' said Lisa, 'we switched over to a poker club, with all winnings goin' to charity.'

'Great idea,' he said.

'We played every other Wednesday night, and everybody brought a covered dish.'

'It was just way too much,' said Tammy, 'to, you know, every other Wednesday come up with a new dish.'

'Takeout,' said Cynthia.

Debbie lifted her glass to Moira. 'So Moira reorganized us as a travel club, she is *very* good at travel plannin'.'

'We've been friends for forty years,' said Tammy. 'We met in a Scrabble club. We're crazy about Scrabble.'

He noticed Tammy wore bracelets which did a good bit of jangling.

'So, y'all like to fish?' asked Pete.

'All our husbands trout-fished,' said Lisa. 'We never did, we were too busy raisin' kids. While Johnny could still talk, it was throat cancer, he said, Lisa, honey, learn to trout-fish.'

'Good advice,' said Pete.

'He said it was great for th' central nervous system.'

Tammy put on a swipe of lipstick without looking in a mirror. 'Moira's husband, bless 'is heart, had fishin' on th' brain 'til th' minute he passed.'

'Check out Lough Arrow, he said, plain as day.' Moira dabbed her eyes with her napkin. 'Those were practically his last words.'

'His last words,' Pete said, reverent.

'His parents brought him here as a boy and he came twice after college. We had fishin' husbands in common, for sure.'

'Had,' said Pete.

'We're all widows,' said Lisa.

'Sorry,' said Pete.

'Right,' said Tom. 'Real sorry.'

Hugh nodded, respectful.

'Another thing we have in common,' said Lisa, 'is . . . guess what.'

'They'll *never* guess,' said Debbie.

'You're all Irish,' said Cynthia.

Debbie shrieked. 'How did you *know*?'

'A hunch.'

'Third generation,' said Moira. 'County Tyrone.'

'*Fifth* generation,' said Debbie. 'County Mayo.'

'Maybe fourth, maybe Sligo,' said Lisa. 'I'm not totally sure.'

Tammy sighed. 'I have no clue, but my great-grandmother was named O'Leary—not th' one with th' cow.'

Hugh raised his glass. 'Limerick. Fourth generation.'

Tom raised his. 'Sligo. Third.'

'All my connections are pretty much Sligo,' said Pete, 'except for a crowd on my mother's side that moved up to Tyrone. Okay, here's one for you. What's th' connection between us lads that has nothin' to do with fishin'?'

'You're all losin' your *hair*?' asked Debbie.

'Cousins!' Cynthia and Moira chorused.

*'Slainte!'* said Pete.

There ensued a discussion of emigration dates, the sprawl of kin over counties and continents, the Kavanagh bloodline, fife-playing in general.

'I'm wonderin' why y'all turned up here,' said Pete. 'Out in th' sticks an' all.'

'We took the advice of a dyin' man,' said Tammy. 'Googled World's Best Trout Fishin', then Googled Lough Arrow and found Broughadoon. Liam and Anna were great to work with, and ta-da'—Tammy's bracelets jangled—'here we are.'

'Ready to fish like *maniacs*,' said Debbie.

Pete turned his chair to face the club table. 'Where do you fish back home? New England? Colorado? Montana?'

Moira looked Pete in the eye. 'Th' country club lake.'

'Catch a lot of golf balls that way,' said Hugh.

Dessert was served amid a bombast of lectures by the anglers—Spent-gnat, Sooty Olive, Connemara Black, Invicta, Green Peter, feeder streams, buzzer hatches, Bibio, murroughs . . .

'What are they talking about?' whispered Cynthia.

'We don't need to know,' he said.

'So,' Pete inquired of the club table, 'how about some help with your gear in the morning?'

'We have ghillies coming, thank you.'

'Well, then, ladies'—Pete hoisted his glass—'may it be yourselves bringin' home our dinner tomorrow evenin'. We'll just be sleepin' in, if you don't mind.'

Laughter at the fishermen's table.

'By the way,' said Tom, 'when we registered our catch in the fishing log, we saw Tim Kavanagh's name, but no record of your catch.'

'Fishing log?'

'The fishing log by the dining room door. What was it, now, a fifteen-pound salmon?'

He felt the heat in his face. 'Good Lord! I thought I was signing the guest register.'

Laughter all around; he was laughing himself.

'Reverend,' said Liam, 'may I speak with you a moment?'

'Of course.'

'Excuse us, Mrs. Kav'na. Only a moment.'

They passed Pud, stationed at the door with his shoe, and walked up to the library. Coals simmered in the grate.

'I went out to the power box to see if I could

make heads or tails of this thing,' said Liam. 'The lines have been cut.'

'Nothing to do with the storm?'

'No, no. Cut clean through.' Liam appeared stricken. 'I don't want to alarm the household; I don't know what to make of it.'

'Looks like you've enough candles to go around, and I believe you said the power company comes tomorrow.'

'But who would do such a bloody wicked thing?'

That was the trouble with being clergy—people often believed you knew it all. Then there were those who believed you knew nothing, which had its own set of aggravations.

'I'm sorry, I can't imagine.'

'Of course, of course, righto.' Liam furrowed his brow, dazed. 'But thanks. It helps to tell somebody.'

'Anything I can do?'

'Don't say anything, please; 't will alarm th' house. I'll try to get the ESB out first thing tomorrow, and the Garda, as well. 't is a right cod.'

Coffee was served in the library, where William had taken up residence at the checkerboard. Seamus arrived from his walk downhill, bringing a scent of pipe smoke and hedges into the room. He felt a certain completeness in this patchwork company.

'Figs are my favorite,' Cynthia said when Anna joined them by the fire. 'And your ice cream with verbena . . . I can't find words. It was the loveliest of desserts. Thank you.'

'So glad you enjoyed it. We want you to be happy here.' Anna lowered her eyes and said, 'I'd like to apologize.'

'Whatever for?'

'For Bella's attitude. She's not as gracious to guests as we'd wish. She's . . . in training, you might say. I hope you'll overlook any faults.'

'You needn't apologize,' said Cynthia. 'We shall pray for things to go well.'

Anna glanced up sharply. 'Yes. Thank you.'

'Your father is a handsome fellow,' he said.

'He's an oul' dote, yes. He was quite the prize-fighter in his day, and a fine storyteller when you get him started. He also likes to tell of seeing Mr. Yeats's funeral cortege when his body came back to Dublin in '48.'

William and Seamus had set up their board and were leaning over it, each with a pint by his elbow.

'Da has his one pint of Guinness each evening, as does Seamus. They're two of our more temperate guests.' He thought her smile engaging, a giving out of herself.

'By the way,' said Anna, 'how's your jet lag?'

'I thought we'd cured it with a long nap this afternoon,' said Cynthia, 'but I'm fading again.'

'Let's go up,' he said. He would finish the letter tonight and post it tomorrow with the drawing. Henry would be eager to hear and to see.

They said their good nights to all and walked along the stone-flagged corridor and up the stairs. Shadows cast by the chamber stick leaped ahead of them on the walls.

'This is a dash too *Wuthering Heights*,' she said. 'Maybe I'm ready for the power to come on.'

'Maybe I am, too.'

He opened their door and set the stick on the night table, grateful to see their bed had been turned down.

'Tell you what. I'm going to run back and get a flashlight, the one I used this morning wasn't top-notch. Back in a jiffy, okay?'

'Okay,' she said. 'Should I close the window?'

'Leave it open; it'll be good to have a little fresh air after the turf smoke.'

He had reached the foot of the stairs when

he heard her scream. It pierced his heart like a knife, froze him to the spot.

Again, she screamed.

He was up the stairs and across the landing and up the second flight in what seemed an instant.

'My God!' he shouted into their darkened room. 'Are you all right?'

A pale light shone from the hall sconces; she was clinging to the bedpost.

'Are you all right?' He took her in his arms.

'A man in the armoire, he jumped out the window.'

'Are you hurt?'

'My ankle,' she said. 'When he came out, I stepped back and knocked the candle off the table, it was dark . . .' Her body was racked by violent trembling.

'Reverend!' Liam with a flashlight. 'Did we hear a shout?'

'There was a man in the room, he came out of the wardrobe.'

'God above! Are you all right?'

'My ankle,' said Cynthia.

'Where did he go?'

'Out the window,' he told Liam. 'What's down there?'

'The herb garden. What did he look like?'

'He was covering his face with one hand,' she said, 'but I know he was tall. It was so dark . . .' She shook like a jackhammer; her teeth chattered as he held her.

'I'll send Anna up, and get Dr. Feeney out to have a look—or should we drive you to hospital?'

'No, please. No.' She was crying, soundless.

'The candle is somewhere on the floor. Could you look it up and get a light going?'

'Righto. For th' love of God.'

The wick flamed; the room came dimly back to them.

'I'll ring the Garda. 't will alarm the house but can't be helped. I'm sorry, Mrs. Kav'na, Reverend, I have no idea . . . Jesus, Joseph, Mary, an' all th' saints.' Liam crossed himself, and disappeared into the shadowed smudge of the hallway.

He helped Cynthia to the green chair, his heart still racing, then turned to shut the window. The smell was familiar to him from his mother's Mississippi gardens—it was the heavy, languorous scent of crushed mint.

# Seven

'There, now,' said James Feeney. 'Nothing broken as far as I can tell.'

The silver-haired, blade-thin doctor was
seated on the footstool by Cynthia's chair, her
foot resting in his lap. Several chamber sticks lit
the room.

'But that's only as far as I can tell. It's swelling more than a bit. 'T would be wise to have
X-rays. That would be best.'

'No, please,' she said. 'Can't I just stay off it
awhile?'

'My best advice is for X-rays.'

'Please, no, I'll do anything.'

Feeney gave a kind of sigh. 'Then you must

stay off it, of course. For some days. Perhaps a boot . . .'

'No boot,' she said, dismayed. 'I just had one. I promise I'll stay off it.'

His wife was not known for being a model patient; the doctor's face registered frustration.

'You'll need crutches, then; I can lend you a pair.'

'Déjà vu all over again,' she said, quoting a ballplayer whose name she could never remember.

'There's no way around the use of crutches unless you confine yourself to your room. And you don't appear to be a lady who enjoys confinement.'

'I'll use the crutches, of course. Thank you, Doctor. Will you forgive me?'

Feeney smiled. 'Absolutely. We'll do what we can and hope for the best.'

Through the closed window, voices in the garden below. An occasional arc of light glanced across the panes.

'Anna, bring a glass of water, please. Reverend, see that she's given one of these every four to six hours, as needed.' Feeney rummaged in his case, fetched up an envelope, shook out a pill.

'You should sleep well tonight, but the pain

may give you a fit 'til the medication gets going.'
The doctor stood and took her hand. 'As in
most of our travails, Mrs. Kav'na, patience will
be the best cure.'

She swallowed the pill with a long draught
of water. 'I'm a dab short on patience, Doctor,
but quite long on endurance.'

'Can't I talk you into having it x-rayed? I
could take you into Sligo myself, if that would
help.'

'May I just see how it goes for a day or two?'

'Very well.' Feeney looked his way, amused.
*So this is what you live with*, he seemed to say.
'I'm afraid you must give a few minutes to the
Garda. They've done all they can without hav-
ing their chat with the eyewitness. Are you up
to it?'

'I am,' she said.

'I see you're reading the oul' journal,' said
Feeney. He opened the cover, peered in.

'A page-turner, actually.'

Feeney laughed. 'Never had more than a
minute or two to sit with it. Perhaps when I
retire.' He closed the cover, hefted his black
bag. 'Well, then, I'll be back with the crutches
first thing in the morning, and of course, if you
need me, give us a shout. Anna, why don't you

stay with Mrs. Kav'na while the reverend and I have a moment?'

'Of course.' Anna's face was blanched. 'Thank you, Doctor.'

'See that the Gards make it brief with Mrs. Kav'na, she needs her rest.' Feeney kissed Anna on the cheek. 'Take care of yourself, Anna Conor, you're working too hard and we can't have you poorly. I prescribe two weeks in the Ibiza countryside.'

He went with Feeney to the landing. Murmurs, occasional merriment from the library. The scent of pipe smoke.

'She must stay off the foot,' said Feeney. 'Absolutely—I don't know what's going on in there. My guess is it's a sprain, but no way to know without the X-ray.'

'I'll see to it,' he said.

'I regret the terrible fright you've had. I've been a friend of the Conor family for more than forty years, and must say I feel the upset very keenly for all of you. While I'm thinking of it, your wife will need help on the stairs. Crutches are bloody suicide on stairs.'

'I'm wondering . . . we have family coming in a few days. They'll be at Broughadoon for a night, then we've a car trip planned.'

'Give me a notion of your itinerary.'

'A few cemeteries, the ruin of the Kavanagh family seat . . .'

'Where is that?'

'Fourteen kilometers east and across a sheep pasture.' He knew the verdict already. 'Then Borris House, the Connemara coast . . .'

Feeney pulled at his chin. 'No, no, I don't think so. Not at all. But we'll talk tomorrow. By the way, do you play bridge?'

'Bridge? Roughly the same way I sit a horse.'

'And what way is that?'

'With great trepidation.'

Feeney chuckled. 'Once a month, Liam's mother has the local priest and myself in for lunch and an afternoon of bridge. We're always scouting for a fourth.'

He felt indebted to a man routed from his armchair at a late hour, to attend a willful patient. But, as for sitting at a bridge table, he'd rather have a root canal.

'Perhaps I'll think about it.' He shook Feeney's hand. 'Our warmest thanks for your kindness.'

'Hope you can join us day after tomorrow. Seamus turns out a fine lunch. 't would be champion of you.'

Feeney trotted down the stairs, passing Liam and the uniformed officers coming up. 'Try to make quick work of it, gentlemen. The lady has had a great fright.'

He felt her anguish as if it were his own—indeed, it was his own.

'Anything gone missing?' asked Liam.

'I did a quick search—don't think so.'

''t will be crowded in there. I'll just be in the hall if you need me, I'm tryin' to run down the ESB on th' mobile.'

He went in with two officers and a photographer from the Crime Unit and stood by her as they asked questions and made notes. Bursts of light from the camera flash lit the room.

Tall, quite tall, yes. He covered his face with one hand and it was very dark, only a candle burning, she had no idea what he looked like. She had no memory of his hair color—it seemed his head was covered in some way. He must have been young, as he was very quick going over the sill and out the window. She had come into the room only moments before opening the door of the armoire. When he bolted out, he'd thrown his other hand in front of him and struck her arm, all of which caused her to stumble backward and turn her ankle.

Had the Kav'nas discovered anything missing? They had not.

A Gard pulled on a glove and opened the right-hand door of the armoire. Peered in, closed it. Opened the door on the left—drawers only.

'Anything missing?'

'Haven't looked carefully, but don't think so.'

Cynthia speculated that the intruder had been in the room when he heard them coming along the hall earlier than expected, and had hidden himself in the armoire. The Gards speculated that the intruder may have been looking for easy pickings while the guests were at dinner, and since no one at Broughadoon had found anything missing, perhaps he was frightened off at the top of his rounds. Very likely, they agreed, the intruder had not singled out the Kavanaghs.

Was Mrs. Kav'na known to travel with jewelry?

Only her wedding band, a watch, a strand of pearls, two pairs of earrings.

Was Mr. Kav'na known to travel with cash?

No more than a couple hundred euros, in this case. And he always kept his wallet in his pants pocket, never in a guest room.

Had their room door been locked?

There were no guest-room keys at Broughadoon.

A Gard reported that the soil beneath the
window was freshly raked of footprints; a rake
was found propped by the gate which opened
to a gravel path; the herbs beneath the window
were trampled.

Had the Kavanaghs seen anyone in the hall?
Noticed anyone suspicious about the place since
they arrived? Would the Kavanaghs mind being
fingerprinted, and having fingerprint work
done on various surfaces in their room?

They wouldn't mind.

Cynthia leaned her head against the back of
the chair and closed her eyes. Anna appeared
at the door with a pot of tea. The travel club
passed along the hall with chamber sticks, peer-
ing into the room and speaking in hushed
voices. This would be a long night.

He stepped out to the landing with Liam.

'I asked them to dust the power box for fingerprints while they're at it,' said Liam. 'God's
truth, I hate this for you. We won't charge you
anything, 't is on th' house entirely.'

'Don't think about it, please.'

'Nothing like this ever happened before.
We're a very quiet, very decent sort of place.'

'Of course.'

'Anything missing, Reverend?'

'I don't think so. Please call me Tim.'

'Ah, no. I've never called a clergyman by his Christian name, Catholic or Protestant.'

'Give it a try when you feel up to it.'

'Yes. Well. A whiskey, then?'

'Not for me, thanks.'

'Seamus has gone to fetch our Maureen McKenna to be fingerprinted. He said tell you he's ready to give a hand if needed.'

'I appreciate it. How are the other guests?'

'O'Malley's dead asleep in th' library; the other lads have signed off for the evenin'. As for the travel club, they thought th' Gards were real dotes in their new uniforms. So'—Liam shrugged—'they all took it in stride; I was afraid the women would be checkin' out. There'll likely be a wing chair or two pushed up to their doors tonight.'

'Anything missing from the rooms?'

'Doesn't appear to be.'

'I'd like you to know I'm praying about this. All of it.'

Liam looked startled. 'After my father died, I forgot that sort of thing—praying. I put it behind me. Some call it lapsed. As for me, Reverend, I'm pure fallen. Fallen entirely.'

It was a quarter to one when he reached to the night table and looked at his watch. It was close in the room—the body heat and commotion had churned up the peace of it—but he had no intention of opening the window.

He thanked God that nothing worse had happened tonight, and wondered again if they should have made the trip at all. From the very outset, their Ireland plans had been hindered by cancellation and delay, and now this terrible fright for her, and pain into the bargain.

He listened for a time to her whiffling snore, a musical sort of sound, actually, which had always charmed him. She would make the best of it; she was good at making the best of things.

Across the Pond in Mitford, tourists were strolling Main Street, languid and bemused in mountain air far sweeter than the August haze they'd left behind. Dooley would have finished up his day as a vet's assistant, and gone into Mitford, perhaps, to take his three brothers and sister for pizza-with-everything. He thought of the tall, lanky boy with inquisitive eyes and the way he laughed and the way his laughter infected others. He prayed for Dooley's wisdom and discernment, and for the safekeeping of all the siblings, reunited after years of loss.

He had just found the sweet spot in his pillow when he felt movement beneath their bed. He lay frozen with alarm, listening.

Then, the rapid thumping sound, known to him as the Scratching of the Odd Flea.

'Pud,' he hissed. 'Come out of there.'

# Eight

'I'm so sorry for all of it,' said Anna. 'Most guests would have been dreadfully upset by last night, and no power to boot. They'd be packin' up this morning, sure enough. You're a very kind man.'

He was often called kind, and never knew what to say in response. He certainly didn't think he was *very* kind—curious more like it, interested enough in what was going on not to complain of discomfort within reason.

'And then to have our dog sleeping under your bed. He's done it only once before—adopted himself out to a schoolteacher on holiday from Cavan.'

'I'm his first Yank, then.'

Anna smiled a little. 'We got him from a shelter. They said he belonged to a very hard man; Pud doesn't like the raised voice.' She sighed, then straightened herself. 'Still and all, I shall give you rhubarb every morning if that would make it up a bit.'

'No need to make it up,' he said, 'but I'll gladly take it.'

They sat at the breakfast table, waiting for Liam to bring out Cynthia's fry.

'How is Cynthia this morning?'

'She slept well, and was singing a little before I came down.' Where Christ is, Dorothy Sayers had said, cheerfulness will keep breaking in. A description, *in toto*, of the woman who shared his bed.

'Do you think she might like to move rooms?'

'She hasn't mentioned it.' Unloading drawers, schlepping their jumble—an aggravation he wasn't up to.

'We don't have an extra room available, but one of the anglers may be willing to make an exchange. I could ask Pete, his room would give you a larger bath and a lovely writing table.'

'Same view?'

'Ah, no. Blocked by the beeches, I'm afraid.

I've given you our prettiest room, really, with hardly a twig to obscure the scenery.'

'Thanks,' he said. 'Unless you hear otherwise, we'll stick where we are.'

'Two of the travel club will be bunking together tomorrow to free up the room for your cousins. That was understood when the ladies booked.'

'Musical chairs,' he said.

'Always.' Anna ran her fingers through a reckless mass of red curls. 'Forgive my appearance, Reverend, I've somehow not put the comb to my head this morning. It's as much to keep as the garden.'

She was a beautiful, big-boned woman, intense and present to the moment, with eyes that appeared to take in a horde of details and sort them at lightning speed. Their eyes met as he lifted the cup and polished off his coffee—she looked worn, conflicted, and for a brief moment made no effort to conceal it. He felt there was something she wanted to say to him—four decades of counseling had honed a certain skill at sensing trial behind the forced smile, the hard jaw, the stiff upper lip.

'I hope you won't regret not getting about 'til the cousins arrive. There are so many grand places to see—Ben Bulben, of course, and the lovely Knocknarea walk to Queen Maeve's grave, and Lissadell House and Inishmurray Island, and, oh, the Tubbercurry Fair coming . . .'

She went on, dutiful in limning the list. Even if they could get about, he lacked the grit to look at anything grand or affecting just now—the view of the lake was enough. He'd never been much of a tourist, and anyway, he'd seen a lot of Sligo on the previous trip. A day in the library would be a banquet of sorts, with a jog by the lake in the afternoon. He had no idea what to do about Walter and Katherine showing up full of vim and vigor, unscathed, as usual, by jet or any other lag. Bottom line, James Feeney was in possession of their immediate future. If Cynthia couldn't ramble over hill and dale, neither would he.

He was leaving the dining room when Anna dropped a fork, which hit the wood floor, bounced, and skidded under a dish cupboard. He set the tray down.

'I'll get it,' he said, dropping at once to his hands and knees.

'No, no, please,' she said. 'Let me, please.'

'I can see it, it's right back . . .' He tried to reach the thing, but it eluded him. 'A broom,' he said. Peggy had taught him the efficacy of the broom handle—useful for everything from removing spiderwebs in ceiling corners to adjusting a high-hanging picture on the wall. Anna supplied a broom.

He retrieved the fork, embarrassed that he couldn't shoot to his feet like a young curate. Halfway up, he took the hand she offered.

'There,' she said, smiling.

'There,' he said, handing over the fork.

They burst into laughter, the nonsensical kind that felt good and didn't strain anything in the process.

He was passing through the library with the breakfast tray, noting that the fire had been poked up.

'Yoo hoo, darling, over here. Scooted down the stairs on me bum, then found an umbrella in the stair hall and used it as a cane.'

There she sat in a chair by the open window, looking up-for-anything. He was foolishly happy. 'You heedless woman.'

He set the tray on the lamp table and rounded up one of the several footstools and placed the tray on it and shook out her napkin and draped it across her lap.

'Wait,' he said, ''til your doctor hears about this.'

'I've just heard about it from Maureen.' James Feeney strode in from the hall with a pair of crutches and propped them against the wall. 'Good morning to all. We have here a very clever woman. Stays off her foot, as the doctor ordered, and still gets about like a field hare. Did you rest?' Feeney asked his patient.

'Well enough, thanks—the little pills are a godsend.'

'Sorry to interrupt your breakfast, I'll have a quick look if you don't mind.' Feeney squatted by the chair. 'Have you ever used crutches?'

'Yes, just recently. And before that, when I was ten years old. I painted one red and one yellow, and added green ribbons.'

'A harbinger of things to come. I'm told you're a famous children's book illustrator.' He examined her ankle. 'Swollen, inflamed, stiff. All to be expected.' He gave the ankle a slight turn. 'How does that feel?'

'Not bad.'

'This?'

She flinched. 'Ugh.'

'When you were ten—was it your ankle that put you on crutches?'

'Yes. The same one. Sprained badly.'

'And your recent fracture. How did that happen?'

'Missed a porch step,' she said.

'I broke my ankle entirely when I was nine. I was learning to fly with my older brother, Jack.'

'Did you learn?'

'Ah, no, but Jack did. Royal Air Force. We lost him in France.'

'I'm sorry.'

Feeney cleared his throat. 'Yes, well, I recommend you stay off it for at least ten days. You have history with this ankle and must treat it with due regard. Ten days should do the trick, but absolutely no hobbling about or you'll put it in a worse muddle than we have here.

'As for the other piece of business, I can't recommend you go on the car trip. Sorry. 't would be begging trouble, in my opinion.' Feeney stood more slowly than he'd squatted. 'Practice with the crutches before going full steam, if you will, I'm no good at mending bones. Reverend, if you'd give a thought to our bridge party tomorrow, I'd be delighted. You'll make me a hero in the eyes of our hostess, not to mention the village priest.'

He looked at Cynthia—she would bail him out; she knew how he felt about bridge.

'Oh, do go,' she said. 'I'll be so happy staying here with the journal. I'm headed into the mysterious spread of an unidentified bacteria.'

'You'll regret it,' he said to Feeney. 'I'm no thumping good at it. Believe me.'

Feeney laughed. 'Our hostess relishes a good slaughter now and then. I should know—I've been the poor pig more than once. Well, then, many thanks, Reverend. See you up there at one o'clock tomorrow.' Feeney gave his hand a first-rate pump and turned to his patient. 'And no more depending on the odd umbrella.'

The doctor was gone as quickly as he'd come.

'Dadgum it, Kavanagh. See what you've done with your meddling?'

'You don't want to go?'

'Do I enjoy playing bridge?'

'Well, no. But think how interesting it will be to see the house, you can tell me everything. And of course, look how nice he's being to us. You made him quite happy, I think.'

'Seems to me he was happy enough to begin with.'

She asked a blessing she'd learned in child-hood, tucked into her eggs, ignored his huff.

'You won't miss all the roaming about we've looked forward to for nine years?'

'Eight,' she said. 'It's actually the best of

birthday presents, just staying here. No contracts to fulfill, no dear James on the phone gouging a calendar or gift book out of me. And my retired husband off on a wonderful adventure.'

'That remains to be seen.'

'I regret it, of course, for Walter and Katherine's sake—all their best-laid plans upset.' She looked at him, appealing. 'I regret it for you, too. Are you terribly disappointed?'

'Not in the least. Not even a little.' He saw the pain in her face, the stress of last night. His wife was a better man than himself. 'I'll ring them in a few hours; it's the middle of the night in New Jersey. There'll be rooms to cancel, that sort of thing.' Katherine had arranged all details of the car trip.

'When this ankle business is over, we can visit the family castle and all the other places we've talked about—even Yeats's grave.' With a look of mock severity, she recited Yeats's self-written epitaph. 'Cast a cold eye on life, on death / Horseman, pass by.'

'Whatever that means,' he said.

Liam hurried in. 'The ESB just arrived. We'll have power before lunch, please God. And I've a grand idea, see what you think.'

'Say on.'

'We've an old estate wagon, a Vauxhall. William bought it before we converted to kilometers, makes th' Rover look brand-new. You could practice drivin' up and down th' lane for a warm-up, then venture out to the highway—and if you scrape a fender, there's nothing lost. 't will be a piece of cake. Give it a thought, I'm at the power box if needed.'

'What a terrific idea,' exclaimed his wife. 'You should do it, darling.'

Why was everyone after him to be *doing*? The notion that he might loll about was appalling, he supposed, and this after forty-plus years of running himself ragged. Apparently one must sustain an injury in order to loll unmolested by the well-meaning.

'Are you out of your mind?' he asked when Liam left the room.

'Not yet, but I know you. You only think you want to spend a day in the library. You need to get out and about, Timothy, stir your bones. That's what makes you tick.'

God help him—now he had no mind of his own.

'All those years wearing out shoe leather on the streets of Mitford—it made you so happy to walk the beat, see your flock, *mingle*.'

On the other hand, the fellows in the pub

had certainly enjoyed a good laugh over his fear of driving on the wrong side. 't isn't th' wrong side, they howled, har, har.

'We'll see,' he said. 'And what about you for today?'

'I'm sticking in this chair, where I can watch all the coming and going.'

'In the thick of things.'

'Correct.'

'So much for Thomas à Kempis.'

'If you'd please go up and get the journal and my sketchbook and watercolors, and the Patrick Kavanagh poems and the book on the hunger years . . . just bring the whole darned thing, I'll be living out of it for a while.'

In the room, he looked for the cell phone and charger, pawing through the drawers, his suitcase, her suitcase, his jacket pockets, his shaving kit, aggravated by the amount of plunder they'd dragged over. He'd never be the one sailing through air terminals with a suitcase the size of a Whitman's Sampler.

Had he even brought the blasted phone? He hardly used it, except for the occasional call home while doing errands in Wesley, but Katherine had insisted he must have it, along with the phone company's international package.

He was not amused to find the charger cord stuffed into a sock.

'There you are, Rev'rend!'

He looked up.

'Maureen! And there you are!' The open narrative of her face drew him in at once.

'We're glad to have you an' Mrs. Kav'na.' She set the laundry basket by the door and came to him with a bobbing gait and shook his hand. He liked the feel of her callused palm in his.

'Maureen McKenna, Rev'rend.'

'A pleasure to meet you.'

She put her hand over her mouth like a child, dubious. 'Mrs. Kav'na says I'm to call her Cynthia?'

'Absolutely, she likes that.'

'M' husband's youngest brother married a Kav'na from Wexford, and my great-grandfather's second wife was a Kav'na.'

'Small world.'

She beamed. 'Did you like my drawin', Rev'rend?'

'Very, very much.'

'Maureen, she says, I'm drawin' your inner beauty, an' I says, all th' beauty I've got is th' inner. Then she puts th' oul' hump in m' nose, an' I say, can you erase that off, mebbe? Ah, no, she says, 't is a *lovely* hump. 't was th' same as lookin' in th' mirror, that drawin'. She made me a gift of it this mornin', 't will go in a nice frame over th' telly.'

Mere wisps of pale red hair remained on her head, like the Velveteen Rabbit in its age.

'Did we meet when I was here ten years ago?'

'Ah, no, 't was th' death of me poor husband, Tarry, that kept us away then.'

'I'm sorry.'

''t is a lonely washin' that hasn't a man's shirt in it.'

'I'm sure.'

'But I've never missed a day since. I was with Anna from the first, when she started out alone to fix the oul' place. 't was a ruin, Rev'rend. She was slavin' for Mrs. Conor up Catharmore by day, and us workin' down here in th' evenin' like menfolk.

'Then Herself gave Anna th' boot an' Liam, God bless 'im, came with her. They were married in th' library with all th' rubble an' plaster lyin' about an' their guests lookin' through th' roof at th' blue sky. I said, 't was open to God an' all 'is angels for pourin' down blessin's on us. Aye, an' they've poured down through bad times an' good, with Anna's gift for pinchin' th' penny.'

Tears pooled in her eyes. 'Troth, she's a queen, Anna Conor. An' look at me jabberin' when I'm after collectin' your laundry.'

She held out the basket as one might present the wafer, there was grace in the gesture.

'Cynthia says send th' shirt you wore on th' plane and your personals; she wants her wee bit in the top drawer, she says.'

'The fishermen got away early, I take it?'

'Oh, they did. An' th' ladies an' their ghillies will be out all day to the Lung Valley, so 't was a big fry this mornin'. Everybody was speakin' of th' terrible thing that happened to your lovely wife—please God, it shouldn't ruin her holiday.'

He deposited Cynthia's offering in the basket and rummaged on the floor of the armoire for his own bit.

'Mr. O'Malley was searchin' everywhere this mornin' for 'is orange pullover with a hood, but surely nobody would steal such as that, he says. I thought mebbe he sent it down with 'is laundry an' Bella folded it with th' family wash, but 't was no pullover to be found. Mr. O'Malley calls it 'is lucky fishin' shirt, so we're all on th' hunt for 't.'

'And I've been tearing up jack looking for my cell phone.'

He delivered the Mobile Library and Snack Hamper to the patient, found Liam, took him up on his offer, listened to a tutorial on the idiosyncrasies of the vehicle, collected the keys, had serious second thoughts.

Then again, why not? It was a beautiful morning, cool as mid–May in Carolina, and what did he have to lose? He and Walter had talked about Katherine needing a backup driver, just in case. One thing was clear—he did not want Walter to be the backup driver. When Walter looked away from the road, as was his wont, the car veered in the direction of his gaze.

William sat by the fire studying *The Sligo Champion*, Cynthia was absorbed in the journal. A true library, he thought.

'You're looking fit this morning, William.'

'Same as y'rself, Rev'rend. I hear you'll be takin' a turn in m' oul' clunker—she was a beauty in her day.'

'I've decided to step up to the plate and drive like an Irishman.' He jangled the keys.

'Ye are an Irishman,' said William.

He kept forgetting that.

''t is a grand, soft day for runnin' about. Might I go with ye, then?'

'Why, yes. Of course.'

''t isn't th' automatic Yanks are after drivin', she's a stick.'

'I drive a stick at home.'

William collected his cane, buttoned his cardigan. 'Your missus says she's comin' along with th' ankle.'

'She is. Dr. Feeney had a look this morning. She just needs to stay off the foot.'

'We're ruined entirely by such as that—jumpin' out of cupboards at defenseless women an' all. Anna, she'll make it up to ye some way.'

'No need. I'll just say goodbye to my wife and we'll be off.'

He wasn't so sure about this.

'Okay, Kav'na. I'm out of here to practice driving on the wrong side. Do you need to practice with your crutches before I go? You can't sit there forever without moving around.'

Through the open window, the distant sound of a bleating sheep. She looked up in the dreamy way she had when her mind was elsewhere. 'It'll be three times in a half century I've raced around on the wicked things; I'll be fine, just set them closer.'

He set them closer, leaned down, and kissed her. 'Stay off that historic ankle.'

Anna came in from the entrance hall with a

trug of purple iris. 'Da,' she said, anxious, 'are you off somewhere?'

'I'm goin' with th' rev'rend to help with 'is drivin'.'

'I need all the help I can get,' he told Anna.

'Are you sure, Reverend?'

'If somebody around here would just call me Tim,' he said, mocking the wistful.

'I've never—'

'I know—you've never called a clergyman by his first name.'

'Yes. I mean, no. Never.'

'Try it,' he said.

''tis th' Protestants don't mind th' first name,' declared William.

She took a deep breath, smiled her engaging smile. 'Tim.'

'See there?'

'Put on your ones an' twos an' come with us,' said William.

'No, Da, I've got my work to do. Go and enjoy yourself.'

She pressed his hand, he smelled the faint scent of iris. 'Have a good time, then, and come back safe, please God.'

They crunched over the gravel to a faded green vehicle unlike anything he'd ever seen, and clambered in. William sat with his cane between his knees, expectant.

He fumbled with the ignition, stepped on the brake, pushed in the clutch, fired the engine.

A cacophony of shrieks and moans, and they were off.

He glanced in disbelief at William, who was laughing, and tried to wrench the stick out of first gear into second, but could not; it might have been set in concrete.

'You got t' *torment* th' bugger!' William shouted over the roar and babble.

'Pull back on 't, 't will squawk like ye're strippin' it. Are ye heavy on th' clutch? Bear down!'

He bore down and wrestled the stick into second. Perspiration blew from all pores. Then, the gear grooved into its sweet spot and they were out of the car park and into the narrow lane.

Green fields furled away on either side of the track, the broad lake gleamed on their right. He got a deep breath, looked at William, laughed.

'Runnin' like a top!' shouted his passenger.

The intense green of Ireland had become a cliché, he supposed, with all credit going to the goodness of rain. But it was composed of more, he reckoned, than a plenitude of moisture—

something supernal was ever rising from the core of this ancient land carved by glaciers.

A goulash of gear rattled on the backseat—hubcaps, spare tires, a jumble of waders and Wellingtons, a jar of nails, a couple of salmon nets.

'Any morning traffic in the lane—to speak of?'

'Maybe th' lad as tends th' deer comin' in, maybe not. Can't say.'

'What about the steering?' The wheel was behaving like a loose tooth.

''t is a lazy wheel, ye'll have to show it what's what.'

He should have taken a swing around the car park before setting off. When bombarded by other people's agendas for his time and energy, he lost entirely what feeble mind he possessed. But that was all spilled milk and no use bawling; he was doing this thing.

Somewhere toward the end of the hedgerows, he did what he feared—ran too close to the masquerade of moss and ivy and struck the stone beneath. There was the horrific sound of scraping metal, as the side mirror was ripped from its hinges.

He killed the engine. The jet lag which he'd

largely ignored, together with the upheaval of last night, crashed in. He had no strength even for humiliation.

'I'll replace it,' he said. 'I'm sorry.'

'Ah, now, every dog's a pup 'til he hunts. 't is no matter. Crank 'er up an' keep goin'.'

He cranked her up. Stuck the smashed and dangling mirror back on its thingamajig. Wrestled the stick into reverse. Backed away from the wall.

'Hold it!' shouted William. 'Ye'll be knockin' off th' taillamp. All right, now, pull ahead.'

He crossed himself. He pulled ahead. They were off.

Somehow—he didn't know how—the whole equation started to work once they clamored past what Aengus Malone called the landlord walls.

'I'm going out to the highway,' he said, 'if it's all right with you.'

'Go out!' said the old man. In the strong morning light, William's hair was a blaze of white fire.

'Left or right?' he asked.

'Left!'

Once they hit asphalt, the rattle and bang of the thing had a kind of music, after all. The noise was similar to the effect of taps on a shoe—letting a man know he was alive, and breathing, and going where he had to go.

'Hallelujah,' he said.

'Ah-men,' said William. 'An' there's a pub down th' way.'

'Not for me, thanks.'

'Ah, no, for me,' said William. ''t is a long month of Sundays since I drank a pint with th' sun up.'

Roughly three miles on the wrong side, and so far, so good, he thought, as they topped the hill and pulled onto the gravel of the roadside pub.

They sat at the bar with the morning sun warming their backs through the open door.

'I was a livin' terror,' said William.

'I'd fight a bear if there be one about. 't was a monstrous thing reared up in me as a lad. It frightened even m'self, an' scared th' wits out of th' boys I roughed about with. When it came on, 't would send 'em runnin' home to their oul' mothers.

'I felt all th' rage of Ireland in me, fierce to come out. I'd have been a happier man if it'd come out in farmin' th' land, or somethin' more peaceable. My oul' da used to say a bit he got from your man Virgil: *If I can't move heaven, I'll raise hell.*

'An Irishman in those days had no chance of movin' heaven, so a number of us tried the other device.

'Back then, young an' old still collected at th' crossroads in these wild regions, to talk an' joke and play th' fiddle—but me, I'd go there to fight. I'd hardly a shoe to me foot those days, but all th' while, th' name of William Donavan was goin' round th' townlands an' villages 'til th' whole of Sligo knew it. Now an' again, I was smokin' grapevine an' dinin' off seaweed, but I earned a quid or two—an' every man I fought, Irish or no, I pictured in m' mind as English. 't was the *incentive*, m' father called it, an' bedad, if it didn't work most of th' time.

''t was all a savage piece of business, Rev'rend, an' a miracle I'm sittin' here in your face today with these ears modeled off a cauliflower.

'I was seventeen yares old when they promoted a fight as they had in th' early times, though 't was by then against th' law to fight in such a brute manner. They went up an' down th' roads from Ballysadare to Curry, talkin' it up. 't was to be three rounds—one with swords, one bare-knuckle, one with th' cudgels, as they did in th' former century. My oul' father called it *cum gladiis et fustibus*, he spoke the odd bit of Latin learned from my grandfather.'

William took a draught of his Guinness.

'I'd handled a sword a good bit an' it came easy enough. First round I made a deep cut to 'is left buttock an' drew th' blood they were lookin' for; second, I done 'im up with my bare fists in three minutes. Third was th' cudgels, an' th' most violent brawl a man could ever hope to see, m'self included. 't was like I stepped out of me flesh, walked out of it like an oul' overcoat and was fightin' on th' side of the angels. If it came to th' worst, I said, 't would be my own way of dyin' for Ireland.

'He dealt me a crushin' blow to th' ribs, I heard 'em snap like twigs, an' th' breath went out of me altogether. But I managed to deal him a blow to th' knee. Smashed 'is kneecap, I remember th' sound of it, an' down he went.

'Mother of God, I only did such as that th' once, I niver did it again to any man. At th' end, they were cheerin' an' liftin' me up, a great bag of wicked pain an' bleedin' flesh, an' 't was William Donavan who won th' match.

'That one got th' name abroad, an' a cunnin' man from Enniskillen to manage th' all of it. It put a head on me, th' uproar an' blather—I was

thinkin' m'self next in line to th' great John L.
Sullivan. 't was Sullivan who said when he
started boxin', he felt he could knock out any
man livin', an' so did I.'

William hauled forth a handkerchief, gave
his nose a fierce blow. 'Th' sinuses!' he said.
'From m' nose bein' broken th' three times.

'And here we went, then, to Bundoran, Long-
ford, Roscommon, Ballina, Boyle, Carrick-on-
Shannon—every place there was a man to fight,
an' th' Irish were fightin' men. Then there was
Collooney—an' 't was in Collooney I met th'
woman I proposed to marry.' William's blue
eyes were bright, as with fever.

'William,' said the bartender, 'introduce me
to th' father.'

't is no father, 't is th' Rev'rend Timothy
Kav'na from th' States. Meet Jack Kennedy.'

'A pleasure,' said the bartender.

'Named for the Irish Jack who became our
President?'

'Ah, no, we've Jack Kennedys by th' legions.
Throw a cap in th' air, 't will come down on a
Jack Kennedy one way or another. I hear you
had a bit of noise at Broughadoon last night,
some fellow in your cupboards.'

'The bad news is th' quickest to go round,'
said William. 'How'd you hear such?'

'From th' Gards who came by for a bit of late supper. Any harm done?'

'Only to th' rev'rend's lovely wife. Havin' a man jump in y'r face at a late hour is harm enough, I'd say.'

'Sorry to hear it. He'll not be back, is my guess. I take it you're stayin' down the way, then.'

'My wife and I are at Broughadoon for a week or two, yes.'

'Fishin', are you?'

'No fishing.'

'He's learnin' to drive on th' wrong side of the road,' said William.

Jack Kennedy had himself a laugh. 'And how's it goin'?'

'Only one side mirror so far,' he said.

'Remember the old days, William, when you walked up and back from the lodge to have y'rself a smoke?'

'Aye, an' when a man had to step outside with his fag in a hard rain, I quit tobacco altogether.'

''t was th' smokin' and drinkin' laws gave us th' hardest blow,' said Jack. 'For m' father who opened this place, 't was the telly as corrupted the pub system by keepin' customers at home, and so we put the telly in the pubs an' that helped bring 'em back, don't you know, an' things were lookin' up—then along comes the punishin' limits on drinkin', an' while they're at it, they take away th' smokin' inside.' Jack threw up his hands. ''t is one heavy blade after another.'

'Saints above, Jack, you're exaggeratin' th' truth.'

'Th' truth, William, cannot be exaggerated.'

''t is savin' lives, if you read th' papers. We'll live longer to cheat th' devil.'

Jack laughed. 'You've a point, William, you've a point. An' never let it be said Jack Kennedy has th' tight fist. Your drinks are on th' house.'

'Ye never stood me a drink in me life.'

'You never came in with a rev'rend before, nor a man havin' a Diet Coke when he could have himself a pint.'

They were pulling out of the car park when he saw the bicycle moving along the highway at considerable speed. He braked for the bike to pass. Orange pullover, hood up. Rider sitting tall on the seat. Dark glasses. He waited for a time, staring after the southbound cyclist, then pulled onto the highway, confused for a moment about the side of the road he should occupy.

A couple of miles out, it dawned on him that this contraption would fly if you gave it its head. 'Where's the speedometer?' he shouted.

William pointed.

He whistled. 'Eighty miles an hour?'

''t is broke,' said William. 'More like forty.'

'You said your father spoke Latin?'

'Aye, a bit, and proud of it. My grandfather was a pupil in th' last of th' hedge schools where a lad got a proper education in th' classics. Of course, 't wasn't in th' hedges by then—'t was in a cow barn with th' stalls mucked out. Many a potato farmer in th' oul' days could quote your man Virgil. As a lad, I knew off a line or two, m'self.'

'Can you recite any of it?'

'Don't know as I can, but let me see, now.' William closed his eyes, bowed his head, thumped his cane in a long meditation. 'For th' love of God, 't is like scourin' for a needle in a haystack.'

'Don't fret yourself,' he said. 'I can read Virgil in Broughadoon's own library.'

'Here it comes!' shouted William. He threw his head back, eyes still closed.

*'In th' dawnin' spring,'* he orated over the clamor of the engine, *'when icy streams trickle*

*from snowy mountains, and crumblin' clod breaks at th' Zephyr's touch, even then would I have my bull groan o'er th' deep-driven plough, and th' share glisten when rubbed by th' furrow.'* William looked at him, nodded in triumph.

'Well done, sir, very well done. The deep-driven plough. The glistening share. Very fine.'

'An' that's th' end of it. 't would be squeezin' water from a stone to give ye another word. Are ye poet-minded, then?'

'Since I was a boy. I like the old fellows who wandered over hill and dale with their knapsacks. John Clare, Wordsworth, Cowper. My brother's a poet.' Speaking of Henry gave him an unexpected rush of pride, something like happiness.

He turned off the highway, into the long lane to Broughadoon.

'Where does your brother keep 'imself?'

'Outside Holly Springs, Mississippi. He's retired from the railroad.'

'I was after goin' to America as a lad an' ridin' your railroad. I had a mind to see Texas, but too late now.'

'Can't do everything, William.'

'Aye.'

'Were you at Broughadoon when I was here ten years ago?'

'Anna says I was off to visit my oul' brother, John, who passed two years back. I'm th' last of five, so.'

They were hitting the rain puddles pretty hard.

'You were saying you met a woman in Collooney.'

'Th' most beautiful woman you could imagine, if you was to imagine a woman.'

William was sullen for a time, gazing ahead.

'I promised her I'd come back an' marry her, 't was what I wanted above all else, an' she wanted it, too—so she said. But I was makin' a name for m'self, an' they were callin' for me in Dublin an' Wicklow an' Waterford an' all th' rest.

''t was th' agent after th' Enniskillen chancer had th' big dream, said he'd fashion me as th' modern Gentleman Jim Corbett. So he takes me an' m' swelled head an' we make th' crossin' from Dún Laoghaire to Angelsea, an' board th' train to London. I was feelin' royal by then, struttin' th' streets in me first pair of dacent shoes and money janglin' in every pocket.

'But I should've stuck where I was, Rev'rend,

for then they ran me up to Scotland for a full two yares, which is where I got th' lovely nose I'm wearin' an' th' scar on me forehead. Mother of God, th' Scots were a brutal lot.

'I was niver much of a drinker, I'd like ye to know. Love of th' drink is th' curse of th' land—makes a man shoot at 'is landlord, an' makes you miss 'im.

'Instead of leakin' me money away, I was savin' for a cottage—on a hillock proud of a little bogland, where a man might raise a family. I remember I could see it plain as day—a bench by the door an' a byre to th' side, and a clock with weights an' chains.

'Wherever I was, I would go out in th' night and look up at th' great swarm of th' Milky Way an' talk to th' heart of th' girl in Collooney. Aye, an' she would talk to me—not in a voice you could hear outright, but I felt th' sweetness of it in my blood, an' I'd tell her to wait for William Donavan. Wait for me, lass, I'd say, I'm comin' back.'

'And did you get back?'

'Ah, no, not for seven yares.' William gave him a fierce look. 'She was married to another.'

They passed the cow barn with its single blue shutter.

'I don't know much, William, but I do know this: Talking to the stars will not get the job done with a woman. I can personally vouch for it.'

William's face was dark with memory. 'The oul' termagant,' he said.

# Nine

'Didn't know if it was worth mentioning,' he said, 'but there you have it.'

'Tall, you say?' Liam's blue eyes had the gray look.

'Yes.'

'And thin.'

'Very.' Ichabod Crane personified.

'Riding a black bike.'

'Yes.'

'Would there have been a basket at the rear?'

'There was, actually.'

'God help us.'

'Someone you know, then.'

'Jack Slade. Th' blaggard I booted off th'

job. He worked up at Paddy's a few times, that's how I found him. I had a hunch about him, figured he was using drugs of some sort, but there's a lot of that in th' trade.' Liam rubbed his forehead. 'I turned a blind eye to 't because he was a star at th' coping.'

'He was wearing sunglasses, if that means anything.'

'He worked in sunglasses, almost never took them off. I'll call th' Garda, see what they think. Which direction was he headed?'

'South.'

'He has a place a few kilometers south. Did he see you, look your way? He would have recognized the vehicle.'

'He may have seen us as he topped the hill, but no, he didn't turn his head our way. O'Malley's shirt is still missing, I take it.'

'We tore the place apart this morning. Nowhere to be found.'

He wouldn't mention his cell phone yet— he wasn't absolutely certain he brought it. 'Any word on the fingerprints?'

'They said it could be a while—a lot of latent fingerprints from previous guests. I know a detective at the Garda station in Riverstown, a fellow named Corrigan. I'll give him a call with this.'

'Another piece of bad news,' he said, handing over the keys and hating the remorse. 'I drove too close to the wall and ruined the driver's-side mirror. I'll replace it. I'm sorry.' He couldn't remember so many regrets being exchanged in such a short span of time.

'If that was all the bad news to be had around here, I'd be dancin' at th' crossroads. How did it go?'

'Always the silver lining, as you say—I think I nailed it. But—we met only eight or ten cars on the highway and nothing in the lane, so no great challenge.'

Liam managed a smile. ''t is what's in th' lane that makes th' Irish driver. Have another go, anytime. William behaved himself?'

'We made a short visit to Jack Kennedy. Hope that was all right.'

'Aye, William will be talkin' about it for days.'

'I'll need to use your mobile to call New Jersey.' He checked his watch. Still a bit early. 'Will pay for the call, of course. Can't seem to find my cell phone.' For all he knew, it had gone the way of O'Malley's pullover.

'I'll call th' Garda. Let me know when you're after usin' my mobile, and thanks for being buggered into the bridge game. Feeney's without mercy when it comes to scaring up a fourth.

I'll drive you up a half-hour early tomorrow, if you don't mind. Seamus is after givin' you a tour of the place.'

'Perhaps my wife could come along, just for the tour?'

'Ah.' Liam closed his eyes a moment. 'My mother doesn't care for attractive women, and your wife is a very attractive woman. If we could wait 'til another day—when Mother's havin' her drop-down, as she calls it, I'm sure we can work something out. God's truth, my mother's a terror.'

Liam fidgeted, uneasy.

'And Rev'rend . . . if you could possibly wear a tie tomorrow . . .'

'I would normally wear a collar.'

'Ah, God help us, she likes th' Protestant cleric to wear th' tie.'

'Not this Protestant cleric.' He said it mildly enough, he thought.

Buying time, he browsed a recent *Independent*, then rang Walter. Hurtling through midtown Manhattan in a cab at seven A.M., his cousin expressed dismay over the peevish star this trip had come under; he and Katherine were nonetheless looking forward to connecting at Broughadoon and reworking the schedule; and love to Cynthia who would be in their prayers, God bless 'er.

He hailed Maureen as he came along the stair hall. 'How did our patient get on while we were out?'

'Bella was after givin' her a hand, but she went up th' way she came down, except in reverse! She's a dote, she is, an' no wonder, with a drop of th' Irish in 'er. I've just done a good cleanin' on th' side she goes up an' down, to keep th' dust off her skirts. How was your drivin' lesson?'

'We made it in one piece.'

'I hear Jack Kennedy stood you a glass.'

'He did.'

'Did Liam tell you we've a big surprise for th' guests tomorrow evenin'? Cynthia says she's up to it, if th' rev'rend is.'

'Consider it done, then.'

She was sleeping, curled like a cat beneath the comforter, the armoire door open, the window closed. He undressed and crawled in beside her and was out like a light.

He woke when he heard her cry out in her sleep, and rolled over and put his hand on her shoulder. 'It's all right,' he said.

She turned to him; he was alarmed by the look on her face.

'The man . . .' She covered her face with her hands.

'It's all right, it's okay. It won't happen again. Would you like to get out of here? Just say the word. We can take a hotel in Sligo.'

'It was only a dream, I'll be fine.' She shivered a little.

'You always say that when something goes wrong.'

'And, of course, I'm always fine.' She sat up and rubbed her eyes and squinted at his watch. 'I'm hungry as a bear, and it's time for you to eat something, too. Did you take the raisins with you?'

'I did not.'

'Did you smash into anything?'

'I did. Tore off the driver's-side mirror. But I think I got the hang of it.' He told her about the bike rider he'd seen on the highway, which made her mildly anxious, then reported his phone call to Walter. Her relief was as palpable as his own.

'I asked the operator for charges,' he said. 'Sixty bucks.'

She wasn't currently into finances. 'I missed you,' she said.

'You did?' He was a sucker for being missed.

'I was stuck with Bella as my caregiver.'

'Tell me everything and I'll bring our lunch up.'

'The little wretch. Needs a swift kick in the pants.'

'On the order of what you used to give Dooley.'

'Yes, and of course it worked; they beg for it, I think. Needless to say, she's starving for love—and since I've nothing better to do, I've decided to give it to her, though she'll put up a terrific fight.'

'You're amazing.'

'She's very bright. I asked why she chose the butterfly tattoo, what it means to her. She opened up a little, then, but only a little. The butterfly, she said, has a very short life span. I took that to signify her teenage angst, which can definitely have a suicidal edge.

'She's partial to the monarch, which flies from Canada to Mexico, covering two thousand miles in two months—isn't that amazing?—but only when conditions are perfect and against the most terrible odds. So maybe she's thinking to fly the coop when the timing is right, and the further away, the better.'

'How do you know these things?'

'Very simple. I was a teenager. She did something I wouldn't have expected. She recited two verses from Frost, from his poem My Butterfly.

She seemed to . . . grow softer, somehow, when she spoke the lines.

'There's a collection of Frost poems in the library, so I wrote down the verses.'

She took her sketchbook from the bedside table, and read aloud.

*'It seemed God let thee flutter from his gentle clasp / Then fearful he had let thee win / Too far beyond him to be gathered in / Snatched thee, o'er eager, with un-gentle grasp.*

'And so in the poem, the season ends and the flowers die, and the butterfly, too, and she quoted this:

*'Then when I was distraught / And could not speak / Sidelong, full on my cheek / What should that reckless zephyr fling / But the wild touch of thy dye-dusty wing.'*

The sound of a power saw keening beyond the window.

'Such a sorrowing in her,' she said.

He saw the sorrowing reflected in Cynthia's face. If there was ever one to say, *I feel your pain,* and mean it, it was his wife. 'Lunch!' he said in what she called his pulpit voice.

'Yes. Well. Any sort of sandwich on soda bread with a bit of fruit and tea, and I'll be your slave.'

'You'll forget that heedless remark, but I'll remember it.'

He pulled on a pair of jeans, a shirt, tennis shoes. 'Back in a flash,' he said. 'And by the way . . .' He flipped the light switch at the door—on, off, on, off.

'Hooray!' she said.

'The hot bath you've been dreaming of.'

He knocked on the kitchen door. Bella opened it, but said nothing. Lunch wasn't usually served at Broughadoon, but Anna had made special arrangements for the Kavanaghs.

'If we could get a couple of sandwiches? Anything on soda bread, with fruit and tea.'

She stared, cool.

'Thank you,' he said.

She closed the door. Robert Frost or no, it would take more than a swift kick to get that job done.

He sat at the table and looked out to the view, noted the faint scent of insect repellent, and remembered hearing that all fishing lodges smell that way, especially in August when the midges are out.

Tonight he would finish the letter—find an envelope large enough for the drawing to be mailed flat, take a wild guess at the weight, put stamps on the whole business, and sayonara. No wonder the postcard was such a popular item when traveling.

Bella entered the dining room with the tray. 'Shall I take it up, then?'

'Many thanks, but no, I'll take it.' He was pleased to return her attempt at being civil. 'Mrs. Kav'na loves your soda bread.'

'Is there anything Mrs. Kav'na doesn't love?'

Her tone was chilling, he felt the venom in it. 'Men jumping out of cupboards would be one,' he said, seizing the tray.

In their room, he set the tray on the foot of the bed.

'Love her if you like, but leave me out of it.'

She was clearly amused. 'She's a terrible pain.'

'Man,' he said, quoting Dooley. He needed to get out of here—be a tourist, see a castle, anything. 'Are you sure you don't want to get a room in Sligo? We can call Aengus Malone to drive us.' He'd be happy to dodge running up the hill tomorrow to the den of a fire-breathing dragon who devours Protestants and sucks the marrow bones.

'Calm down, sweetheart. She's testing us. She'd be thrilled to know she's upsetting you like this.'

'What happened to her, anyway?'

'There was a divorce years ago. She lived with her mother until she was twelve, then went off to Dublin to her dad, a very famous Irish musician. Apparently, his influence hasn't been the best; she was quite free to do as she pleased, and now his new girlfriend has moved in. It's someone Bella despises, and so she's back to her mother after six years.'

'Eighteen, then.' His heart was oddly moved, if only a little. He'd been through this himself, through years of Dooley's arrogance and rage— and then the miracle issuing forth, albeit slow as blood from stone. 'How do you know this?'

'Maureen.'

'She volunteered it?'

'I asked her.'

'When it comes to meddling, my dear, you make clergy look like amateurs.'

'Maureen believes in her. I think Maureen is the unofficial grandmother—Anna's mum, she says, died in childbirth. Oh, and Bella's Irish name is K-o-i-f-e, pronounced Kweefa . . .'

Two castles. A ruin, even.

'Eat something,' she said, laying into her sandwich.

Yes. He didn't want to rile his diabetes, anything but.

He was washing up when the knock came.

Liam's piercing blue eyes were gray. 'Corrigan would like us to come to the station at Riverstown. They want to hear what I know about Jack Slade, and what you saw on the highway.'

Come here, go there, do this, do that. 'What I saw could be told on the phone.'

'Aye. Of course. I'm sorry.'

He couldn't tolerate another apology, from himself or anyone else.

'If they want to talk to me in person, I'd be glad to do it here.' He would mention the business of his cell phone then.

'I'll see to it,' said Liam.

'Before dinner, please.'

How simple it was to say no. And it had only taken seventy years.

'I have an idea,' he told Cynthia.

'I love ideas.'

'After dinner this evening, I'm taking you out.'

'Where are we going?'

'It's a surprise.' They would have daylight until nearly ten o'clock.

He shifted what had become 'his' wing chair to face the view, and sat with his notebook and pen.

*. . . are staying here at Broughadoon.*

He completed the sentence that had dangled for—how long? It seemed weeks.

*Much has transpired since this letter was begun.*

*In brief, Cynthia was surprised by an intruder in our room, which caused her to wrench her bad ankle—all this followed by police, fingerprinting, and the visit of a local doctor who ordered her to stay off her foot for up to ten days. This, of course, cancels a good bit of our tour with Walter and Katherine.*

*Happily, W and K don't mind the upset of plans. They arrive day after tomorrow to spend one night, then on to Borris House and beyond, after which we join up for the last leg (north to Belfast, down to Dublin).*

*A bit of an expense to cancel rooms on short notice, but worth it, and fortunately our room here remains available. W and K insist they're grateful for time to themselves, W having been consumed for months by a disagreeable legal case.*

*C in good spirits and learning to navigate on crutches and true grit. She sends her love along with this watercolor view from our bedroom window. As ever, the very soul of her subject is called forth by her brush.*

Goethe said, 'One ought, every day at least, to hear a little song, read a good poem, see a fine picture, and, if it were possible, to speak a few reasonable words.'

*I have heard a little song, as my good wife rattled off a verse or two of Danny Boy this morning. I have read what I believe to be a good poem by Patrick Kavanagh, and looked out to a fine picture on every side. Further, I have spoken, and am trying to write to you, a few reasonable words. In this way, Goethe might agree that I have enjoyed a full day's pleasure though it is but four in the afternoon.*

*Just learned that I'm to be questioned by a detective, yet another component of our vacation saga, so will sign off for now with an Irish proverb useful to all:*

*'A light heart lives*

Something nudging his leg.

'Pud?'

The little guy was looking up at him, the shoe fastened in his jaws.

'I forgot to tell you,' said Cynthia. 'He slipped in when Liam came to the door and hid under the bed.'

In terms of never giving up, this was a very Churchillian dog. No, go, get away, heel—what difference would it make? No dog had ever obeyed his commands; his Bouvier-wolfhound mix, in the long years of puppydom, was disciplined only by an emphatic vocalizing of scripture, preferably from the KJV.

*Lie . . . down*, he might have commanded early in the game.

Result: Walking about, licking the empty food bowl, possibly scratching.

For God so loved the *world*, he learned later to proclaim, that he gave his *only begotten son* . . .

Result: Instant lying down or, if required, bounding forth into a despised torrent of rain to take care of business. Dog Disciplined by Scripture—it was a show people lined up to see, worth taking on the road. His gut feeling was, it wouldn't work in this application.

'Drop the shoe,' he said.

Pud did not drop the shoe.

'Roll over.'

Pud blinked.

'Sit,' he said.

'He is sitting.' Obviously starved for entertainment, his wife was watching this hapless demo.

'Try fetch,' she said.

'Fetch.'

'You have to throw the shoe first, Timothy.'

'If I throw the shoe, there'll be no end to it, I won't have a minute's peace.'

'You don't have a minute's peace anyway,

since what transpired the other evening. I would throw the shoe.'

'So you throw the shoe,' he said.

'He doesn't want me to throw the shoe.'

He threw the shoe.

Glee and jubilation, full Jack Russell style. Pud returned the shoe, placed it at his feet, looked up. Two shining brown orbs of hope and expectation . . .

He sighed; thought of his own good dog; calculated how long he could hold out against a terrier.

'We'll be back,' he told his wife.

On his passage through the entrance hall, he gave a salute to Aengus Malone's hat. Then he and Pud crunched over the gravel and around the lodge to the head of the lake path. The water's surface was golden now, hammered by afternoon sun. Bees droned in the flower beds; the trunks of the beeches convened like patient elephants.

It was a wonderland out here, in summer air moved by a breeze off the water. In Blake's words, his soul felt suddenly threshed from its husk. With no effort, he drew a deep breath; the straitjacket fell away like William's overcoat.

When he stepped to the mound, the crowd

rose to their feet, cheering. He was pitching for the Mitford Reds, and they were winning.

Before he delivered the pitch, Pud was racing ahead of it on the path.

He burned the shoe straight down the middle. Pud leaped like a salmon, spun in the air, caught it.

'Man,' he said.

Pud dashed back, dropped the shoe at his feet, looked up.

A curve shoe up and away.

A fast shoe high and in.

A sinker low and away.

The aerodynamic of a shoe was unpredictable, to say the least. A rivulet of sweat ran along his backbone.

He smoked a high, looping pitch down the path, sank to his haunches, watched Pud bring it back.

'Way to go, *buddy*!'

After the game, the Pitch would have a hot dog with everything but onions, thanks. Ditto for the Catch.

He turned his Reds cap around with the bill shading his neck from the beating Irish sun, and gave Pud a good scratch behind the ears.

Vacation. He was finally on it.

# Ten

They lingered at their table and watched a boat on the evening lake. On his first visit, he'd never sat still long enough to watch a boat on a lake. Such lulling meditation as this gave room to an interesting possibility—all Feeney wanted, after all, was a warm body.

'Anybody play bridge?' he asked the anglers.

'I'm a poker man,' said Pete O'Malley, pining toward the empty travel club table. 'But I play a little gin with these turkeys.'

'My mother-in-law's a bridge nut, my wife's a bridge nut,' said Hugh. 'Me, I'm gin and poker all th' way.'

'No bridge for me,' said Tom. 'I'm a bloody

eejit at that game. Say, how about th' guy stealin' O'Malley's pullover?'

'That pullover caught many a big one,' said
Pete. 'I'd rather he stole my Rolodex.'

'Your Rolodex?'

'Rolex,' said Pete, who had, in his own
words, been at the jug. 'We saw the detective
come in, heard you may have spotted th' guy
who did it.'

'Maybe. They can't pull somebody in without hard evidence. The good news is, the so-
called suspect has a record of aggravated assault
and unlawful possession of a firearm—they'll
be looking to see if his fingerprints match any
they found here.'

'They dusted my room,' said Pete. 'Asked for
a complete description of the pullover. Lands'
End, maybe 1998. Tear on right sleeve from a
fishhook. Stain on front, fish blood.'

'Overall smell,' said Tom, '—fishy.'

'So, how did it go today?'

'No fishin' today,' said Tom. 'Saw a castle,
drove over to Rosses Point, fooled around.
Spent the afternoon with Jack Kennedy up th'
road. You ever sample poteen?'

'No way.'

'It'll turn you forty shades of green,' said
Hugh.

'So I've heard. My barber says whatever I do, stay away from poteen.'

'With advice like that, I'd be lookin' for another barber,' said Pete.

Laughter at the fishermen's table.

'We're sorry about th' crutches,' Pete told Cynthia. 'Sorry about th' whole thing.'

'Yes, ma'am,' said Hugh.

'Terrible,' said Tom. 'Really sorry.'

'Thanks. I'm glad to hear nothing else was missing from your rooms.'

'Zero,' said Hugh.

'Nothin' in Finnegan's room to go missin',' said Pete. 'A sweater with a moth hole you could stick your leg through, a pair of britches he wore in high school, a pack of Camel Lights.'

'Always keep your valuables on your person,' said Hugh. 'That's my motto.'

From the dining room they made their way to the bench he had spotted in the afternoon. From somewhere along the lake came the faintest keening of a violin. Or perhaps it was the sough of wind in the trees.

'So lovely,' she said, gazing around. 'It stuns me, I have no words for it. And look!—the dear old beeches.'

There was an affecting lull in the light, as if

the day resisted the settling dusk. A butterfly
was at the buddleia.

He took her crutches and propped them
against the back of the bench, and they sat for
a time, musing, looking toward the silvered
lough.

'Pete O'Malley has a crush on Moira,' she
said.

'What?'

'Pete. Moira—the book/poker/travel club
organizer.'

'How do you know?'

'I just know.'

'Is he married?'

'Separated. Maureen said he wanted to take
Moira buzzer fishing.'

'What's that?'

'It's a kind of fishing you do at night.'

'I think he'd be rushing things.'

They laughed. 'You're a regular evening gazette, Kav'na.'

'You love me,' she said, amazed and certain.

It was like her to say such things, completely
out of the blue. 'I've always loved you,' he said.
'From the time I was born.'

'How did you manage that?'

'I think I came into the world seeking something not absolutely tied to this earthly realm. Your open mind, your curiosity, your reverence promised that and drew me in.' He put his arm around her, felt the cool of her flesh against his.

'My mother had it, you have it,' he said. 'She took red dirt and made gardens that people came from miles around to see. No earth-moving equipment, just a wheelbarrow and shovel. No money, just hard work, ingenuity, and passion. All the time, everywhere you go, you know how to make something out of what most people see as nothing. You've made something out of me.'

'No, sweetheart, you were quite the finished product.'

'Never. I was an overworked, underfeeling man growing old alone. I thank you for teaching me not to fear intimacy; for making me do this thing we call marriage.'

'I made you do it?'

'I quit, but you didn't. Of course, I was praying you wouldn't, but I fully expected you to.'

He put his hand under her chin and lifted her face to his and kissed her. 'Happy birthday, glimmering girl. Sorry it's been such a hassle.'

'It isn't such a hassle, really. It's just life— quirky and scary and lovely and immense. The beauty to be seen from our window can't be diminished by the dark soul that crawled out of it last night. I wouldn't have it any other way; I wouldn't have you any other way. You let me be the woman I am. No one has ever let me be that before. And another thing . . .'

'Say on.' The scent of wisteria . . .

'You listen. Really listening to someone is a very tender and generous gift. Sometimes I'm frightened by what we have together.'

'Don't be frightened. There's so much in the world to frighten us—let's leave that one thing alone.'

The clouds above the lake were disappearing in the fading light; the air quickened with the scent of something fresh, electric.

'Tomorrow morning's rain,' he said. 'Announcing itself.'

They went in then, through the dining room illumined by the light over the painting, and through the library where Pete O'Malley snored in his wing chair and Pud slept off the narcotic of today's big game. There had been no sign tonight of Seamus and William at their checkers.

It took a while for her to navigate the stairs in her inventive way, a way that seemed to him a kind of liturgical act of trust and humility.

With each of the stair steps, he recited a line from the Compline:

> Before the ending of the day . . .
> Creator of the world we pray . . .
> That thou with wonted love wouldst keep . . .
> Thy watch around us while we sleep . . .
> O let no evil dreams be near . . .
> Or phantoms of the night appear . . .

At the top of the stairs, he helped her up and gave her the crutches.

'Keep me as the apple of Your eye,' he said, concluding the old prayer.

Her breath came fast. 'Hide me under the shadow of Thy wings.'

Their bed had been turned down, a lamp glowed in the corner. As he closed the door, he was glad to hear the sound of the club coming in with much laughter and talking.

# Eleven

3 November 1861

    Earth hard as Iron

    Men framing

    One wants a Name for this mighty effort—it is ever gnawing at me to find the pleasing name—Inistiorc perhaps—Irish for Island of the Boar.

    When Keegan came to us we rowed to the Island & found a wild Sow and her sucklings—where the Boar had gone, we couldn't know, perhaps to a table hereabout— Keegan wanted a suckling for his own board, but I couldn't stomach the killing of it—he

didn't disguise the sour look he had for me
nor his disdain for the fact that once dressed
& properly cooked I would agreeably eat the
innocent Creature.

The People along the water are calling it
Cathair Mohr or Big Fort—Caitlin declares it
a good name, easily disguised in English as
Catharmore—we must not appear to think
too highly of ourselves with a 'Big Fort.'

Clar House, meaning Plain House—that
will do it for Balfour no doubt—but tis
disagreeable in the extreme on the page & on
the Tongue. We consider Cluainaigh or
Cloonee, for it is mostly pasture land. Then
there is Caiseal Mor, or large stone fort,
which anglicizes to Cashelmore. I am fond of
Tullagh Mor or Tullachmore, for great hill—
but perhaps after all, Catharmore, letting the
People be the judge—a pesky business to tag
the work of one's heart & hands.

As wether permits, we labor on the large
building sited near the Lough in a grove
of ancient Beeches. Six bay two-storey
Limestone on the rectangular plan with
projecting end bays to the East elevation—
hipped slate Roofs, clay ridge tiles, mitred
hips, roughly-dressed stone Voussoirs to

arches, stone sills, square-headed door openings to North and South, square-headed central threshing room & Loft.

Keegan has made a fine temporary stall for Adam off the Surgery which confers a secondary benefit—though but a mite of equine heat escapes through the wallboards, it is welcomed by all—Caitlin wished our good mount to be blanketed at night with one of Uncle's Turkey rugs but Keegan ascribes to the Country way of warming a horse from the inside which he accomplishes with a daily feed in Winter of heat-producing corn— Adam is the sleekest Steed in these Wild Regions.

Tis a most humble satisfaction to be the source of economic improvement to families of this Region. Near twenty men take home wages from Cathair Mohr & many learning trades to which they would not otherwise be exposed.

We pray toward the completion of the house by Spring & thank God Who is the one true Source of all our Blessings.

After praying the Morning Office at five-thirty, he had opened the window to the patter of rain among beech leaves, then sat with the journal, reading pages at random.

20 November

A virulent Maladie has lately run amok though the Countryside, especially infecting the young—we can find nothing like it in the many journals on these shelves.

Twill run its course, says old Rose McFee when we despair of our helplessness—Rose is believed to be of great Age, perhaps beyond the century mark—she has but snags in her head, alarmingly revealed in a roguish Grin used to frighten unruly Children.

Balfour noses about overmuch, walking among the men, playing the Cock, suggesting improved ways to do the work at hand—he also sends a steady stream of servants from his household presenting every offense from Bunion & Sty to Gout & Goiter, all to be treated gratis—we often see angry welts & bruises on the skin but they decline to comment. If anything should aile the family we are called to come at once & minister as best we can in a small, foul Compartment without windows or good light. We have twice rid his stout wife of Hemoroids using the homeliest of methods—a procedure requiring the Hemoroids to be opened externally with the subsequent application of a poultice of boiled Onion—this was not learned in Philadelphia but from my dear Mother, a natural Physician who swore by it—I have not seen it fail. As for Balfour—the old Proverb, He who marries for money earns it, reminds us that he who receives Land without charge pays for it—til the Lord comes with His trumpets.

C & I are swamped beyond our Mortal Energies yet she vows she has never been happier nor have I. May God have Mercy on us in this impossible Calling.

In turning the November pages, he found a scrap of paper folded in half. He liked finding the odd scrap in old books; he recently came upon a list of his mother's in the devotional she wore to tatters. *Qt milk 5 lbs potatoes cake flour 1 coconut Ovaltine*

The few words had startling power—he had tasted her coconut cake, smelled the Ovaltine in her cup.

The ink on the scrap was more faded than that of the journal entries, and the handwriting distinctively different. He put the flashlight to the task.

My dearest F, I found this in my reading
last evening of Mr. Dickens' Little Dorrit,
Uncle's last book purchase before his passing.
It reminds me of you. <u>He went like the rain,
among the just and the unjust, doing all the
good he could.</u> Your loving C

12 December

By dint of unstinting Sacrifice amongst the
People, Caitlin has been obliged to take to her
bed—She has forged her own Lenten season
through an exhaustion both utter and
complete—I have not watched over her
properly—am sick at heart for the frightful
turn in her Health—She hardly sips Tea. She
gives until there is nothing left in her store—I
now know that it is I who must mind her
store. The eldest child of O'Leary the
Shoemaker, a scantling of a Girl just turned
fourteen, comes to address C's needs while
I'm about the business of Doctoring—as well
as minding the labors of twenty men as
Wether permits. To have the fine Surgery in
the basement of the new house will be a
Blessing beyond telling to us & to the People.

The shocking lore about Dr. Wilde reaches
even to these Remote Quarters—if a man is
paying his due portion of service under God

he should have no time nor even spunk to sire an Infant in every cabin as all say of him—Tis the heartless and self-serving fool who would add to the world more mouths to be fed in these desperate times.

Father Dominic has delivered the Host today on his mare Fiddler, finding ice still moored in patches along the bleak Road—ice on the Lough thinning somewhat—have brought our seven Red Hens inside lest their few Eggs be frozen—am thankful that C finds the hens an amusement though young Aoife is not amused in the least. As A has no shoes to equip her in this wether—(I am reminded of the proverb)—we have paid her father to fashion a pair with great haste.

Prior to Tuesday's mild Thaw I had broken a slab of ice in Adam's watering Trough on nine consecutive mornings.

A grinding hard Winter.

He laid the journal on the table and got up and cranked the window shut, petitioning God for the grace to adopt a more agreeable attitude toward the day at hand. With Fintan and Caitlin O'Donnell making themselves useful, who was he to carp about a card game?

He eyed in the far corner of the room the

carton of books they'd schlepped across the Pond. They were both fearful of being stuck without a decent book, and who knew they would find everything from Virgil to Synge on the shelves of a fishing lodge?

Returning to his chair, he opened his notebook, uncapped his pen.

'. . . longest.'
*You and Peggy are faithfully in our prayers.*
*Will write again soon, reporting the outcome of said ruckus.*

*God be with you, my brother.*
*Timothy*

He folded the letter with the watercolor, licked the envelope he'd rounded up, laid on more Irish stamps than were probably needed, checked his watch.

Six-thirty; the sun had been up for a half hour. He wanted coffee.

He also wanted soda bread with local butter, and rhubarb compote cooked to perfection on an Aga the color of a fire engine.

That was the trouble with vacations. At home, he was perfectly content with cereal and a banana, or the occasional poached egg. Here, he was ravenous from first light onward and eating like a field hand—while his sole exercise consisted of tossing around a shoe, no pun intended.

He glanced at his wife, burrowed like a vole into the bedclothes and as dead to the world as any teenager. 'A clean conscience,' she said when he made envious remarks.

He dressed in waterproof running gear and stepped out to the hall, greeted by a zephyr of cooking smells from downstairs.

While Cynthia read last night, he'd used the kitchen phone to call the erstwhile secretary who served during his years as Mitford's working priest. Then, when he retired, she didn't. Known by some as the Genghis Khan of church secretaries, she was Velcro that wouldn't unstick.

No, he couldn't remember his cell phone number, because he never called it. And no, he couldn't remember his PIN number or even if he had one.

But yes, she would try to reach Dooley and get the phone number from him, and yes, she would take care of calling the phone company ASAP, but keep in mind that she'd be put on hold 'til she was old and gray, as if she had time to waste, thank you, didn't he know she'd been rooked into organizing the Bane and Blessing at Lord's Chapel this year, and if it was all the same to him, would he bring her a really nice souvenir, her preference being a vase from Waterford?

If anyone could get the account unplugged, it was Emma Newland, who would go after Sprint like Turks taking Cairo.

No Pud in the wing chair; he was disappointed.

He placed the outgoing envelope in the box on the sofa table, and took a minute to examine the sepia prints of the fishermen. Boats in the background, no houses yet built on the opposite shore, a black Lab seated in front of the lineup of men in boots and tweed, their catch on display at their feet—all looked particularly happy, he thought. Perhaps one day even he would cast a line, send it singing over the water . . .

In another photograph, two boys in shorts and sweaters and buckled shoes, the taller one sober, the other smiling and shy, each with a large fish in one hand and a net in the other, most likely Liam and Paddy. He wondered which of the men was their father.

'Rev'rend.'

He started.

'I heard back last night from Corrigan.'

He saw that Liam hadn't slept well.

'No matches to Slade's prints. No evidence to warrant a search of his place.'

'Sorry,' he said. 'Somehow, it felt too easy.'

'But they're sending a Gard to question his whereabouts the other night.'

'Thanks for the update.'

'You're going out?'

'Need to get the heart pumping.' As if recent events hadn't done the job. 'Back in half an hour, maybe less, it's still raining.'

'Take care,' said Liam.

'Don't worry about this,' he said. A useless comment in the world's view, but thoroughly scriptural and all he had just then.

In the entrance hall he pulled the hood over his head, tied the drawstring, and stepped out into the misting rain. The path to Catharmore was almost completely engulfed in fog. He jogged across the gravel and around to the garden bench, where he warmed up before beginning his measured lope down the path to the lake.

Someone had said that in Ireland there's no such thing as bad weather—only the wrong clothes. He was prepared. In his hood and jacket, he was as hidden as a turtle in its shell, yet he felt more at one with the rain than if he were naked to it. Halfway along the path, he stopped running and lifted his face to its quenching sweetness, opened his mouth to it like a child.

He had known for a long time in his head, and knew now in his marrowbones—his spirit was dry as dust. He hadn't completely realized that 'til this moment. Dry from giving out for months and even years, and failing to take in.

*Create in me a clean heart, oh, God, renew a right spirit within me.*

It was a prayer borrowed from the psalmist, but too long to sum his great need. It was a breath prayer he was after.

*Clean me out, fill me up, please.*

Running again. The woods on either side fell away; the lake opened itself to him—gray water devouring gray clouds, immense.

He could see the absurdity, even the comedy of his feeling about the bridge afternoon, see that it didn't matter enough to be resisted.

*Clean me out, fill me up, clean me out . . .*

He drew the smell of water on water into his lungs, felt the fulsome air enter the tissues in a way he'd never experienced, heard his living breath suck in, pump out . . .

He reached the shore, heart hammering, and stood looking over the great swell of the lough, palms lifted to the rain.

He saw something, then, moving in the heavy mist beyond the reedbeds, someone walking his way and nearly upon him. Probably one of their gung-ho fishing guys. Without his glasses, which would be no better than windshields without wipers, he was clueless. He threw up his hand, didn't look to see if there was a response, and headed toward the path.

'Reverend.'

He turned. Anna was wearing a raincoat, the hood pulled close about her face.

'I hope I didn't startle you,' she said. It's my day off.'

'Not at all.'

'Well, then, let's hope it clears up and gives you sunshine.'

'Reverend . . .'

Why harp on this foolishness of having people call him Tim, let them call him what they bloody well pleased.

'I can't call you Tim,' she said. 'I did it the once to be brave and modern, but I'm not at all modern and certainly not brave.'

'I'm sure one must be very brave to operate

a fishing lodge!' This was no place for a jocular chat; he wanted coffee.

'Could we . . . could I possibly talk with you? I won't keep you, I'm so sorry to ask. I've been wanting . . . but I didn't know . . .'

He saw a kind of agony in her face. 'Of course. Where shall we . . .'

'Our fishing hut just there, in the beeches. God bless you. Thank you. I won't keep you.'

'You lead, I'll follow.'

The hut was a small, parged building with a couple of stone steps to the door and a single room. A table with anglers' magazines and an ashtray, a few books on a shelf, a candle in a bottle, chairs, a mantel clock stopped at twelve minutes past three. Rain streaked the windows.

'We could sit,' she said, anxious.

'Good idea.' He untied his hood, shook water from his jacket, hung it on the back of a chair. She hung her raincoat on a hook by the door and sat across the table from him.

'I didn't know I would see you this morning,' she said, 'but I was hoping . . . I'm so sorry to do it like this.' Tears welled in her eyes.

'Tell you what—no more apologies. Not for anything.'

She put her hands over her face and wept, silent.

As a curate, he'd tried using words against tears, yet something he thought wise often came out as banal. Later, he learned to be silent, praying.

Rain pecked the roof; she wiped her eyes with the palms of her hands and looked at him. She was brave after all, he thought.

'I don't know where to begin.'

'Begin anywhere.'

'Yes.' She was silent again, looking at her hands on the table, palms down. 'My mother died when I was born. That has always haunted me, I always felt I had to apologize to my father, somehow, and of course there can be no making up for such a loss. I think he loved her, but more than that, I think he needed her, yes, that's what it was, he needed her. She was a kind and lovely woman, everyone said, very deep—and they say I look like her. There are long days when I miss her; 't is a punishing want, and yet I never knew her at all.' She looked at him, appealing.

'I never saw what was needed to be a mother, I had no model for it. I bungled the job.' She turned away. 'But I love my child.' She wept again, soundless.

He drew a bandanna from his pocket and handed it to her and she took it and wiped her eyes and blew her nose. 'I'll wash it,' she said, earnest. 'Bella is hurting and I can't reach her— she won't let me in. She was angry with me for leaving her Da, she was only four at the time, but a very bright and deep and sensitive four, she begged me to stay with him, but I could not. Niall was very loose with his affections those years we were married, and I couldn't bear what it was doing to all of us. When Koife—Bella—and I left, we lived for a time in Dublin, but it wasn't a good place for her to come up, and so we moved here to be with Da in what's now the kitchen wing. He had bought the oul' place long ago when Liam's mother had to let it go. Da had invested his boxing money in a haulage business in Dublin. It did very well—seventeen lorries on the move; in good times, day and night together. When someone bought him out, he came back to Lough Arrow, just five kilometers from where he lived as a lad.

'I hadn't a car and couldn't get about for work—I heard that Catharmore was looking for someone to cook and clean. Da said, don't speak th' name William Donavan in that house, and I didn't, and I was taken on. Lough Arrow was the terrible opposite of Dublin, I suppose— Bella hated it here, there were no children about, and she was very lonely. Until she entered school, my da watched out for her during the day. I was working up th' hill from early morning 'til late afternoon, and at Broughadoon at night. 't was my dream to turn th' wreck of it into a fishing lodge to make us a living, so I didn't give Bella the attention she craved. She was but six when she took up the fiddle; 't was her boon companion and she was brilliant at it, it came as natural as the waxing of the moon.

'She left to live with her father when she was twelve. I couldn't stop her, Reverend, it's what she wanted, she was fierce to do it. She and Niall have the bond of music, which is her life—but I never forgave myself for letting her go.'

'God gave me a boy to raise,' he said. 'We'll talk about it later, I hope, but I tell you now that it's not too late—no matter how deep the wound.'

She wiped her eyes with the bandanna. 'I've lived for years thinking it's too late. Too late for Bella and me, too late for Liam and his mother, too late for . . . too late.'

'Never,' he said. 'Please know that. When did you leave Catharmore?'

'I continued working up the hill after Paddy

and Seamus came. She wanted me to stay because I did very personal things for her—washed out her undies, altered her clothes to keep them in fashion, moved her jewelry around to various hiding places in the house—sometimes but a step ahead of Paddy, who was after selling it.' She lowered her eyes. 'I don't know whether I should tell you everything, Reverend. I want to tell you, but it is so frightening to tell everything.'

'I understand.'

'Each morning at first light, I pray the Lord's Prayer, and often the decade of Sorrowful Mysteries—but Liam and I stopped going to Mass long ago. He gave up so much that reminded him of his father, and when I moved here, I told myself it was the work that was on me seven days a week. Liam says we're more than lapsed, Reverend, we're fallen altogether. As a girl, I wished so terribly to satisfy God . . .'

'A good Scot named George MacDonald said God is impossible to satisfy but easy to please.'

'I think I've forgotten how to do pleasing things—except for our guests.' She looked away from him. 'All these years, there's been no one to . . . to . . .'

'Hear your confession?'

'Yes. Confession was always important to me, I was schooled in a convent and took it seriously as a girl.'

'Confession brings pardon and peace,' he said. 'We all need it. St. John says, If we confess our sins, God is faithful and just to forgive us our sins, and to cleanse us from all unrighteousness.'

'It's all right then, to speak . . .'—she seemed dubious—'my heart?'

'God asks us to do it. But you know I can't grant you absolution.'

'I know. But you'll hear me?'

'I will.'

'Liam's mother was always after the gin, and sometimes she would be . . . out of her head with me. She never cared for me, though I worked very hard for her. By the time she learned who I was, she had come to depend on me, but despised me even more for what she called my wicked deception in not telling her I was William Donavan's daughter.

'Liam used to come home at the weekends, and I fell in love with him altogether—I couldn't imagine how he turned out to be such a lovely man with such a deep spirit—he's like his father, they say. She was always angry with

Liam for his admiration and love for his father—
she wanted her boys to love only her. And yet,
she couldn't feel love, Reverend, she couldn't
feel anything at all.

'She hated me for loving him—Paddy says
she could never get on with women who love
her sons—but I wouldn't let her hurt me, I shut
myself from her so coldly that I hardly had any
feelings left. I turned my own heart to stone.'

She rose from the table and walked to a window, her hands plunged into the pockets of her
loose dress. 'Sure, she had a terrible blow when
she was young, a tragic accident in her family,
but that's no excuse, Reverend, for inflicting
her outrage on others, it doesn't give one license . . .' She turned to him. 'Not at all.

'I held myself away from Liam for more than
a year; it was a torment to us both. I held myself away because . . .

'My da met Evelyn McGuiness in Collooney, when he was just a lad trying to earn
his way as a boxing champion. It was a brutal
sport, and he was very brave and hardworking
and determined to make something of himself,
a boy with hardly a shoe to his foot. At the
time he met her, he was just beginning to get a
leg up, as he says, and was soon traveling all
over Ireland, then England, and up to Scot-

land. When they fell in love he promised her he would come home again and marry her. And he did come home again, but 't was seven long years that had passed, and she had seen two sisters and her mother die a horrible death and no one to turn to in her grief. She had married Mr. Conor—Mr. Riley, we all call him—and they had a son, Paddy. She had been nursemaid at Catharmore to Mr. Riley's first wife who died of cancer.

'She was very bitter towards Da for not coming for her as he promised, and he was bitter towards her for not waiting, though heaven knows he had handled matters in a gormless way. So off again he went to Dublin, and then, some while before he married my mother, he came back and . . . there was something between them. Da would never say what, he refuses to talk about it, but Paddy thinks . . .'

She wrung the bandanna in her hands. 'Nine months later, Liam was born.

'And so I held myself from Liam. 't was agony to find myself in love with my half-brother—'t is against the church and against the law, a misbegotten thing. And yet I loved him so, I thought I couldn't bear the pain.

'To his mother, I was but a lowly servant girl, just as she'd been when she worked for

Mr. Riley's first wife. For Liam to love me was a deep sting to her, and because she couldn't hurt me with her tormenting, she tried to hurt Liam, instead. One night when she was very drunk, she told me something that was—in its way—as . . .'

Her face colored with an old fury. 'She told me Mr. Riley wasn't Liam's father.'

'She confessed to you, then.'

'But 't was another heavy blade entirely. She said Liam's real father was Mr. Riley's business partner . . . someone who came here for fishing parties.' She caught her breath sharply. 'He's in the pictures in our library, God help us.'

She came and sat at the table. 'I don't know if it's true, there's no way to know. She often said crazy, mindless things.'

'Why do you think she told you this?'

'I think she believed I would tell Liam in one of the dreadful fights he and I had in those days. But of course I would never tell him such a terrible thing.' Her voice shook with the trembling in her. 'The truth is of no importance in the end, Reverend, because Mr. Riley loved Liam very much. I'm sure he never knew he wasn't Liam's father.'

'How did you feel about what she said?'

'I felt suddenly free . . . that maybe it was all

right for us to love, maybe it was God's way of giving us permission.' She drew in her breath. 'I decided to take the risk.

'I left Catharmore and Liam came with me, and we were wed in the library with the roof nearly gone above us. He began helping me resurrect Broughadoon. He worked so hard and is gifted in so many ways; 't is all because of him that we have such a lovely place.'

'He gives the credit to you.'

'Aye, he would.' He saw for a moment the light in her eyes. 'I love my husband.'

'Your husband loves you.'

'I've lived all these years knowing the truth, and the hatred I feel for her is so cruel, it devours me even yet. Sometimes I feel as if my heart would break for Liam—knowing the truth doesn't always set us free, Reverend.'

Not always, perhaps, but often. Learning he had a brother from his father's intimacy with the dark-skinned woman who helped raise him had been, after the initial shock, liberating—scary, but liberating. He had a brother now, that was the important thing, and he and Henry had the rest of their lives to puzzle out the mystery of it, to give thanks for it.

'Liam loves Bella as best he can, he wants to be a good da to her, but she shuts him out.

And there's a coldness in Liam towards Da, though he tries to hide it from me. I think he resents that Da was allowed to buy his birthright. All around us, there's a shutting out of love, so.'

'I sense there's hard feeling still between Evelyn Conor and your father.'

'My da bought Broughadoon anonymously, after Mr. Riley died and she came up against it. Perhaps Da was trying to make up for his misguided ways and help her; perhaps he was only bitter, and bent on taking away something she loved—I don't know. But when she found it was Da who owned what had been hers, things went to pieces altogether.

'And then there's Paddy, always after Liam to give a hand with the roof, the gardens, the guttering, to loan him money—and Bella with such a fierce and dangerous rage, and myself thinking she got it from me, after all, that it's in the blood, this brutal fury, perhaps I'm the one who . . .'—she put her hands over her face and sobbed— 'infects others with it.'

He waited.

'I confess, Reverend, my weakness of faith, my hurtful selfishness, the sin of this consuming hatred that withers my bones. I want to let it go.' A long keening came out of her. 'I want to let it all go.'

He looked at the grainy light slanting across the floor, and wondered where Ibiza might be, that place for which the Irish yearn when it rains.

# Twelve

'Wicked-looking stuff, his art, collected when he lived in New York.'

'Did you visit New York?'

They were driving up the hill in the Rover.

'In my late thirties,' said Liam. 'I couldn't wait to get home. Don't like a lot of frizzing about, horns blaring, that sort of thing.'

'A bumpkin like myself.'

'And our father's gardens have run riot, of course. Seamus is no hand with a spade, nor Paddy, either.'

'Gardening is civil and social, Thoreau said, but it wants the rigor of the forest and the outlaw.'

'This one's all outlaw. I'd love to get my hands on 't, but there's no stoppin' th' force of a goin' wheel—I'd be up to my eyeballs, an' Broughadoon runnin' wild.'

'Any hope for the country house hotel to happen?'

'No hope a'tall as I see it. Paddy can't boil water, much less cook a decent fry; he's rude to everybody and a bloody terror with the cheque book. So he's after writing a novel to make his fortune. Says a lot of ad blokes have done th' same—James Patterson, Salman Rushdie, Peter Mayle, Elmore Leonard . . .'

'Dorothy Sayers,' he said. 'She was in the ad business. Mystery writer, Christian apologist. A great success.'

'So there you have it,' said Liam. 'Paddy's convinced he's next in line.'

'This bridge club—it's been around a few years?'

'Feeney and Father O'Reilly have paid a monthly call to Mother since Father passed. He was generous to Feeney when he was coming along in his medical practice, and openhanded to th' parish altogether. They were with him when he died; one of the last things he said was, lads, keep an eye on Evelyn. God knows, they've been faithful, they've done their bit—

but none can wean her of the drink or the step-stool.'

'The stepstool.'

'Goes up it like a monkey—pops herself onto a counter or table or whatever's at hand—an' squirrels her jumble in cupboards. She's after keepin' her last bit of jewelry from Paddy, who'd be off to the pawnshop in th' blink of an eye. When Seamus came, she hauled the family plate to the top shelves, forks, knives, spoons, and all. Up she'd go to get herself a fork, and after the washing-up, Seamus would leave it out for her to put away again. That lasted for a year or two.'

He might have laughed, but Liam wasn't amused.

The misting rain of the morning had turned to a pelting; he reached to the backseat and grabbed his wet umbrella. 'By the way, where's Pud?'

'Shut up in th' family quarters.'

'Why is that?'

'To give you your peace!'

'If you're putting him up on our account, please turn him out. We like the little guy.'

'You're sure of it?'

'Absolutely.'

Liam grinned. 'Righto, then.' The engine idled at the front portico; Liam stared ahead. 'Perhaps one day we could . . . that is . . . ah, no, a foolish thought. Dinner this evening compliments of the travel club.'

'Can't seem to think of them as anything but the poker club. No eel, I trust.'

'Trout, salmon, an' plenty of it. There'll be long eatin' in that, as William says. After dessert, we move to th' library for Anna's surprise. 't will be grand, I hope.'

Liam's mobile buzzed; he squinted at the ID. 'It's Corrigan. Hallo, Conor here . . . Well, then . . . Did you check in with Jack Kennedy, he dropped a good bit of his wages there. Yes . . . No . . . Of course. Will do.'

Liam snapped the phone shut. 'Nobody's seen Slade in two weeks. Corrigan says there's nothing more can be done, call him if anything turns up.'

Again, the weight on Liam, the stricken look. He remembered what Peggy often said when he was a boy and things were hard. 'Ever'thing gon' be all right.' It had always consoled him, even when he didn't believe it.

'Everything's going to be all right,' he said.

Liam looked surprised. 'That's what my father used to say—just like that. 't is a wonder to hear it again.'

He climbed out and shot up the umbrella.

'You're a lovely man, Rev'rend. Don't take our mother's ways too personally, an' enjoy your visit.'

The Rover rattled down the drive.

'Seamus! Is that you?'

Seamus hailed him from the portico. ''t is m'self in my butler's equipage, fittin' tight as a sausage casin'.'

The Catharmore dogs burst from the house, an eruption of Vesuvius. He bounded up the steps, lowered the umbrella, shook hands. 'You're looking very smart in that gear, my friend.'

'You can see your face in th' shine of it, but Mrs. Conor likes me to wear it for company. Can't gain so much as half a stone without rippin' th' seat of it.' Seamus pulled a small comb from his pocket and hurriedly assailed his mustache. 'Haven't had two minutes to rub together, but we're ready for the bridge club and glad to have you join us, Rev'rend.'

'Tim, Seamus. Try Tim.' He dropped a few dog biscuits onto the porch decking.

'Tim it is, then. I'll just lean your brolly against the rail here. As you can see, we're standing at the west portico, which Dr. O'Donnell adapted from that of Bellamont Forest in County Cavan. They say the design was derived from Palladio's Villa Rotunda in Vicenza—the historians who visit make quite a bit of that. But come inside, I'll tour you around; Dr. Feeney and Father O'Reilly are on their way—runnin' a bit late, I'm afraid.'

The front door stood open as Irish doors might in a land presumably free of bugs. He stepped inside, adjusted his eyes to the shadowed space. He hadn't expected such a vast entry hall, nor one so handsomely proportioned.

A high ceiling with elaborate cornices. Pilasters on either side of two double doorways. A low fire on the hearth at the right of the hall, and in the center, Doric columns flanking a broad stair that ascended to a landing and a bank of dim windows.

'Very beautiful, Seamus. Very grand.'

As for the art, Liam was right. Odious stuff. Smears of black, red, white, ocher, on unframed canvases of immense size.

Seamus gave him a discreet look. 'They keep th' devil in his rightful place.'

'To each his own.'

'Aye. He tried to sell it off, but 't wouldn't sell. Now, then, you're seeing Catharmore at a good time of year—in winter, the hall is perishin' cold. Paddy and his mother like a fire here on Christmas Day, but in no time a'tall, they're off to th' kitchen for th' heat of the Aga.

'This is the room as completed in 1862 or thereabout, everything done by Irish workmen. Mr. Riley carried out a restoration of the place in the 1940s—nothing changed save the add-on of closets and loos. Then Paddy did grand work on the main floor when he came home from New York.'

'And you came with him, Liam says.'

'We met in a pub, Paddy and I, in lower Manhattan. I was there with my employer, Michael Kerr—an Irish gentleman of means who emigrated as a lad and lived to be ninety-eight years and a day. Mr. Kerr liked to visit this particular pub at the weekend, to have himself an Irish whiskey and a good cry about the oul' country—a lovely man, he was, and like a father to me. Paddy would come in with his riotous crowd from the advertisin' shop and all th' Irish among us would end up singin' the old songs of the Eire; 't was a great highlight of Mr. Kerr's last years. When Mr. Kerr passed, Paddy had sold his business and was comin' home to Sligo a rich man. Come with me, Seamus, he says, I'll buy you a suit of butler's clothes and you'll have a pint and three meals a day for the rest of your life.'

Seamus laughed, patted his midsection. 'Three is one too many, but I took the offer and never looked back. I had longed for home, but had nothin' saved to give myself a start—I confess th' habit of sharin' my earnings with Irish down on their luck.'

'There are worse habits.'

'Wouldn't have minded bein' poor if I hadn't been so short of cash.'

They had a laugh.

'But here I am, thanks to God and Paddy Conor. Now, that's th' Doric-style columns that's holdin' up the ceilin' there—and a good thing it is, as th' two floors above need all th' holdin' up they can get.'

'Is that an engraving?' On a pane of glass in a window near the front door, something chiseled—a date, very likely. He walked over and looked, stooped, adjusted his glasses.

My dearest love
Always and forever
Evelyn

He glanced at Seamus, who appeared abstracted.

'Mrs. Conor scratched that in as a young bride, with the diamond Mr. Riley gave her. He was very pleased—they say. You'll see the drawing room and dining room at drinks and lunch, so if you'll come this way, I'll show you the kitchen.'

They walked along the stair hall, lined with display cases of mounted fish, and turned left into what he reckoned may be Catharmore's crown jewel.

'Paddy put a bob or two in th' kitchen, as you see. 't was the oul' kitchen and maids' quarters they combined into one.'

A wall of windows looking out to the ruined garden; decorative tile work surrounding a blue Aga; limestone floors, a coved ceiling, an enormous iron rack hung with copperware. Impressive.

'Paddy was after letting guests dine in th' kitchen, he said, th' way they do in th' States. They would pay a deal more for th' privilege, he said, an' cover the cost of a roof altogether.'

The cooking smells could stand against any at Broughadoon. He realized he was ravenous.

'I'm hoping to meet Paddy. Will he be with us?'

'Paddy's after doing some business or other, haven't seen much of him in several days. Make yourself comfortable, now, I'll just stir up the pot.'

Seamus took an apron from a hook, tied it on, lifted the pot lid, looked in, replaced the lid. 'I hope you don't mind being treated like family, Tim.'

'I'm honored to be treated like family.'

Seamus opened the oven door. 'I hope I didn't overstep my bounds bringin' you into the kitchen.'

'Not in the least.'

Seamus used a long fork to poke whatever was in the oven; by the smell, roast lamb.

'This will be the end of the tour, as the old scullery has been turned over to Mrs. Conor and the paneled library to Paddy, for there's no livin' a'tall on the upper floors. As for me, I'm in the laundry which I've fitted out quite snug, if you don't mind th' washer cyclin' as you watch th' telly.'

'How about the basement? I believe O'Donnell's surgery was located there.'

''t was, yes, but we never go below unless at gunpoint; 't is a calamity with the risin' damp. On occasion, Paddy's forced to do something about th' plumbing or such, and then we're in for it, 't is like openin' a hole to China and pourin' in euro by th' washtub.'

'I have one of those holes myself,' he said. Their new heating and cooling system had cost twice a year's salary in his first parish. 'Have you read O'Donnell's journal?'

'I've made a stab at it, but my eyes are unfit for th' faded ink and he goes on too long about th' least thing. My da inherited a journal from his grandfather. Wind rising, it might say. Figs ripe. Annie bilious. Farrelly ploughing.' Seamus laughed. 'That would be my style of a journal.'

'Is the doctor's old cabin standing?'

'A pile of rubble in the sheep meadow, they say.' Seamus removed his apron, hung it on the hook, buttoned his jacket. 'Well, then. Everything's under control; the rolls will pop in after the other guests arrive. I hope you've an appetite.'

'You can count on it.'

'Drinks will go for a half hour or so, you could probably do with a nibble.' Seamus cut a slice from a round of cheese on a platter. 'Our own sheep. Very fine.'

The cheese was proffered on the blade of a knife, the way his father had done years ago.

He bit into the cheese—aged, mildly tart beneath a mellow sweetness. 'Hits the spot.

There's a lot to be said for being treated like family.'

Seamus gave him a paper napkin. 'A taste of Irish to wash it down?'

'No, no, thanks.'

'Liam says you're light on th' drink—a good thing. Thirst after the drink, m' father said, sorrow after th' money.'

'I was never much for spirits. A glass of burgundy or Bordeaux, a sherry now and then.'

'I seem to remember a bottle of sherry at the back of the cabinet; it may have aged a good deal.'

'All the better.'

'I feel the need of a pipe, m'self. Would you step out with me? We've a bit of time before I show you to the drawing room. You might have to stick it out with Herself—ah, sorry, Tim, please forgive that—with Mrs. Conor—'til the rest of the party show up.'

The rain-soaked terrace was bare, save for a huddle of plastic chairs stacked together and anchored with a rock. 'Th' wind carried off th' good stuff long ago. Probably somewhere in Easkey, on the porch of a stout fisherman and his wife.'

They stood well back of the rain pouring in a sheet from the terrace roof. Ever the earnest home owner, he suspected leaking gutters or none at all.

Seamus lit his pipe, puffed, kept the match to it, puffed, flicked the match. The scent of tobacco curled into the damp air.

'I should warn you, Tim, if Liam didn't. She'll be after trimmin' your sails.'

Seamus drew on his pipe. 'She came up grindin' poor in a mud cabin in Collooney with four brothers and two sisters, all dead now—two passing with their mother in a most tragic manner. And there were certain other . . . matters, as well. She's been takin' th' hurt out on th' rest of th' world for many a year.'

A loud buzzing in the kitchen.

'There she is.' Seamus checked his watch. 'Five 'til one.'

In the kitchen, Seamus pressed a button near the Aga. 'Yes, mum.'

'Show our guest into the drawing room, I'll be along directly.'

'Yes, mum.'

'Well, then.' Seamus took out his comb, looked at it a moment, doleful. 'She likes it groomed,' he said of his mustache.

At the drawing room door, Seamus shook his hand gravely, as if seeing him off on a coffin ship.

# Thirteen

It was a beautiful room, graceful in proportion, though smelling of stale cigarette smoke, mild damp, dogs. A fire simmered on the hearth.

A table in front of a large window, its view to the lake obscured by rain. Framed photographs. Bottles. Glasses. A vase with roses. Behind the sofa, a game table and four chairs—where the blood would be let, he reckoned. Much furniture in the room; a massive ottoman stacked with books, stationed on the medallion of a worn Aubusson. Dog beds in a far corner.

He glanced up, then, and drew in his breath. The portrait above the mantel was stunning in the true sense of the word.

A slender, dark-haired young woman of uncommon beauty looked directly at the observer. Penetrating brown eyes, a necklace of pearls, a gown of aquamarine satin, a pale arm draped casually over the upholstered arm of the French chair in which she was sitting . . .

He approached the portrait, examined it closely. It had the finesse and style of a Sargent, but surely no Sargent would be hanging in these remote regions.

He couldn't take his eyes off hers; there was a palpable sense of the sitter's presence; something of iron resolve, something, too, of anger or remorse. As if loath to invade her privacy or stare too brazenly, he stepped away.

The insistent gaze drew him back. *Look here, I have something that must be said.*

In the strong cheekbones, the chiseled nose, the anxious brow, he saw Liam.

He moved to the fire and turned his back to the soft blaze. August, and the warmth felt good to him.

Above the double doorway, another portrait—Riley Conor, he presumed. Short, portly, muscular, bemused. Wearing boots and jodhpurs, a tweed jacket—holding what appeared to be a small prayer book and leaning on the back of a leather chair before shelves of books rendered carefully by the brush. His brown eyes squinted, as if set to the task of puzzling out a riddle.

He walked to the ottoman at the center of the room; looked again above the mantel and again above the doorway. The subjects of the portraits coolly assessed each other across the divide.

*Look here, I have something that . . .*

The doors opened, his hostess entered. He felt the odd fear and excitement of a child who imagines a monster living beneath his bed.

'Missus Evelyn McGuiness Conor,' boomed Seamus, 'the Reverend Timothy Andrew Kav'na.'

The heavy doors were closed behind her.

She was petite, erect, severe, with the piercing gaze of the portrait nearly intact. He bowed. It was a completely involuntary gesture, and very slight, but she recognized it at once; it had been a good thing to do.

She extended her hand. 'Mister Kav'na.'

'Mrs. Conor.' So she was skipping the reverend business. 'Thank you for having me.' He pressed her hand lightly—he might have captured a small bird. 'I was just admiring your portrait.'

'Thank you for coming, Mister Kav'na. It isn't every day we can round up a fourth.' She leaned on her cane.

'I'm afraid you'll find me a very lame duck.'

'You'll make up for it with interesting conversation, I'm sure. As for the portrait, it was done in this very room, by an Irishman—after Mister Sargent's rendition of Lady Agnew of Lochnaw.'

'And very well done, indeed.'

'Mister Conor and I had lately returned to Catharmore from our honeymoon on the Amalfi Coast. I was twenty, but my waist'—she smiled thinly—'was eighteen—like your Scarlett O'Hara, I'm told. Let us be seated, Mister Kav'na.'

He offered the smile he relied on when parishioners commented on his sermon and he realized they'd heard something entirely different from what he'd said.

Evelyn Conor walked stiffly across the room with the aid of her cane and sat in a high-backed chair by the fire; at her direction, he occupied the end of the sofa to her right. She was a woman of considerable beauty even now, though better than sixty years had passed since she sat for a painter who knew what he was about.

Her long hair was loosely bound at the back of her head and dark, still, though with a wide streak of silver above what his mother had called a 'widow's peak.' Her cheeks were palely rouged, her long-sleeved black dress simply cut; she wore no ornament. He could not imagine this woman clambering up a stepstool.

'Because of my fine nose, the painter wished to render me in profile after Mister Sargent's Madame X. But my husband and I preferred to realize our money's worth by having it done straight on.'

'A wise decision.'

'That is my late husband's portrait above the door.'

'A very agreeable-looking man. Liam speaks of him with affection.' He hadn't meant to say that.

'Liam speaks eagerly of his father, but scarcely mentions his mother. I don't suppose they've told you I'm dying?'

'They haven't.'

'They never do. It's left to me to do the telling.'

'I'm sorry to hear it.'

'No use to be sorry. We must all go sometime.' She briefly drummed the chair arm with her fingers, gazed past him.

'But death is not important, Mister Kav'na.' She gave him a fierce look. 'It cannot frighten me, for I have been purified by suffering.'

He didn't know where to step with this.

'Doctor Feeney and Father O'Reilly will be late. I trust you have some expertise at making drinks? Our man is occupied in the kitchen.'

'Of course. What sort of drinks, Mrs. Conor?' Nothing with small umbrellas or fruit, definitely not.

'Gin and tonic for myself. Would you be up to it?'

'Absolutely,' he said, shooting from the sofa.

At the table, he adjusted his bifocals, stooped, peered at labels on the several bottles, located the gin. Two bottles, different labels. Tonic very handy, no problem. A small dish with wedges of lemon and lime. Glasses in two different sizes.

'What measurements do you prefer, Mrs. Conor?'

'Two to one, thank you.'

'Would that be two of tonic?'

'Of gin, Mister Kav'na.'

Maybe he should use the short glass.

'And what label, if I may?'

'The green label, if you please.'

The English were known to lay off the ice, but perhaps that custom didn't extend to these shores.

'Ice, Mrs. Conor?'

'No ice, Mister Kav'na. The ice is for you; I'm told Americans enjoy the curious habit of watering down perfectly good spirits.'

'Let's see. Short glass or tall?' He had expected a root canal, and he was getting it.

'Have you *never* done this, Mister Kav'na?'

'Not really.'

'The short glass, as you so quaintly put it.'

'Almost done—lemon or lime?'

'Lime, thank you.'

'Coming up.' He let out his breath, which he realized he'd been holding, and stirred the drink with a silver muddle.

'No *stirring*, if you please. It bruises the gin.'

This was no root canal, after all; it was brain surgery. He managed to deliver the thing, with a napkin.

She looked up at him, raised an eyebrow. 'Do you teetotal, Mister Kav'na?'

'No, ma'am, not at all. I'm a sherry man.' He felt the perfect fool for saying it. A sherry man.

'Sherry,' she said with distaste. 'An English habit.'

Spanish, too, he might add.

'You're in Ireland, Mister Kav'na, you can't go about as dry as the bones of Ezekiel.'

'Cheers,' he said, terse. The morning with Anna had hardly quickened his regard for Evelyn Conor.

'*Slainte!*' She lifted her glass and turned to a contrivance by the mantel, pressing a button.

Seamus's voice boomed into the room. 'Yes, mum.'

'Do we have sherry in some remote quarter?'

'Oh, yes, mum, we do, indeed. Only a moment.'

Why couldn't he be like everyone else instead of standing out like a sore thumb? But he'd never been like everyone else; he'd always stood out like a sore thumb.

'I enjoyed my tour of your handsome rooms. The entrance hall is a great tribute to classical form—a privilege to see it.'

'It is an Irish house.'

'Yes.'

'Historians tell us that Catharmore was a fine school of architecture. Doctor O'Donnell had access to a few very skilled men, who tutored a legion of the unskilled. Many trades were learnt here.' She drank with evident thirst.

'Have you read O'Donnell's journal?'

'I have not. I admire him for what he accomplished, but find his ramblings tiresome. A very inward-seeming man, in my view.' She dabbed the corners of her mouth with the napkin. 'I trust you and your wife are enjoying your stay.' She appeared to lack interest in his reply.

'We're enjoying it very much, thank you.' He glanced at his watch—he was needing backup.

'In your Protestant religion, sir, I hear there is great distress.'

'Well, of course, we have the same religion, you and I, Catholic and Protestant—we both believe in the divinity of the Christ, the head of the Church, the one who entered into death that we might have life. As for great distress, I believe it is fully shared between Catholic and Protestant.'

The Great Distress. He would have to remember that.

'And to what do you account such disarray?'

'Disobedience, Mrs. Conor.'

'The Protestants were in disobedience against the Irish for more than seven centuries. What do you say to that, Mister Kav'na?'

'I say that we were gravely mistaken.'

'The Irish are suddenly quick to forget. I shall not forget.'

'I feel the need is not to forget, but to forgive. Where there is forgiveness, the heart of stone becomes a heart of flesh.'

'I'll thank you not to preach to me.'

'I was not preaching, Mrs. Conor, I was making an observation out of my own experience.' To be precise, out of his father's experience of unforgiveness, and the calamity it caused on all sides.

She drank, appeared abstracted. 'I dislike late arrivals.'

'The rain,' he said.

The realization had begun when he took her hand, and now came all of a piece—he had known Evelyn Conor for most of his life. Nearly every parish had one, though he couldn't recall that any had been so proficient at the acid tongue. He was reminded, too, of his father's lacerating coldness, which rendered Evelyn Conor's behavior somehow familiar; the thought that they had met in other times and places, shared some sort of past, was oddly relieving.

She drew in her breath. He checked his watch.

'I had hoped to meet Paddy.'

'Paddy is in Sligo on business. You can see him in the portrait of my late husband, if you like. The spit image.'

Rain streaming onto the glistening panes. The fire smoldering. A clock ticking.

'I don't suppose anyone from Broughadoon has sent their compliments?' she asked.

'Why, yes. They did. Thank you for reminding me. Mr. William Donavan sends his compliments.' What William actually said was, 'A tip of me cap to the oul' scrape.'

'You must pass mine along to him, and to the rest of the household,' she said. 'And Mister Kav'na . . .'

'Yes, Mrs. Conor?'

'I hope you won't need reminding.'

'You can count on it.'

The doors opened. Three rain-soaked dogs burst into the room, followed by James Feeney and a stout and laughing priest wearing a dark suit. Seamus and his silver tray brought up the rear.

*Deo gratias.*

He stood, took a deep breath, buttoned his jacket. Tonight, he would be the evening gazette.

# Fourteen

Messages at Broughadoon.

<Googled your lodge and got email address. Pray for Lew Boyd he has prostate cancer it's a good thing he married that little Tennessee woman when he did. Saw Dooley and Lace—Dooley was filling up the truck, they were headed to the lake for a picnic. He is tall as a chimney and she is pretty as a speckled pup—looks like I may have to buy a new dress, ha ha. Knowing you I called Puny and low and behold she found your cell phone ON THE HALL TABLE. Have canceled yr

international plan, etc since you won't need
it. You should make a list when you travel
and CHECK IT TWICE!!!

<PS—I already have a small Waterford
vase, so large would be great.>

<Unable to contact yr cell, emailing u at
B'doon from LaGuardia. K needs hair
appt tomorrow—will C ride with her? Blow
dry. Pls make arrangement as necessary
for after one pm if possible. Looking
forward, W>

<Hey, Dad, whats the deal? Can't connect
w/ yr cell phone. Dooley>

The afternoon nap—he was perishing for
want of it.

Thinking of Lew, he prayed his way upstairs, slipped into their room, undressed, and
climbed into bed next to his napping wife.

But he couldn't sleep. He was wired from
the coffee he'd slugged down at the bridge
table. At Catharmore, they didn't know from
decaf.

'Home is the hunter from the hill . . .' She
turned to him, smiled. He was ever amazed
that she appeared glad to see him.

'It's hard being too beautiful to get invited anywhere,' she said, propping on an elbow.

'You're invited up one afternoon before we leave; Seamus will show you around. Except for bridge days, she naps from two 'til four.'

'Well done, darling. It's a little cool, I'll just put on my robe and you can tell me everything.' She sat up and slipped into the Shred, then thumped down beside him, expectant.

'Emma says Lew Boyd has prostate cancer.'

'Thank God he has Earlene. I'll pray. I'm so sorry.'

'Puny found my cell phone.' He felt sheepish; he'd almost rather it was stolen. 'She saw Dooley and Lace on their way to the lake. Dooley emailed to say he couldn't contact my cell. And Katherine would like a hair appointment for tomorrow after one o'clock—she hopes you'll arrange it and ride with her.'

'Only Katherine would fly all night, change planes, drive to Lough Arrow, then race out to get her hair done.' She drank from her water glass. 'I'll take care of it; surely there's some place around here. Okay, get going.'

'Where to begin?'

'The house.'

'As handsome on the inside as it is plain without.' He told her about lintels, cornices, columns, pilasters; stuffed fish in glass cases; the windowed kitchen, the tumbled garden.

'Did you see the surgery?'

'Seamus says they don't venture belowstairs except at gunpoint. More than a little dereliction going on at Catharmore, but most of it out of view.'

'What does she look like?'

'A little like Rose Kennedy, and a lot like Liam. You'll enjoy seeing her portrait as a young woman—it could pass for a Sargent but was done by an Irishman. She told me she's dying, but Feeney said later she's dying in the same way we're all dying. He said he's trying to get her in for blood work, he's concerned for her liver, but so far there's nothing seriously wrong that leaving off the drink wouldn't cure.'

'Was she the ogre?'

'She was eviscerating, to say the least. I was alone with her for maybe twenty minutes, but it seemed an eternity.'

Rain streamed against the windows.

'She eased up over drinks and lunch—maybe a bit sloshed, and quite the coquette. But as soon as the cards hit the table, she was a terror all over again.'

'Who was your partner?'

'Three guesses. I dealt the first hand, and if you could have seen mine, you'd have foundered yourself with laughter. Talk about dying.'

'A bust.'

'And then some. But her cards were good and I managed to provide a little help, after all. They couldn't set us—we won.'

'Hooray!'

'An amazing piece of business with the dogs. They bounded into the drawing room sopping wet—she looked them in the eye, pointed to their beds, and away they slunk with nary a yap. I'd pay cash money for that trick.'

'How is my good doctor?'

'Feeney inquired about you at length, he'll drop around tomorrow evening. He told some great stories about his country practice, but I must say Father O'Reilly was the life of the party. His Irish name is Tadhg O Raghailligh—call me Tad, he says. Told me that Tadhg translates to the anglicized Timothy.

'He seemed to take pleasure in something Freud said, that the Irish were the only people who couldn't be helped by psychoanalysis.'

'Makes me prouder still of my drop from Connemara,' she said.

'He grew up in a two-room cottage with his parents, five brothers, three sisters, and a pony.'

'A pony? In the house?'

'Only in winter. Tad was the eldest, and right from the get-go, set apart by his mother for the priesthood. From infancy up, she introduced him as her son the priest. In seminary, said he slept in a room with only two other boys and felt lonely as Longfellow's cloud—missed the body heat and the roughhousing. 't was no comfort bein' rich, he said. A charming fellow.

'We went on a bit about Irish poetry—in the old days, he says Ireland's standing army of poets never fell below ten thousand.'

She drew in her breath, marveling. He relished the role of Gazetteer.

'Then we talked about the pull Ireland puts on its scattered people, the way it has of calling us back. Tad says no use to look for our ancestors in the cemeteries and church registers—we meet them in the DNA of the folks across the table, in the street, in the pew. I realized I was breaking bread with people whose ancestral blood was spilled with that of the Kavanaghs. It was affecting.'

'And these lovely men keep coming to her bridge table, year after year?'

In a way that's almost certainly conflicted, I think they care about her. Hard to imagine, but . . . in a nutshell, glad I went. How about you?'

'Painted like a house afire.'

She took her sketchbook from the night table and opened it and held it up for him to see.

Pud.

He laughed outright.

Pud sitting in the wing chair near the fire, looking at the painter—solemn as a judge, as Peggy used to say.

'You're an amazing woman. This is extraordinary. We'll have to frame it and hang it over the telly.'

'Something's going on with my work—it's getting better, I think. It started with the portrait of Maureen—some huge step has been taken, I don't understand how or why. You know I've always been comfortable painting animals but afraid of painting people. Today, I kept waiting for the fear to come back, but it didn't. It's thrilling. Look.'

He was knocked out by a close-up of Bella's face, it filled the page. Another pair of eyes that expressed a deeper context than he could read. *I have something that must be said . . .*

He stared at the curious way she had set her

mouth, as if holding hostage a secret power and defying any search for it.

'Out of the park,' he said.

'We had a long talk; she softened toward me. I told her how I tried to take my own life. I don't know why I told her that, except I felt she needed to hear it, that it would mean something. I painted while we were talking. She took her mask off once or twice; I watched the way her feelings shifted. She's a very deep and profound young woman. And she knows something, Timothy, something she's desperate to talk about. It's like a worm gnawing at her.'

'And isn't that the way with all of us? Remember me telling you about old Vance Havner?—he said everybody's tryin' to swallow somethin' that won't go down.' He'd seen it in his years of counseling parishioners; he'd seen it in himself, again and again, and this morning in Anna. The gnawing worm was ever-present in a broken world.

'I'm probably imagining things,' she said. 'Maybe I've been too shut-in, too close to everyone here.'

Their habit of telling each other everything did not include all he was told in confidence as a priest; they were in agreement early on about that sticky business—so far, he'd said little about the meeting with Anna.

'How's the ankle?'

'Swollen. Aggravating. Aren't you going to take a nap?'

'Can't,' he said, getting out of bed. 'Maybe I'll read awhile in the journal, there's plenty of time before dinner. What about you?'

She held up a paperback. 'Patrick Kav'na, the old dear.'

'Tad is a great fan of Kav'na, likes him for his harrows and ricks, the provincialism Yeats chastised. And by the way, St. Patrick didn't drive out the snakes, there were never any here to begin with.' Tad had been a fount of information.

He sat in his chair by the window and turned to the page he'd marked with a sheet from his notebook. Rain sang in the gutters; the scent of something baking drifted up from the kitchen ovens.

21 January 1862

My heart is greatly rejoiced—I have gone on my knees before God at the Mass Rock & thanked Him with everything in me—Caitlin sitting up & looking alive as if woken from the dead.

I had been condemning myself most painfully for the failure of the many methods used to revive her, including a variety of nauseous Tonics recommended by Jones Quinn. I am thankful that the Great Physician dissuaded me from the practice of leeching—a practice I abhor, but was ready to use if her languor persisted.

I walked into the Cabin this morning with an imaginary mount on an imaginary rope & handed the rope to Caitlin—She knew at once what I was promising for she had heard the hammering & commotion as Keegan framed the addition to Adam's stall.

Capall she said to A who shrieked with joy—I wept as C gave a fond kiss to the old scar on my cheek, always a sign of her fondest favor. It was the first word she had spoken since Sunday a week & into the bargain she was pleased to choose the Irish word for horse.

Tis a fine bay mare on which C can go abroad on her own Rounds—alone or with Aoife as need be. She says she will call her Little Dorrit after the Dickens novel she so enjoys.

She has tonight supped a little poached trout, a little tea—it is A's every desire that tomorrow her mistress will relish an egg from one of the hens & sop the yolk with a mite of A's fine soda bread.

I have rolled up my pallet from the floor & will sleep again beside my wife. When she saw me doing this she smiled. Baile, I said, pointing in the direction of the house.

Baile, she said, her eyes very bright with happiness.

Soon, I said in English for I do not know the Irish for what is imminent.


A nudge against his leg. He looked down.

'Out on bail,' said his wife. 'I let him come up and sleep under the bed. By the way, he doesn't hear well—it's his age, says Maureen.'

'Where's the shoe?'

'I have it. He gets it back when he leaves the room. This way, you can sit and read in peace.'

'A great idea.'

'We'll see,' she said.

24 February 1862

Balfour has a most Poisonous tongue— he is often drunken & moves among the workmen as someone carrying the fever & infecting all who abide his foul ravings. He has twice refused payment for the Land

deeded me—I am sick with anger for my
witless impulse to take what cost nothing in
order to more greatly supply the Needy. I may
as well be a tenant in his view—he has long
forgot his child who suffered near death until
God wrought a miracle & enabled me to spare
her life—nor does he seem to recall the many
years of his dysentery which C fervently
hopes—though she declines to pray—returns
with a vengeance! But then I must strive to
cure it again.

I have gone to the Mass Rock this day &
prayed to God who didst teach the hearts of
His faithful people by the sending to them the
Light of the Holy Spirit & asked that He
might grant me by the same Spirit to have
right judgment in all things.

I trust it is not too late to have beseeched
God for right judgment—C says that with
God tis never too late.

Many delays in construction due to long
sieges of punishing wether.

Keegan hung a young doe in the half-built
stall & dressed it—A has never cooked deer
loin thus Keegan will himself do the honors
and has rigged a spit in the firebox. A Feast
will bring much needed merriment to our
hearth.

President Lincoln last month issued a war order authorizing aggression against the Confederacy. I had near forgot that country which educated and prospered me. I am saddened by the horrific tyranny of slavery, recognizing in it much that our own Irish have endured. Uncle freed his twelve slaves well before his passing, though our good Cook, Sukey, stayed on & was much accomplished in reading & writing. Her Cookery book writ in her own hand will come with our furnishings when we complete the many labours demanded by Catharmore.

'What is this Mass rock business?' he asked.

'I've been meaning to find out,' she said. 'Help me remember to ask.'

'And who will help me remember to help you?'

'Please try.'

'Righto. What happened to Balfour's place, do you know? Might be something to see before we leave.'

'Keep reading,' she said.

12 May 1862

While one may despise the Oppressor, one clings to his language—it is spoken

everywhere the print of his Boot is made—
Keegan says the English is for 'mekkin war &
the Irish for mekkin love.' Keegan has been
twelve years widowed & I see him cast his eye
about at the Women—he tells a rough joke on
occasion which makes the old women laugh
& the young hide their faces behind their
hands.

He is correct in asserting that I should be
handier at the doctoring if I chose to speak
Irish with the people—though twas Mother's
milk to me until seventeen or more, I carry
no blood memory of it—to have spoken it
in America would have marked me as a
simpleton. Keegan's own English is good & he
speaks enough Irish to have assisted in finding
a Name for the place & to interpret when we
stir about the Region—he is indispensable
among the workmen.

A is a bright thing who wishes to teach us
in the Evening—we point like dunces to this
& that—the packed earth floor, the hearth,
the chickens, the cooking pots—& she gives
us the Irish in return. At the same time she is
learning a bit of English from us, all of which
turns the speech of this narrow household into
a stew of befuddlement, causing Laughter to
break out like measles & excite the Chickens.

| Candle | coinneal |
| Baby | Leanbh |
| Finger | miar |
| May | Bealtaine |

She brought very few personal items when she came to us, save for her most prized possession—her mother's old three-legged milking stool. She sits on it before the fire conducting her language lessons, happy to have something to give beyond earnest common labor.

When I speak with Keegan about independence, he says tis a speabhraidi, a pipedream. I hope to soon turn him from this lazy-minded notion—it is a blasphemy.

John Mitchel said it for me—'England is truly a great public criminal. England! All England! She must be punished; that punishment will as I believe come upon her by & through Ireland; & so Ireland will be avenged.'

Many casualties in the recent battle of Shiloh, well above ten thousand either side. It seems to me this war is not over human flesh but Greed as is the case in every armed conflict. God help the brothers who war against one another.

1 June

A fine, soft rain throughout the day—in America I had forgotten how often it rains in the Eire—gratifying nonetheless to be making the Rounds & seeing so many lift their Caps as we pass—Adam was given two apples by the children at O'Leary's cabin, so well do they love my Mount & the fact that their Sister has a good home with the doctor & his wife.

Such a day is a Pleasure when one is haunted so gravely by the many one sees of Suffering.

Have hired on Danny Moore who is deft with the stump & gets about smartly on his crutch—though unskilled, he seems fitted for the plaster work & will apprentice to James Murray, a man of parts—I have given him a wage above that of other unskilled plasterers—he has given in turn his vow not to speak of it to the men as it would incite ill feeling—his mother came on foot to thank me—she & C having a fine tea together.

Will go down to the Dublin Apothecary Monday next, with further intentions of seeing our Solicitor & having a new coat with hood & warm lining fashioned for C—A shall also have something warm for her back—she is small & thin as a reed as are all her family from long years of poor nourishment.

Have today agreed with C how we shall divide our Estate as one never knows when one's Call may come. Having no child of our own, I will name my orphaned nephew & namesake, Padraigin, as heir to Catharmore— he shows good sense in business affairs & is thrifty as a Scot. He has visited once at my decree—quite silent & cold as a trout but perhaps overstrained by travel undertaken on roads nearly in ruin—I would fain do for him what Uncle did for me. Only one of my brothers living & he in good fettle with fat cows & sufficient Bogland & a hale daughter to care for his needs. C's widowed niece & her many offspring benefit in our lifetime rather than when we are laid in the Grave.

Without further delay of bad wether, we shall move our modest household into the manor no later than year's end. Keegan will turn his cottage over to an ageing sister & lodge in a small room adjoining the Surgery.

C proposes that A should have the care of our lamps when in the house—she is deft at trimming wicks to produce a sweet flame &

washing the chimneys without breakage. She
will also have sole care of the laundry, the
carrying out of ashes, emptying of slop jars &
other general chores. A is pleased at the
prospect of expanding her duties.

He came awake from Fintan O'Donnell's
complicated life and noted the simplicity of his
own—Pud's chin rested on his bare foot. Made
him miss the Old Gentleman. He could say
anything to Barnabas, read him the Romantic
poets or discourse on the politics of the day; his
good dog inevitably listened with grave interest. An elegant soul.

4 June
    Balfour treats his servants the way slaves
are said to be treated in the southlands of
America. I doctered a southern slave on two
occasions in Philadelphia—a striking figure of
a black man with a voice as deep as that of a
church organ & attired nearly as well as
his Master in a vest of striped satin with
a woollen frock coat & dove colored
breeches—I recall that he carried a pocket
watch & suffered from tumors of the mouth
which we were able to address with some
success—he oversaw the business dealings of a

planter in the Carolinas & had a nobel
manner about him.

Yesterday treated the head wound of a lad
who was kicked by a horse while mucking
Balfour's stables—I learned that he was badly
beaten twice when Balfour was in a drunken
rage—He broke down in a fit of sobbing &
pled with me not to tell it abroad else he be
more fiercely treated & sent off the place.
Having come from England with his father,
now deceased, he would have no Family to
turn to nor any place to lay his head.

From my experience in America & in my
own Country, tis clear that Alcohol has
wrought more misery than can be reckoned—
it is as merciless as any plague in the taking of
both lives & souls.

The caffeine was wearing thin. He trooped
to the bed, Pud at his heels, and crawled beneath the duvet.

As he punched up his pillow, Pud stared at
him, unblinking. Needless to say, there would
be no balm in Gilead. None.

'On or off?' he asked his reading wife.

'Why don't we just cut to the chase?'

He patted a spot by his feet; Pud leaped onto

the bed, nailed the proffered territory, lay down, sighed.

'Only one problem,' he said.

'What's that?'

'We don't know where this might lead.'

She turned a page, laughing. 'Since when do we know where anything might lead?'

'You have a point,' he said.

# Fifteen

Showered, shaved, and dressed for dinner, he opened the journal to his bookmark.

> Fair
>
> Having cured a sty on the eye of my own milch cow, the word has spread like brush fire—for everything from cow beetle to the infected teat, they are at me for treatment. No bastes, I tell them, no bastes! Old Rose McFee is determined I should deliver her calf.
>
> Fair days—the men working at a pace—we shall take occupancy of Catharmore by early August or I'm damned.
>
> I mark here Keegan's report—that Balfour

has twice made foul comments to the men about Aoife.

'You're all dressed.' She limped from the bathroom on her crutch, steaming like a clam in the Darling Robe.

'Why don't you go visit in the library? Just come back in a half hour or so and give me a hand down the stairs.' She leaned to him and fussed with the silk handkerchief in his jacket pocket, and he stood for any further improvements.

'You're looking very sexy,' she said.

Until she came into his life, such a thing as looking sexy had never occurred to him—the notion would have seemed absurd.

There he'd been, tied up at the dock for better than sixty years, the waves occasionally swamping his boat, but safe at harbor, nonetheless. Then she'd moved next door and in no time at all he was unmoored completely. He was terrified of being dashed on the rocks, or adrift on the deep with no way to read the stars of his frightening passion—he was the old man 'way out at sea, in the thrall of a woman who found him romantic and clever. St. Matthew had asked, Which of you by taking thought can add one cubit unto his stature? Ha. He had grown ten feet tall in the first months of his fumbling courtship.

'I mean it,' she said, kissing him for a fare-thee-well. She drew away and laughed. 'You're blushing.'

'Tight collar.'

'I haven't wanted to say anything, but you're a little out of control with your diet.'

'I'll watch it.' He hated watching it, but she was right.

'Thirty minutes, then? Don't forget me.'

'No chance.'

Pud accompanied him downstairs, shoe in mouth. On the landing, he peered out to the garden—the rain had ended, thanks be to God.

In the library, Pete O'Malley, looking sour and wearing a tie patterned with fishing lures.

'How did it go today at the river?'

'Was supposed to fair off by noon,' said Pete, 'but not a stir.'

He sat in a wing chair. 'Where did the poker club do their damage?'

'Lough Key. Hardly any rain at Key. Caught enough fish to sink a freighter—they could go commercial.'

'They're that good?'

'Maniacs, those women. Cast a line, hook a trout, cast a line, hook a salmon . . .' Pete swirled his drink, drained the glass. 'I'm havin' th' Irish T-bone this evenin'. Medium rare.'

'Come on. It's the poker club's night to shine.'

Pete looked repentent. 'You're right. I'll have th' T-bone tomorrow evenin'.'

'That's the spirit.'

Pud sat at his feet, unblinking. 'Give it up, buddy. I'll catch you tomorrow.' Seducing aromas from the kitchen. Gray flakes of burned turf rising in the draft.

'Maybe I should get a dog,' said Pete.

'You can tell dogs anything, and they'll still love you.'

'If I told a dog everything, that dog would be gone in a heartbeat. Guess it's different with clergy, not much to tell.'

He laughed. 'Guess you don't know much about clergy.'

Pete adjusted his tie, eyed the stair hall. 'We're out of here Friday before sunup.'

'Sorry to hear it.'

'A pretty good life at ol' Broughadoon. Like Ireland used to be. Anyway, I'll be goin' home to a Manx cat my wife left when she moved out, an' a parrot named Roscoe that sings Beatles tunes.'

'You're kidding.'

'Serious as a heart attack. Ol' Roscoe lives at the office; my secretary treats him like Michael Collins resurrected. He's been on th' telly three times.'

'What's his specialty?'

'Yellow Submarine. Want to see his picture?'

Pete pulled a cell phone from his jacket pocket, glowered at it, fiddled with it, handed it over. 'Roscoe.'

A photo of a parrot looking grouchy. 'Amazing,' he said. 'No grandkids?'

'It's hard to get grandkids these days, have you noticed? My daughter has a pig that sleeps on her bed, my son has a wire-haired terrier—that's all she wrote in that department.'

'What do you do in Dublin?'

'Insurance. Family company founded by my great-granddad in nineteen aught nine.'

'Aught. Haven't heard that in a while.'

'I've been seein' a lot of it on my bottom line. Too much stress in th' business today—I remember what my dad used to say, he owned a cattle operation on the side—stress toughens th' meat and sours th' milk.'

'I'll buy that.'

Pete looked at him intently. 'You're a lucky man.'

'Can't say I believe in luck, but why do you think so?'

'Your wife, she's a great lady.'

'She is. Thanks. Puts up with me.'

'That's bloody hard to find—somebody to put up with you—in spite of your mess.'

'Putting up with somebody's mess works both ways.'

'I couldn't put up with my wife's mess—I don't blame her for walkin' out.'

A burst of laughter from the dining room; they were finishing the table setups. Something electric was in the air—something to do with Anna's surprise, no doubt.

'I have bad luck with women. But, hey, if I didn't have bad luck, I wouldn't have any luck at all.' Pete manufactured a laugh.

He knew the feeling. Balding, overweight, and stuck in a remote parish at the age of forty, he had resigned himself to the fact that it was all over for him in the marriage department. What he couldn't know was that twenty years later, a children's book author with great legs would move next door.

'You know what it'll take to save my marriage?' asked Pete.

'What's that?'

'A bloody miracle.'

They heard the poker club coming along the stair hall. He saw the hopeful look on Pete's face, saw him close it down and try the sour look again.

'Refill,' said Pete, getting up and heading to the honesty bar.

In the dining room, newly starched linens; candles and garden roses on tables and sideboard; doors open to the summer evening. A pretty good life at ol' Broughadoon—definitely.

Though the anglers were full of praise for the club's fishing skills, they were quick to point out that ghillies and decent weather must nonetheless be given their due.

'What*ever*,' said Debbie. '*Slainte!*'

Glasses lifted all around. '*Slainte!*'

He gazed with his wife at the lough, silvered in the gathering dusk. 'Maureen calls this the moth hour,' she said, half dreaming. 'The moth hour . . .'

'I've been thinking,' he said. 'I haven't committed anything to memory in quite a while. You've inspired me; I'd like to memorize a poem. Maybe Patrick Kav'na. It would be a souvenir we don't have to pack, and would last us as long as our wits hold out.'

'Which we pray will be a very long time,' she said.

Decked in his butler's garb, Seamus on his night off from Catharmore was standing in for Bella on her own night off.

'Fresh peach tart this evening, in a rosemary cornmeal crust . . .'

Seamus paused for effect.

'. . . or Blackberry Semifreddo—ripe blackberries blended with fresh mint, verbena, homemade ricotta, and local sweet cream, frozen in a nest of dark chocolate.'

'Now, *that's* poetry,' he told his wife.

He remembered being seven years old and working along the creek with Peggy in the blazing Mississippi sun. The handles on their tin buckets creaked; heat shimmered off the water.

Pick a berry, slap a chigger, pick a berry . . .

'We gon' be eat up,' said Peggy.

'I'm done eat up.'

'I'm *already eat*-en up,' she corrected in the voice that never sounded like Peggy. When he was old enough to know better, he realized she never corrected *herself*, not one time, it was always him she was after with the English lesson.

'You gon' beat me, you keep pickin' so fast,' she said.

'I ain't gon' beat you, 'cause I be eatin' all I pick after I get to right here.' He tapped the bucket three-fourths of the way to the top.

'Peoples say don' eat while you pickin'. If you does, when you eats yo' cobbler this evenin', it won't taste half as good.'

'How come?'

''cause you done spoiled th' taste in yo' mouf out here on th' creek.'

He looked up and rolled his eyeballs as far back in his head as they would go. That's what he thought about that dumb notion.

Peggy laughed pretty hard; he liked to make Peggy laugh. 'You *know* what *you* is,' she said.

He did know. He was th' aggravatin'est little weasel she ever seen . . .

'The peach tart,' said Cynthia.

'The thing with blackberries,' he told Seamus.

''t is a grand evening you'll be havin' in th' library with your coffee.'

Cynthia adjusted her glasses and peered at their server. 'You're looking quite distinguished, I must say.'

''t is th' candlelight—it softens th' shine on my butler's oul' duds. We'll bury you in it, Seamus, says Mrs. Conor. Aye, says I, for you'll outlive me and all th' rest.'

'What would you know about the Mass rock?' he asked. 'Where is it located? O'Donnell speaks of it in the journal.'

'You'll have to ask Anna or Liam. I saw it years ago, but can't remember whether it's right or left of th' lake path.'

When Seamus walked away he saw it coming.

'Cream. Cheese. Chocolate,' said his wife, reciting a litany of his offenses.

'Righto. And mint, verbena, and fresh berries. Six of one, half dozen of the other.'

She raised an eyebrow.

'Now, Kav'na. Look at all the fish I'm having. Very good for the diabetic. And all the fresh vegetables. *Locally grown*,' he said, losing the battle.

The anglers' table was engrossed in recitation of one sort or another.

Tom raised his glass to the room. 'May the most we wish for be the least we get.'

'Hear, hear! *Slainte!*'

'Oh, give me grace to catch a fish,' said Pete, 'so big that even I, when talkin' of it afterwards, may have no need to lie.'

'*Slainte!*'

'*Slainte* here, *slainte* there,' said his wife, definitely in the spirit of things.

'To look for a moment on th' *serious* side . . .' said Debbie.

'As if there isn't enough of that in the world,' said Hugh.

'. . . I have a question—what is *work*? I mean in th' true *philosophical* sense.'

'The true philosophical sense.' Hugh looked blank. 'Beats me. I haven't hit a lick at a snake in three, maybe four weeks.'

He pitched in his two cents' worth. 'According to your man Oscar Wilde, work is the curse of the drinking classes.'

'The answer is simple,' said Moira. '*Work* is for people who *don't know how to fish.*'

Laughter all around.

Pete raised his glass. 'No offense to you, Tim. In your callin', you're fishin' twenty-four/seven.'

'Righto,' said Hugh. 'You're off th' hook in a manner of speaking.'

'I've got a great idea,' said Pete. 'How about we all get together again next year, same time, same station? I'll bring Roscoe.'

The door from the kitchen swung open—Maureen and Anna, flushed from the heat of the Aga, entered with William, who brought up the rear.

'Hullo, everyone,' said Anna. 'We're just going in to arrange the chairs. Enjoy your dessert, and please come along when you hear the bell.'

'Need any help with th' liftin'?' asked Pete.

'We've three strong backs for 't,' said William. ''t is your job to lift th' fork.'

'Th' bane of my days,' he heard Anna say as the trio walked up the hall. 'I can do nothing with it this evening, nothing at all.'

And there was William saying, ''t is beautiful hair ye got from y'r own mother, Anna Conor. Stop aitin' y'r face about it.'

At the sound of the bell, they left their tables and trooped to the library, happy to see the small fire poked up and lamps gleaming against the dusk.

# Sixteen

Maureen patted a couple of wing chairs angled toward the hearth. 'Your poor ankle wins th' prize of th' front row.'

'You're a dote,' said his wife. 'Will you sit with us?'

'Aye, with pleasure, and thank you for your comp'ny.' Before he could give a hand, she drew a chair from the game table and sat next to him. 'There'll be fifteen of us this evenin'—like family.'

'It's my guess,' he said, 'that you had something to do with our surprise.'

'Aye. For many years now.'

He found the disorder of her teeth compelling, in a way; her smile was more engaging for it.

Anna had disappeared; Liam and Seamus served coffee.

He nosed the dark, fragrant brew, took a sip—full-bore, precisely the way he liked it. At home he played it safe, drank the eunuch decaf every evening; here, he rolled the dice, and so far had slept like a log. He'd been hooked on coffee from an early age; had searched for decades since for anything remotely similar to what his mother perked in a beat-up pot on the woodstove that stood alongside the electric range. Often with a grind of wild chickory root, it had the heedless taste of the campfire, something of backbone and daring that he could never replicate.

The club took the sofa; the anglers nailed favorite wing chairs; William and Seamus assumed their posts at the checkerboard; Liam sat nearby, distracted.

Anna entered from the stair hall as the mantel clock struck a quarter 'til nine, and stood before them on the hearth. Because he was accustomed to seeing her in clogs and work gear, her frank good looks in a green dress gave him a kind of jolt. He saw in her face the softening that follows earnest confession.

'With the exception of my departed mother, Roisin, I cannot think of anyone I'd rather share this special evening with. All of you here tonight love life and its many possibilities, just as they say my mother did.'

She spoke slowly, measuring her words. ''t is a rare gift you'll be given this evening—a wondrous thing of heart and mind and soul that we can't completely understand, for it comes of God alone.

'Ladies and gentlemen . . .' Her voice broke; she lowered her eyes briefly, looked up again. ''t is with great honor and joy that I give you . . . my daughter, Bella Flaherty.'

Bella strode from the hall and stood where her mother had stood. She gazed for a moment above the heads of her audience, brought the fiddle up, rested it beneath her chin, poised the bow. Her body was rigid, every energy concentrated.

She drew the bow across the strings in a single long, piercing note. Lifted the bow, laid it again to the strings, sounded a note that shimmered in the air, fragile as a moth.

He took Cynthia's hand.

The music came at them abruptly, and with such raw force that he was rocked back in his chair. Raging, wounded, feverish music, with the volume of a dozen fiddles at work in the room. He looked at his wife, who sat with her mouth slightly agape; glanced at Maureen, who covered her mouth with her hand.

God above, he thought. The unleashed spirit of the music had something in it of unchecked risk and gamble; perspiration gleamed on Bella's face, half turned from them to her fiddle. He closed his eyes to sharpen his hearing of the music, was astounded again by its flash and intensity, backed by the drumming of William's cane on the floor. It was a wild ride with no roll bars.

The piece ended suddenly. There was a long, stunned silence—then, an explosion of applause as Bella looked without expression above their heads.

''t is th' trad music she plays, like her father,' said Maureen. ''t was a hard one, that, with what they call th' tongued triplets.'

'Brilliant,' he whispered.

Bella looked at William. 'Daideo, this is for you.'

William gave a nod, crossed himself.

She placed the fiddle under her chin, raised the bow. Then came the grieving music, pouring over them like a vapor, like a shroud. He was standing by the fresh mound in Hill Crest, alone at his mother's grave, wondering how he could go on.

Cynthia glanced at him, wordless.

Now the music was no longer the shroud, but comfort to the ones surviving, pleading with their sorrow, ending with promise.

Their unhindered applause poured into the silence left by the voice of the fiddle. He was moved that anyone so young could interpret wrenching loss, then remembered the child removed to Lough Arrow at the age of four.

His nerves had come alive, he was fully awake in some hidden place in himself that he hadn't remembered.

Maureen leaned to him and whispered, ''t will be Bonny Kate comin' up, mebbe, or Dear Irish Boy, if she takes th' notion.'

He clasped Maureen's hand with its leathered palm, raised it to his cheek. 'Well done,' he said.

'She's not my own blood, but she's my babby for all that!'

'Aye,' he said.

Bella turned her gaze to Maureen. 'Mamó, this is for you.'

Then, something he could only define as anointed—with her bow, Bella Flaherty called forth music of sweetly fluent temper; tenderness found its opening and was transformed into something akin to yearning, or longing; he heard in the notes the drone of the bagpipe. Maureen wiped her eyes with the back of her hand.

If they could hear this back home, he thought, where countless Irish had immigrated all those years ago, where the color of the old speech lingered, and the old tunes resonated still . . .

Applause, then, and Maureen throwing a kiss to the fiddler.

'Will ye sing with me, Mamó?'

'Oh,' said Maureen, her breath gone at the idea.

'Will ye?'

Maureen flushed, looked at him, at Cynthia. 'Jesus, Mary, an' all th' saints . . . I wasn't expectin' . . .'

'Please,' said Cynthia.

''t would be a *féirin*,' said Anna.

'Th' Nightingale, then, and God help an' oul' woman.' Maureen rose from the chair and joined Bella.

William looked disapproving. ''t is a tune of the English.'

'They borrow from us, we borrow from them,' said Bella. 'Niall plays it.'

'Niall,' said William, with obvious distaste.

At the opening notes, Maureen closed her eyes, tilted her head, and joined her dusky voice with the music of the fiddle.

As I went a-walkin' one mornin' in May
I met a young couple who fondly did stray
An' one was a young maid so sweet and so fair
An' the other a soldier and a brave grenadier.

An' they kissed so sweet and comfortin' as they
    clung to each other.
They went arm in arm along the road like sister
    and brother.
They went arm in arm along the road till they
    came to a stream
An' they both sat down together to hear the
    nightingale sing.

From out of his knapsack he took a fine fiddle
An' he played her such merry tunes that you
    ever did hear
An' he played her such merry tunes that the
    valley did ring
An' they both sat down together to hear the
    nightingale sing.

Hers was a face which had been fully lived in, he thought, and while he was no fan of

aging, it had done a grand work on Maureen
McKenna. Bella turned from them to the
woman she called grandmother, bending low
into the croon of the music.

> . . . an' if ever I return again, it'll be in the spring
> An' we'll both sit down together an' hear the
>       nightingale sing.
>
> An' they kissed so sweet and comfortin' as they
>       clung to each other.
> They went arm in arm along the road like sister
>       and brother.
>
> They went arm in arm along the road till they
>       came to a stream
> An' they both sat down together to hear the
>       nightingale sing.

They rose to their feet, even William, ap-
plauding, cheering.

'Give us another!' cried William.

'Do, Mamó.'

'Johnny, I Hardly Knew Ye!' said William.

'You know I can't sing it for bawlin' me eyes
out. What'll it be, then?' she asked Bella.

The fiddle answered.

Maureen laughed, nodded to the fiddler, and sang.

> I'll tell me ma when I go home
> Th' boys won't leave th' girls alone.
> They pull my hair, they stole my comb,
> But that's all right 'til I go home.
> She is handsome, she is pretty,
> She's th' belle of Belfast city.
> She is courtin', one, two, three.
> Please won't you tell me, who is she?
>
> Albert Mooney says he loves her.
> All th' boys are fightin' for her.
> They rap at th' door an' they ring th' bell
> Sayin', Oh, my true love are ye well?
> Out she comes as white as snow,
> Rings on her fingers, bells on her toes.
> Ol' Jenny Murphy says she'll die
> If she don't get th' fellow with th' rovin' eye.
>
> Let th' wind an' th' rain an' th' hail blow high
> An' th' snow come shovelin' from th' sky . . .

Bella tapped her foot, bore down on the tune, and circled back to the opening lines.

'But that's all right 'til I go home!' The music ended on a high, comic note that gave them all a laugh.

Maureen stood unmoving for a moment, spent and breathless. Seamus bowed to the fiddler and then to Maureen. William thumped his cane, and all the rest put in their money's worth.

The concert was over. Bella lowered the fiddle and bow. A smile played at the corners of her mouth.

'Brava! Brava!' yelled the club, as Bella disappeared along the stair hall and Maureen returned to her chair.

'Thank you,' he said with feeling. 'Well done.'

He wanted it all to happen again, the music had flown so quickly. They had been given rage, mourning, hope, laughter—and joy—they had also been given joy.

Cynthia was embracing Anna, Anna was kissing Maureen, Seamus was slapping William on the back.

'What did you make of that?' asked his astonished wife.

'Camp meeting.' The finest half hour of camp meeting he'd ever seen, and he'd seen a few.

He embraced Anna with great feeling. 'There,' he said.

'There,' she said, laughing through tears.

'Will she come back and join us?'

'She gave us all she had just now.'

'Rev'rend,' said William, who was dressed to the nines in a sport coat and tie, 'have an Irish whiskey, 't will be good f'r ye.'

'How good for me do you think it might be?' he asked.

''t will give ye a good laugh and a long sleep,' said the old man.

'A very attractive benefit, but I'm going to hold off. However—before I go home, William, we'll have a shot of the Irish together, just you and me.'

'At Joe Kennedy's or Broughadoon?'

'Broughadoon. I'll challenge you to a game of checkers.'

'Done, sir,' said William.

Maureen handed around a tray. 'If you won't slake th' thirst, have a sweet, then.'

'I'll pass, and thank you. God's blessing on you, dear lady, you've helped raise a young genius.'

'She's not a bad girl a'tall, Rev'rend, not deep down. As for m'self, I was a very bad girl.'

'I'm not believing that.'

'You should have seen th' tricks I was up to with th' lads hereabout—there was a Daniel, a James, two Roberts, an' a Paddy—an' all after marryin' me. I turned my mother's hair white as any fleece. A willful scut I was.'

'I can't imagine . . .'

'Aye, an' save your tryin'; I've done my con-fessin' an' he's put the all of it as far as th' east is from th' west.'

'What happened to change things?'

'My oul' mother prayed for me, and m' grandmother, to boot.'

'That'll do it,' he said.

'I lived forty happy years with Tarry, an' niver a bitter word between us.'

'Now, Maureen,' said Anna.

'Ah, well, one or two is all. So you see, Rev'rend, there's always hope, for I don't think I came out too badly, thanks to God in 'is mercy.'

'Amen,' he said. 'You were wonderful to-night.'

Maureen laughed. ''t wasn't only th' guests got a surprise out of th' evenin'.'

He glanced up then and saw Liam, standing by the sepia photographs as if dazed, his face wearing the flat, pasty look. They made eye contact; Liam lifted his hand in a gesture which he didn't understand.

He excused himself and went to him. 'What is it?'

Liam grasped his arm; they walked along the hall and into the dining room.

'The Barret,' whispered Liam.

But there was no Barret.

Except for the sconces and two empty picture hooks, the wall above the sideboard was bare.

# Seventeen

*7:15 a.m.*
    *Warm, clear day predicted*
    *Broughadoon*
    *Dear Henry,*
    *Up later than usual—having coffee at our table by the window and taking advantage of the rare quiet moment around this place.*
    *There's nothing so bad it couldn't be worse, say the Irish, and turns out they're right. After the shock and nuisance of the cupboard business, comes the theft of a valuable painting from the dining room while guests and staff gathered in the library, innocent as babes.*
    *Appears to have been lifted off the picture hooks*

and ferried out the side doors to the garden, with no footprints to be found anywhere on the property (due in part to a considerable amount of pea gravel around the lodge). No tire tracks in the lane leading to the main road. It's as if the picture, valued at roughly 350,000 in American dollars and largely uninsured, was taken up in the air.

The Gardai (or perhaps it is Garda, I can't seem to get it straight) swarmed the place. Photos taken—a rogue's gallery if you ever saw one—four guards, a detective, and a video of all interviews with guests, etc., keeping the lot of us up past one in the morning. I slept so poorly that I rose at the usual time just to have the misery over with, and prayed the Morning Office—you, Peggy, and Sister faithfully in my petitions. Fell asleep in the chair and reduced the deficit by two hours.

C and I haven't discussed it yet, but I'm all for packing up and getting out of Dodge when W and K, who arrive at eleven this morning, depart tomorrow. They could drive us to Sligo or thereabout and surely we can find a room in a pleasant inn or hotel—I will do some phoning after the breakfast rush clears the kitchen. Another few days and we'll be done with this most recent Long and Unlovely Confinement.

You and I should learn to fish, Henry, it would

*give us something to talk about in our dotage. The sport appears to hold its fans in thrall, they can't get enough of it—they've been known to depart this mortal coil promoting fishing with their final breath. All our anglers out this morning at sunrise, ready to go again full throttle.*

*Have been adopted by yet another dog—this fellow a Jack Russell of the Pudding variety, long in the tooth like the rest of us, but up for anything. He sleeps under or on our bed, depending on circumstances.*

*We plan to read the southern writers again when we get home—Flannery O'Connor for one, to look at what happened to the great Irish literary tradition as it traveled across the Pond and slipped under our Magnolia Curtain. My guess is that it wasn't greatly transformed, which is a good thing.*

*A fine library at my fingertips, yet have cracked only two covers on its many shelves—a journal kept by the builder of the house on the hill above, and an old volume in which I found this observation of the Irish by Edmund Campion, martyred 1581:*

*'The people are thus inclined: religious, franke, amorous, irefull, sufferable of paines infinite, very glorious, many sorcerers, excellent horsemen, delighted with warres, great almes-givers, surpassing in hospitalitie . . . They are sharpe-witted, lovers of*

*lerning, capable of any studie whereunto they bend
themselves, constant in travaile, adventurous,
intractable, kinde-hearted . . . '*

    *So there you have in a nutshell the Gaelic side
of our heritage. Though written in the 16th century,
the description isn't much out of fashion would be
my guess.*

    *Never waste a crisis, said Albert Schweitzer
(I think it was Al), but what the kind-hearted
people here will do with this latest brouhaha is
beyond me. I don't know much, but I do know this:
I will never open a lodging for guests, it is 24/7 and
hell to pay to make a bit of heaven for other people.*

    *Take care of yourself and do all that the
doctors—and Peggy—tell you to do.*

    *Dhia dhuit, my brother,*

    *Timothy*

He had glanced at the nearly bare dining room wall and seen the darker rectangle of paint which the Barret protected against fading. He'd chosen to sit with his back to the sideboard while having breakfast and writing the letter, thus hiding from view another sight he didn't care for: a barricade of yellow tape across the doors to the garden.

He walked to the library, Pud at his heels, dropped the stamped envelope in the box at the sofa, saluted Malone's hat in the entrance hall, and stepped out to a shaft of birdsong. He stood for a moment, imagining glaciers lumbering through these regions, carving out what they pleased—valleys, coastlines, mountains, lakes, the astonishing Ben Bulben.

Anna was at her flower beds, crouching among the iris with a pruner.

'Good morning, Anna.'

'Good morning, Reverend.' She didn't look up.

'Did you rest a little?'

'A little,' she said. 'And you?' Not looking up. A rooster crowed beyond the beeches.

'Well enough. Liam?'

'He's out with the sheep, the damp has started a bit of foot rot. He likes tending the sheep.' She turned to him, her eyes red with the little sleep. 'It takes his mind off things.'

She dropped spent blooms into a trug; there was a close scent of catmint and lavender.

'I believe Dr. Feeney would be prescribing a real day off for you.'

'With all due respect to Dr. Feeney,' she said, 'he has never managed a guest lodge. One must keep a pleasing front no matter what comes, and be full of smiles into the bargain. There's always a scrap one can pull from the deep.'

'Always a scrap, yes.' Like the rest of the human horde, he had pulled many a scrap and would doubtless pull more. 'Counting ours, you'll have had nine frys this morning.' He didn't envy her the labor of it.

'And box lunches for our anglers and ghillies. But I've seen the lean days we were building our business, when there were no frys to be made a'tall at Broughadoon. I'll take th' nine over the none.'

He wanted to ask if her roses were troubled with black spot and beetles, as were his, but . . . 'If there's anything I can do . . .'

She stood and handed him a stem of iris, the bloom golden in color. 'Thank you for hearing me yesterday; 't is a great gift to be heard. You really listened, and your prayer—I shall always remember it. I felt I was starving unto death, and it fed me.'

He lifted the curved petals to catch a scent he'd favored since childhood. 'Something from *Macbeth* came to me in the night—give sorrow words; the grief that doesn't speak whispers o'er the fraught heart and bids it break. Thank you for trusting me.'

'I feel sad for Liam, 't was the truest link to his da, that painting. Such value can't be appraised nor replaced and the books are small consolation.'

'Yes.'

''t is in a way like losing his father again. And the final blow is that we hadn't insured it properly. Loss upon loss. We had meant to . . .'

They were silent then, looking toward the lake.

'There's never any privacy, really, in keeping an inn, even when one lies in one's own bed. Personal life and possessions are so blended into the business, there's no telling where one stops and the other begins. One is ever in the company of others.' She looked at him. 'But it's what we love, of course, and one pays a price always for what is loved.'

'Yes.'

'In the end, the guest sees everything, it's all so . . . intimate; I wish we could protect you from that.'

'A pet occupation of the Enemy is to distance us from intimacy. Such intimacy is a sacrifice for you and Liam, but a gift to us.'

The cloud moved off her face, she nearly laughed. 'You're a very different sort of man.'

'There,' he said, laughing.

'There,' she said, somehow relieved.

'The Mass rock—we read about it in the journal. Is there a chance of seeing it?'

'Past the fishing hut and into the wood a half kilometer. You'll have a stone wall to climb over. 't is in a grove, hard by a beech with a limb looking like an elephant's head. You'll see the doleful eye and the long trunk.'

'I saw the anglers going out.' He had no idea why he was forcing conversation on this stricken woman.

'The club wanted to sleep in, but the ghillies were paid in advance and so they're off to get their money's worth. As for the men, they invited themselves to tag along with the ladies, they'll be leaving us tomorrow.' Anna gave him a half-smile from the deep.

He saw movement along the lake path—a man with a camera emerged from the bushes.

'Garda,' she said. 'They're everywhere.'

He should go about his business and leave Anna about hers. He was glued to the spot, brainless as any eejit.

'Da wants you to have use of the Vauxhall—if you'll take the use of it. A terrible old thing, the Vauxhall; still and all, 't is safe enough to take you round to see th' beauty.' She drew off her work gloves. 'We're gormless not to have thought of it before.'

'You're kind. Thank you.' He didn't want to say that the anglers weren't the only ones having their last day. 'I regret that the uproar took some of the shine off what Bella did for us. It was a great privilege to hear her.'

'Her day off yesterday was spent practicing, so I'm giving her today. We're going busking tonight at the Tubbercurry Fair.'

'Busking.'

'Playing the old music for whoever walks by or will listen. Setting out the hat. A lot of musicians do it.'

'How far away?'

'Thirty-five kilometers. Bella is isolated here, she needs to be among friends, other musicians. She's after going alone, but I'm going with her. 't will give us time together.'

'Always a good thing.'

'Seamus and Maureen will stand in with Liam at dinner. Seamus has many holiday hours due him by law. He'll spend a few with us over the next days, though Lady Agnew will not approve.'

'Lady Agnew.'

'Sorry. It's what Paddy calls his mother, after the original painting by Mr. Sargent.'

'If I know my cousin, he'll sleep the day away, Cynthia and Katherine are going off to Sligo for hair appointments, and I'll be no trouble. Perhaps you can get a break.'

There would be no good time to tell her; he should do it now. 'I haven't talked with Cynthia about this, Anna, but I think we should . . .' He hesitated.

'Move on?'

'Yes.'

''t is what I would do in your place.'

'I'm sorry.'

'Please don't be sorry, you'll get me started on all the apologies you're owed, and we'll be at it a fortnight.'

He was wilted cabbage. If he sat on that bench, he would not get up.

'Would you like your fry now, Reverend? Cynthia says your diabetes . . .'

'I would, yes. Thank you.'

She walked toward the kitchen door, leaving her trug among the iris.

'Anna,' he said.

She turned. He saw the exhaustion in her face, in the slump of her shoulders.

'I believe there's a silver lining in this.'

She made no response and went in.

Why couldn't he keep his trap shut? He did

believe that, but there was no proper solace in him—why did he strive to dredge up the skills of priestly consolation which he'd apparently lost or never had?

He sat on the bench, weighted by all that had happened. And why had it happened, anyway? He'd gone on maybe five vacations in his life. The very word had for decades been foreign to him. There'd been a couple of summers at Walter's in Oxford, an occasional summer in Pass Christian as a boy, the long-ago trip to England, and of course the initial visit to Broughadoon. That was it, unless his honeymoon counted as a vacation. But why this upheaval in what should be a refreshment? And, Lord, why the ankle business into the bargain? This was, after all, Cynthia's *birthday gift*. And what about Anna and Liam, who had most to suffer in this monstrous snare? They were *good people* . . .

He realized he was whining; that these were the very questions put to him unceasingly during his years as a priest. Why me? Why her? Why us? Why them? Why now? Why then? Endless.

It was nearly eleven when he woke from a nap and found his wife sitting beneath the open window in her green chair, dressed and reading the journal. He sat up on the side of the bed. 'I think we should leave tomorrow with Walter and Katherine.'

There was a long silence. His heart beat dully; his legs felt like a couple of pine logs.

'A terrible thing has happened,' she said.

'Yes.'

'In the journal, I mean. I saw your book-mark, it's just ahead.'

'Don't tell me.' He had zero interest in an-other terrible thing. 'They offered us the Vaux-hall, I could have taken you around a bit, driven you by a castle or two. I hear there's a car park close to Yeats's grave, you could have made it over without any trouble.' She didn't appear to be listening. 'Lunch at a pub, even—we might have done that.'

She was staring at the wall above the bed, at the print of sedge warblers in a thicket of reeds.

'Did you rest?' he asked.

'Sort of. Ready to get something done with my hair—I'm tired of standing in the shower on one leg like a heron.'

He left the bed and dressed quickly. 'Com-ing down?'

Her mind was still elsewhere, she looked perplexed.

'Coming down, Kav'na?'

'Yes,' she said.

'Do we agree we should leave?'

'Probably. I suppose so. Yes.'

He checked his watch. 'They'll be arriving anytime.'

'Have you told Anna or Liam?'

'Anna.'

'What did she say?'

'That she would do the same.'

'Where will we go?'

'I called around before I brought your tray up. Emailed Dooley, by the way. Talked with a four-star inn in Sligo, but no dining and nothing on the ground floor. Two hotels were booked solid—high season, as you know. I'll make more calls this afternoon; we'll rent a car, of course.'

'Do you think you can do it, the driving on the wrong side?'

'I *will* do it,' he said.

His cousin was true to form. Knocked out and ready for a decent sleep, Walter gave him the so-called cousin's kiss, joined him in exclaiming the Kavanagh family motto, and hied to the room until dinner. He watched him climb the stairs, feeling strangely moved, even startled, by his cousin's evident aging in the years since Walter served as his best man. To his mind, his first cousin had always been twelve years old—the only kid he ever knew who could make straight A's and just as handily make short work of anyone who bullied him.

Katherine was also true to form. After a bit of washing up and two cups of Conor coffee, she slid back behind the wheel of the rented Fiat and was off like a shot. His wife waved from the passenger window.

Pud followed him into the lodge. In the kitchen, he sat at the pine table where the family took their meals, and ate the lunch left for him. There was the sense of being in the wake of a storm—but for occasional birdsong through the open windows, the place was as silent as stone.

Having found the number in his notebook, he dialed his distant cousin Erin Donovan who, on his previous trip to Sligo, had hosted the tea at which most of the liquid refreshment was ninety-proof.

'Hullo, everyone. Don't look for me in Killybegs 'til August thirty, I'm in Ibiza—no phone, no email, no worries, have a great summer!' That place again. He didn't leave a message.

Using Anna's list of recommendations, he rang a couple of innkeepers—both jovial as all get-out, but no availabilities. Then, bingo, a double room with in-house dining and a spectacular view of the ancient cairn on Knocknarea, available tomorrow night only. Walter and Katherine would have no problem with driving them to Strandhill, where he would rent a car and find the wits to make further plans. He took out his credit card and booked the room.

He looked at Pud; Pud looked at him.

He changed into shorts and a T-shirt and in ten minutes was headed down the lake path at an easy gait. The very air was a lough, a deep swim of moisture and heat that moved like silk against his bare flesh. Things were shifting forward now—a room with a view, a new outlook; he felt the release of it. He was running along the shore near the hut when he glimpsed something moving in the reeds. A white swan pushed out upon the breast of water, soundless, the elegant, curved neck repeated in the looking glass below. 'Hey,' he said under his breath. 'You're beautiful.' As with rainbows, he counted the sight of a swan a good omen.

He hung a right past the hut, Pud at his heels. Slapping midges and pouring sweat, he pushed through the woods, hopeful that Ireland was as free of ticks as of snakes.

As he reached the stone wall, he heard the distant mourning of the fiddle. Bella had gone before him to the Mass rock.

Pud growled, then barked.

'Reverend Kav'na?'

He turned, startled. Liam's detective connection, who had been on the scene last night—a stocky fellow with a bulbous nose and heavy eyebrows, wearing what appeared to be a wool suit over a turtleneck.

Corrigan held a wallet open to his credentials. 'I hardly recognized you out of your collar, Reverend. Guess you don't need to see this.' He closed the wallet.

'You gave me a start.' Pud still barking.

'May I ask what brought you into the woods?'

'Looking for a Mass rock on the other side of the wall. Anna Conor gave me directions.'

'My grandfather had a Mass rock on his place, called it an altar rock. 't is sometimes found in a pair with a hollowed-out stone for a font. Do you know the history?'

'Not entirely, no.' He squatted and gave Pud a rub behind the ears.

'Our priests used them in secret to conduct Mass. When th' English were after exterminatin' th' Catholic church altogether, there was a

price on the head of every priest—they were
hunted like fox.'

'How may I help you, Detective Corrigan?'

'Merely wondering what you were about,
Reverend. It seems all this began the night after
you and Mrs. Kav'na arrived at Broughadoon.'

'Correct.' The poker club had done their
own arriving before things began—but he said
nothing.

'Seen anyone about the place on a bicycle?'

'Only the bicycle on the main road which
we discussed earlier.'

'Would you call yourself an art lover?'

He stood again. 'Most definitely. My wife is
an artist.'

'Do you collect art?'

'Hers.'

The fiddle keening in the long distance . . .

Corrigan smiled, ironic. 'Were you familiar
with the work of the senior George Barret before coming to Ireland?'

'Enough to know his importance in Irish art
history.'

'Exiled himself to England.'

'Yes.'

'What are your plans for the remainder of
your holiday?' Corrigan had closed his wallet,

was kneading the leather between his fingers as if by long habit.

'We're leaving tomorrow.'

'I believe you were booked for several days yet.'

'We were. But the recent business of the man in the armoire followed by last night's distressing episode is hardly fodder for a pleasant holiday.'

'Most unfortunate. And where would you and th' missus be headed tomorrow?'

'To Strandhill, I can't recall the name of the place.'

'I'll get the name from you before we leave. You'll be around?'

'I will. Anything else, then?'

'Not at the moment.' Corrigan wiped his face with a handkerchief. 'Close.'

Was there no seersucker to be had in the Eire, nor open collars? 'If you've done with me . . .' He headed for the wall.

'No one over the wall, I'm afraid, 'til the Garda have a chance to get in and make a sweep. Cheerio, then.' The ironic smile, and over the wall went Corrigan himself, as if he owned the place.

He retraced his passage through the woods and up to the lodge, then showered, dressed, and went downstairs, hearing in some distant quarter an electric drill. He poked around the library until he found a volume of Synge's plays, and soon after sitting in the wing chair fell soundly asleep.

He heard the crunch of gravel in the car park, the slamming of the Fiat's doors, voices. Thirty minutes of shut-eye had helped.

'Did I snore?' he asked Pud.

Cynthia careened in on her crutches. 'We need to talk,' she said. Through the open front door, he saw Katherine digging around in the trunk of their rental car.

From the throne of her chair, his wife told him everything.

'I cannot *believe*, not even in my wildest imagination, that you would ever, I repeat, *ever* have allowed me to ride in the same car with your so-called Stirling Moss. It is a *grave* discredit to the memory of Mr. Moss to compare him with a perfectly crazed, lawless, and out-of-control *imposter*.'

'Okay, okay,' he said, holding up a hand in surrender. 'Your hair looks great.'

'My *hair*,' she said, 'is standing on *end*. Why did you ever, I repeat, *ever* think I'd be willing to tool around an entire *country* with this person at the wheel?'

He knew the feeling.

'Are you out of your *mind*?'

'A perfectly good question,' he said.

'As for the jolly plan for us to travel together in the same vehicle when my ankle is knit—*never*. You should have seen the face of the shop owner when she opened the door and *Stirling* pulled the car practically up to the *washbasin*.'

What could he say?

At six-thirty, Katherine appeared at their door in her bathrobe, pleading sudden and utter exhaustion, and reporting Walter still incoherent. They wouldn't be down for dinner, they were having it in their room, please forgive—but they'd be up at the crack, ready for a lovely long chat at breakfast before heading over to the ruin of the family castle and off to the cemetery for a gravestone rubbing and then down to Connemara, though heaven knows they'd love to stay and help the Garda solve the mystery of the missing painting, and what a scramble their long-awaited trip to Ireland had turned out to be for all concerned, proving once again that truth is immensely stranger than fiction.

On Katherine's heels had come Corrigan, nosing out the name of the inn at Strandhill, and then Feeney, on his way home from the free clinic he'd pulled together two years ago.

Feeney showered praise on the patient who had obviously resisted every temptation to rile the ankle by witless conduct.

Following dinner, they declined the trifle or chocolate torte and opted for coffee at their table.

'I can't do it,' she said.

'Can't do what?'

'I can't leave.'

'Can't leave?'

'Because these people mean something to me. They need us.'

'But we can't be providence for other people, Kav'na. Oswald Chambers says that's one of our hardest lessons—learning that we mustn't interfere in other people's lives.' There wouldn't, after all, be a checkers game with William . . .

'I'm not trying to be their providence, I'm their friend. Bella needs someone, Timothy—someone who isn't her overworked mother or Maureen. It's not that I'm in any way better than these two good women, not at all, it's that I was once as frightened and frozen as she is.'

'But this is a vacation,' he said in something akin to his pulpit voice. He'd never see the Mass rock or finish Fintan O'Donnell's journal or row her to the forested island in the middle of the lough, but so be it.

'What is a vacation, anyway? Two or three weeks of sucking up every good thing for yourself? And even with all that's happened, I love it here. It feels in a way like home, like family. You know I never really had a family. Just my parents and myself in this sealed envelope, each of us desperate to break the seal. I don't feel our stay is over yet, something isn't right about leaving.'

'But what can you do if we stay?'

'About what?'

'About anything.'

'I don't think I'm needed to do anything except be here.'

He said to her what Anna had said to him. 'You're very unusual, Kavanagh.'

She shrugged, laughed a little. 'I remember sitting on the big stone in the schoolyard with my teacher one day, it was fifth grade. Everyone had gone and we were waiting yet again for Mother to come for me. Miss Collins asked if it made me sad for my mother to forget me. I said it made me sad that Mother herself felt forgotten.

'She looked at me and touched my hair and said, Cynthia, you are most unusual. I was afraid that being unusual wasn't good, then she said, And that's a good thing. Sometimes I think Miss Collins might have been my first taste of God.'

She sipped her coffee. 'Besides, I'm not interfering any more than you interfered by hearing Anna's testimony.'

'She asked me to hear it.'

'And in a way, they've asked me to be here, to stand with them . . . though of course they haven't said that in so many words.'

His wife had a mind unlike any he'd ever encountered, a fact he blamed, if any blaming were to be done, on the nature of artists in general. Her instincts often raced ahead of his own to the quick of things.

'My work is going so well now—the best in years. I'd like to tough it out, Timothy—live it out, pray it out, paint it out.'

'This trip is your birthday gift, not mine. All I want is to do what's best for you.'

'But what's best for me right now is what's best for them, I think. Don't you see?'

He did see. But it angered him.

In the library, which he was coming to account as the central nerve center of the universe, Seamus and William were at the checkerboard, the Labs by their feet; a couple of club members sat at a game table, having coffee with Tom and Hugh.

'Hey, y'all!' Tammy threw up a hand, jangling the redoubtable bracelets.

'Pull up a chair,' said Debbie, 'we're just *shootin' th' bull.*'

'Thanks. Maybe later.' He couldn't shoot the bull right now if someone gave him cash money. 'Come,' he said, offering his arm to his wife. 'I'm taking you out.'

She eyed him, solemn, then laughed. He saw the forgiveness in her, and laughed back. Caving to the siren call of dispute was the last thing they needed.

'Look,' she whispered, as they stepped out to the garden.

In the last of the light, the silhouette of two people who had been quicker on the draw.

'Busy bench,' he said.

'Shall we go in and start a jigsaw?'

It was definite, then, engraved in stone— they would not be leaving. One didn't start a jigsaw without hope of seeing it through.

'I have a call to make.' He expected to pay for the room in Strandhill, an expense accountable to a birthday made happier. But there would be no accounting of such expense. A couple from Kerry had called, said the innkeeper, and would be thrilled to get the room—

been to your Philadelphia, saw the bell, deposit refunded, and thanks very much.

He scrawled a note for Liam and Anna—*Would like to stay as earlier planned, hope our room remains available, Tim*—and left it on the enormous slab of limestone that served as the kitchen prep station.

On the way to the library, he suddenly remembered seeing Bella on a bicycle the morning after their arrival. He hadn't meant to lie to Corrigan—until now, he'd forgotten that brief glimpse entirely. Besides, that was days ago, so how could it have anything to do with last night?

At the puzzle table, four pieces out of five hundred already fitted together to form the hindquarters of a ram lying among a flock downhill from a thatched cottage. He studied the image on the box lid: In the foreground, a young man and woman on bicycles, pedaling home from the turf field with side baskets loaded. The woman wore a bandanna over her hair; the man, a beat-up hat slanted at a rakish angle.

He sat with her and looked for border pieces; he liked to start with the borders. She Who Would Start Anywhere the Notion Struck busied herself with turning pieces face-up.

'For a moment,' she said, 'I thought it was Anna and Liam on the bench, but of course Anna isn't here tonight.'

'Not to mention that they never sit down.'

She slid another piece onto the ram.

'I hate it when you do that,' he said.

'I wonder who it was.'

'It was Pete and Moira.'

'Surely not.'

'Trust me.'

They were picking up steam with a portion of thatched roof when Pete and Moira breezed in and stationed themselves by the hearth.

'Ta-*da-a-a*!' Moira alerted the assembly at the top of her voice.

Pud woke up and looked about.

'We have great news, everybody!'

He noticed the high color of Moira's face, the necktie with the fishing-lures pattern sticking out of Pete's jacket pocket.

'So that's buzzer fishing,' said Cynthia.

Pete looked dazzled, or perhaps dazed. 'You're not goin' to believe this.'

'*Way* not,' said Moira. 'We can't believe it ourselves.'

'Troth, 't is a guessin' game,' said William, who didn't appear to care for guessing games.

'Wait, wait, don't tell us,' said Debbie. 'You're

goin' to meet in Atlanta and see how things *pan out!*'

'Or,' said Lisa, 'Roscoe is flyin' up from Dublin?'

'Try again,' said Pete, rocking on the balls of his feet, grinning.

Nobody tried again; they were dumbfounded.

His wife leaned to him, whispered, 'Moira said she wouldn't go out with him if he was the last man on earth. What *happened* on that bench?'

He didn't know, but he and Cynthia were next in line to check it out.

'Get *on* with it,' said Hugh.

'Okay, okay,' said Pete. 'Ready?' he asked Moira.

'*We're cousins!*'

Tom whistled. Pud barked.

'My great-great-grandmother Margaret on my daddy's side,' said Pete, 'went with a crowd of O'Malleys from Sligo to Tyrone, where she married a Tommy O'Beirne—'

'O'Beirne bein' my maiden name,' said Moira. 'And Tommy bein' my great-great-grandfather—it's in our old family Bible plain as the nose on your face: Tommy O'Beirne of County Tyrone to Margaret O'Malley of County Sligo, emigrated 1869 to Boston. I used to study all those names when I was a little kid, I loved that stuff.

So I just called Atlanta and my daughters looked it up in th' Bible, and ta-*da-a-a*, I was right!'

'Oh, Lord,' said Debbie. 'This is *way* too much.'

'And,' said Moira, 'since Pete is cousins with Hugh and Tom, maybe, just maybe I'm cousins with them, too.'

The din grew in volume and pitch. William thumped his cane. At the anglers' request, Seamus brought forth a tray of Guinness.

Amused, they worked part of the thatch, two sheep, a bit of hedgerow, as one by one the exhausted club made their way to bed.

'I'm callin' it a day, too,' said Hugh. 'We're up with the roosters and off to Strandhill first thing in the morning. Tim, Cynthia, sure great to meet you, hope everything goes slick as grease from here out.'

'Ditto,' said Pete. 'Hope you'll come over again next August, same time, same station, we'll help you finish your entry in th' guest register.'

Back-slapping. Hand-shaking. Laughter.

Hugh handed him a card. 'Give me a call if you're ever in Annapolis. Got a nice guesthouse with a pool, you'd be welcome.'

'It's been a pleasure,' said Tom. 'Here's a little something to remind you of this rough crowd.'

Tom deposited a fishing fly in the palm of his hand. 'Connemara Black. Might come in handy someday.'

'Why . . . this is beautiful. Thanks.'

'Tied that myself. That's a feather off th' crest of a golden pheasant, that's black seal fur right there, an' th' beard hackle's off a blue jay. You can use that for sea trout or salmon.'

'Great,' he said, 'Thanks again.'

Tom gave him a serious look. 'That's your classic pattern for that fly.'

'God be with you,' he said, shaking Pete's hand.

'*Dhia dhuit*,' said O'Malley. 'As for my Irish, that's th' whole kabosh right there. Take it easy.'

He held on to Pete's handshake, feeling an odd regret. Somehow, he and Pete O'Malley hadn't finished being together in the same place at the same time.

The library was empty. Strangers had come into their sphere, shared a connection, and vanished into the remainder of their own lives. The anglers had been like a wallpaper pattern that took some getting used to, followed by the realization that one had grown fond of it.

They went to the garden and sat looking up into the great hall of night. The laughter in the library had been relieving; an ice floe had melted. Her bare shoulder fit neatly into the cup of his hand.

*'There is no light in earth or heaven,'* he quoted, *'but the cold light of stars; and the first watch of night is given to the red planet Mars.'*

She mused. 'Not Yeats.'

'Longfellow. Tomorrow, Ben Bulben, Yeats's grave, and lunch in a good pub. We'll go out every day and see the sights, but never anything to stress your ankle.'

She was off in that world of hers. 'You know how the Irish say nothing's so bad it couldn't be worse?'

What could be worse than the painting being stolen? He didn't want to think about it.

Even in the dark, he could see the flash of her smile. 'How about this, instead? Nothing's so good, it couldn't be better.'

She turned to him and kissed him. Then kissed him again. He thought it might be the scent of the golden iris, but it was the fragrance of wisteria.

On their way through the library, she turned off to the powder room and he discovered Pete in a wing chair.

'Guess I'll be sittin' up awhile. I never drink coffee at night—then on these fishin' trips, I start rollin' th' dice.'

'It'll catch me, too, before it's over.' He sat in the chair facing Pete.

'I'm always rollin' th' bloody dice—with alcohol, women, business, life in general.' Pete furrowed his brow. 'I'm goin' home an' call my wife.'

'Glad to hear it.'

'All I can do is call. As for seein' her, that's up to her. Out on th' bench, Moira talked me into it. Before I found out we're cousins, I was comin' on to her, Reverend, I admit it. I put my hand on her leg, I mean, what did I have to lose, us leavin' tomorrow and all that? Touch me again, she said, and I'll kill you. Can you believe it?'

'I can believe it,' he said.

'So we got to talkin' about me being such a badass, and what was my problem, anyway, and first thing you know, I'm bawlin' like a baby, because she's right. I'd been wanting to have another shot at things with my wife, but I didn't have th' guts to go to her, hat in hand. I'm not wired that way.'

'You love your wife?'

'It'd be a flamin' lie if I said I didn't.'

'Let her know it,' he said. 'I'll pray for you.'

'I need it. I'm goin' to try, I swear to God. I'm tired of bein' th' bloody walkin' wounded.'

'While you're at it, stay in touch with the one who wired you. We're all wired for love, all wired to go hat in hand if that's what it takes.'

Pete looked at him, looked away, sighed.

'Talk to him about everything, Pete—your wife, your business, what ails you. One of his jobs is to listen.'

Cynthia was making her way out of the powder room.

'Nothing to lose,' he said.

They stood; shook hands again, embraced.

'Next year,' said Pete.

'Maybe,' he said. 'I'm open.'

He made the slow ascent of the stairs with her, carrying the crutches. As they reached the landing, he heard someone below.

'Reverend?'

He couldn't see Liam's face in the shadowed hall, but the despairing tone of his voice was familiar.

'Could I see you when Cynthia is safe in your room? It's extremely urgent.'

'He's after disproving my edit of the Irish proverb,' Cynthia said under her breath. 'Trust me.'

He did trust her—as well he might. While playing the fiddle at the Tubbercurry Fair, Liam said, Bella had been approached by a drunk who became obscene and aggressive. Jack Slade had appeared out of nowhere and brutally stabbed the man. Slade was being held without bond, Anna was with Bella at the Garda station in Tubbercurry—could Liam come at once.

# Eighteen

He had gone upstairs for a map to give Walter, pondering the issues of last night.

Slade's victim hadn't died but was in critical condition. Sobering, this cascade of incidents since they'd stepped foot on the place.

They gathered in the car park, their wives laughing over some private joke.

'Broughadoon is wonderful,' said Walter, 'but too much drama this time around. If I were in your boots, I'd be out of here.'

'It's her birthday, she gets to choose.'

'A point of considerable merit,' said his cousin. 'And speaking of age, I think we're all holding up well enough, though I deeply re-

gret looking more like Dad with each passing day.'

'He was a handsome fellow, my uncle. Good
looks trump age.'

They had spent the morning remembering
their Mississippi rites of passage and hacking
through Kavanagh history cobbled together in
recent years. He'd also taken the Vauxhall for a
practice run around the Catharmore circle,
flinging a few dog biscuits while at it.

'What's the plan?' he asked Walter, who always had one.

'Let's say Belfast a week from today. An overnight there, then head south, taking our time.
Katherine's up for Guinness pie at that terrific
pub we stumbled on in Dundalk, still talks
about it. Anyway, we'll finally see the family
drinking horn at Trinity, and the Book of
Kells—a long time coming. You have the hotel
phone numbers; do what you can at once, given
the season.'

'That works,' he said. The fact of separate
cars had been established; all concerned seemed
relieved. 'Maybe we can squeak out of here a
day sooner than we think. Let's stay in touch.'

'What happened to your cell phone, by the
way?'

'Don't ask.'

Walter laughed. 'To the four winds, would be my guess.'

'Close enough.'

They recited the family motto—'Peace and plenty!'—gave the high-five, and, following a round of the cousin's kiss, which resembled the European greeting model embellished by back-slapping, Katherine scratched the Fiat out of the car park and into the outer lane.

Walter waved from the open window; Katherine honked three times.

'Father, Son, and Holy Spirit,' he informed Cynthia. 'Her signature honk.'

He opened the door of the Vauxhall, which he'd parked next in line for takeoff, and helped Cynthia into the passenger seat. He was frankly consoled that Maureen had offered to pray for the 'brilliant performance' of their loaner.

'Rev'rend! Cynthia!' It was Maureen, leaning from an open window on the second floor. 'Come back safe, please God.'

The side mirror had been reset in the thing-amajig and there was nothing on the backseat but the blasted crutches and their versatile snack hamper. He even smelled leather polish, though precious little leather was left to polish.

They were off with a rattle.

For five days, his wife had entertained scant

notion of where she was in the universe, save for views from the dining room or a garden bench. She cranked down the car window, poked her head out, gawked. He loved the reflex of her open mouth.

'Amazing,' she said. 'Unbelievable.'

To their right, the easy green slope to the lake and its several islands, and the hovering hills beyond. Then the stone walls overtaken by scarlet trumpet vine, wild fuchsia, purple buddleia.

'I'll have run out of adjectives by the main highway.'

'Understood.'

'And Timothy . . . now that we're not committed to flinging ourselves around in the backseat of a car with Stirling at the wheel, I'm crazy about Katherine all over again.'

'Also understood.'

She fell for the cow barn with the single blue shutter, as he thought she might.

'How lazy of me not to be more curious about my own Irish connection. I have no idea how we knew that my double-great-grandmother played the fife—Mother tried to trace the line when I was at Smith, but she got nowhere. It's such a lot of trouble, genealogy.'

'Next time,' he said, 'we can look up your crowd.'

'Just think, darling—you and I could be cousins.'

Following Anna's directions, they left the main highway and meandered about for an hour, stopping to sketch a lamb drinking water from a green tub. It was a greater provision than he'd hoped when they found a grassy sward with shade, a dead-on view of Ben Bulben, and a parking spot on the verge.

He helped her to a stooping tree with a massive trunk—a horse chestnut—then went back for the hamper and its cargo of lunch. 'Just in case,' Anna had said. 'It may give you more freedom to roam.'

A light breeze shifted through a patch of blue flowers; across the road, sheep dotted a hill. Perhaps this was divine compensation for the ankle and all the rest of it, this day abroad in a world of mild temperatures and easeful shade and no haste in their bones.

He spread the blanket and sat beside her, as he'd done those years ago in a pasture when the bull chased him and they'd eaten raspberry tart and he'd surrendered his defenses without meaning to.

They'd gone to the country on the red motor scooter he used for eight years after giving up his

Buick for Lent; he remembered how she'd clung
on behind him and the thrill he felt that such a
thing could be happening to him, Timothy Kavanagh. With cornfields zooming past and her
warm flesh pressed to his back, he remembered
praying that he wouldn't suffer a heart attack or
stroke from such frightful happiness. It had been
their last day together before he set off for Sligo.

'Beann Gulban, the peak of Gulba. What do
you think?'

She turned to him with the dreaming look
in her eyes. 'It's too beautiful. Far, far too beautiful and mysterious. I'm sitting here trying to
believe it's real. What is it, exactly?'

'A mountain with a level plateau. Limestone
and shale, sculpted by glaciers. Stands seventeen hundred feet above the plain. Our guide-
book calls it *a great satisfaction to seekers of the
picturesque.*'

'I don't see how one can call it anything at
all—it defies logic and language completely.
Look.' She flung her arm out to him. Goose
bumps.

'The megaliths would give you a few bumps
into the bargain, and so would the Carrowkeel
cairns.'

He filled their glasses with Anna's tea. 'From

the cairns, you can see more than a third of Ireland on a clear day.'

'I'd love to visit the holy wells.'

'Holy wells, dolmens, crannogs, caves; Stone Age, Bronze Age, Iron Age, Ice Age—name an age, the landmarks are all here, but nearly all involve walking. Next time,' he said, raising his glass to hers. 'Eat your Wheaties.'

'I like it when you talk about next times. Getting you on an airplane is right up there with getting blood from a turnip.'

'I'm doing better,' he said. 'And speaking of turnips, let's eat.'

They devoured their lunch with appetite, then used the hamper as a headrest. Lying together on the blanket, they watched clouds navigate the canopy of leaves and branches. This was what they needed—the proverbial life of Reilly.

'How's the ankle today?'

'Good. I'm tempted to throw away the crutches.'

'Don't do it.'

'I won't. But I'm so sorry about all this, really I am.'

'Don't be sorry. Otherwise we'd be racing around like chickens with our heads cut off. Believe me, if you've seen one or two castles, you've seen them all. The way things have worked out—it's better, really. More . . . idiosyncratic.'

She laughed, traced the bridge of his nose with her forefinger. 'Tell me what Broughadoon was like the first time.'

He told her of the plainness of the place and how that had suited him in his bachelor days, and the morning he stood at his bedroom window and glimpsed Anna behind the lodge, hanging wash on what she had called her drying bushes—aprons, dish towels, shirts, a child's jumper. She had hooked items of women's underwear on twigs behind the bushes, and he'd turned from the window as if caught in some indecent act.

And there was the day the cow got into the garden, and he'd never seen such flapping about of arms and shouting in the unknown tongue while the cow chewed, solemn as a judge, and would not be moved. Someone had brought a halter and rope and managed to drag the creature from the garden, but the damage was done and quite a lot of moaning and groaning was lifted onto the brim of the morning along with a scent of trampled leeks. In true Irish fashion, a kitchen helper had the wits to appreciate the offering the cow left behind, forking it off to the side to cure. Paid 'er dues, he said, pragmatic. They had all got behind a spade or a rake and busied themselves until the garden looked nearly fit again. He'd pitched in as well, and later enjoyed the evening's special: braised leek soup. 'Bruised, more like it,' he'd said, which raised a laugh.

The memories were a movie playing in his head, something slow and indistinct with a tone of sepia to it.

They hadn't spent much time at the lodge, for they'd been out and about trying to see and do it all, to swallow it all down without chewing. As for the menu, he said, he didn't remember anything like homemade verbena ice cream or the semifreddo business. Supper had been delicious enough, though compared to the comestibles of this visit, unremarkable. Breakfast was usually brown bread, coffee, jam, and fruit, at a table with a short leg propped up by a packet of matches. He vaguely remembered the young child with dark hair and large eyes whom he knew now to have been Bella—she had not mingled with the guests.

He didn't remember any dogs, though he had recently got one, or more precisely, one had got him. Nor could he remember anything in particular about the guests—then again,

come to think of it, there'd been a Mrs. McSo-
methingorother, who wore overwrought hats
and looked like a character from a Victorian
pen-and-ink drawing.

'It's coming back to me,' he said. 'She traveled with twelve place settings of sterling flatware.'

'*Surely* not.'

'She recited a child's poem, something like,
I'm tired of eating bread with crusts and going
to bed too early, and something, something,
something about her hair being curly.'

'But why did she travel with twelve place
settings of flatware?'

He pondered. 'I think it was to prevent anyone at home making off with it.'

'Why did she come to the lodge? Did she
*fish*?'

'Like a maniac, as I recall.'

'Ah,' she said, wrinkling her brow.

'So,' he said, ending his narrative of former
days at Broughadoon.

'Everything's certainly different now,' she
said. 'Anna says Bella is in a terrible state—but
then, Anna doesn't look so well herself.'

'Let's not dwell on it,' he said, taking her
hand. 'Where shall we worship on Sunday?
Church of Ireland or Tad's place?'

'Tad's place, don't you think?'

They gazed at Ben Bulben, feeding what would soon enough be memory.

'I'm painting William this evening—by firelight. He said he'd have a nice wash today, and Anna will trick him out in his Sunday best. I've never painted anything at all by firelight— so many shadows, and most of them moving. Maybe I can't do it.'

'You can do it.'

She turned her head and looked at him, solemn. 'Thanks. I adore you. Who do you think stole the painting?'

'I've heard a good bit about Liam's brother and his urgent need for money.'

They hadn't really talked about what happened. The idea of leaving and then staying, plus the coming and going of Walter and Katherine, had largely occupied their thoughts since the Barret disappeared.

'Jack Slade,' she said. 'Let's say he did it. Then comes the awful thing at the fair and he gets himself locked away, and it stays wherever he hid it, and when he gets out of prison, he fences it and he's a very rich stone coper—I think that's the word Liam used.'

'I saw Liam this morning. He says Slade is done for—for a few years, anyway.'

'How was Liam, I haven't seen him.'

'Beating himself up. Not only was it something he loved, but it was important to his dad. Then there's dropping the ball on the insurance—they'll get something from the business coverage, but not much. Throw in the armoire business and the Tubbercurry incident, and it's been a while since I've seen such a hailstorm.'

The clouds today were swift; sunlight broke over the green hide of the ben, vanished, reappeared.

'The question is how anybody got it off the place at all,' he said. 'No fingerprints, no footprints, no tire marks. If someone could figure that out . . .'

She slapped at a midge. 'That's too hard for me. I'm more interested in who, not how. Maybe a former guest. Or a neighbor?'

'I haven't seen any neighbors,' he said. And Seamus was not in the lineup of possible thugs, he thought, absolutely not. 'Given the size of it, it would be awkward to carry any distance. Managing it would probably take two people. How about the wine merchant we met coming out when Aengus was driving us in? He parks his truck off-road, and he and a henchman slip down to the lodge . . .'

'But if he walks down the lane, he leaves footprints—the Garda said the lane was muddy.'

'Right. Anyway, if he managed somehow to get there without leaving a trace, he and the henchman pop into the dining room, and in a flash they lift it off the two hooks and away they go.'

'How would he know the dining room would be empty then?'

'He watches through the French doors.'

'But he still wouldn't know that everyone was in the library, that nobody was likely to come back to the dining room and catch them at it.'

'Then it's an inside job. The wine guy knew when people would be out of the room and for how long.' He felt suddenly foolish in the guise of amateur sleuth.

'Would they have done it, Anna and Liam, for the insurance money? It's a horrible thought, I can't believe I said it. But would they?'

'If they'd done it for money,' he said, 'they would have beefed up the insurance policy. Anna says the coverage was minimal. Besides, I'm convinced Liam loved that painting.'

'I'm sorry I said it,' she confessed. 'Then what if Paddy insured it?'

'Could be. Who knows?'

'I wish I'd read more P. D. James. By the way, I don't think they say henchman anymore—you are so quaint.'

'Quaint,' he said with distaste. Being a village parson had turned him off the word entirely—it was something tourists occasionally said not only of Mitford but of him when trooping through town like they owned the place.

She was still laughing.

'Help yourself,' he said.

She narrowed her eyes, looked at him approvingly. 'It's been ages since you let me paint you.'

'You made me look like Churchill.'

She pulled a face.

'Or maybe it was Mussolini.'

'I could do much better now. What I'm after is that little quirky thing about your mouth, the one your mother had in pictures I've seen of her. It's so fleeting—but I feel I could catch it now.'

Save for her, he would have jumped ship on all this. But he was in and he was glad; it felt right.

'I'm excited about painting William—all those lovely wrinkles around his blue eyes, and that wicked scar on his temple. A fine nose, too—perhaps it was Roman before it was bashed in. Did the Romans come through Ireland?'

'The Romans came through everywhere.'

'William blames the Vikings for red hair, which he says isn't Irish at all. It came from th' bloody murderin' Vikin's, he says—from th' numerous rapes an' rampages that sullied th' black hair of th' Gaelic nation.'

'There's a view of history for you.'

She slapped her arm. 'I see how Liam has taken to you, just like your parishioners in Mitford—even people who weren't your parishioners. You attract that sort of thing like I attract midges. You never seem to mind.'

'Maybe it's some assurance to me that I exist, or have meaning—who knows? It's always been that way.'

'You're like both father and priest to Liam, Anna says. That's a lot to put on someone.'

'Like you're breath and life to me. That's a lot to put on you.'

'But I don't mind it. Not ever. Besides, you try so hard to keep that need hidden. You seem afraid it will take something from me. But it doesn't take anything away—it gives me something.

'That's what you do for people. It's a wonderful gift, but it drains you. You see someone in need and take the plunge—that's what God does, of course. But when you told Liam the police could jolly well come to you, I think you hit a home run.'

'A first,' he said, wry.

A young woman with an infant in her arms appeared on the narrow road, trailed by a border collie. The collie stopped, eyed them, barked. The woman lifted the tiny arm of the baby in a wagging salute to the couple at the chestnut tree, who waved back. He watched the trio disappear around a bend, praying for them as he had often done for the odd stranger or passerby, and even, on occasion, for the crew and passengers of a plane droning overhead. It was a private and instinctive thing, having little, or perhaps nothing to do with being a priest.

'I love Ireland,' she said.

'You haven't seen much of it.'

'But I feel much of it, somehow. What if every day had a title, rather like the title of a poem—Psalm of Life or The Wild Swans at Coole, like that?'

'Ah. So, what would today be titled?'

'You go first.'

'Free at Last.'

'Perfect!' she said. 'You win.'

The mild zephyr that shook the blue flowers trifled with her hair. 'I'm supposed to be painting Ben Bulben.'

'Never mind. Legions have already done it, I'm sure. Getting down to brass tacks—shall I have Liam drive me to Sligo and rent a decent car?'

'The world is full of decent cars,' she said. 'Let's rattle around, we'll remember it all'—she looked toward the Vauxhall—'more vividly.'

'Speaking of which, I just remembered . . .'

'Tell me.'

'We didn't go to the country on my motor scooter.'

'When?'

'When we were courting—the time the bull chased me and we ate the raspberry tart.'

'Who said we went on your motor scooter?'

'I was thinking about it a few minutes ago, about you clinging on behind me, and it seemed so real. What I remembered was my fantasy about us going on the motor scooter. We went in the car.'

'I would never have gone on that motor scooter.'

'Right,' he said. 'By the way, when I asked

you about seeing Balfour's place, how did you know what happened to it? You asked Anna?'

'I skipped ahead to the end of the journal. Just for a peek.' She slapped at a midge. 'But I've decided to read it in proper order, roughly in sync with you.'

'Do we want to keep reading it?'

'We do,' she said.

'What if it was an inside job?'

'Balfour's place?'

He stood up, stretched. 'The painting.'

'I wasn't going to talk about that anymore. But, yes, what if . . .' She sat up. 'I mean, why was Jack Slade at the fair when Bella was there, and why did he stab the fellow for talking out of turn to her? What business is she of his?'

'Good question. The Garda probably asked that, too. Speaking of—what is it, anyway? Garda with an *a* at the end or Gardai with an *i* at the end?'

'Beats me,' she said. 'I've seen it with two *i*'s at the end.'

'Anyhow, let's up and away, Kav'na. *Tempus fugit.*' He checked his pant pockets, discovered the Connemara Black with its jagged barb— not a good thing to tote around in a pocket.

He helped her from the blanket; she looked curiously sober. 'Are we nuts to stay?'

'We're a little nuts even if we don't stay,' he said. 'So what's the difference?'

'Do we really want to visit a graveyard today?'

'Probably not today. Besides, you already know the epitaph.'

'Cast a cold eye,' she said, collecting the picnic leavings and stowing them in the hamper.

# Nineteen

The party was over—the caffeine had caught up with him.

He had fallen asleep around midnight, trekked to the bathroom at three, and woke himself snoring at four. Awake at his usual hour of five, he wrestled briefly with the notion of getting up and unpacking their book carton, then slept again and dreamed. He watched his hands break the whole-grain loaf—*look on the heart by sorrow broken, look on the tears by sinners shed*—smelled the sour yeast as crumbs scattered onto the fair linen. The dream wheeled to the stone arch of Sewanee's Heaven's Gate and the sight of an old school chum—he threw up his hand—but no, it was Dooley, his mortal flesh radiant in a patch of light. Dooley at Sewanee!—so he hadn't gone down to Georgia with all those peaches and incinerating summers. A great happiness came to him, he called Dooley's name and woke himself.

He wondered if he'd disturbed Cynthia, but no, Rip Van Winkle was having at it.

Disgusted with the whole affair, he threw off the covers and made himself useful—splashed his face, shot the insulin, prayed the Morning Office by the floor lamp Maureen installed, then took the leather-bound journal in his lap and opened it to the placement of his bookmark. A cumbersome piece of work, this, not for casual reading at the beach.

The bulb blazed like the headlight of an eighteen-wheeler; he could see the weave of the linen in the yellowed pages.

14 June 1862

Have returned from Dublin to find matters here in utter ruin.

Unable to write these last days for the sick shame & rage I suffer at the upheaval in both home & worksite. C exhorts me to allow the fury to subside before I act—I cannot believe it will ever subside.

In my absence Balfour came to our Cabin
& sought to have his way with A. Keegan was
fishing & C had been at the garden—she said
she felt some dull heaviness on her heart &
hurried to the Cabin where she found A
weeping & backed into the chimney corner
fearing for her life. Balfour drunken &
demonic—threatened A with worse if she
cried out—C brandished the poker at him,
not watching her words & drove him off the
place. A heavy blade to us all. At the Mass
Rock again pleading God's wisdom in how
this unforgivable act should be avenged. I
confess savoring the notion of putting him
down with a single shot to his heart in which
is housed a roiling nest of vile intentions.
Have sent by Keegan an urgent letter of
appeal to Father Dominic seeking prayer &
counsel.

I remember my mother saying There's
nothing so bad it couldn't be worse & thus
Danny Moore has disobeyed my warning &
betrayed our trust in his character. While I
was away he told a stone mason of the higher
wage he receives & the men went to pieces
about it. Danny beaten & brutally kicked—
theres one for yr bloody stump, they said—the
worksite sundered by petty thefts.

A sullen & bellicose group now working away with no one confessing the blame. Keegan had broken up the violence toward Danny & suffered a crack which dislocated his jaw—though re-located it troubles him yet We have given the boot to two perpetrators— Keegan & I anxious for what unemployed men might do in retribution, even our own Irishmen in such a case. Have sent Danny off the job until further notice, not wishing to rush to judgment in a matter which concerns the wellbeing of seven people. His mother in complete agreement & as stricken by his action as by the loss of wages to their household. I take the matter as a grievous lesson for future dealings.

Some evictions going on east of us. When we think we have seen the last of this blasphemy the Enemy once again raises his head.

Holy Mother of God have Mercy on the Souls of all Your people in this Wild & Remote Region.


18 June 1862

Both Father Dominic & Caitlin advise me to do nothing. It is outside all convention that I refrain from avenging wound to my household. Balfour may forget the incident altogether, says Fr Dominic & C agrees.

As no possible good can come of confronting Balfour at this time, I am willing to receive counsel asked for.

Having disabused myself of the notion to put a bullet in Balfour—& confessed this impulse to Fr Dominic—I now harbor the continual image of slapping his face so violently as to send him reeling—in this waking dream, I have seen the snot & blood issue from his nose like a shot. He stumbles backward & falls onto the stone floor of the entrance to his stables thereby cracking his skull—& is dead within minutes. I am haunted by the face of his daughter appearing at the doorway as this murderous incident occurs.

Such grusome images so interfere with my Supplications that I am continually pleading God's forgiveness. Seventy times seven is a hard lesson to be learned.

I seldom write here of those lost to Death under my care, for C & I have done all in our might to save them.

God have mercy on the soul of Connor Gleason age 46 without kith or kin to mourn his passing.

1 July

Blistering heat, no rain in near two weeks

I had begun to believe we were well rid of him but he came again today—the snake in the Garden. He was all hail fellow well met & I decided to leave it at that. There has been rumor of fever outbreak in cabins some distance from here though I have seen no vestige of it in this Region. This rumor breaks out on occasion like a case of measles. Balfour made it clear to me that he wanted no contagion brought on land contiguous to his. As I do not consider the fever an actual threat, I agreed that I would not treat patients here with any true sign of yellow fever.

As I looked at him on his unfortunate mount, I confess I was murdering him with my very eyes. He went away without getting down & without the usual foul jollity with our men. Twas as if he knew the violent cast of my thoughts & was in a scramble to be gone.

May God give us faith & strength to finish the race here.

4 August

Warm, humid, rain in afternoon

In gratitude for the completion of the

house & stables & in honor of the coming
Feast Day of the Blessed Virgin I sent funds to
Fr Dominic for the repair of the Church roof
& other pressing needs. I am greatly relieved
to thus thank Almighty God for the new
home to which we have moved these last
days. Twill be comfortable indeed if we can
improve the kitchen firebox which smokes
the plaster far along the stair hall. A great
dither for the women.

Following Mass on Thursday 14, Fr
Dominic to come and give us a proper
blessing. All neighbors hereabout invited to
share in a Feast. We shall have a crowd
numbering that of the Roman legions.

C scoured the countryside & found five
able women to man the cooking with herself
& Aoife—Keegan has got us a labor force to
roast the pig, the sheep & goats. Irish whiskey
& barrels of Guinness (Keegan and I in
disagreement about # of barrels) will be
offered & that's the end of it. Although I am
loth to do it given their recent behavior, have
sent word to the workmen to attend with
their wives & children. Danny Moore's family
eager to come. Twould be wrong to keep
them away but have warned him that the men
will not suffer him kindly. The incident he

caused has taught him a sobering lesson. He came to me hat in hand, proposing to play the Fiddle for the occasion & offering further entertainment by his sisters who sing the old songs in harmony. I am reminded that such as soothes the savage breast may be balm to the recent fury.

Keegan & I abroad these last weeks checking the quality of livestock & fowl raised for us for this occasion. I look at a fat ewe to be roasted & it is coughing. Keegan, I say, tell Paddy O'Reilly we will not pay for his ewe, it is coughing like a man. That's what sheep do, he says in his dry way—they cough.

He thinks I have been ruined by American living.

Keegan teaches me how to buy a pig. I tell him I do not need to know how to buy a pig as he will buy any pigs in future. He says it is good to know what to look for in man or beast.

He recommends the eyes be animated & the ears upright. He contends the neck must be thick & deep with a 'graceful arch.' Thin skin is wanted in a 'lively' shade of pink. The two raised for us meet these high standards &

I regret the eating of them rather than the breeding—Padraig McFee will keep one of them on til frost & cure its meat for our table. In any case, I walk away feeling we have got our money's worth from McFee.

Have had the notion of transplanting wild Lilies to the Mass Rock—I saw the scene vividly in a dream & smelled their scent.

I am at last able to keep this Journal well hid—each evening when I have done with scribbling it is put away where no one however clever might find it. I could not keep it so private at the Cabin.

Aoife stitching herself a Frock these last evenings. I see she is not wearing the shoes made upon her father's last, as I hoped she might in our new surroundings. She vows she prefers the bare feet in nearly all wether.

She has somehow wormed her milking stool into the parlor where she sits with her cloth and needle. In dying light from the west window I observe her face—it is unusually pensive & I try to imagine her thoughts— thoughts perhaps of a suitor? or some jollity she shared with her sisters on their monthly visit? Perhaps she imagines herself in this new gown the color of ripe peaches mulled with cream—& conceives the way the lads will catch their breath in their throats & speak too loudly among themselves when she passes.

He raised his head and listened for a moment to Cynthia's breathing, and the rattle of beech leaves beyond the window. In the deep shadow of their room were gleaming sheets of thick paper, heavy with images. She had stood the watercolors on the chest of drawers and leaned them against the wall to dry. In the afternoon, he'd twice pulled off the road for her to sketch the landscape—but she asked to go back to the horse chestnut, and the only subject making it to the top of the chest was the loaf-shaped out-crop of Beann Gulban.

9 August

Very warm day; full moon—war news from America deeply agitating

Keegan not himself these last weeks—whistling one minute & the next silent & gaping as if struck by a vision of The Blessed Virgin herself.

C suspects he is in love. I cannot imagine Keegan in love.

C has written out the list of dishes to be served & I transcribe them here for my own good pleasure when in ould age I sit by the hearth enjoying the hospitality of beard & pipe. I shall be astonished to read of the great strength with which God equipped us to do all that has been wrought at Cathair Mohr.

I have asked for Roast Swan which many find delicious, but C will have none of it—I will not devour beauty, she says, twill bring doom upon us. Aye, Keegan says, siding with her, we have doom enough without looking for it. I remind them both that all is beautiful, even the fine pig we'll be roasting, but I have lost this dubious battle.

She reminds me that since we arrived from Philadelphia well over two years past we have delivered forty-seven Infants into this sere & indifferent world, thirty of whom survive & flourish & will likely be among us at the Feast. Twill be a proper blessing to hear the laughter of children about the place.

Twenty roast Geese
Twenty roast Hens stuffed
One hundred Hens Eggs boiled hard
Forty loaves Bread
Two hundred Yeast Buns
Ten pounds Goat Cheese
Ten pounds Cow Butter

1 roast Pig
1 roast Mutton
2 goates
4 bushels Potatoes roast in ash
2 bushels Beans with pork hock
20 mix berry Pies
20 apple Pies
3 tubs bread pudding
20 gallons Goat Milk (from Aiden Marsh)

I am reminded of the mammoth iron kettle by New York brazier John Trageser which we have stored in the stables. It is capable of holding two grown men & came to Uncle by way of a debt owed him. I declined to sell it for it is very novel indeed & Keegan will have the men fashion a kind of tall sawhorse from which to suspend the kettle above the fire. C & Keegan & I discuss how it might be used & agree on Fish Stew. We are quite merry at the prospect of such a wondrous thing as the Great Kettle having its part in the Great Day.

Keegan argues we need not do so much, but God has done so much for us, how can we not joy in seeing the pleasure of those who have near nothing at all? Rose McFee swears

she will dance like a Hare to have such a fill
of her ancient belly, though I wager it holds
but a cupful.

Give or take a few, we expect two hundred
men, women & children. The lawns shall be
trampled to bits from the coming & going of
the people & the cooks at the spit & the
digging of the pit for our meate. We give
thanks there is nothing yet in the lawns to
be ruined save two young Beeches and a
wild Bilberry. Horticulture is a decided
weakness—I have no Eye nor learning for it
yet do not wish to hire someone for the
planning if I might by the grace of God do it
myself. C & I agree that we did not come
here to be the Lord and Lady of parterres nor
to run great herds of any beast.

Keegan in Sligo for remaining provisions,
including cut-rate tin plates & bowls from
which host & guest alike will sup. Keegan
does not approve the Expense of the afore-
named items as he says they will not be
used again. Oh but they will, I say, they
will be used again when we gather to
celebrate the liberty of the Irish people from
centuries of Mayhem & Treachery. Before he
turns his head away I see the look on him—

perhaps he is not so hard against this notion as before.

Keegan does not mince words—he says the Missus O'Donnell must have a woman of all work if she is to manage such a pile as Cathair Mohr. I confess I still carry the burthen of a Cabin mentality which disposes me to count A as help enough— unless we were to entertain Society which I cannot imagine doing with the roads in their present condition. I continue to prove my indifference to C's needs, thinking her capable of anything. Keegan's counsel is well-taken & I will be applying for such when I am next able.

Uncle's furnishings arrive by boat tomorrow at Dublin, to be loaded onto wagons and transported to Lough Arrow in time for the Festivities. What would Uncle say at the sight of his handsome carpets, paintings & many books displayed in a house such as God Himself and Uncle's own fortune have provided? Arriving also will be Uncle's carriage which I shall make use of daily. As it is a fine city carriage, we have but to countrify it a little—making it road worthy for such Regions as these.

We run to catch up with our plenteous blessings.

10 August

Rain at first light

Balfour's man arrived at noon with a basket of fly-bit hares & a sack of bruised apples. I had not thought for a moment that Balfour might show himself at the Feast. Yet when I saw his offering on the cart bed, the thought of his intentions spread within me like a poison.

I handed these so-called neighborly provisions off to Keegan who gave the lot of it a hard look & handed it off to Fionn Connelly who is setting up the great Spit. Take this off the Place, he told Fionn.

Rain throughout the afternoon and into the evening.

11 August

Fairing off

I was called out last night to deliver two infants into this world—one from each of two sisters occupying the same Cabin at some distance from Cathair Mohr. Infants lusty & mothers hale. A girl named Biddy & a boy

named Colm. I have once before seen how
the close confinement of two women can
spawn the conception & delivery of infants
at the same time—it is a puzzling sort of
contagion.

The new fathers who have scarcely a rag of
flesh on their bones brought forth a mite of
whiskey kept back for Fr Dominic and myself
as looking ahead to this occasion. The lads are
brothers both hardworking and these are their
first born. They have promised to be at the
Feast for they can get the loan of a pony &
cart from their grandfather. As C was
suffering one of her headaches, she sent A to
ride with me as nurse. With naught but
natural instinct, A proves herself competent &
steady.

It is a time in this Region of few
desperations—Besides the Melancholia which
is ever doing its devilish work among a
famished people stripped of land, tis but a sty
here, a bit of pus there, bowels that refuse to
move or move too freely—the very sorts of
things my old mother enjoyed. I remember
how she slit the throat of a Hedgehog which
she commanded me to capture & bring to her
in a sack—the creature was rolling in fat for

the spring & summer had been especially wet
& lush and I had often seen him outside his
Burrow at the moth hour surveying the land.
He sniffed the air like a lad whose ploughing
is done for the day & appeared to lack nothing
but a pipe for his contentment. Yet for all his
seeming leisure he was cunning as they come
& hard to run to ground. All this commotion
so Mam might render his fat to be rubbed
inside the ears of the numerous deaf in our
Region. When the deed was done & a crock
of it put up, off we go in the trap with the
crock between my knees. We went round to
young & old with the hearing problems &
before God, Mam succeeded with this
measure on several occasions—not with the
stone deaf but with those having something
left to recover.

How dearly I recall our rounds to the sick
& poor, & Ourselves hardly better off than
they—She was thinking of others always.
When she passed, my brother Michael wrote
to say there was a wake such as this part of the
County had never seen. It wrenches me yet
that her Death from Pneumonia was sudden
& no way for me to attend her last hours. My
father set out a grand portion of whiskey for

all who came to pay their respects & many
twists of good tobacco as well for he knew
that Generosity would be pleasing to her.

I must go again to her Grave before winter.
Though it broke my young heart at the time,
I honor the sacrifice of her third son to
Uncle—it was no easy letting go for either of
us, though my Father was proud to see me off
to America & into the fostering care of a rich
relative. I remember sobbing into my pillow
the night before—me a strapping lad of
seventeen—& then the brothers verily
pushing me onto the boat thinking Thank
God its him & not us leaving every common
thing we know to live in a strange land &
suffer the cruelty of learning from Books.

I remember how Mother regretted not
getting round to do more & how she often
said, If I had my life to live over I'd have a
strong young mare & saddlebags full of
nostrums & herbs of great variety & I would
go over hill & dale til all were cured, but I'm
only a small Woman with a small pony. She
saw the enormity of the need—it snapped &
gnawed at her like a feral thing. Father would
say, A little fire that warms, Bessy, is better
than a big fire that burns.

On the approach of the Blessing of this

house and land & the Grand Feast to follow,
I remember my mother who set the little fire
in me & when the fevers & the infant
deformities & the crucifying amputations
come & I suffer the grave inadequacy of my
resources, I remember the little fire that
warms & am able to go on.

  Elizabeth (Bessy) O'Donnell, b. County
Cavan 1773, d. County Sligo, 1823


It was an unfamiliar odor, layered in the way
perfumes were said to be composed. He sniffed
the air of the closed room—definitely a top
note of fried bacon, his Mississippi nose wouldn't
mistake that, then a middle note of something
sharply caustic, maybe shellac, and bringing up
the rear, the smell of coffee.

O'Donnell's journal was definitely growing
on him. He laid it on the table by the chair and
eased to the armoire, creaking only one floor-
board. Pud stuck his head from beneath the
bed skirt.

'Timothy?'

'Good morning, Sunshine.' It was his
mother's and Peggy's old greeting at the top of
the day.

'What are you doing?'

'Dressing.'

'What time is it?'

He picked up his watch, squinted in the gray morning light. 'Gaining on six forty-five.' He shucked his pajamas into Maureen's basket.

'I loved yesterday,' she said.

'And another grand, soft day predicted, according to William.'

'I'm glad you got the reservations done.'

By the skin of his teeth. 'Coffee's on.'

'Did you sleep?'

'Well enough.' He found the knit shirt folded in the drawer, shook it out, pulled it over his head.

'I feel so guilty being able to sleep.'

'As you should, Kav'na, as you should.'

'What are we doing today?'

'Maybe out to Easkey—stone houses abandoned during the famine, a broad expanse of gray sea, a view to Donegal on a clear day. Just the ticket for artists, it seems to me.

'Or there's a castle in Collooney. Gardens. Ancient trees. Only a few stairs in to lunch.' He zipped his trousers, buckled his belt. 'There's Lissadell House, of course, they say Yeats enjoyed the place. However—too much walking, would be my guess.'

She yawned. 'I'm trying to think.'

'Anna said she forgot to mention roads up

the side of Ben Bulben—very rough tracks with sheep galore and turf fields. A dash on the primitive side, but great views, and the Vauxhall could make it.'

'I love the primitive side.'

He took the comb from his pocket and ran it through what was left of his hair—felt the stubble on his chin, regretted the incessant bother of shaving.

'I like your pictures of Ben Bulben,' he said, pulling on his watch. Worn from the long day, she had forgone sketches of William last night, rescheduling for this evening.

'There's something benign about it,' she said, 'the way it broods over the landscape, but I couldn't catch it. Of course, I never can really catch what I'm after, just fragments, like when small clouds break away from big clouds and little shreds go floating off. I get the little shreds.'

'Little shreds are good.'

He sat on the side of the bed; Pud shot from his quarters as if squeezed forth by the sag in the mattress. 'You remind me of something Washington Irving said about traveling—in Spain, I think it was.' He eased his bare feet into his loafers. 'I copied it out for you years ago.'

'Umm,' she said, burrowing in for another round of sawing wood.

'Let others repine at the lack of turnpike roads and sumptuous hotels and all the elaborate comforts of a country cultivated into tameness . . . but give me the rude mountain scramble, something, something, something, that gives such a true game flavour to—in this case—Ireland. There you have it, and thank heaven, no senility yet.'

She was drowsing into sleep. He leaned toward her side of the bed and touched her cheek. She had added true game flavour to his life, a fact which he didn't take lightly.

Going down the stairs with Pud at his heels, he might have whistled, but didn't want to wake anyone.

In the dining room, he identified the smell— the wall above the sideboard was freshly painted. A picture in oil, smaller than the Barret, hung between the sconces.

He filled his coffee mug—hair of the dog— and squinted at the figures of three men fishing in a broad, dark stream overhung by trees rendered in the taste of the nineteenth century. Above the trees, an illumination of silvered clouds—he was finicky about clouds, these were up there with Constable's. He leaned forward, adjusted his glasses. There, nearly invisible on the shadowed bank, a spaniel and a wicker hamper. No signature.

A fresh start, then; life goes on. Good for Liam.

He took his coffee to the open French doors, now relieved of yellow tape, and wondered what he would write at the top of today's entry if he were keeping a journal. *A mild morning, mist rising.* In the early light, he saw Anna at the flower bed farthest from the lodge. Stooped and intent, she reminded him of his mother and the gardens she wrought from Mississippi clay.

After Peggy disappeared, he had been the one cheering his mother on. He had fetched her tools, helped her dig the holes, joined her in the endless battle against leaf minors in the allée of century-old boxwood. All this under the strain of his father's view of gardens as time-wasting indulgence—Matthew Kavanagh had been known to walk as if blind by a newly planted bed of astonishing possibility.

As the gardens expanded, the curious began showing up at the gate, total strangers sometimes, then came the busloads during Pilgrimage, to see what Madelaine Kavanagh had done. What she had done was to take nothing and turn it into something. That was the first time he witnessed that particular kind of miracle.

He was twelve, maybe thirteen, and reading *Les Misérables* when he found a line that would help him in the cheering-on:

> *The patch of land he had made into a garden was famous in the town for the beauty of the flowers which he grew there.*

Proud, he had gone to his mother, carrying the open book. 'Look, Mama. Just like you.'

In an unforgiving north light from the washhouse window, she read the words he pointed out with his finger and nodded a little and smiled. He saw something then, for the first time—the lines in her face, and the unbearable thinness of her eyelids, blue and transparent as a moth's wing.

He looked out to the flowering beds of Broughadoon and gave thanks for her life, then crossed himself and prayed for this household, his cousins on the road in the Flying Fiat, Henry and Peggy in the house with the swept yard on the road from Holly Springs . . .

'Reverend.'

He turned to see Liam at the kitchen door,

and made a gesture toward the dining room wall. 'Well done, Liam.'

'Seamus and I washed out th' rollers around one o'clock this mornin'. Then the other walls looked so bloody grim, we're after paintin' th' whole business when time allows. I hope you passed a good night.'

'Good enough, thanks.'

The clock in the library chiming the quarter hour.

'The painting came from our family quarters down th' hall, 't was hangin' above our couch these last years.'

'Not a Barret,' he said.

'Not a Barret, no.' Liam joined him. 'But Father loved it, nonetheless. He was a man after a nice touch to clouds, said most artists weren't up to the job of th' human hand or th' heavenly cloud.'

'Agreed. No signature, I see.'

'It wasn't so unusual for the time, leavin' off th' signature.'

'How do you feel about having it on public view . . . the possibility of . . . ?'

'This was always th' wall for hangin' his favorite paintings—he seldom hung them at th' house 'til they had a good run here. I was after bringin' the baskin' whales from the library,

but Anna said 't would be too violent a scene
for guests at their food.'

'Very thoughtful.'

'Blood on th' water an' all.'

'Yes.'

'But 't wouldn't seem right without something there, something he enjoyed. So.' Liam
shrugged. 'I like to believe . . . I have to
believe . . .'

'That it will be safe?' The nail that sticks up
gets hammered down, his father liked to say.

'Yes. Our money goes back into th' business
for now, there's none to be raked off to extra
insurance. Will you have your fry?'

'Think I'll wait. I'll finish my coffee, then
maybe a run. How far around the lake, by the
way?'

'You'd not be back 'til th' moth hour.'

'Settles that. Any word?' He hadn't asked
last night.

'None. Corrigan's working with Tubbercurry to see if there's a connection to what
happened here.'

'Do you believe there's a connection?'

'I have a hunch, yes, about Slade, just some
gut feelin' I can't explain. Whatever th' truth,
I feel better he's under lock an' key.'

'Did the Gards do any looking around up the hill? Since the property adjoins . . .'

'They did. Thought the lane could have been a flight path, but found nothin' a'tall. Queried Mother an' Seamus yesterday—an' Paddy, of course, when they caught up with him, he'd been in Dublin. Nothin' to be learned there, as I could have told them.'

'I suppose Corrigan thought of contacting art dealers.'

'He says they've sent a teletype to th' Garda in Belfast, Dublin—places with th' big dealers, he says. His personal guess is that it might have gone over to England; they're seein' what can be done with that.'

'I was wondering about Slade's bank account, if there might have been some large deposit.'

'All looked into. All a dead end. 't is a right cod.' Liam rubbed his eyes.

'Sorry about Anna and Bella having to suffer the fair incident.'

'Ah, Bella. Eighteen goin' on forty.' Liam heaved a sigh. 'Seems a hundred years since I was eighteen.'

'What were you up to at eighteen?'

'Runnin' wild as bindweed.'

He had been eighteen during what Walter

once called 'Tim's sport with Peggy Cramer.'
He had been wild enough himself.

They looked out now to the massive beeches.
A bird dived by the open doors.

'The poker club says they're leaving us tomorrow for Italy.'

'Righto.'

Anna came up the path, not glancing their
way, and entered the lodge by the door to the
kitchen. He would stir himself, get a move on,
but for the languor in his bones.

'Rev'rend.'

In Liam's voice, an anguish barely expressible.

'Sometime, if you could . . . if you might
possibly be willin' . . .'

A silence gathered between them; Liam's
breath was ragged.

'Willing?' he said at last.

'There's a thing pressin' me like th' Black
Death.'

'Would you like to talk?'

'I would. Yes.'

Since a boy, he'd been called out of himself
by the needs of others. He'd never known what
to do with that until long after he became a
priest.

'We could do it now,' he said.

'Th' travel club is off to Sligo today for

shoppin'—no breakfast, they said, they're after savin' their calories for Italy . . .' Liam ran his fingers through his hair, anxious—'so there are no frys to be made but your own . . .'

'Cynthia's good for a while, and so am I.'

'Still and all, there's th' shutter by the front door that wants th' hinge since spring, an' turves to be hauled up . . .'

He set his mug on the sideboard, saying nothing. He was willing to let the matter drop.

Liam appeared edgy. 'Feels strange to think about just walkin' away when th' notion strikes.'

He nodded.

'But . . .' Liam's smile was sudden, unexpected. 'I guess I remember how.'

'The trick is to put one foot in front of the other,' he said. He hadn't realized until this moment that Liam Conor's smile had a way of improving the air at Broughadoon.

'I'll tell Anna,' said Liam.

*A bright and pleasant morning with a grand, soft day predicted.* That's what he would write if he were keeping a journal.

# Twenty

'We hauled these stones one at a time, on a sled behind Billy th' horse.'

They sat on a gob of limestone, one of three deposited along the shore.

Liam slapped his arm. 'Bloody August and th' midges are out in hordes. My father used to blow pipe smoke into my hair to give me a bit of relief. He always liked a smoke by the lough; we had some of our best talks right here.'

'What did you talk about?'

'When I was a wee lad, about fish. After bein' confirmed, about girls. Before he died, we talked about fish again—not fishing, but fish; their feeding habits, and how it seems they have th' human understanding at times, that sort of thing. I liked that.'

He had no access to this sentiment. As a boy, he wasn't allowed to fish, and when he was old enough to do as he pleased, he lacked the yen. The only lasting image of the sport had come from his Grandfather Kavanagh's counsel on what to do when you catch an eel. One of several tactics cited was to grab hold of it, cut its head off, and skin it. Another was stuff it under a bucket and lift up one side—when it sticks its head out, sit on the bucket. This kind of talk had put him off the notion of catching anything wet and slippery.

A breeze lapped the reeds. He looked for the swan, but didn't see it.

'Before he got too sick to walk about, we came down to this stone for th' last time. He was quiet that mornin', just lookin' at th' lake, th' mist was risin' off it. Then he said . . .' Liam looked away. 'He said, Beauty is enough.

'He said it as if talkin' to himself. The idea seemed to please him. But I'm no philosopher— to tell th' truth, I don't know what he meant.'

'Fathers are good at saying things we can't understand. My dad's last words were, He was right. I'd spent a long time by his bedside, talking of a God he never professed to know or care about, then drove back to school, believing he'd pull through. A man named Martin Houck came in after I left, an old enemy who caused our family much suffering. He spent a few minutes with my father and begged his forgiveness. When a nurse went in later, Dad was dying; he spoke his last words to her. Did he mean Martin Houck was right? Did he mean I was right? Did he mean God was right? One hopes for the latter.'

They watched two ducks dive onto the water. 'Scaup,' said Liam. Small waves purled against the shore.

He was quiet, at peace, waiting for Liam.

'We must give th' travel club a right send-off this evenin',' said Liam. 'They've been dotes.'

'That they have. Anyone else coming in?'

'Not for a few days. We're five percent over last year, but probably losin' ground now, given th' look of things in th' news.' There was the gray in Liam's eyes.

'Who's coming?'

'A woman from the States, and a niece or nephew, don't remember which. Writes books, she says. I don't trust people who write books.'

He didn't remind him of Cynthia's calling.

'When th' book comes out to th' stores,

there's yourself in it lookin' like an eejit, but with a fictitious name to keep th' solicitors off.'

'You've found yourself in a book, then?'

'Not m'self, but it happened to Toby Gibson who lets cottages in Wicklow. They made him into an English lord durin' the evictions—had 'im done in by an Irish gardener who sticks a hayfork in 'is ribs. Modeled th' lord after Toby, clear to his waxed mustache an' th' receipt for his mum's soda bread.'

They made small talk as Liam gathered courage.

'Given what's on your plate, I wouldn't worry about showing up in a book.'

'Aye, but I worry about everything, Reverend, 't is a curse. On the other hand, Paddy worries about nothin' a'tall. You said you have a brother. Are you anything alike?'

'We're definitely alike in our faith, in our taste for poetry—anything more remains to be seen. He's a half-brother. We haven't known each other long, scarcely two months.' He saw the decaying barn outside Holly Springs, saw himself climbing the ladder to the loft, shouting Peggy's name, busting a gut to find her, trying not to step on rotten floorboards that would eject him into the cow stall below, out of earshot of any living soul and maimed for life. Sixty years would pass before he discovered why his mother's maid had left, saying nothing to anyone. He'd been devastated by the loss, unsure of himself without Peggy's measured way of reining him in or letting out the rope, always at the right time; she had been his second mother.

Liam gave him a sharp look. 'If I don't say it now, 't won't get said. The only place I know to start is at th' beginnin'.'

'The best place.'

'I've never confessed to a Protestant.'

'I confessed once to a Catholic when I was a young curate; thought I might be struck by lightning. He was a wonderful man. Confession is for reconciliation with God, it has little to do with denomination.'

The muscle of Liam's jaw clenching. ''t is likely William is my father.'

He wasn't expecting this.

Liam raised his voice, as if he hadn't been heard. 'Anna may be my sister.'

'Why would you think that?'

'I remember th' oul' people sayin' you could tell whose young was whose, by eye color.'

'I've heard that. It's not scientific.'

'Brown and blue make blue. Mother's eyes are brown—William's are blue and so are mine.'

'Ah, but brown and brown can also make blue, and your father had brown eyes—if the portrait I saw is accurate. The eye color business is wildly uncertain—the only thing you can count on is that blue and blue make blue.'

'My Christian name is th' diminutive of William.'

'There's many of both in this country,' he said, feeling a mild nausea.

Liam's anger flared, a third party suddenly between them. 'An' here's a known fact—William came home to Lough Arrow nine months before I was yanked bawlin' into th' world.'

Liam appeared to want something of surprise or condolence. He could give neither.

'He'd never say so to me, but one of his claims to fame is bein' swain to my mother when she was a girl—and who's to say he wasn't at it again when she was a married woman with Paddy just six years old an' his ears big as pitchers? It appears I'm livin' under th' same roof with a man who makes me a villain in th' eyes of th' law an' a heathen in th' eyes of th' church.

'But th' worst of it is, th' man I loved as a father is but a man who raised an' provided for me an' talked to me about life as if 't was a good thing instead of th' bloody terror I see it as bein'.'

He'd heard the sound before, the upheaving of rage and grief long hammered down, loosed in a crucifying howl he found chilling. Liam pressed his hands to his face, sobbed.

There was no saying, *It's all right, you aren't making love blood to blood, your father is one of the sepia figures in a photograph, perhaps the one in tweed knickers holding aloft a brown trout.* He had no right to say what Anna had told him. Indeed, there was no saying that at all, for the truth, if that's what it was, could be more mocking than the lie.

'Jesus, Joseph, an' Mary.' Liam wiped his face with the palms of his hands. 'I knew William an' my mother had feelin's for each other when they were young. I knew she hated his guts because he left an' never came back to marry her. He was a proper stuke about all of it, or maybe he knew he was dodgin' a bullet by stayin' away. But nobody ever said he'd been back to Lough Arrow nine months before I was born.'

'The nine months could be a coincidence. Where did this information come from?'

'A couple of years ago, someone William

knew in th' past turned up at Jack Kennedy's. He was askin' about William, said he'd driven to Lough Arrow with William many years before. He remembered th' date because his twin nephews were born while he was stoppin' here.'

'What do you know about the person who said this?'

'Nothin' more, he was passin' through to Belfast. Paddy said when he heard it from Jack Kennedy, he flashed on a memory from when he was six years old, said the scene sprang on him clear an' sharp as yesterday. He remembers comin' on th' two of them, Mother an' a man on a bench Father set in th' woods. He remembered th' scar on th' man's temple, he said, an' the odd nose.

'Th' man had his arm around Mother, he said, an' they were talkin'. Somethin' about goin' away to Dublin an' he would give her a fine house. She laughed an' said she already had a fine house an' that's when Paddy marched up an' demanded the arm be removed from his mother at once or he would knock th' man's head off. Paddy was forward like that—I would have run like a hare an' brooded on th' shock of it.'

'You believe Paddy was telling the truth?'

'Paddy's ever stickin' th' blade to somebody,

he's like our mother in that. But I have a feelin'
I can't shut away, that he was tellin' th' truth.'

'And so Paddy gets the house, he gets the
father, he wins. Is that it?'

He was sick of this Paddy-on-the-hill, king-
of-the-mountain business. 'Let's say Paddy saw
your mother with a man on a bench. And more
than a half century later, he meets the older
William who bought and moved into Broughadoon. There's no way Paddy could have recognized the much older William as the young
man on the bench all those years ago. Would
you say that's true?'

'But there's th' business of th' scar an' th'
nose.'

'Has anyone confirmed William's presence
in Lough Arrow nine months before you were
born? Your mother? William?'

'I don't ask that. Maybe I don't want to know.'

'Does your mother know Paddy talked with
you about it?'

'No, he says. He remembers she scolded
him as a lad, slapped 'is face an' boxed 'is ears
an' said he'd seen an' heard nothin' a'tall. 't was
his imagination bein' fervid, she said.'

'Fervid? He remembers such a word as that
from the age of six?'

''t is th' word we always used for Paddy's imagination.'

'You said you worry about everything. Perhaps you've got this out of proportion. An arm about your mother is merely suspicious; you have no proof of anything more.'

'I know my mother. I never saw any proof of her love for my father. She was a bloody shrew, and yet he loved her. I used to feel embarrassed for him that he loved a woman so hard in her ways. He was gentle with her, he made excuses . . .'

'Have you talked to Anna about this?'

'There's pressin' enough on Anna without pilin' this rubbish on. She was educated in a convent an' has a proper way about religion—she would think hard of her Da, and God knows what it would do to us. 't would be an upset of th' worst sort.'

'Perhaps you need to risk that upset, trust her to be brave enough to . . .'

'She has upset in plenty; she's ever havin' to be brave, lookin' after William—it's herself that irons his shirts an' makes 'is bed an' cuts his hair—then there's mixin' it up with Bella an' runnin' this place an' puttin' up with me, for God's sake. As for th' Barret, she was always after insuring it for its full worth—I fought her on it, so there's that, as well.'

It was a foolish question, but so be it. 'Can you talk to your mother?'

Liam laughed. 'You spent an afternoon in her company. You know there's no talkin' to my mother. I've had no peace, none a'tall; th' heaviness of it comes between Anna an' me sharp as any blade. I don't know how to run from th' truth like some people do—it's always there, festerin'.'

'What are your feelings toward William?'

'I can't see how to love him like a father, it can't be done. I can never keep th' anger down when I think of how he betrayed a good man with a bad woman. There's th' rare time when I do feel love for William—like a son, you might say, but then 't is a blight on my love for Riley Conor, an' I feel guilty as a thief an' angry again at William's fornicatin' soul. What right did he have to my mother, I say, an' all over again, there's my fury risin' up against my mother for her heedless ways. 't is a dog chasin' its tail, a cruel heap of rubble, all of it.

'Maybe I was feelin' some better, then came th' cupboard business, as William calls it, an' Garda swarmin' th' place, an' all th' rest . . .'

Liam slammed his fist onto the stone. 'God above, what's to be done?'

'Let's start where you started. I believe the beginning needed here is forgiveness.'

'I don't follow you.'

'Peace is what it will take to release you from the bondage of this thing. Forgiveness is a direct link to peace.'

'I don't get your meaning.'

'I mean you need to do some forgiving, Liam.'

'For the bloody horror of th' whole mucking business, *I* need to do some forgiving?'

'Starting with your mother.'

'For God's sake, you can't mean that—'t is a bloody Protestant joke.'

'I do mean it. One must begin somewhere, sometime, to let go of the bitterness, or be eaten alive and the marrow sucked out.'

Liam looked away, angry, and stood down from the stone. 'I can't do this. Sorry for your time. Terribly sorry.'

Liam hurried along the shoreline, away from the path to Broughadoon.

He felt in his chest Liam's crushing heaviness mingled with his own. Through carelessness or blunder, he had estranged a man who needed

God's wisdom, which was precisely what he'd offered. He believed what he had said; he hadn't tried to wrap it in frill or poesy.

What George Steiner had called 'the terrible sweetness of Christ' was needed here. Grace upon grace was needed here. Three men were vying for the fathering of a single boy, and two of them more than enough.

He closed his eyes, breathed in the lambent air of the lough, tried to collect thoughts scattered like leaves before a gale. The grace to forgive Matthew Kavanagh had literally saved his life, his feeling life. What he hadn't known was that it would have to be done again and again over the years. A nuisance, really, like the continuous labor required to keep a garden from running wild, or a bed made, or a machine oiled. Most often, the forgiving of his father had demanded an act of sheer will, there was nothing sappy or sentimental about forgiving a bitter wound, one had to go at it head down. Late in his forties, he had come awake to a key word in the petition, 'forgive us our sins as we forgive those who sin against us.'

*As* was the word on which the petition turned. As we forgive, we are in that same instant forgiven. It was a sacred two-for-one, a hallowed tit for tat.

He wanted that for Liam.

But perhaps the whole thing was beyond his feeble energies as friend or cleric. Perhaps he should take his hands off it altogether, let it go. He prayed to be able to sacrifice the dark weight on his spirit, begged for Liam's deliverance from a darkness far greater than his own had been. He had, at least, known—

'Speak your piece, then, Reverend. I've spoken mine.'

Liam looked at him, then climbed again onto the gob of stone. Blood smeared the knuckles of Liam's right hand.

He felt a shaming impulse to weep, and, through some license barely understood, gave way to it.

# Twenty-one

<Dear Fr T:

<Thanx for yr email of five words total. Cynthia's ankle on all prayer chains. Harold and I attended service at Lord's Chapel last Sunday. They baptized the niece of Dooley's old teacher, Miss Pearson, who visited twice after my gall bladder op. Be glad you are not at LC anymore. For one thing they are using TRUMPETS. Three of the things blaring at once! What in the world they'll fall back on at Easter is beyond me. Somebody said if the Search Committee had used you as a roll model they would not be in this mess. Glad to be

a Baptist again, ha ha. Large Waterford vase.

<Love to all, Emma>

<Hey Dad

<Hey Cynthia

<A foal out of Brown Betty last night. No problems. Miss you guys.

<Hal says he'll be proud to see my name on the business. Wish I could jump over the four years of vet school. Hey, Cynthia hope your ankle is ok. Lace sends love. She spent a week at Meadowgate. Barnabas doing great don't worry about anything. Hal and Marge and Rebecca send love. Sammy and Kenny and Jessie and Pooh send the same and so does Harley. Mush, mush and more mush.

<Love,

<Dools>

The emails were on the bed when they returned from their wanderings. He grabbed Dooley's and read it avidly; he was starving for it. *Don't worry about anything.* He liked that.

After his walk to the lake with Liam and a demoralizing breakfast of yogurt and fruit—his idea, not Broughadoon's—he and Cynthia had taken off for Ben Bulben, where the Vauxhall climbed a rude track along the flank. They slowed for sheep in the road, searched the views. Then lunch at the tea shop in Drumcliff and out to the churchyard where she sketched Yeats's headstone. Covered by a layer of common gravel, his grave had looked bereft among those better-tended.

Through it all, Cynthia was subdued. The prolonged ankle business—the crutches and the craving to toss them—had gotten to her; she was struggling through an inevitable patch of depression. He seldom saw her out of sorts, it was mildly alarming, he would do anything—stand on his head, whistle Dixie—to help her through.

She stood at the chest of drawers, leafing aimlessly through the work of the day. He looked over her shoulder.

'That's a good one,' he said. 'The great Ben as the prow of a ship steering through a green sea.' He thought she might enjoy the imagery.

'I'm afraid I can't do it,' she said, not hearing.

He shucked change from his pocket to the tray. 'Do what?'

'William's portrait by firelight.'

'Worst case, let's say you really can't do it. What difference does it make?'

'All the difference.'

'All? Isn't that carrying it a little far?'

'His face is the best of faces, I won't find another like it'

'Then why not a portrait by daylight or lamplight? Why heap on coals with the firelight business, no pun intended?'

She looked up at him. 'Because that's the way he should be painted. It's the way it needs to be done'

This was making him crazy. 'But you're anxious about it.'

'It's all right to be anxious. A bit of stage fright is good for the performance, don't you think?'

Well, yes—he agreed.

'So you pray and I'll paint and together we'll get the job done. Okay?' She smiled, innocent as any babe.

Thank God, he'd hardly had a smile out of her all day. 'You're a bloody nutcase.'

'Mush, mush, and more mush.'

He pressed her close, wordless. That he could hold to himself all the comfort in all the world was sometimes nearly too great a thing to believe.

At Anna's suggestion, the poker club and the Kavanaghs joined tables at dinner. Cynthia ordered a bottle of Prosecco, which Liam kept for the Italians who sometimes came.

'To a safe and happy journey,' said his wife, 'for the Book Poker Fishin' Irish Widows' Travel Club!'

'That's *us*!' said Debbie.

'*Slainte!*' he said.

'*Salute!*' said everyone else.

Moira adjusted her glasses, shuffled papers. 'Okay, time for th' language test we've been talkin' about—let's hear everything you've learned so far.'

'Um,' said Lisa. '*La dolce vita!*'

'Ferragamo, Armani, *por favore*!' said Tammy. 'What else could we possibly need?'

'We've hardly had time to learn a whole other *language*,' said Debbie. 'I only have one word.'

'Go for it,' said Moira, who was making the rules.

'*Magnifico*?' said Debbie.

'Say that anywhere, it will get you points.'

'I hope we're not going to conjugate any verbs this evenin',' said Lisa.

'On th' plane tomorrow. Now—for a night out in Positano, this is all you need, th' whole nine yards; I made a copy for everybody: *Ciao. Falanghina. Risotto. Tiramisu. Espresso. Il conto. Ciao.*'

'*Two* ciaos?'

'One for hello, one for *sayonara*,' said Moira. 'As for our night out in Naples, we'll be addin' this to our vocabulary: *Vada via che sa di aglio.*'

'Meaning?'

'Buzz off, garlic breath.'

'Idn't she *terrific*?' asked Debbie.

'Bilingual,' said Cynthia.

'Y'all goin' to meet here next year?' asked Lisa.

'We don't know yet,' said Cynthia. 'Are you?'

'Maybe. We really like it over here, th' lake fishin' an' all.'

'I really like workin' with *ghillies*,' said Debbie.

Hoots, cackles, the usual.

He raised his glass. 'Happy fishing in Italy!' This launched a din that made his ears ring.

'You *are* quaint,' said his wife, patting his hand.

'Tim and Cynthia'—Tammy lifted her glass; bracelets jangling. 'Safe travel, strong ankles, and may th' dollar clobber th' euro, pronto!'

'*Salute!*'

'Amen,' he said.

Liam came to the table. 'A phone call from your son. Take it in the kitchen, we'll hold th' noise down at th' sink.'

He passed through the swinging door in a blur and picked up the phone.

'Hey, buddy?'

'Hey, Dad.'

Something was wrong, he could hear it. His heart seized.

'I messed up.'

'Talk to me,' he said.

'She hit me. That's it, I'm done. It's over.'

'Why did she hit you?'

'I told her she was ice sculpture. She's cold, Dad, frozen like Mitford Creek two winters ago. You could skate on her ice.'

The up email, the down phone call. Roller coaster.

He eased himself into the corner behind the desk, turning his back to Maureen and Bella at the sink, Liam at the stovetop. 'She hit you because hitting was what she learned all the years she was being hit.'

'It's time she got over those years.'

'Why are you done? Why did you end it?'

'What else could I do?'

'You could talk.'

'No way.'

'Do you love her?'

A long silence. Then, 'I wish I didn't.'

Before Dooley was ten years old, his mother had given away four of her five children; his father, a violent drunk and erstwhile highway laborer, vanished along the severe slab he'd helped pour. Cleaving asunder was hard for anybody, especially for kids who had felt the cleaver again and again; he could sense Dooley's anguish clear across the Pond.

'Where did she hit you?'

'Slammed me in th' gut.'

'It wasn't the first time.'

Soon after the two met, Dooley had hidden Lace's hat—a despoiled affair which she wore with ominous pride. She'd let him have a big one in the solar plexus.

'Ice,' he said, 'is what you turn into when you're trying to protect yourself. Ice is what keeps you from feeling anything.' Dooley Barlowe had shown up on the rectory doorstep a decade ago, his anger frozen in a glacier of his own. It was melting, drop by everlasting drop, but only in the temperate climate of love and with a staggering amount of patience. 'Are you with me, buddy?'

'I guess. Not really. Gotta go.'

'Wait. Give me a minute.'

Silence. A minute begrudged.

'Can you forgive her?'

'Why invest more energy in somebody who thinks slammin' you in th' gut solves everything? She brought me to my *knees*, Dad.' There was the boil—there was the sticking point.

'Hitting you wasn't a good thing, I admit. But if you think about it . . .'

'I don't want to think about it. Gotta go.'

The transatlantic cable hummed; he set the receiver on its charger.

He was a wreck.

'You're a wreck,' she said. She was waiting for him at the garden door; he went to her and they stepped outside and sat on the bench.

'Dooley and Lace,' she said, knowing. 'At it again.'

He shrugged, shook his head. 'Til the cows come home, I suppose.' This was more than a lovers' quarrel, it was something deeply poisonous that both Lace and Dooley carried like a virus. He'd seen Lace the first time several years ago; she was stealing Sadie Baxter's ferns— digging them with a mattock, shoving them into a sack to sell to a mountain nursery. Watching her eyes beneath the brim of her ruined hat, he asked her to replant everything she had dug, but she had stood him down. I'll knock you in th' head, she said, if you lay hands on my sack—I don't care if you are a preacher.

She grabbed her goods and ran then, the hat flying off her head. He'd taken it home and when she came looking for it at the rectory, Dooley hid it, taunting her. That was the first punch. She had come again after that, beaten brutally by her father. It had taken hours for Cynthia to dress the bleeding lacerations riven upon old wounds.

'All that pain for all those years,' Cynthia said.

'They can't trust each other.'

'Time can be healing. Will you buy that?'

'Not at the moment,' he said. He told her about the ice sculpture.

Why did he care so much about Dooley and Lace as a couple? In recent weeks, he'd finally swallowed the lie that two damaged lives couldn't possibly be fashioned into a whole. Faithless as a heathen, he'd given up hope.

'They have the same enemy,' he said. 'Fear.'

'But they have the same God—love. They'll manage. We were a couple of ice sculptures ourselves.'

'Remember your cold feet a couple days before the wedding?' he asked.

'Remember your cold feet for a whole two years?'

'You win,' he said. He realized that he wanted again to hope.

In the library, Liam prodded a burst of flame from the turves, then stood away from them by the photo gallery. At the lake, Liam had asked him to speak his piece and he'd done that as simply as he knew how. Liam had listened, saying little—from there, the results were beyond anything priest or friend might do. They'd walked back to the lodge together, sober, not talking. 'Partridge,' said Liam at a sound in the hedge.

The club was busy ordering espressos, no decaf—'Gambling again!' said Tammy. Anna removed her apron and found a seat with the club; after serving coffee, Seamus chose the remaining wing chair; Maureen entered, peered around, and sat by Anna. Bella slipped into the room, a shadow gliding past the bookshelves to a chair at the open window.

Cynthia looked stricken.

'What?'

'I think William and I are the evening's entertainment.'

He pondered the expectant faces, the hush over the room. Definitely.

'I thought everyone would go about their

usual after-dinner business while William and I worked by the fire.'

'You'll be fine.'

She gave him a look, mildly ticked at this remark. 'Easy for you to say.'

He had to laugh. 'I worked for forty years with people watching.'

William entered with the aid of a silver-handled cane, wearing a starched shirt, pressed trousers, a jacket, a vest, a blue necktie.

Spontaneous applause. The poker club gave an all-thumbs-up; the scent of Seamus's pipe smoke sweetened the air.

'Anna says you're after capturin' me on paper. So, aye, I'm ready to be captured.' William's face was pink from the scrubbing, from the newness and pleasure of it all.

'Can we *watch*?' asked Debbie.

'Well,' said Cynthia.

'Where d'you want me?' asked William.

'Right there in your chair, comfortable as anything.'

'I see m' fire's been poked up. 't would be Liam thinkin' of that.' William saluted Liam, settled himself by the checkerboard. 'Can a man have his pint while gettin' his likeness struck? I've a ragin' thirst.'

'There by your elbow, Da, ready and waiting.'

''t would be Seamus thinkin' of that.' William lifted his glass to Seamus, took a long draught, wiped his mouth with a handkerchief. 'If you wouldn't object, Missus Kav'na, would ye leave off th' scar an' touch up the oul' nose? An' if you'd be so kind, take a year or two off th' eighty-some that's accumulated while I wasn't lookin'.'

'Ah, no,' said Maureen. ''t is her style to render th' truth.'

'Th' truth,' he said, glowering.

Cynthia was already sketching, her hand darting for this brush or that, the ferrule chiming against the water jar. He sank into prayer like a swimmer into familiar water.

'If you'd like,' Cynthia told William, 'you may take off your coat and tie.'

'You don't care for me coat an' tie?'

'I like them very much, but wouldn't you be more comfortable?'

'A man wants a dacent coat an' tie to get 'is face done up in a picture.'

'You're being painted by someone very famous at her drawing, Da. 't is a privilege she's givin' you. Be a dote, now.'

William gripped the arms of the chair as if it might lift off and fly. ''t would be good to have a fag to settle me nerves. But I'm off tobacco since Jack Kennedy closed down indoor smokin' an' ran us to th' tarmac in a drivin' rain. Beggin' your pardon, Missus, do I need to keep m' trap shut?' William drew forth the handkerchief, gave a honking blow.

'You may talk up a storm, William, it's the shadows I'm wrestling with.'

'Talk about th' good oul' bad days,' Maureen said to William.

'I've but one thing to say about th' oul' bad days—if th' current crop of young was to be up against it as we were, they'd perish with none left standin'.'

Seamus gave his white mustache a quick comb. 'May I tell a joke, then, if it wouldn't interfere with the proceedings?'

'Please,' said Cynthia. 'We love jokes.'

'I generally try to bring one down at th' weekend.' Seamus rose and buttoned the jacket of his butler's garb, clasped his hands behind his back.

'So. There was this gent from Ballyshannon who all his life was after ownin' a BMW sport coupe. So when he retired, first thing he did was fulfill his dream. A few days after this mighty purchase, he was out for a spin an' decided to see what it would do if he opened it up.

'Ah, but you can guess what he saw in th' rearview mirror.'

'A Defender of th' Peace of Ireland!' said William.

'Gent pulled over, knowin' this was not goin' to be a good thing. Th' Gard gets off his motorcycle, comes up to th' gent's window, says, You know how fast you were goin'?

'Gent says, Triple digits?

'Gard gives him a tough look, says, Here's what I'll do. Tell me one I haven't heard before an' I'll let you go.

'Gent thinks a minute, says, My wife ran off with a Gard five years ago an' I thought you were bringin' her back.

'Gard gets on his motorcycle, cranks th' engine, says, Have a nice day.'

The poker club hooted, Maureen slapped her knee, the old man threw back his head and guffawed.

'That's it, William!' said Cynthia. 'Keep laughing!'

Absorbed by what she was doing, he watched her at her work and found himself suddenly happy. Dooley and Lace would manage, she had said. For now, that would have to be enough. His prayer for Cynthia floated beneath the surface of his thoughts—she could do this.

'Don't stop,' she whispered, not looking his way. 'We must keep William laughing,' she said to the room. 'Why don't you tell an Uncle Billy joke, darling?'

'Yes, please,' said Anna.

'Hear, hear,' said Seamus.

'The one you told at the funeral,' urged his wife. 'You remember.'

There he'd stood under the funeral tent in front of God and everybody, forgetting the punch line of Uncle Billy's favorite joke. Miss Rose had called it to his memory in a squawk heard all the way to Main Street. He remembered, all right.

He followed Seamus's lead and stood, buttoning his jacket.

'Uncle Billy Watson was one of my best friends, and a type of uncle to everybody. He was born and reared in the mountains of North Carolina, where many Irish found a home after immigrating to America. I believe he told me his mother was a Flannagan. I know for a fact we've got Hogans and Rileys and O'Connors and Wilsons in our coves and hollers—some very gifted at playing the traditional tunes of their ancestors, by the way. Wish you could hear their fiddle music, Bella, and I wish they could hear yours.'

Bella moved from the window, silent, and sat next to Maureen.

'Uncle Billy devoted most of his life to making people laugh. He believed that laughter doeth good like a medicine, as scripture says, and it must have done him a world of good, for he lived into his eighties.

'I remember the day he called me at the church office and said, Preacher, I done fell off a twelve-foot ladder.

'Good Lord, I said, did you hurt yourself, any bones broken?

'No, sir, he said, not a dent. I only fell off th' bottom rung.'

William laughed, raised his glass. 'To Uncle Billy!'

'Uncle Billy!' said Seamus, raising his.

'Uncle Billy was married to a fierce woman named Rose. Here's something that may have had special meaning; I'll try to tell it the way he told it.

'Well, sir, a feller died who'd lived a mighty sinful life, don't you know. Th' minute he got down t' hell, he commenced t' bossin' around th' imps an' all, a-sayin' do this, do that, an' jump to it! Well, sir, he got so dominatin' an' big-headed that th' little devils reported 'im to th' chief devil, who called th' feller in, said, How come you act like you own this place?

'Feller said, I do own it, my wife give it to me while I was livin'.'

A prodigious roar, he thought, considering the size of the crowd.

'Give us another!' cried William.

'Well, sir, there was this census taker a-goin' round, don't you know. An' he come to this house an' he knocked on th' door an' a woman come to th' door. He says, How many young 'uns you got an' what are their ages?

'Well, let's see, she says, we got Jenny an' Benny, they're ten. We got, uh, Lonnie an' Johnnie, they're twelve, we got Timmy an' Jimmy, they're—

'Census taker says, Hold on! You mean t' tell me you got twins ever' time?

'She says, Law, no, they was hundreds of times we didn' git nothin'.'

There was the light again in Anna's eyes, and Maureen's unhindered laughter. Applause, even.

William thumped his cane. 'Another, if ye'd be so kind!'

He appealed to his wife, who was hammering away on the damp paper. 'Um,' she said, furrowing her brow. 'The gas stove?'

He reeled it off, brought the house down. This was heady stuff.

Maureen wiped her eyes. 'We're starvin' for entertainment.'

'Obviously,' he said.

'Last man standin' gets a pint on th' house,' said William.

Seamus put forth another; Moira rendered one with the full Georgia accent; Maureen stood, smoothed her apron, drew a breath.

'O'Shaughnessy,' she said, 'had emigrated to America an' done well for 'imself, bein' made th' actin' foreman . . .'

'Actin' foreman,' said William, approving.

' . . . an' with th' grand rise in pay they give 'im, he decides to share his good fortune with th' folks back home in Sligo. So he rummages about for a grand present for 'is oul' mum an' da an' settles on a lovely gold-rimmed mirror for th' parlor.'

'Good thinkin',' said William.

'An' so he parcels an' posts it, an' before long his oul' da is openin' it up an' lookin' into th' mirror. Come here, Mary, he says, an' see how your son has aged since he went to that Protestant country!

'And so the mother leans over th' father's

shoulder an' looks in an' says, I'm not surprised a'tall. Look at th' oul' hag he's livin' with.'

He was oddly moved by the laughter, the ease of it. 'Give us another, Maureen!' he said.

'Aye, Rev'rend, an' don't you know Mike Gleason is fetchin' his long-lost brother from th' airport tomorrow? Mike says he hasn't laid eyes on 'im in thirty years. So I say to Mike, An' how will ye recognize 'im, as he's been away that long?

'I won't, says Mike, but he'll recognize me, 'cause I've niver been away a'tall.'

Encouraged by the ensuing ruckus, Seamus set aside his pipe, combed his mustache, and stood, bowing slightly. ''t was a quiet night at Jack Kennedy's.'

'Seamus likes to put on th' local color,' said William.

'Only two oul' gents at th' bar, who had gone at their pints quite fierce an' would need th' cab to get home. First one looks over, says, I'll stand ye a round, 't is me birthday.

'Well, now, says the other, there's a coincidence f'r ye, 't is my birthday as well.

'If that don't take th' cake, says th' first, and how old might ye be?

'Sixty-seven, says the other.

'That's bloody amazin', says the first. I'm sixty-seven meself.

'A twist of fate if I ever heard it, says the other. An' where were ye born, then?

'Enniskillen, says the first. And yourself?

''t was Enniskillen for me, th' very same. What a blinkin' fluke.

'The phone rings, Jack answers, his wife says, Any business down there, darlin'?

'Ah, no, he says, not much. Just the guzzeyed O'Leary twins.'

Miles from Yeats's pavements grey, in what had been stables in a once-isolated corner of his paternal homeland, they were hooting and cackling like maniacs—all without help from TV, CD, DVD, or any other gizmo. Such merriment wouldn't last, of course, but that was life and they were grabbing it and holding on.

He was the first to see it finished. The watercolor was the laughing William Donavan, the very breath of him.

Cynthia looked up, and he stooped and kissed her forehead. 'You did it,' he said. 'The shadows might have been painted by the firelight itself.'

She leaned forward, holding it up for William to see.

'Aye, God!' William said.

Anna put her hand on William's shoulder, pleased. 'Mr. Yeats himself was never so handsome.'

Maureen drew Bella into the circle around Cynthia and her paints. 'Look, babby. Th' spit image!'

'Brilliant!' whispered Bella. ''t is yourself, Daideo, with th' necktie matchin' your eyes.'

William gazed at the damp paper, mesmerized. 'A prodigious fine work, Missus. I don' know how ye did it.'

'I had help,' said his wife, looking a mite dazed.

As they heaved their way upstairs, Pud in tow, he felt her exhaustion as palpably as his own. Bouncing around in the Vauxhall for two days running made the prediction of tomorrow's heavy rains sound welcome.

But it wasn't weariness he was feeling. He realized he was bracing himself for something to do with her work. He would risk ferreting out the truth instead of tensing for the unknown.

They put on their nightclothes and lay in the dark, looking out to the sheen of the moon in a mackerel sky.

'What are you going to do with this new ability to paint people?'

'What do you mean, do with?'

'It seems you'd want to do something with these wonderful portraits—perhaps an art show.'

'An art show? Where? In the Local behind the produce section? On our clothesline where the garage used to be?'

'You have contacts in New York.'

'But I don't want a show, Timothy. It's too much work, it's insanely too much work. And then the critics go after you and find you provincial, which I am, and who would want to buy a portrait of someone they don't even know?'

'Ah,' he said, feeling some relief. He had pressed Uncle Billy to give an art show—Andrew Gregory had framed more than twenty of the old man's early pencil drawings of wildlife and hung them in his antiques shop. The show had been such a hit that Uncle Billy pronounced himself 'nearabout killed.'

'What I want to do is give the portraits away. I want Bella to have hers, she seemed so pleased with it. And William must have his, to show off sometimes, or just look at and remember how gay we were this evening by the fire. I still can't believe how well it came off tonight—William has a very busy face.'

No art show, then. He breathed out. However . . .

'I know what you're thinking,' she said. 'You've never been able to fool me.'

He would like to be able to fool her on occasion, but so be it. 'What was I thinking?'

'That I'm going to dive into another book, and abandon you for months on end.'

'Correct.' And shame on him, he was two cents with a hole in it.

'I am going to do another book. I just don't know when.' She gave him a profoundly steady gaze. 'Books—that's what I do.'

'Of course.'

'You do people, I do books.'

The faint chime of the clock at the end of the hall.

'Before I retired,' he said, 'I think you sometimes felt abandoned.'

'As hard as I tried not to, I did. You were always caught up in dozens of other lives, and I had to make my peace with it, knowing that's what you do. And look what came of it—you rounded up the Barlowe children, and saved Lace's neck—that wonderful, beautiful, talented girl who might have been ruined but for tangling yourself up in her terrible life. So I long ago gave you permission to keep doing that, and you should give me the same.'

'I do, of course.'

'But you give it from your head, not your heart.'

'You're right,' he said. 'You take no prisoners.'

She drew his hand to her mouth and kissed it. 'So when we grow old—what shall we do besides people and books?'

'We are old,' he said, rueful.

She turned over and buried her face in the pillow. 'Speak for yourself, sweetheart.'

She had gone at William's portrait like a hound after a hare. He felt the tight muscles in her neck and right shoulder—this was old territory, he knew it like his own flesh. How often had he rubbed the tension from the muscles that did the heavy lifting of her calling? He was ashamed of his peevishness.

'Who's next under your unremitting brush?'

'Anna and Liam. That feels good; don't stop.'

'But they almost never sit down, and certainly not at the same time.'

'Anna said they would do it, she seemed happy about it.'

'You know Seamus invited us to Catharmore on Monday afternoon?'

She yawned. 'I'll be the nosiest guest imaginable.'

'No news there.'

'And Feeney's dropping by to see you tomorrow.'

Beneath the bed, Pud sighed. He heard birds stirring in the trees beyond the window, and soon, her whiffling snore.

# Twenty-two

Cynthia sat reading amid a wave of books washed onto the shore of the duvet. He was stashed in the wing chair, imbibing his own pleasures.

'Timothy.'

He looked up.

'This is heaven,' she said.

'Aye.'

'You know how we've talked about the lake, how it looks when it's filled with sky. A pal of Yeats wrote this: *The waters hold all heaven within their heart.* A good way of putting it, don't you think?'

'It is.' He loved this woman.

She returned to her book, he to his.

Rain pounded the roof tiles, lashed the windows. A gully-washer.

12 August 1862, Tuesday

A persecuting heat—midges & horseflies bedevil man & beast

C & I rejoice to see the Parlor fitted out & A declares great wonder & astonishment at the sight—she has never before set eyes on a dining table nor any bed with head & footboard nor clothes cupboard nor chamber pot enclosed beneath the hinged seat of a chair.

Keegan & I & some of the men arranged the many Furnishings both our own & Uncle's & hung paintings whilst the draper did up the windows.

C bedazzled by the fresh beauty of our own Accoutrements so long languishing in storage. The two fine Newport chairs together with the Boston loveseats & mahogony Game Tables have been placed on the best of the Turkey carpets. The 1773 Philadelphia tea table with porcelain tray— Uncle's pride—is positioned near the hearth & the mantelpiece fitted out with export ware as is the taste. The Paul Revere wine cooler and

Pickering salver are particular favorites, but no one with whom to crow over their merits.

In the overmantel I have hung the painting of Niagra Falls that excites the imagination more than I remembered—it captivated the workers to such a degree that all labor was suspended for a full half hour, which they obligingly made up at the end. All their lives they have seen only Water lying flat in a lake or River or spouting from the spring of a Holy Well & now they observe it gushing down a precipitous inclination with a fine Rainbow into the bargain. One of the men could but utter a blasphemy, being his way of approving the astonishing Sight.

When C & A were at last fetched, the Turf Fire was alight & the chimney drawing sweetly as a man's fondest pipe. It is beyond my dreams, C said & did not reserve her tears. In no time past was I was so over-joyed, I think we would all say the same.

As for the Library, there is much to be done. I shall strive to catalog the books after the manner of Mr. Jefferson whom Uncle greatly admired—Anatomy Agriculture Architecture Botany Chemistry History Horticulture Medicine Philosophy & so forth. It is a library well furnished with eminent works on Architecture, a passion which Uncle shared with the third American President. I am reminded yet again that an Irishman designed the White House & have related this to the men & showed them a photograph.

With the burthen of the Great Move taken from me, I find I cannot savor the relief of having finished, for indeed it is not finished by any means. The two upper floors—including servants rooms—remain to be completed at a cost beyond reason. Thanks to God for my restraint on the exterior details.

Keegan has taken to looking at Aoife in a most unsettling manner. While fixing his gaze on her yesterday he muttered something in Irish. A bitter gall rose in me & I ordered him to translate at once.

She's a Beauty, he said not looking my way.


14 August 1862

With the last of my enfeebled strength, I mark here the passing of a most Blessed & Joyous & Memorable Day which I trust will forever endure in Lore hearabout.

Today came the Legions soon after Mass was dismissed at noon. Every form of locomotion known to man—from unshod foot to rude sled, pony cart & horse—even a quaint buggy cobbled together like a toy but large enough for several solemn children riding behind a father who drew the thing along with great pride. There were whistles & a drum at the lead as if all had convened at the foot of the hill with the notion of giving us a parade. C, A & Keegan & myself stood at the front portico gaping as the Great Smoke of roasting meates beckoned them up the lane. We looked toward an end to the stream yet it flowed on. It seemed every soul in Sligo was drawn to Cathair Mohr as the tides to the moon!

There's naught left to home but th' Wee Folk, said Keegan. C put her hands to her face, alarmed—There'll not be enough, she said. There'll be enough, said Keegan—Enough & more.

I record here that the heat of the early afternoon was crucifying, I was after mopping my brow the livelong day.

Our eyes searched the lane for Balfour & his party but they did not appear. Then at the tail of the procession came my nephew Padraigin in a carriage exasperated by age & intemperate cargo—Himself overdressed & overfed, his new & clearly costive bride of one year with a suckling babe, the bride's sharp-

faced mother, two glum sisters-in-law, a lad of
seven or eight years & the poor fellow who
drove them in this hired contraption with two
massive trunks lashed atop.

We were greatly dismayed to learn of their
intended stay of a full month. Yet—Where
there be a country house, the droves will
arrive to occupy it—it is a law unto itself.

I confess I feared a mild Pandemonium at
the food & was astonished by the solemnity
with which our many guests dressed their
bowls & filled their cups & punished at once
any child out of order. They sat everywhere
about the place—along the hedges & on the
porticos & leaned against the garden wall &
even climbed with their rations into the trees
where a number of children sat like monkeys
eating with fierce appetite. Father Dominic
stood on the portico & in a voice as loud &
clear as Chas Wesley was said to possess
pronounced a blessing which I copy out here.

O heavenly Father Almighty God, we
humbly beseech Thee to bless & sanctify this
house & all who dwell therein & everything
in it & do Thou vouchsafe to fill it with all
good things; grant to them O Lord the
abundance of heavenly blessings & from the
richness of the earth every substance necessary

for life & finally direct their desires to the
fruits of Thy mercy—deign to bless & sanctify
this house as Thou didst deign to bless the
house of Abraham, of Isaac, & of Jacob & may
the angels of Thy light, dwelling within the
walk of this house, protect it & those who
dwell therein. Through Christ our Lord
Amen.

Then came a blessing upon the barn &
stables, the nearly-completed Carriage House
& last but not least, all those who cross these
boundaries & threshold.

As many as could then recited with Fr
Dominic a portion of the Breastplate—

> Christ be with me, Christ within me,
> Christ behind me, Christ before me,
> Christ beside me, Christ to win me,
> Christ to comfort & restore me,
> Christ beneath me, Christ above me,
> Christ in quiet, Christ in danger,
> Christ in hearts of all that love us,
> Christ in mouth of friend & stranger.

Sometime in all the pomp I stood & gave a
talk of sorts shouted at the top of my lungs &
felt nearly faint for it. It is not what I do best,
oratory.

And then Danny Moore brought out his fiddle & soon the dancing began & the lifting of cups to the doctor & his good wife & even to the Great Kettle for its bounty, after which began the pony rides & as C later said, twas the Pandemonium after all!

I was at last filling my plate when Rose McFee sought me out—the sight of her was astonishing. The left jaw was swollen beyond belief for such a scrawny face as was now wrenched with suffering. Without a word she opened her maw & pointed to the black cavern within. I reeled from the stench.

Have it out! she commands. 't is a savage pain—I can bear it no longer.

Now, Rose, I say, I am no puller of teeth. Your man Aidan Murphy is the one for that—I saw him only minutes ago at Biddy Fitzgerald's mouth.

He wants a shilling, she says. An' he's known to yank th' bloody wrong one out. Then you're left with th' misery you had in th' first place an' back ye trot to th' oul' dosser for th' real thing.'

Heaven only knows what Germs might be loosed upon the Region while mucking about in so monstrous a hole. I was after giving her two bob for Murphy & be done with it when

she says, Do ye see y'r man Balfour didn't
come to y'r feast?

Yes, yes. A weight gone off us all!

Ye can thank me f'r that, if ye please.

And why would I thank ye for that?

For all he done to ye, she says, I set a curse
on 'is privates.

The ructions caused here by Balfour had
been noised about to the entire Region.

She gives me one of her dooming looks. Ye
owe me th' comfort I'm after, she says.

And would ye do such a thing to me,
Rose, if I decline what you're askin'?

Ye niver want to learn th' answer to that,
she says, wincing with pain.

I confess I trembled. How shall we do it
then? I say.

Nippers is what I'd say. But if you've not
th' spunk to do it I'll do it meself an' th' devil
with ye.

I grew faint as any woman. I can amputate
a limb or remove a rotten appendix, but a
tooth is another matter altogether & especially
if residing in the mouth of Rose McFee for
nigh a century.

I looked about for C or A, but did not see
them. Thus I passed my dinner plate off to

another, all appetite quelled for the day if not Eternity itself.

In the Surgery I lit the lantern & hung it above the chair & she tipped her balding head back upon the slat. I washed my hands & looked in, holding her mouth on either side & prayed my own dear Mother would assist me in this Torment.

In a region of severe dental disease, I had never seen such an orifice—its contents but one black stump in a perilous swelling of the lower left quadrant. I held my breath against the reek & covered her withered chest with a scrap of linen.

Are ye fearful, Rose McFee? The sweat poured off me.

Do as ye must, she says.

We'll pull it with the nippers, I say, then lance the abcess & drain it. Try not to swallow til after we rinse or ye'll be fillin' yourself with poison.

Out comes the ould stump like a cabbage in November.

Aye, God! she says.

Spit, I say, holding the bowl. Rinse, I say, offering the cup. I regretted my failure to tie on an apron.

When she puts her head back again I slit
the angry gum & Great God what a letting of
blood & pus—it splatters my shirt front as if
flung from a bucket. She reels off a
thoroughly medicinal amount of Irish
epithets.

I hold the bowl, offer the cup, relieved that
my hands have stopped their palsy.

I'm going to press your cheek, now, I say,
at the point of the abcess—we must force it
all out of there. Are you with me, Rose
McFee?

I'm with ye, ye brute!

There comes a gurgling sound as air &
fluid are expressed. I vow never again to do
such hog butchering.

I washed up then sterilized a needle at
the flame of the lamp & pushed the tip
of it in where the pain was originating.
Again the bloody pus pouring forth & the
spitting & gargling & supplications to the
Holy Mother & Her Blessed Son.

When the worst of it was past, I did as I'd
seen Mother do—swabbed her mouth with
peroxide, then fetched a potato from the cellar
with instructions to peel & cut it up & every
two hours hold a piece against the incision to
draw out infection.

May God himself give ye a blessin', she
says.

I sent her off with a vial of peroxide &
further instructions & went up to scrub myself
& dress again. I noted the sense of satisfaction
God sends often enough to keep a man at
such a calling.

The dancing continued beneath a three-
quarter moon until nearly midnight, with the
Moore sisters singing til spent. All the Sweets
had vanished & even the crumbs. Trageser's
Great Kettle hung dry above the coals, &
gathered from around the spits & piled in
baskets for the road home were the bones—
every half-starved dog & not a few children &
elders would have the amusement of them on
the morrow.

Little by little & save for Father Dominic
who would abide with us overnight, they
went their way, carrying sleeping children, a
few swinging lanterns—we stood at the open
windows of the parlor, listening to the rattle
of carts in the lane, the nickering of a horse or
pony. Some reeled & staggered, some sang
until they passed out of hearing, whole
families lay down by the lane to sleep until
sun up—but all went away as happy as we had
human ability to make them.

A clearly does not fancy herself a beauty, which adds to her grace. In her frock the color of peaches stirred with cream, she was a sight such as I have never before seen & such as words could never express.

To Mass tomorrow, the Feast Day of The Blessed Virgin.

19 August
Unseasonal damp & chill

From dawn until dusk yesterday, the new Surgery received a horde of visitors—many out of simple curiosity, for it was not opened to the publik on our own Feast Day, except to Rose McFee. To abuse the Damp, we kept a turf fire on the Hearth which gave a note of Cheer to sick and hale alike. One old fellow stood hat over heart, looking about with Wonder. He swore he had never seen a lovelier place outside the sanctuary at Drumcliff!

Lovelier than Palmerston's place? I jest.

Th' divil with Palmerston, he says, offended, & curses the name of England's former Prime Minister whose work at Classiebawn is a spectacle of men & materials. Twill be a castle, they say, brooding on its barren ridge & claiming the eye for miles around.

As I earlier refused to doctor beasts, I must now refuse requests for dental doctoring—my fame has rapidly spread & I shall likely be pestered unto death. A woman came at me this morning with her mouth open wide as any cellar door.

C & I feeling our great age, myself of 52 years, she of 48.

At a little past noon today, Balfour sent his man to summon me.

I must come at once, he said, to see his master. When I inquired after the trouble, the fellow looked abashed. A scaldin' stream, he said.

I took Adam & arrived at half past one o'clock to see Balfour in his bed chamber. Would I wish such a Pox on my worst enemy? I would not. I did what I could & learned from a stable boy that Balfour spends a deal of time hanging about Palmerston's work site which is largely a pile of Donegal stone. He says B treks the 40-odd miles horseback every other fortnight & lodges in taverns. Good riddance.

While there, I was enjoined to see half the

population of Balfour's place—they lined up
belowstairs, man, woman & child, with
everything from goiter to blood in the stool &
ructions of the gut. I was then summoned
upstairs to Balfour's wife & her Diarrhea.
Having no ready Nostrum I must go again on
the morrow. I learned from a doctor in Phila.
that Mr. Jefferson was afflicted much of his
life with Diarrhea. How in God's name a man
could be so discomfited & yet give speeches &
attend fine dinners, I do not know.

While I was away, C answered at the
Surgery & kept A as busy as any bee.

Nephew & the lad were fishing, it is said.

C experiencing a return of the headaches
suffered so frequently in Philadelphia. I have
sent to Dublin for *Passiflora Incarnata* which
works chiefly upon the nervous system & is
said to be relieving of the Sick Headache. It
should come up to Sligo by train in the next
week or so.

20 August
A lowering sky

Keegan has told me he will wed in
September—the Bride being Fiona, our Head
Cook at the Feast.  He says I should consider

both of us lucky men as he will have a wife to cure him of his long face, & C & I will have an able Cook & House Keeper. You could not do better, he says, in the whole of Ireland. He confesses he has looked both far & near for a suitable Wife & there she stood in the kitchen under his very nose, baking 40 Loaves as easy as rolling off a log. Her husband has been dead these four years & no children—a fact which relieves Keegan for he has little patience with the Young. I was obliged to get out the whiskey & sat with him in some amusement as he told his tale of Courtship over a period of but four days thus far—to a woman seven years his senior & easily twice his girth.

Keegan says it came about the day before the Feast—he had passed through the kitchen & nicked off a chunk of dough to mollify his famishing hunger. When caught in the act he says a large woman flew at him with an iron rolling pin which she vowed to use if he laid another hand on her rising dough. He replied that he would make her dough rise, bedad. Thus commenced a chase down the stairs & through the lower halls & when she was nearly upon him he surrendered by waving a scullery rag. He says he was taken prisoner then & they fell down together laughing. I did not press him for Details.

I am eager to have Sukey's Philadelphia Cookery book put to use here. A freed mulatto slave brought from Jamaica to America by Uncle, Sukey was a cook like nothing known before or since. Thus my earnest inquiry of Keegan—Can Fiona read? He assures me with a gushing pride that she can both read & sign her name with a flourish.

I have found Keegan a decent judge of character but suggest he move forward with caution. He says he has waited many years for such a stirring as Fiona provokes & declines the proper use of either Patience or Common Sense. He is merry as a whiskey priest—& this a man inclined to be sour as a Protestant.

Two large roasting hens, a pike & the greater portion of a ham employed this late afternoon at our supper for eight. The infant was brought to table with his mother & cried bitterly the whole duration. The lad has hardly spoken a word & looks at me with doleful eyes.

As C passed up to bed this evening with

another of her Headaches, I observe her lips & fingers moving. What are you doing? I ask.

I am counting the days, she says.

20 September
Mild

I cannot but wonder why the War between the American States is of such grave concern, disturbing my sleep. C says it is a simple matter—I thrived on the Hospitality of that Soil for thirty-three years & became the ardent supporter of its many just causes. Yet in these years at Lough Arrow I have sought to invest all my powers—of hope & strength & knowledge & affection—in the dire needs of my own people. If this incendiary conflict were indeed roused by the right or wrong of slavery I would side with the North. But as in everything in this world it is but Greed & more Greed which requires the issue of slavery to mask the wicked truth.

May God have mercy upon Union & Confederate troops alike, & upon President Lincoln in this crucifying Struggle.

Balfour's condition appears remedied. I would have him feel indebted to me—but we shall see. I have diagnosed his wife's condition as stemming from a disreputable kitchen &

have advised the frequent sterilizing of knife blades, basins & tableware. This counsel met with eyebrows raised to the brim of her cap. Thus any good I might have done with Balfour may be undone by my bold come-uppance of their Yorkshire cook & scullery maids.

As Nephew has lodged with us many days beyond the month, I ask when he intends returning home. He says he is having difficulty getting the carriage brought out. I say I will send Keegan to inquire though it will be some days hence, as Keegan is to wed tomorrow at noon.

I believe Keegan expected me to rouse a celebration but C & I not yet recovered from the one roused earlier. I will provide a fair portion of whiskey, & tobacco to lift a haze over the celebrants. C will send ahead a large pot of Apple Dumplings. I've no more to give, she says—I am given out.

21 September
A grand day

I took some time in making my toilet this morning & was dashed when I looked in the mirror to comb my graying beard. It is every morning of every day that I look upon this face & yet this time saw it more soberly.

My brow displays the furrows of a potato field! I examine my pate—tis growing as bald as Uncles—& recall that Father possessed a head of hair to equal any privet hedge. It must be true that the persecution of baldness travels down the maternal line. At the long mirror in the upper hall, I pause to judge my physique. Taller, in the main, than most & fit enough—with no paunch thanks to God. I do heartily despise the paunch.

Having a few minutes to spare I sit to this journal—it has become a warm friend who hears all, sees all & forgives all.

Keegan's Bride will be moving into the little room next to the Surgery as she's 'after being close to the housekeeping.' It was never meant to lodge two people, but we have nonetheless furnished these tight Quarters with a good bed, a floor mat, two chairs & a bureau. The turnips & potatoes have more room in their cellar than the newlyweds will enjoy in this cranny. Fiona to bring 'a wee drop' of her own things, according to Keegan. We will then be at full house until Nephew & his legions depart, please God.

Speaking of the legions, they wish to

accompany us to the Wedding today. How on earth we are all to be transported I cannot say—I shall not risk the ruination of my Carriage by adding even one more passenger to the load over four miles of rough track. As to why they must attend the Wedding of a complete stranger, I posit they are following the scent of Whiskey & Apple Dumplings.

Late evening—

As Adam cast a shoe this morning & no time to remedy the circumstance, there was naught to do but walk, as Little Dorrit is not yet broke to the Carriage. I had managed to round up a wagon for the Multitudes but the women of that party declined such a rough amenity & then C was stricken with the Headache. All this whittled our party to Nephew & the lad & myself. Knowing that A had looked forward eagerly to the occasion, I asked C if I might take her along. C was lying on the chaise & did not turn her head. As you please, she said.

The lad who seldom utters a sound became a regular magpie along the route.

Do ye have th' Wee Folk? he says, casting his gaze about in the hedges. He wore his

stubbed shoes slung about his neck by means
of the laces tied together.

I'm afraid I don't believe in Wee Folk,
I say.

He looks at me with astonishment, then
recovers himself & says deferentially, They're
there nonetheless.

We walk on & he says, Aren't they, Aoife?

A looks at me, suppressing a smile. I wager
she believes in them.

Twas the peach frock she wore & the shoes
her Father made.


23 September

God have mercy. The wee drop that
accompanied Fiona was a wagon load piled to
the heavens. I have never seen such a look on
C's face as the whole of it appeared in the lane
pulled by a horse nearly dead from privation.
Then came more than several of the Missus
Keegan's women friends & their children
skipping along behind with a passel of dogs &
a pig at the rear.

I insisted C leave the surgery & rest herself
in our Bedchamber.

I cannot, she said, the oul Flanagan Sisters
have waited since early morning & the Bailey
infant has a miserable case of Thrush. She

stood rigid as a broom handle, but I persisted, for the wagon load & all the rest would soon be spilling into the little room near the Surgery, surely provoking another of her Headaches.

Send A to see me through, I said & wondered at the look she gave me for the relief I offered.

God help us, there is no strength to tell the rest of it—a farce if ever there was one. The jumble is forced into the small room as a sausage into a casing—one might fear to open the door lest the flotsam of cupboards & coat pegs & crockeries spew forth & strike one down.

Arrival of the *Passiflora* anxiously awaited. Though found to be salubrious in Philadelphia, Valerian & Peppermint Oil now have but weak effect.

A now complaining of blisters raised by the wearing of shoes on Wedding Day.

They're from your father's own last, I chide. Tis a discredit to fling about the talk of blisters.

I am lately persuaded that we are overly insular here—I have no Discourse with anyone save Keegan & our patients. C has but A for company & the work of two upon her

shoulders, though I pray the Missus Keegan
will lift the burthen. There remains the issue
however, of the several unfinished
guestchambers. Thus if more guests are
attracted than we can immediately handle,
we'll be hanging them up by a horseshoe nail.

In any case we must somehow introduce
Society into the halls of Cathair Mohr.

Day following
Fog heavy o'er the Lough

Rose McFee came late yesterday with a
basket of Burdock Root, & Nettles which
she calls Devils Claw. She named her price
for something I had not asked for nor
required.

Why, Rose McFee, I say, how can ye
charge a man who eased your pain & dunned
ye nary a penny for the service?

That sarvice, she says, was paid by what I
fixed on your neighbor.

I gave her a coin which she grabbed from
my hand while instructing me in the proper
use of her gleanings. I turned the raw stuff
over to Aoife with a request to make a tea of
the Burdock, as Rose attests it will unblock
the sweat glands & urinary system which may
help with the Headache.

It never arises in conversation, yet Nephew
is clearly pleased to be my Heir. He swaggers
about as if he owns the place in advance of my
demise, suggesting where the pig sty be
located & giving Keegan the business. Keegan
gives it back. Th' Young Bladder, Keegan
calls him, being full of th' piss, he says, tells us
the goat is a most profitable animal & we
should buy a flock of two hundred to begin.
Keegan stalks away without a word & Young
Bladder tells me Keegan must be dismissed—
God have mercy. It is Nephew & his flock of
hungry mouths who must be dismissed. I
wonder at the numerous mistakes I have
made here—chief among them, accepting
land from a man who is no Christian
neighbor, & now the issue of Nephew as heir
to Cathair Mohr. It was the right thing to do,
to pass my estate to the eldest son of my eldest
brother & my Namesake into the bargain. I
only wished to do as had been done unto me
by Uncle. I will soon discuss the matter with
my Solicitor.

Fiona on duty at an early hour—I have
never heard such Rattle & Bang as she
commandeers the arrangement of the kitchen
to suit her taste. I'm told by a patient that the
Missus Keegan can bottle a full Orchard in a

day. A has fled to her family til the morrow, barefoot as any waif.

I did not return home to be a man of Show yet I require a horse for Keegan so that he needn't take Adam when he goes about my business. And then I must provide a Carriage for C's ministrations among the people, for oft times we are called out separately in any wether & she has her monthly rounds of near twenty miles, to boot. A could do with a cart & pony to visit her family & make the occasional call on a patient.

There is as well the problem of sheep & cattle—all these things I am able to see clearly now the house is liveable & the long labor essentially done. One wants a bit of mutton & beef for the table without dashing about to fetch it from others. And how then shall we have cattle when the pastures of Cathair Mohr are so long overgrown? And how then shall we manure the fields to restore their vitality if we have not cattle?

At the end, I am a town man lacking even the heart for tramping about in neglected fields wounding the Game. My father was a Sawyer whose husbandry ran to cultivating a patch of Turnips & keeping a bay mare, & no use to look for the bucolic influence from

Uncle, a gentleman chiefly disposed to business, an interest in architecture, & the private life. Clearly I must furnish myself with a man to oversee further Improvements here. Keegan bright enough & industrious but not one to grasp the Long Picture.

I am reminded that Balfour employs roughly twenty or more men and women, tis a factory over there to feed and keep but three people, though I hear their entertaining of guests is near constant.

One concludes that it is not enough to have a comfortable house & a roof over one's equipage—the monstrous thing begets itself like the common hare, adding up to the full Plantation & rendering a man as impoverished as his neighbor in the windowless cot.

Day following
Mackerel skies

Nephew & his legions departing day after tomorrow, thanks to God.

The lad says to me this morning, How do you cut off a leg?

I say to him, Why do you ask?

He says, I seen Danny Moore's stump. He shown it to me, took th' wrap off it.

Aye, I say, he likes to do that.

How do you cut off a leg? he says again.

A sharp knife for the flesh & muscle, I
say, & a saw for the bone.

I have never seen a more solemn look on a
young face.

I'd like to do that when I'm a man, he says.

Are you sure of it? There's blood & guts to
cutting into people, it's a messy business &
neither Doctor nor Patient relishes a minute
of it.

I should like to do it, he says, very firm.

Well, then, I must go out in the carriage
tomorrow. Would you like to come along?

He thinks about this. Thoughts move over
his face like shifting clouds reflected on the
lough.

Yis, he says. Yis, sir.

Very well. Twill be raining cats & dogs &
we'll get a good soaking in & out of the
carriage.

He looks at me, expectant.

We won't be cutting off any legs
tomorrow. Will you still come?

He thinks again, puckering his lips. Yis, he
says & gravely takes my hand & shakes it.


Day following

The lad & I got away early & the rain held

off until we were nearly done with our calls.
We had a bite of mutton stew with Granny
Moore & a fine soda bread to sop the gravy.
He ate as if famished, then watched intently
my ministrations to a nasty sore on Bridie
Flaherty's knee. Bridie had limped to the
Moores to meet the doctor. Here, I said,
offering him the nasty bandage that had been
on near a week. He looked at it, aghast, then
took it. Put it in the fire I said & he did. And
wash up in the basin, I said & he did. In any
case, the wound was nearly healed. To
celebrate Bridie did a jigging hop on the other
leg, which caused the lad to laugh.

We drove homeward in a misting rain.

After a long silence, he says, I don't care to
go back to Mullaghmore.

And why is that?

I like it here very fine.

His mother is one of the glum sisters—I
could understand his reluctance.

We were trotting along by the great stand
of bracken, on one of the smoothest carriage
roads hereabout—I had my own men render
it so.

How did you come by the name Eunan?

Me granda got it off an oul' saint.

The boy looked over at me, serious as a
monk.

Where is your father?

Me da has got no legs.

No legs!

But stumps like Danny Moore.

My God, I say. How did it happen?

't was th' stones fell on 'im when he was
layin' a wall.

He's a mason, then.

Yis. His legs was trapped under th' stones a
full day & th' part of a night.

Can he work?

No. He has th' coughin'. He's with my
oul' granny who makes medicine for 'im to
stop th' coughin'.

Does it stop, then?

No. Yis. Sometimes.

My thoughts fly to the many aggravations
of the Lungs.

If it had been me at th' cuttin' off of 'is
legs, he says, twould be a better job than them
butchers done.

He looks suddenly thrice his age & turns
his head & stares at the lough.

How do you get by?

Mam takes in sewin'.

Aye.

For them as goes from thin to fat & back th' other way.

Twould be mostly the other way these days, I say.

I nick out the oul' stitches, she puts in th' new, too fine for th' naked eye to see, they says.

How old are ye, lad?

Siven, soon to be eight.

Are you the eldest?

Yis, an' th' onliest.

Just yourself, then?

He turns to me now & smiles but weakly. Mam says they only done it th' once.

To be polite I laugh at the little joke he has clearly been trained to put forth.

Are you schooled, then?

Yis.

I'm sorry about your Da, I say.

With all the suffering I've seen I should be able to deliver a greater consolation but I am dumb as a spoon for all that.

There's a man, I say, Arthur MacMurrough Kavanagh, whose Seat is Borris House in Carlow. He was born with stumps for legs, an' only a bit of arms. Tuck your thumbs deep into your armpits.

The boy looks at me, wondering.

Yes, do as I say I'm going to show you something.

I drop the reins & tuck my thumbs into my armpits.

Follow suit I say, & he does.

Are your thumbs deep in your armpits, so?

Yis.

Do your fingers meet over your chest?

No.

I pick up the reins.

Exactly! I say. Tis the kind of arms MacMurrough was born with. Very short & no fingers to speak of, yet he's fearless for all that.

The lad looks desolately at his hands upon a thin chest.

He's traveled to India & hunted tigers & according to the talk that goes round, he's a very fine shot.

This sets the lad to thinking long thoughts.

Fishes, too, & quite fierce on horseback, I say, aspiring to suggest some hope for those without proper limbs.

The boy's face is frozen with astonishment.

Well, now, there's more to the story of Arthur MacMurrough Kavanagh, would ye believe it? Into the bargain, he's said to be a poet & an artist.

He gawps at me. How does he hold 'is brush, so?

In his mouth, I'm told.

What about his gun, does he do it th' same?

I'm dashed if I know, I say.

How does he ride if he has no legs to grip 'is mount?

In a little chair strapped upon the horse's back, they say.

The rain pelting us now, drumming the top of the open carriage.

Giddyap, ye brute, I say to Adam, which is what Uncle's driver Mercy always said to his horse, & always in a kind manner.

At the house, Keegan is there to greet us with a gnarly apple for Adam. I hand over the reins.

Drive to Rose McFee with all speed, I say. Take a large jug & tell her to make a fresh portion of her cough Nostrum. First thing the morrow, fetch it back to me—tis going with the lad—& easy on the carriage, I say, for Keegan has little patience.

We were greeted in the rear Hall by A & a blast of cooking odours to make the mouth water—twas roasted pork shoulder & the sweet scent of baking bread. I lately learned

that Fiona has taken a shine to the lad & is
trying to put meat on his bones.

Come & wash, A says to Eunan, & tell us
about your doctorin'.

She takes the lad's hand in hers & they
walk away, chattering.

I burned th' rag, I heard him say as they
went along the stair hall. Twas a desperate
fester on her oul' knee.

She turns then & looks back & smiles
at me.

I watch them pass out of view & find my
heart thundering strangely. I do not know the
cause & then—I am suddenly enfeebled by
the power of a yearning long hidden.


A pesky turn for O'Donnell, he thought.
And amazing, this reference to a man believed
to be of his own Kavanagh line. A small-world
sort of thing, which he would tell Henry in a
forthcoming letter. He removed his glasses and
rubbed his eyes—the faded ink demanded a
price.

He thought of his own lad who, like Fintan's, hadn't wanted to go home again. Dooley
had instead come to live at the rectory, and
both their lives were changed forever.

He closed the journal and gazed at the innocence of Cynthia's utter absorption in the book. She moved her lips, silent as any schoolgirl at memory work. Her ankle had given severe pain in the night, shortening their sleep. She confessed she had slipped in the shower the day before, felt a twinge, but thought little of it. It was only a small slip, she said, and nothing to worry about.

He stood and stretched his limbs, yawned. 'I'm going down and call Dooley.'

'Dooley?' she said, not looking up.

'You remember him. Tall, skinny as a rail, red hair.'

'Um,' she said from the distant continent she occupied.

'Freckles.'

Rain drummed the panes.

'Anything I can bring you from below?'

'Did you say something?' Still reading, brow puckered.

'Anything I can bring you from below?'

She looked up, blinked, smiled. 'A pot of tea.'

'Any swelling?'

'A little. Nothing to worry about.'

'Have you come to the piece in the journal about the Kav'na with no arms or legs?'

'I'm a few entries short of your bookmark—they're just getting ready for the Feast. The one who was a member of Parliament and the father of seven?'

'The same.' He slipped his feet into the brown loafers; Pud appeared from beneath the bed.

'Feeney will be along this evening.' He went to her side of the bed and kissed her forehead. 'Back in a flash.'

'If you see Bella, tell her I send my love.'

He was mildly startled—it seemed a trivializing gesture.

'What will she think of such a thing?'

'I don't know. But she needs to hear that word today, I just feel it.'

'Well, then,' he said.

He had been given more unlikely missions, though not many.

# Twenty-three

He stepped into the dining room as she came in from the kitchen.

'Bella! Good afternoon.'

He felt the perfect fool; regretted the unwitting use of his pulpit voice. 'I bear a message from my wife. She sends her love.'

She glared at him, scornful. 'You'll get nothing from me,' she said, wheeling back into the kitchen. The door swung behind her.

An encounter with Bella was right up there with having your face slapped 'til your jaws rattled. Perhaps Anna had told Bella of their talk in the fishing hut. Maybe she knew Liam had confided his own concerns. It hardly mattered.

Bella Flaherty was fenced by a thicket of nettles; he wouldn't invite her sting again. And no
way would he stick his head in the kitchen and
order a pot of tea, much less try to ring Dooley.

He walked up to the library, scanned the
bookshelves; Fintan O'Donnell's long disserta-
tion had put him off the notion of reading.

Rain oiled the windows, obscuring every
view. He examined the sepia photographs,
searched a group shot. Did Liam resemble any
of these men? He squinted at a tall fellow in
the back row, eyed the angular face. But why
waste time on nonsense? Did he, Timothy,
look like his tall, exceedingly handsome father?
Of course not—he was the near-image of his
portly, balding Grandpa Kavanagh.

He paced the room. He wasn't good at having nothing to do, and having nothing to do
for days on end was losing its luster. Whatever
zeal he'd entertained for memorizing verse had
definitely waned.

'Reverend?'

'Anna!' He was glad for the sight of her at-
tentive face; even her clogs were consoling.

'Was she rude to you?'

He smiled.

'I'm sorry.'

'It's all right.'

'She's in very bad sorts, something gnaws at her dreadfully. I always believe it's my fault, that if I only knew how, I could make things better.'

'I understand the feeling.'

'She says she's suffocating from the remoteness of the place, and no one about under forty—an ancient age to her. She told me this morning there was someone who would have taken her away, but it's impossible now.'

'Jack Slade?' He hadn't meant to say that, not at all.

She blanched, offended. 'I have no such evidence.'

No mother would want such evidence—he had overstepped.

She saw that she had put him off. 'I'm sorry,' she said. 'Broughadoon's endless refrain.'

'I'm sorry I asked.' In truth, he could dig a hole and crawl in it. But three apologies in the span of a few seconds? What was there to do but laugh a little?—and so they did.

'The rain puts an end to the roses for a time,' she said. 'And the lavender hates it, of course.'

'There's a price to be paid for being green,' he said, making small talk.

'We've had a postcard from Moira. Hired

cars are too dear in Positano, so she's getting about on a Vespa.'

'Holy smoke.'

'*Ti sei bevuto il cervello* is her war cry, she says, to Italian drivers.'

'Meaning?'

'Loosely translated, Have you swallowed your brain?'

They had a small chuckle. 'Anything at all from the Garda?'

His question put the instant worried look on her face. 'They can find nothing to go on, they say. I don't understand . . .' She pulled forth a scrap, gave him an innkeeperish smile.

'Well, then,' he said, prepared to hurry off.

'The dining room must be lonely,' she said, 'without the anglers. Will you join us in the kitchen this evening for supper? Dr. Feeney will be here for his house call, you know, and Seamus is with us. It's our family night; we do it each month.'

Hadn't she said innkeepers are ever forced into the society of guests? Perhaps he should decline. And yet, he wanted to join them in the kitchen. 'Unless you hear back from us, we accept with pleasure.'

'Grand!' She took a deep breath and drew

herself up and smiled her old smile, revealing a healthy store of what his mother called 'milk-fed' white teeth.

'I'd like to take a pot of tea up to Cynthia,' he said. 'If that's convenient.'

'I just gave a knock to deliver your laundry, but no answer. I looked in and she's sleeping. Shall I carry it up?'

'No, no, I'll take it up in a bit. No hurry.' He would have mentioned Cynthia's loss of sleep from the pestering ankle, but Anna would have said she was sorry and off they'd go on a rabbit chase.

She seemed hesitant, smoothed her apron. 'You said you would tell me about Dooley, how things . . . went along for you.'

She glanced at her watch. 'I've a few minutes off the clock. Would this . . . be a good time?'

'A very good time,' It gave a small pleasure to be asked—he needed the work.

'If it isn't asking too much,' she said.

'Not at all. I like to talk about Dooley.'

Her green eyes were luminous. 'Please come, then.'

They turned left before the dining room, then right, and proceeded along a narrow hall with a bank of windows. The close passageway smelled of something cooking on the red Aga.

'Smells good,' he said.

'Bella's cooking this evening. Italian is her favorite cuisine since she was little.'

A blue door then, which she opened with shy pleasure.

'My Ibiza,' she said. 'Please go in and make yourself comfortable, I'll only be a moment.'

He stepped into the room, heard her clogs sounding along the passageway.

He looked at the tall windows clouded by rain, at images pinned to the wall, of gardens, flowers, reproductions of paintings—one by Cecil Kennedy, whom he admired. He searched for the legendary ladybug that appeared in all of Kennedy's remarkable paintings of flowers, and there it was, of course.

On a long worktable, trowels, pruners, gloves, clay pots stacked by size—the usual detritus of the earnest green thumb. Above the table, pencil sketches tacked to a corkboard. Garden designs. He looked at a large sketch in which islands of space were identified in block letters:

LODGE. KITCHEN GARDEN. LANE GARDENS. HIDDEN GARDEN. BLUEBELL WALK. ORCHARD. MASS ROCK—the elements tied together by a winding pathway.

Facing the windows at the end of the room,

an artists' easel and a high stool. At the end of the table, a jumble of paint tubes, brushes in a Chinese vase, a smeared palette, a tole pitcher filled with roses. A bloom gave way as he stood looking; petals fell silent as nuns to the stone floor.

She came in with a tea tray and set it on the table. 'There!' she said, slightly out of breath.

'I can see why all of Sligo wishes to visit Ibiza.'

''t is a great clutter, I'm afraid.'

'That's its charm.' He felt happy in some new way. 'I didn't know you're an artist.'

'I'm not, really. Just trying to get the hang of it, but there's never enough time.'

She poured two cups of tea, handed one to him. 'No one comes here but myself, and that all too rarely, so I have but the one chair—like your Mr. Thoreau. Please sit; I'll bring my stool.'

She picked it up and brought it over and was perched on it before he could set his cup down and give a hand.

'I was after converting it to a guest room,' she said. 'We could use it in the busy season— but Liam won't allow it.'

'Good fellow,' he said, taking the armchair.

'So please tell me, Reverend . . .' She looked suddenly worn. 'How did you do it?'

'With prayer. A lot of prayer.' He sat back in the chair, inhaled the fragrance of the steaming tea. 'With patience, too, of course—but not enough. As for love, I had no way of knowing how to love a wounded boy—perhaps because I had been a wounded boy myself, I don't know.

'We think of love as warm and cozy, and that's certainly part of it. But it was hard to muster those feelings toward someone who vented his lifelong rage on me. I felt pretty sorry for myself, sometimes.'

'Yes,' she said. '*Yes.*' Her hair was old copper in the rain-washed light.

'It's not the sort of thing romantics wish to hear, but I found that in the end, love must be a kind of discipline. If we love only with our feelings, we're sunk—we may feel love one day and something quite other the next. Soon after he came to live with me—he was eleven years old at the time—I realized I must learn to love with my will, not my feelings. I had to love him when he threw his shoe at the wall and cussed my dog, love him when he called me names I won't repeat, love him when he refused to eat what I'd cooked after celebrating and preaching at three Sunday services . . . you get the idea.'

She fixed him in her steady gaze.

'And so I enjoyed the warm feelings, the stuff of the heart, when it was present between us, as it sometimes was, even in the beginning. And when it wasn't, there was the will to love him, something like . . . a generator kicking in, a backup.

'I learned over a long period of trial and error to see in him what God made him to be. Wounded people use a lot of smoke and mirrors, they thrust the bitterness and rage out there like a shield. Then it becomes their banner, and finally, their weapon. But I stopped falling for the bitterness and rage. I didn't stop knowing it was there—and there for a very good reason—but I stopped taking the bullet for it. With God's help, I was able to start seeing through the smoke. I saw how bright he was, like your Bella, how talented, and how possible it was for him to triumph over so much that hounded him.'

He took a sip of tea, and realized he was trembling.

'To put a fine point to it, Anna—I stopped praying for God to change Dooley; I asked God to change me—to give me his eyes to see into the spirit of this exceptional broken boy.

'I started talking to Dooley as if he were bright and industrious and savvy and trustworthy. I believed it was already real, that he was already whole and able to love. And all I can say is—it began to work . . . for both of us.

'One day he was sent home from school for beating up a classmate. He'd given him a good drubbing. Turns out, he did it because the boy called me a nerd.' He laughed; he loved this story. 'Imagine that. I felt twelve feet tall. The little guy had gone to bat for me; it was a bloody miracle. Did I send him to bed with no supper, ground him for a week? No. Right or wrong, I thanked him. I was never so touched.'

'How good,' she said, laughing a little, weeping a little. 'How good.'

'There's no quick fix, Anna. It's all in increments, the same way our roses grow. Winning someone who's never won anything themselves—it's a long road, and we don't always get it right—not by a long shot.

'When Dooley came to me, he had the hunched look of an old man, his face was set like flint. I remember how much I wanted to hear him laugh. Just getting a laugh out of the little guy would have been right up there with God smiting a rock and water gushing forth. And, of course, one day he did laugh. And then another day, and another. Healing came as little drops of water, and never the mighty ocean when you need it, Anna.

'There's just no way to deal with their suffering, except through love. And there was no way I could gouge that kind of love out of my own selfish hide without the help of God.

'You're Bella's mother, and that's a great power in itself. I have to believe she loves you very much. Trust that, believe that, as hard as it is to believe right now. Act as if it were true, it can change things.'

'Her father speaks bitterly of me,' she said. 'His image of me seems engraved forever on her heart. Dooley's parents—what were they like?'

'His mother and father were both alcoholics. She has since recovered; Clyde hasn't—I've had a couple of run-ins with Clyde. He left the family before the last child was born. In any case, Dooley essentially helped raise the kids until his mother gave them away.'

'Gave them away?'

'Four out of five. They're together again now after many years.'

She closed her eyes. 'There's a sense in which I gave Bella away when I let her go.'

'Yes.'

'She expects me to give her up again, doesn't she?'

'I think she wants you to know she'll give you up, first.'

She covered her face with her apron and wept, silent.

'I know time is what you have very little of, Anna. But maybe you could look for a way to spend time with her. I kept far too busy as a working priest; it was up hill and down dale for everyone else, but I could easily find an excuse to let Dooley shift for himself. I remember when God spoke to my heart about this—about how he shows his love by being as near to us as our very breath. Bella says she's lonely here— that's something to listen to. I feel your time would be the greatest gift you could give her.'

'How will I reach her, what shall I do to get through her terrible coldness?'

'Continue going in to her through her music, as you did the other evening with the concert. Go in where there's common ground. Do whatever you can, Anna, to find common ground, and if you do nothing more, forgive her and pray for her. Whenever she lashes out, when-

ever she draws away, pray and forgive, forgive
and pray.'

'Is it too late?' She wept openly now.

'It's never too late, please believe this. There's
a scripture in the Book of Joel—*I will restore
unto you the days the locusts have eaten.* He's fully
able to do it, and waiting for you to ask.'

'What about . . . Jack Slade?'

'That's in the past. If I were you, I'd put it
out of your mind.'

'It was on your mind . . .'

'But it doesn't matter now. All that matters
is loving her back to you.'

'I can never thank you enough.'

'Please don't try, I beg you. Thank him.'

She wiped her eyes, looked at her watch.
'Forgive me, I must unload the dishwashers and
get the bread in the oven. Maureen's off with
her old aunt for a bit and I'm quite behind. One
more thing, if you would. How old is Dooley
now? What's become of him?'

'He's twenty-one, and recently took my name
as his own. Dooley Kav'na.' He swallowed hard.
'A rising sophomore at the University of Georgia. He wants to be a vet, and circumstances have
conspired to give him his own practice when he
finishes school. A parishioner left him a small

fortune. It covers his education and transportation, and leaves something to share with his brothers and little sister. He handles it pretty well. A good fellow, my son.'

'I'm glad for you.'

'It may look impossible for you and Bella, but it isn't. Ask God's help. He wants to help— it's the way he's wired.'

She slipped off the stool and he stood and set his cup on the table.

'Will you pray for us, for all of us?' she asked.

He took her hand. 'I do and I will,' he said.

He was going up with the tea when the idea struck. He would build such a room for Cynthia, who had for years plied her trade in a minuscule space scarcely larger than her drawing board. He was shamed that his study, in which he hadn't actually studied in months, was the largest room in the house. And all that to satisfy what?—a need to appear busy in retirement? He was dazzled by the suddenness of such thinking, an epiphany.

His step was lighter on the stairs. The room would adjoin his study and have its own view of Baxter Park. The money would come from his pocket, not hers, though owing to their early agreement of not spending large amounts unless consulting the other, he'd have to get her John Hancock. He could see the room clearly: She was bent over her worktable in the southwest corner, the air smelling of sawn wood, the walls lined with her work.

He couldn't wait to tell her everything.

# Twenty-four

'What is it with Mother?' Liam asked Feeney. 'You finally talked her into doin' tests, Anna says.'

'The lab report came back this afternoon, which is why I was late getting here. I was up to Catharmore first.'

'And?'

'Told her what will be no news to any of us—her liver will be her death unless she stops the drinking. She didn't receive it well, of course.'

'Surprise, surprise,' said Liam. 'What about Paddy? Does he know?'

'He does.' Feeney rested his fork. 'On a more

positive note, your mother tells me she wants to live.'

'I can't imagine why, seein' she's so in love with dyin'.'

Anna looked his way, then lowered her eyes. This was family night, all right.

Cynthia enjoyed such dynamics, as long as they were someone else's. He wondered how she was getting on with dinner and the telly Anna had rolled in for the remainder of their stay. He had been sent off quite happily to the Conor table, with instructions to 'watch what you put in your mouth.'

'So the question,' said Liam, 'is will she stop th' drinkin'?'

''t will be difficult, I grant you. Nausea, tremors, hallucinations—even seizures, if it comes to that. Can't know. What we can know is'—the doctor grinned—'she will be exceedingly irritable.'

Laughter. Seamus smiled, discreet.

'You're full of surprises, Feeney. So how would she go about it?'

'There's the treatment option at a clinic, of course, but she won't have it, nor will Paddy agree to it. A costly and persecuting piece of business, in any case. She wants to do it at home.'

Liam forked a mouthful of ziti. 'I don't get

it. How could she do it at home with none but Seamus to give a hand?'

'She'll need full-time nursing care . . .'

'Of course! To be paid for with th' pot of gold at th' end of the rainbow.'

'. . . and I would supervise.'

Liam said something in Irish. 'Who was the bloke rolled a stone up th' hill only to have it roll back again?'

'Sisyphus,' said Anna.

'That's you, Doc. That'll have you comin' and goin'.'

The rain had stopped, though it rattled yet in the downspouts. The August evening was cool, the heat from the Aga welcome.

William had been talkative before dinner but was silent now. Bella picked at the ziti, stared at the wall, unseeing. Glancing up occasionally with a certain gratitude, Seamus ate without hurry.

Bella was the elephant in the room. No one attempted to penetrate the thicket of nettles, save for William. For William, the thicket parted as the Red Sea for Moses.

'Are ye learnin' a tune for your Daideo now?'

'Aye. 't will make you laugh.'

'We need a laugh in this world. Has it got th' strong beat to it?'

'For you, always th' strong beat.'

'You might get me dancin', so.'

'I'd give a packet of striped humbugs to see you dancin'.'

The platter was coming around again. His early training frowned on taking two of anything, and his diabetes demanded such a rigor. On the other hand, the ziti was outstanding and life notoriously short. He defied his upbringing, flouted his wife's instruction—and took seconds. Anna looked pleased

'*Delizioso*, Bella!' The poker club tutorial hadn't eluded him altogether. '*Salute!*'

All glasses raised to the cook. '*Salute!*'

Some flicker in her eyes—of what, he couldn't say.

He saw Anna touch Bella's arm; saw the girl flinch, thought again of Dooley and how he must call tonight without fail.

Liam went across the lodge to work on the unfinished room. Everyone else carried their portion of 'afters' into the library, where the Labs drowsed by the fire. Feeney sat with him on the sofa and swiftly devoured a serving of tiramisu.

'I've asked Bella to come up and assist me in the ankle exam. Stay here if you will, I'll be down directly with a report. You might say a prayer, Tim, for your wife's cooperation.'

'In what, exactly?'

'In doing what has to be done.'

'Which is?'

'The pain tells me she must have an x-ray, and no quibbling.'

William poked up the fire, and there went the combing of the mustache, the placement of the cane by William's chair, the match to the pipe. There shone the pint at their elbows and the old checkerboard in its pool of light from the lamp. He was moved by the grateful satisfaction of the two men, each a harbor for the other.

In the kitchen, he stuffed himself into the farthest corner, away from the gurgle and slosh of the dishwashers, and dialed.

'Hey, Dad.'

'Hey, yourself. What's going on?'

'Not much. Big fly problem in the barn. How about you?'

'Not much. A lot of rain.' He would ask and get it over with. 'Are you still done?'

'Look, Dad, you're worried, I can tell. Don't worry. There's nothing to worry about.'

'The two of you . . . both of you . . . mean so much.'

'What else can I do?'

'Don't quit,' he said. 'Not yet. Hunker down.

Talk. I'll be home soon, we can talk together, the four of us.'

In the silence between them, a cow bawled in the Meadowgate barn.

'Keep going, son. It's too soon to quit.' He heard the odd desperation in his voice.

'Hey, Dad . . .'

'Yes?'

'Thanks. Thanks a lot. Gotta go.'

'Whoa. Wait a minute. We love you, buddy.'

'Love you back.'

He chose a book and took it to the sofa and opened it at random. He wanted to see his boy—Dooley would return to school at month's end. He missed Barnabas, and Puny and her two sets of twins; he wanted to fill up the Mustang at Lew Boyd's and eat a cellophane-wrapped egg salad sandwich and a pack of Fig Newtons and sit around in a plastic chair with Mule and J.C. and Percy and shoot the bull. He found he was completely over the notion of running up and down the road with Walter and Katherine; taking his chances at this inn or that, packing and unpacking. Bottom line, he was no good at vacations, and come to think of it—this was no vacation.

'Will she be able, do ye think, Seamus?'

'If Dr. Feeney can't help her, nobody can.

They say it's up there with peelin' off your own skin.'

'God above,' said William, 'she'll need a priest, for all that.'

'Aye, but she won't allow Father Tad to do his priestly bit in her company.'

'I hope he's sneakin' it in, then, when she's not lookin'.' William gave a honking blow into his handkerchief. 'Th' oul' heathen.'

There was the paw on his foot; the one scratch, the two. He peered down, hardly recognizing the little guy without the shoe. The pleading eyes, and again the paw on his foot; the one scratch, the two. No way was he going to search for the misbegotten shoe.

He patted the cushion where the Labs were sometimes allowed.

Pud leaped up, lay down, sighed. And here he was, three thousand miles from home and scratching another man's dog behind the ears.

Feeney came along the stair hall and joined him on the sofa. 'Studies say we live longer with a dog in our lives. I should get a dog.'

'No doubt about it. How did it go?'

'She says you must take your time, Bella's with her. Now, then—she didn't quibble. I'll fetch you early Monday at eight o'clock. If I'm with you, things may get done more quickly, though granted, hardly anything gets done more quickly these days.'

'What's going on?'

'She told me about the mishap in the shower. There you have it. The pain, the swelling all over again.'

'Anything serious, do you think?'

'I'm thinking a disruption of the ankle joint, which would be good news compared to other scenarios. She has too much history with this thing to suit me. I've given her another pain medication, she'll sleep well and be fine 'til Monday. I should have cracked my bloody whip the night it happened.'

'She doesn't take to whip-cracking.'

Feeney had an affecting, albeit crooked smile. 'I'm a widower with no face across the table in twelve years. Don't know if I could be married again.'

'Why is that?'

'Women are very strong-minded.'

He laughed. 'I'll say. But that's a good thing. I was an old fogey straight from Central Casting—living alone, set in my ways, walking the dog for an evening's entertainment. What she saw in yours truly I'll never understand, but she's made something of me. Definitely.'

'That's the problem, Tim. They want to make something of you.'

More laughter.

'She says you have Type One diabetes.'

'Correct.'

Feeney cocked an eyebrow. 'You went at the tiramisu pretty good.'

'Just this once,' he said, shamelessly reciting the diabetic's unholy mantra.

'Your Irish ancestors were Protestant?'

'Seven generations back we were Catholic, with a couple of priests to our credit. I fear we took the soup in one way or another.'

'But for the soup, you may not have been here this evening.'

'What about Mrs. Conor? Anything you might need from me?'

'Pray, would be my advice. She's not such a bad old thing, if you know her history. Why don't we move to the front hall? Open the door and get a breath of air?'

They stepped out to the entrance hall, to the fishing gear and deer head, where Aengus Malone's hat swung from an antler like a totem.

He opened the door to the washed August night; Pud bolted outside, nose to the ground. Feeney moved boots and waders from an iron bench and they sat down among the clutter of other lives.

'How much do you know?' asked Feeney.

'She was young, met William, they fell in love. He didn't return as expected.'

'Aye. His career as a prizefighter was on the upswing, and soon after their meeting, off he makes for England and other parts.

'She was desperately in love with him, and took a lot of chiding from her family when he didn't come back and marry her, as he vowed. She was a very proud girl, and likely boastful, so the insults and harassment grew, became a kind of sport among her kin and neighbors. Her beauty was probably no help, for all that— you've seen the painting.

'She didn't care for three of her four brothers, but she loved her two sisters a good deal, though they fought like cats. The father had died some years before and the upkeep of the family fell to the women—the boys were not much accountable. Two went over to England, one to Canada, the youngest was finished off in a pub fight. Thomas. He'd been Evelyn's pet, her bright and shining star, she called him, something of a poet and dreamer.

'Evelyn and her mother took in washing, did piecework, kept a few hens for egg money; the two sisters were in service to an Englishwoman. It was a hard life in a cabin with a mud floor and no window. Yet it's the sort of thing the tourists come looking for even today—the famine cabins, the oul' thatched cottage—a torment to live in the bloody things. Evelyn's mother was desperate for a better life for herself and her girls and seemed to think William was becoming a rich man out there in the boxing world. She and Evelyn's uncle put the pressure on Evelyn to find William and somehow force him to marry her.'

'She was expecting a child?'

'Still th' virgin, she says. I tell you all this in confidence, of course.'

'Of course.'

'None of this is talked about in the family— Paddy and Liam refer to the issues of her past simply as Mother's Remorse.

'And so she has this fierce pressure on her. But how does a young woman in the west country of the 1930s make contact with a roving prizefighter who himself didn't know where he'd next lay his head?

'But they kept at her like midges, and one evening they had a regular brawl about it. Evelyn had banked up the fire for the night and pulled their four chairs to the hearth with a wash laid over them to dry. Her mother—

Maeve it was—called her names I won't repeat, and the sisters, who were on their night off from service, sided with their mother. Evelyn did her own bit of verbal damage—it was an unholy thing, she said, there was some physical violence among the three sisters—she trembled like a leaf when she told me this years ago. And so she stormed out of the cabin and went down to the farm pond, thinking she might drown herself like the kittens her mother forced her to dispose of when she was a child. It was a cold night, she said, and she was out in hardly a stitch and no shoe to her foot.'

The distant tapping of Liam's hammer.

'I wonder whether to say it, for it makes no difference to the tragedy of that night, but she was kept warm by a neighbor lad—her first time in the arms of anyone other than William. When it was over, the guilt was on her, as you can imagine—a crucifying thing to a Catholic girl trying to better herself in the eyes of God and man, and, also to the point, trying to keep herself unspoilt for the one she hoped to marry.'

Feeney got up and walked to the door, stood looking into the black night. The air was cool, seasoned with the wild scent of summer rain.

'She felt her life changed forever, ruined in some way beyond what had happened at the pond. She said she forgave her mother and sisters, even Thomas for letting himself be killed, as she put it. She wanted nothing more than their forgiveness, even for her proud ways. She was reminded of how her mother tenderized tough meat by pounding it to shreds with the edge of a dinner plate. She felt her heart ravaged in such a manner, she said, and softened with the need to begin again if Providence would allow it.

'It was the early hours of the morning when she went up to that airless cabin and opened the door. The fire literally exploded. It was of course oxygen flooding into the buildup of unignited gases. 't was an inferno.'

He felt the terrible weight of his living bones. The sound of rain dripped into their silence.

'Her uncle forced her to view the remains. I won't go into great detail, but fire does a wicked thing to human flesh—it leaves only the blackened torso, very little of the limbs. She was driven nearly mad by the sight.'

'I can't imagine what it took to survive this,' he said.

'She learned to survive by withholding love, or any sort of human feeling, from everyone—especially herself. Later, that withholding would affect her husband and sons—Paddy and Liam say they have no memory of any tenderness from her.'

Feeney returned to the bench, sat with his hands on his knees. 'As Liam said, she talks of dying, hopes to die. She thinks it would serve her right, which is why I was gobsmacked to hear her say she wants to live. And yet, faced with the liver business and the very thing she's been keen to do, she's terrified.'

He needed to make sense of this. 'A spark to the laundry and then the chairs smoldering . . . ?'

'Exactly,' said Feeney. 'They may have died of asphyxiation long before she opened the door.'

'But she opened the door.'

'Yes.'

'Her remorse haunts this house,' he told Feeney.

'As it does the house above. I'm sorry to tell you all this, but it seems you should know.'

'I'm glad you told me, it changes things.' The truth always changed things. He wondered how much more Evelyn Conor had confided to her doctor and erstwhile bridge partner, but he said nothing.

'You've been good medicine for Brougha-doon, Tim.'

He had no idea what to say to that. 'Mass tomorrow. Will Cynthia be up to it?'

'Good for the soul, bad for the ankle. I wouldn't pester it in the least if I were you.'

'Perhaps you'll give me Tad's phone number,' he said. 'I'd like to see him before we leave.' But would they ever leave? If it wasn't frogs and flies, it was hail and locusts.

'He's just off to his brother in Wales for two weeks. His annual August retreat.'

'Too bad. I'd hoped to see more of him.'

Pud returned, shook himself, followed them into the library to the bookcases with their fluted pilasters, to lamplight and peat burning against the night, to two gray heads bent over the board. The Labs looked up at them, lay down again, slept.

Only a while ago, he'd wanted the comforts of home. Yet now he felt keenly the kind and solemn spirit of this room, and knew again that he was supposed to be here, that the easy familiarity of Fig Newtons could, if only for a time, be sacrificed.

# Twenty-five

William appeared dubious, distracted; Seamus refired his pipe. The proverbial pin could have been heard dropping as he and Feeney watched the progress of the checkers game.

'Phone call, Rev'rend.' Liam gave a high sign from the hall. 'From th' Dub.'

'O'Malley!'

'Says he has good news an' bad news.'

He sat at the desk in the kitchen; Liam worked on a laptop at the table; the smell of coffee lingered in the room.

'Hey, Tim, how's it goin' at ol' Broughadoon?'

'We're missing the riffraff, Pete. Great to hear your voice.'

'She's back.' Pete breathed into the phone.

'And?'

'For four days. A trial run. But get this—it's scarin' me to death. When I think about it, *ask th' Collar* is th' message I get. I need your help, Tim—I don't have a clue what to do.'

This was a phone with a cord, which meant he couldn't go trotting off to another room for the private affair of counseling. *C'est la vie*— family night is family night.

'You're asking me to tell you what to do?'

'That's why I'm callin'. I'd appreciate it.'

'You're sure of this?'

'Dead sure.'

He crossed himself, breathed out, dived in. 'How about doing nothing?'

'Oh, yeah?'

'Don't tell her you've changed or finally gotten your act together or everything's going to be different. That's what they all say, and then it doesn't happen. It takes time for good stuff to happen.'

Pete's ragged breathing was a minor gale.

'And whatever you do, no flowers, no mushy cards.'

'You can count on no mushy cards, but I thought flowers for sure.'

'Don't do it,' he said.

'I don't get it.'

'Think about it. You send flowers now, make a big noise, and that's the end of it, you go back to doing the same old, same old. Best not to say or do anything you can't live up to down the road.'

He was breaking a sweat. Marriage was serious business, and Pete had taken him by surprise. He'd actually trained for marriage counseling—not because he wanted to, but because he needed to. During his first couple of years in Mitford, marriages were breaking apart like ice caps—mother, father, children, floating off on solitary floes into the ether, and he with nothing much to offer but unctuous prayer for reconciliation.

He'd worried that his counsel wouldn't be taken seriously, anyway—what did a bachelor priest know of such desperate matters?

The more he observed the wreckage, the more anxious he became to effect genuine healing—most anybody could do a Band-Aid, he was in for stanching the hemorrhage. How did the dynamics of marriage differ from other relationships, anyway? What did God want for marriage in the first place? He prayed about it as if his life depended on it, searched the scriptures, attended a series of weekend seminars in Asheville. He received a certificate to hang on the wall, some assurance, perhaps, to the wretched souls who sat on the bench in the church office and spilled their guts.

Over time, he counseled quite a few couples in mild distress, and a total of eight in desperate straits. Ten years later, he'd done a discreet check on the eight. Two were lost on the floes; six were hanging in there, which was way above the national average. When he rejoiced over the results of this survey, however unscientific, Emma had raised an eyebrow and pointed up. It's not like it was all *you*, she said, which went without saying.

'If I can't say or do anything I can't live up to,' said Pete, 'what am I gonna say an' do? I was thinkin' maybe a great dinner in th' kind of place that fries your Amex; I could live up to that when the economy takes a little uptick. An' maybe a nice bottle of champagne, a little foie gras . . .'

'Fish and chips,' he said.

'Come on.'

'Don't show off, don't flash anything around.

Go easy. Besides, you probably did all that the last time she left you and came back for a trial run.'

'You're right.' Pete sounded depressed.

'Forget what it does to your Amex, it takes a lot of energy to go out for fancy dinners and be the hale-fellow-well-met and keep flowers rolling in. For now, how about spending that energy on her, focus it all on her? Just love her, and let her know it. Hold her hand, tell her how much she means to you, and here's a big one—listen to what she has to say, Pete. If you let her talk, and if you really listen, she'll tell you everything you need to know.'

A stricken silence in Dublin.

'Have you tried any of this stuff?' asked Pete.

'Pretty much all of it. But hey, no guarantee on anything. Just my two cents' worth.'

'I don't know. The big dinner an' th' flowers—that was goin' to be my best shot. But I could prob'ly do a bracelet if I have to.'

'Maybe you need to fork over a few euros to a professional.'

'No way. I'm lookin' for a freebie here.'

'Okay, all the strategies I just suggested— that's the small stuff. Here's the big one.'

'Shoot.' Pete heaved a sigh that cleaned out the phone line.

'Ask God every day to give you the wisdom and courage to be all he made you to be—for your wife, for yourself, for him. If you give God a chance in this and do the best you can, he'll help you do the rest. When you were here, you said it would take a miracle to save your marriage. Unless there's something you haven't told me, you don't do miracles.'

The dishwashers beeped—cycles ended.

'And, Pete . . .'

'Yeah?'

'While you're at it, please pray for your wife—she needs wisdom and courage, too. You're a team—think like a team.'

'You're askin' a lot, Tim.'

'I won't kid you—it's going to take a lot.'

'If you would say a, you know, prayer.'

'Consider it done, call me anytime. And regards to Roscoe.'

He drew out his handkerchief, wiped his face. He'd just been through the scrub cycle. 'A desperate man,' he said to Liam.

Liam was amused. 'While at it, he asked my opinion.'

'What was your opinion?'

'A couple weeks in Ibiza.'

'That, too,' he said.

'Great plug for fish an' chips, Rev'rend.'

In the library, the laurel wreath had fallen to Seamus.

'Th' man of th' hour,' said William, poking up the fire. 'Says 't was like makin' hay on a soft day.'

'Aye, but tomorrow, Willie, you'll be makin' hay of your own.' Seamus held up his comb—'Th' oul' flea rake,' he said—gave his mustache a drubbing. 'Well, gentlemen, I vowed I'd unload th' dishwashers before goin' up th' hill.'

'I'll come along and have a visit with Liam,' said Feeney. 'I'll give you a lift.'

'Ever th' comin' an' goin',' said William.

He would stir his bones and run along the lake tomorrow; he'd go farther this time, and definitely to the Mass rock. He sat in a favorite wing chair, checked his watch, wondered at Bella's long stay.

William lowered himself into an adjoining chair, the usual light gone from him.

'Could I have your ear, Rev'rend?'

'With pleasure.'

'Ye heard tonight what's come to th' lass from Collooney—ould an' ruined by th' drink. She needed me in a desperate way with somethin' that happened to her mother an' sisters, but I let her down. I was on th' pig's back in those days, I wanted th' whole world for my-self. Do ye understand?'

'I do.'

'I was th' young buck beatin' men to bloody pulp and livin' to boast of it. As you might imagine, I found th' girls numerous as fairies in Mayo. I thought any woman would wait for William Donavan 'til he got his name in lights.'

William bowed his head, examined his palms as if seeing some truth there.

'And so I married Roisin, Anna's mum, while I still had feelin's for Evelyn McGuiness. Roisin was pretty as a speckled pup; worked like a man at th' turf field, yet gentle as a lamb in her ways. A lovely woman—an' could play th' oul' tunes on th' fiddle.'

'Bella gets it from both sides, then.'

'A double dose, as ye heard th' other evenin'. When Koife plays, Roisin comes back to me, but I don't deserve her company.' William looked up, his blue eyes gray. 'In th' end, I was faithless to two women.

''t was a hard thing to reckon what my self-ish pleasures laid waste. Th' regret is like a can-cer still growin', an' no way to cure it.'

The fire smoldered; Pud snored at his feet.

'I hope this is not considered a confession,

Rev'rend, for I can't take pardon from a Protestant.'

'I'm just hearing you,' he said.

'I thank ye for that.' William sat back in the chair, stared at the fire. 'I made a right hames of it all. An' now I'm an oul' man with all my fortunes spent an' gone, an' nothin' left of th' fled days but regret.' William withdrew his handkerchief and did what he had to do, which seemed to cheer him in a small way.

'Regret an' gratitude, I have to say. Gratitude for my Anna an' her lovin' ways; Anna, who's made us a comfortable livin' out of this place. Gratitude for Koife, who herself has felt th' blade twisted deep. Aye, an' for Liam, who's put th' stamp of success on deer farmin' an' sheep raisin' like you never saw. They're eatin' our lamb an' venison all th' way to Belfast an' callin' for more.

'We always got on famous, Liam an' me, but th' last couple of years . . .' William shrugged. 'In th' end, I regret th' bit about me livin' here 'til I'm carried out in a box. It's made Liam th' bosun in what was to be his own ship.'

He wanted to ask what happened when William returned to Lough Arrow those years ago—he wanted Liam and Anna to know the truth. But how could even William know it?

Evelyn Conor was the only one truly intimate with such a truth.

'Ye need to know I dearly loved Anna's mum, but in a different way. We can't love every woman as I loved Evelyn McGuiness, or 't would kill a man, burst open 'is heart, so. Thank Jesus there's never but one like that in a man's life.

'Pray for Evelyn McGuiness, if ye'd be so kind. I've seen those as try to give up th' drink, an' 't would make ye weep to witness such persecution.'

He heard voices—Feeney, Seamus, Liam—coming quickly along the hall. Nothing so bad it couldn't be worse, he thought, seeing the look on Liam's face. Feeney and Seamus were nearly running for the door.

'Paddy called—it's Mother. Will you go, Rev'rend?'

'Cynthia,' he said.

'I'll send Anna up, please God.'

At the entrance hall, he turned and looked at William, whose face expressed a plea for them to fix things if they could.

'The stepstool, of course,' said Feeney as they crunched across the gravel to the car. "Had to happen. Bloody inevitable.' Feeney tossed his house call bag onto the backseat. 'Paddy said she wasn't drinking; she swears that's why she fell.'

'God love 'er,' said Seamus.

'They'll be wanting you home nights, Seamus. But you've been expecting that.'

'Aye.'

'What do you need me to do?' he asked Feeney.

'Be there. Just be there.'

# Twenty-six

He waited in the entrance hall, eyes closed, praying.

Voices at the end of the hall.

'Did you get her off the floor?'

'Aye.'

'Who is that person?'

'The Rev'rend Tim Kav'na,' said Seamus.

'What's he doing here?'

'Dr. Feeney asked him up.'

'Why in God's name would Feeney ask up a Protestant . . . ?'

'Th' gravity of the matter at hand, I believe, and 't was all we had. Dr. Feeney wants him riding with your mother in th' backseat, no need to get the ambulance out, he says. I'm just after ice to keep th' swellin' down.'

'Have you packed her things?'

'I'm comin' to that.'

A door slamming.

He was willing enough to be all they had, to be here, waiting.

He looked at the broad staircase rising to two floors of ruined and vacant rooms and thought how Fintan O'Donnell's own rooms abovestairs had stood vacant. He wondered whether the O'Donnells had kept a fire on the hearth in this great hall, how they found comfort in the pestering drafts of winter. He thought of the kitchen smells coming out to greet the senses of those who waited here generations ago.

Someone had said a house is a history book, his own former homeplace near Holly Springs being an example from 1853. He had often felt the temper of past occupants in the house and fields, and had, on rare occasion, smelled the cook fires of the slaves who had lived and labored there long before his arrival. Once he had heard laughter—not the ordinary sort of laughter heard from the living, but laughter from a time long vanished. It had seemed as known and familiar as the cooking smells, a palpable link to those gone before.

Feeney came up the hall, charging the air with haste.

'I need you to ride with her in the rear seat, we're taking my car. It's both wrists, and some injury to her left leg, I'm not sure what. It needs the three of us to get this done.'

He followed Feeney along the dark hall to her room. A single lamp burning; a muted television in the corner; the old Lab on a cushion next to a bed with many pillows, and Evelyn Conor sitting in a chair in a nightgown, shocked by pain.

'What's to bundle her in, Seamus?' Feeney had bound her wrists with what appeared to be kitchen towels.

Seamus brought a shawl from a chair, placed it around her shoulders; took an afghan from the foot of the bed and handed it to Feeney, who swaddled her in it, carefully tucking her arms close. She moaned, cried out.

'God above,' Seamus whispered.

'I've given her morphine for the pain. Because of the leg, we'll have to carry her. Slippers? We need slippers.'

Seamus went down on both knees, searched

along the side of the bed, brought up slippers, gently placed them on her feet. 'My God!' she said, agonized.

'Tim, go ahead of us to the car, get the rear doors open, clear the seat of my jumble; we'll bring her down. And ask Paddy to come and speak to his mother, for God's sake.'

'Where will I find him?'

'First door on th' left as we pass up th' hall,' said Seamus.

Seamus and Feeney lifted her; it was a clean maneuver. She did not cry out, but was wrenched and silent, tears shone on her face.

He passed quickly along the hall and through the open front doors and down to the Rover as the Labs came racing up the driveway from Broughadoon. He did as Feeney asked, tossed the jumble behind the rear seats, left the doors open, and headed back to the house at a pace, passing them on the steps.

'Water,' said Feeney, 'bring a bottle of water. And my bag from her bedroom, and her things in the duffel.'

He knocked; there was no answer. An angry blood beat in him and he opened the door. Paddy Conor—standing in the middle of a paneled room lined with empty bookshelves—

grim, glass in hand. It was the man in the portrait, in the flesh.

He said what Feeney had said. 'Come and
speak to your mother, for God's sake.'

He went to the kitchen and looked in the
refrigerator. No bottled water. In the corner,
an open case of it. He put a bottle in each jacket
pocket, one for the injured, one for the resident
diabetic, then crossed the hall to her bedroom,
to the open leather bag with its antiseptic breath
of injury and healing, snapped it shut, and collected it with the duffel.

Paddy waited in the hall, affronted. 'There's
Seamus and Feeney and yourself. You've no
need for me.'

'Come,' he said, meaning it.

He crawled into the backseat. Seamus stowed
the bags, closed the door, signed the cross. The
dogs sat watching. On the other side of the
Rover, Paddy peered through the closed window. 'Mother,' he said. She didn't hear or see
him.

Feeney took it easy along the rain-pocked
lane, but held nothing back on the highway to
Sligo.

In his years as a priest, he'd driven or accompanied more than a few sick and suffering to

the hospital. Each ride had been desperate in its own way, but this seemed something more— or perhaps something other.

'Reverend,' she whispered.

He knew this was not an appeal, not a conversation opener, but some way of connecting with the man who rode beside her, their bodies nearly touching, the heat of their flesh intermingled.

# Twenty-seven

He rang his cousin on Tuesday morning. He had dreaded this.

'You'll never guess,' he said.

Walter guessed. 'How did it happen?'

'Slipped in the shower, disrupted the healing. So now we wait for the swelling to go down, then on with the moon boot. I think the best thing to do is meet you at the airport, as planned.'

'How long for the swelling to go down?'

'Maybe three days. She must keep the ankle elevated. Then he wants to make sure the moon boot is doing its job, that's a couple of days, and who knows what from there out.'

'A bloody marathon for her,' said Walter. 'Doomed from the beginning, this trip.'

'We hate it for you and Katherine. I know it's been a bust.'

Somewhere near the kitchen, fiddle music; at the other end of the lodge, the faint tap of Liam's hammer.

'No bust for us. We haven't had this much fun since we were young and rich in Venice. All that to say—old and poor in Ireland isn't so bad, either. How is she?'

'Angry with herself. Depressed.' His wife was hard to put down, this had done it.

Trying to buck up to the thing, she had turned to him in the night and said, 'I must keep my wits.'

And how would he keep his? Their room had seemed strange, as if they had departed it physically and were mere vapors left behind. More than anything, he wanted her to have a good cry. Not once had she broken—not from the cupboard business, not from the pain, not from the endless aggravation. She was a dam holding back a great force. He would do the weeping for her, if he could.

With Pud, he ran along the path beside the lake, his thoughts scattered like wash blown from a line. Rooms had been canceled and penalties paid; he'd emailed Lord's Chapel, asking the prayer group to fall to. He remembered Rutherford's take on adversity: *When I find myself in the cellar of affliction, I always look about for the wine.*

He made a mental list of wines to see them through:

He would bite the bullet and memorize a poem to amuse her.

He would read O'Donnell's journal aloud—they wanted to finish it before going home.

He would somehow get her up to Catharmore. Given Monday's trek to Sligo and the general rigor of the medical exam and X-rays, she had missed her visit up the hill.

Last but not least, he would remind her that Feeney called the whole thing fortunate. 'Worse could have happened,' Feeney said, alluding to surgery. 'Count it a blessing.'

He prayed for Evelyn Conor's return home this afternoon, and smooth going for the full-time home care required by her helplessness—one wrist fractured and in a cast, one wrist sprained and in a splint—both arms immobilized, one leg severely bruised but no bones broken. ''t is a time of bones,' Feeney said of his two patients at one location. 'A regular field day.'

Bella's confession to Cynthia had been

no surprise—during Slade's three weeks at Broughadoon, she had twice gone to meet him secretly, one of those times being the morning he'd seen her on the bicycle—the morning of the uproar in the kitchen. Slade had promised to take her to Dublin to see her father, then to New York. Bella had agreed to meet Slade in the outer lane, carrying her few things in the bicycle basket. He had not come at midnight, as promised—she had waited 'til dawn. Cynthia asked if it had been Slade in the cupboard, and she said it had been—he was looking for cash, credit cards, jewelry to finance their way to New York. Bella had resisted this plan, but gave in, letting Slade know when guests would be out of their rooms. Cynthia asked about the painting, but Bella had already said too much, and begged Cynthia not to betray her to Anna and Liam.

'She's sick about the way things have gone, and terrified of the consequences if she's found out. She apologized for what happened to my ankle that night. There's more, of course, and she's dying to tell it, but I haven't gained her trust for more—not yet.'

He ran 'til sweat poured like vinegar into his eyes—he'd forgotten the bandanna.

No swans. All at Coole, he supposed.

Back at the lodge, the fiddle music again, definitely near the kitchen.

He realized he'd forgotten to see the Mass rock. His own wits had departed, and nothing left but fog in a jar.

He shucked out of his running clothes, got into a hot shower, and let it go 'til he was boiled as a squab. He decided to begin their wine flight with something definitely new vintage, which was the best he could do at the moment.

He toweled off, took it from the hook on the bathroom door, and put it on. If this wasn't worth a laugh, nothing would ever be. He rolled the sleeves down, belted the thing, made his entrance. Blast. She was sleeping.

He took Fintan's journal off the bed and sat with it in his accustomed chair, and checked her bookmark. She had left him in the dust.

He adjusted his glasses. If he couldn't entertain her, he would entertain himself.

1 October

All have said their goodbyes—A has kissed the lad & wept & Fiona has set up a squawk as if at a wake. As the rest go out to the coach I am standing with him on the front portico.

Would ye want to come again? I say.

He cannot look at me, but gazes away. He

is dressed in the black suit of his mother's making, the sleeves & trouser legs far short of their original mark.

So ye would come again, Lad?

Yis, sir. I like it here very fine, I would come & stay.

But who would nick the stitches out?

Me Da could do it, he says, sober as a cleric.

I am pleased to see how he thinks ahead.

Might you come at Christmas if we fetched you?

He looks up, his face alight as I haven't seen before.

Yis, he says.

What has been your favorite amusement at Cathair Mohr? I say.

Aoife. An' then goin' on th' call an' takin' off th' bandage an' seein' th' scab come away.

You like the sight of such a nasty thing?

I like seein' a nasty thing can be fixed back to a good thing, he says.

The bedraggled coach is waiting. I take my watch from its pocket & look at the time & feel my heart sorely weighted. I might have bidden him come on other calls, or asked Keegan to show him our rosy pig at McFee's.

Well, then, I say, & he reaches up & shakes my hand very gravely.

I watch them pass down the lane, the coach creaking beneath the additional weight of food & plunder given them by C.

I lift my hand, should the lad be looking back.

Before leaving for the airport on his previous trip to Ireland, he and Dooley had said their goodbyes at Meadowgate Creek. Dooley had avoided eye contact, was busy dropping a line with an earthworm attached. The boy didn't want to be left and he, Timothy, didn't want to leave, not at all. But the trip was doctor's orders, and the parish had raised money for the airfare. On his way along the path to the house, he had turned and lifted his hand, hoping Dooley would look up. But no, Dooley was fishing as if his life depended on it.

October
God only knows the date
Lady Balfour has sent for me with a note written in her childish hand—

This time do bring the Onion, she says, as ours are Scant this year.

The pig ready to be slaughtered. Keegan merry at the prospect & the Bride on fire to make sausages & head cheese & all the rest. I have not often felt the rich man but the prospect of our own pig filling crocks & smokehouse gives me nearly a swagger as I go about.

Except for the anticipation of the pig, I have felt a weight on me the livelong day. Something pressing at the heart's core. I seem to be waking from a long sleep & realize I have not walked my Land since stepping off its borders with the Surveyor.

I do not know its Badgers & Weasels, its Oaks & Ashes, its Berries & Brambles, nor even its mite of Bogland—not least, I have failed to put the place under watch for Poachers & have no idea what occurs within its neglected borders, though Keegan does what he can.  I have not sought different vantage points for pleasurable views nor often observed the Lough in its many changes of mood & spirit. I have but twice lifted a trout from its waters & not once explored the several Islands therein as I once thought to do. The Improvement of this demesne—however modest—coupled with our practice among the people, has greatly wearied me. I feel my mind at times full of mist, but would not confess this anywhere save in these mute pages.

While not surprised I was nonetheless dismayed when Nephew approached me for an advance of monies or other assets against his Inheritance. Though cursed with a morbid flatulence & the tendency to sloth, he is not without sufficient sensibility to make his way in the Lumber Business where he is partner. A hot anger flared in me but I made no rebuke, saying only that my Solicitor would not reckon this timely—which is the Truth.

A keeps a kettle on the Surgery hob & brews me a strong cup each afternoon. Should I demur, she tells me Missus wishes it, & thus I drink it to please them both. I found myself staring today at the top of A's head as she stooped to pick something off the floor. I saw where the hair parted from forehead to crown, a path through a dark wood, her pink scalp a living world unto itself.

My Lord & my God, have mercy upon me.

Mid–October 1862

This week past we saw near eighty patients in the Surgery & twenty-four on rounds. I asked for A's assistance throughout the week, thereby robbing C of her most valuable helper. A is like a daughter, says C who could not conceive in our many years of effort. I note here that A is a fine nurse by nature—I believe this may be her Gift from On High.

We must have more hands about Cathair Mohr & have hired on Jessie, a round lass of nineteen who throws back her head & laughs like any sailor. Tis rumored she is unafraid of work & proficient at scrubboard & iron. She will share A's small room back of the Scullery.

I was looking two days past for Uncle's early English fruit spoons in a repoussé pattern that is very handsome. As we were to have fruit compote that evening, I took C's key ring & unlocked the sideboard & found the worn Velveteen box with its small clasp. I opened it & saw the spoons were missing. As C is the only one with access to the board's key, or any key, I assumed she had the spoons in service somewhere but she said she did not.

There are certain things one grasps without head knowledge—tis the gut speaking.

I waited until Keegan was well away from the house & Fiona up to her elbows in dough. If I had seen their room crowded before, it was now so furbished with clutter & disarray that naught but a path, more a tunnel, was open through it.

The stink of the chamber pot was rife. I stepped to the dresser without hesitation, as if led there by instinct & opened the top drawer & there lay the spoons among a scramble of disheveled linens. Though I had gone looking, I was startled by the discovery, could not believe my eyes. My heart pounded like that of any thief. I slipped the spoons into my pocket & took them to C who was rightfully alarmed.

Put them back into the box, I said & let us see how things go. No, she said, let us use them as planned, in plain view. When Fiona served the table, I studied her carefully, not attempting to hide my gaze. I had set the spoons on the board where the compote would be placed. I saw or believed I saw the slightest flinching in her right shoulder as she spied them but when she turned again to the table there was nothing writ on her broad face but nonchalance.

C & I too harried to treat this pestering sore; we are managing to close our eyes to it, believing F would not have the gall to do it again, being so found out. C & A will be making a full inventory of all plate & dinner ware, even to the pots & pans & C will keep the keys with her at all times.

I have of course said nothing to Keegan & do not believe he is implicated—we will bide our time as F is after all a grand cook though slovenly in the kitchen. Further, I find the proximity of their room—to where I now sit to write—a Grievance. *Why do I so often act without thinking?* There stands the cottage with its greater comforts but The Bride of All the World wishes to be in the big house & with the servants' quarters on the top floor yet unfinished, twas the only room available to satisfy her whim.

I find the master and mistress more often pressed to satisfy the caprice of servants than the other way round.

17 October 1862

We learned yesterday why Jessie is so rotund. She is pregnant into the fifth month.

After a morning of loud weeping and hand-wringing with C, all was again calm. If she had told us, she said, we would not have taken her on. She has no home to go to as her people have disowned her and the child's father has run away to Antrim.

Ruse & subterfuge appear to be the ticket these days at Cathair Mohr, but as much to the point—when she came into the surgery seeking work, why did I not perceive that she was carrying a child? And how did C miss this?

I thought she was overly fond of the table, says C.

That alone should have been a warning, I say.

As to what we shall do in this predicament, C and I merely exchange a look—that is all we have time or energy to offer the other.

Keegan recommends a cousin as the man for overseeing the demesne. But taking his wife into account, I have had enough of Keegan's staffing the place and will go down to my Solicitor who knows town puffs & able countrymen alike.

I took Balfour's daughter a sweet when I called up with my Onion. You must thank the doctor, says Lady Balfour to the girl who is slow-witted as any tot. Balfour stands nearby, looking dour.

We've thanked the doctor well enough and bloody more, says Lady B's grinding little consort. He's built his pile upon the thanks we've given him. Balfour laughs, then, revealing teeth the color of sheep dung.

I hardly remember laughter of my own in recent times—yet this morning was able to enjoy the Medicine of mirth such as I had not done in years.

A reported to the Surgery at seven-thirty wearing a cap she had made. That she has never in her life seen a nurses cap is evident. Her version, albeit white, features a starched central peak banded at the base with bits of yellowing lace.

She goes about her work soberly, lighting the fire she laid last evening, putting the fresh linen on the table, pulling the little step stool out for the patient to clamber up.

Three anxious souls wait beyond the door.

And who is there for us this mornin', sir?' says A, bright as any penny.

Edema, Goiter, & Dyspepsia, say I.

Her laughter is generous & unaffected.

That would be Missus O'Bierne, Missus Teague an' Danny Moore's grandda, she says in her careful English.

Tis pride I am feeling for Aoife O'Leary's quick wit.

Before Edema comes in, however, I know I must say something about the cap—it is in the room with us like a whale & no one speaking of it.

Your cap! I say.

Twill make my work in the Surgery more . . . proper, she says, coloring.

She sees I am tentative. I see she is deciding between disappointment & saving face. At once she removes the cap & goes to the far table & pops it on the human skull I keep—tis a wonder to most patients, a fright to others.

The cap is a perfect foil for the vacant eyes and ancient teeth. I start laughing & cannot stop. Tears are soon running down—the Foolishness of my laughter cannot be restrained, it is contagious as any pox for A is also laughing unhindered. I then hear the answering guffaw of Pat Moore beyond the door whereupon I open the door & stick my head out & both women erupt into laughter at the sight of their country physician looking the lunatic.

Something is going out of me—I am a pustule draining poisonous matter. It is the sort of release for which one would pay money.

Laughing yet, I step out & take Missus O'Bierne's crusty ould hand & lead her into

the Surgery & there is C, standing white &
still at the door from the hall.

At the look of her, we fall instantly silent &
she turns & goes—we hear her footsteps along
the flagstones.


I do not know the date
Time it is a- flying, as the poet says

I can confess this nowhere but here. Upon
standing in the yard this morning & seeing
Fiona wring the necks of three hens, I felt
vilely ill & faint. And then came the axe &
the blood. I who have seen rivers of blood
could not bear the sight.


My days of training & practice in
Philadelphia seem as far from me as the
planets from Earth. After arriving Pa. in 1828,
there came the cholera epidemic four years
later, with 900 dead.

I remember C imploring Uncle not to
leave the house in the evenings—from the
cradle both C & I had impressed upon us a
fear of night air, to the extent we imagined it
as veritably writhing with wicked humours of
every type. But away he would go, pulling
the broad lapel of his overcoat about his
face & setting off in the carriage with his

driver, Mercy, a freed slave from Virginia. We knew we may not see him for some days, or he may appear the next morning at breakfast. No one ever showed surprise at his coming & going nor was any mention made of where he had been or might be going. Sukey knew more than the rest of us, but was as remote about Uncle's affairs as he.

And the riots—they were ever at the Riots in Pa., Negroes & Irish fighting for the same jobs, the same housing & wages—300 constables called in to quell the bloody fracases at South Street above Seventh.

Riots in '35 followed by an outbreak of typhus, & in 1849, cholera again with a death toll of 1,000.

Tis making Ireland look the safe place, said Uncle.

I remember this tonight upon the brink of Winter, & think how little prejudice was turned against Uncle for his Irish blood, & how I flourished in his shadow. 'He's not like the rest of your lot,' was said to me on several occasions. It was the first time I felt the menace of something I now erase from memory once for all.

J is a good worker & has quickly made herself useful—we cannot turn her out & so

will have a babby in the house come spring.
God knows if it is not one thing, tis a dozen
more—C again with the headache & the
Passiflora no comfort. I hardly know what is
to be done.

4 November

I have come face to face with the darkness
in myself—has it always been there & I have
chosen to look away? Or has it come upon me
solely because of the ravening hunger I must
deny? I am stalked like prey.

10 November?

Last night was black & starless & no candle
nor firelight in her chamber. Yet there seemed
a Phosphoresence in the room.

I had brought up a Compress of ice & took
it to the chaise where she lay inert as any
corpse. I stooped to apply the compress to
her forehead, but something in her spirit
rebuked me.

What is it, my love? I ask.

I am not your love, she says.

It was as if someone else had spoken.

This house is your love. The Irish poor are
your love. I am your occasional nurse.

The remark was beyond my comprehension.

I thought we shared this dream, I said at last.

I did share it, she said. I did wish to come here, I did wish to live in the little cottage with its dirt floor & red hens & I did wish to come at last to this house & enter into your private dream. But now tis like the fairies have stolen you & I am gone from your heart. I have searched for my place there, the old place I have called Home these many years but the door is closed & I fear it shall soon be locked.

I felt all the known world slipping from me. Suddenly I could no longer stand & I sat in the chair beside the chaise.

Do you want the Oil, I say, my voice nearly gone.

You touch me with the Oil but your hands no longer know me.

We are often weary, I say. It is the long hours & the many obligations . . .

I ken your needs before you know them yourself, she says. But you remember little of mine. When I speak to you, you do not hear—your mind has hidden from me. I once saw myself in your eyes but I am never there these many months.

I gave you this house, I say, for it is all I know to say.

You gave this house to the people, we but live & work here. You gave this house to Ireland as a banner for hope & courage.

I am trembling like an old man. The mist is rising in me.

You are unfair, I say.

I am a woman, she says.

The compress ices my fingers, but I can not put it to her forehead. It is a Benediction that can not yet be offered. I lay the compress on the stone sill of the window & cross myself & make a petition. The Phosphorescence continues—for a very long time I sit frozen, my breast tormented nearly beyond endurance. I know of course what I must do.

I lean close to reckon whether she is sleeping now & hear her ragged breathing—she is awake. I say her name & she stirs.

I must take something from you, I say. I hardly recognize my voice. But I vow to give you myself in return.

She turns on the chaise & in the darkness I see the milky white of her eyes opened to me.

As God is my witness, I say, I never touched her.

After a time her cold hand takes mine & we hold to each other, drawing the little warmth into ourselves.

He inserted his bookmark next to Cynthia's, sobered. He and his sleeping wife were now at the same hard place in the life of Fintan O'Donnell. He closed the journal and went into the bathroom and removed the robe.

# Twenty-eight

The email sailed in under the door as he dressed for dinner.

<Dear Fr Tim,

<I cannot BELIEVE you emailed Lord's Chapel for prayer without going through me. You know you do not have to go direct to ANYBODY when I can go direct FOR you. I cannot believe you did not ask me to pray for Cynthia and that this request had to come from a person I don't even KNOW at LC. There are way too many people NOBODY knows down there, you have to

go over to the PRESBYTERIANS to find
somebody you ever laid eyes on. It's all the
DEVELOPMENT our fancy schmancy
Mayor is so crazy about, which is what we
get for not appreciating Esther Cunningham
who practically gave her LIFE to keep out
the HORDES.

<Emma

<P. S. The Waterford pattern I like is
LISMORE>

He passed the email to her and waited.

There! Laughter unhindered. He would hug
Emma Newland's neck when he got home. As
for what he'd say about the absence of a $300
vase, shipping not included, he would cross
that bridge when he got to it.

'Will you be all right, then?' he asked. She
was watching an Irish game show from her
wing chair, obediently elevating the Historic
Ankle.

'Go and be as the butterfly,' she said, waving
him off.

He stepped out to the hall, closed the door
behind him, opened it again. 'No fair reading
the journal ahead of me, Kav'na.'

In the library, Anna introduced a merry

party of Sweeneys and the woman who writes books—tall, with a cloud of graying hair, accompanied by her ten-year-old niece, who had learned Gaelic for the trip.

'*Gaelic?*' he said, astonished.

'Only enough to get by,' said Emily.

The sunshine had returned to Broughadoon. When Maureen came round with a tray of cheese biscuits, he kissed her on both cheeks.

'And how did you find your aunt?'

'Ninety-four she is, with every tooth her own an' Mass twice a day. I took me paintin' along, 'twas seen by th' half of Ballina.'

'Cynthia will be happy you're home.'

'I'll be takin' up her dinner. I can hardly turn my back on th' poor darlin' for th' trouble she's into.'

William sported a tie he hadn't seen; Liam was his personable self, chatting up the newbies, delivering drinks. Feast or famine, this lodging business—a full house was a very good thing.

He was spooning up the last of his sugar-free afters when Seamus called. Into the kitchen and the gargle of Dishwasher #1.

'Mrs. Conor is askin' you up tomorrow at eleven.'

'What's that?'

'Mrs. Conor. She's askin' for you.'

He was surprised. They had spoken but once on the night ride to Sligo. He had said, 'I'm praying for you.' White with pain, she had snapped at him: 'Do as you please.'

'I'll be there.'

'Dr. Feeney's on his way down, said he'd meet you at th' front hall, if you'd be so kind.'

'How is she?'

'Th' tremors an' all th' rest. 't is killin' me to see it.'

'Let the nurses do the seeing,' he said. 'Your being there is enough, I'm sure it's a comfort to her.'

'So.' Seamus sounded desolate in that desolate house.

'Anything I can do tonight?' he asked.

'Ye could say a bit of a prayer for us.'

He went to the library, realizing that in a way he couldn't understand, it was killing him, too. He felt the force of something coming down, falling to pieces.

When the Rover wheeled in, he was waiting at the door.

'She's still determined to go off th' drink,' said Feeney. 'This is serious business for someone her age; she could die, I told her that. She said she was dying anyway—she wants to go through with it.'

Feeney removed his jacket, hung it on an antler.

'But Paddy must be out of the house. They drink together, he'll figure a way to get it to her. So I've asked him to leave.'

'What did he say to that?'

'He's scared out of his wits by the screaming, the look of her in such a fix. He's willing to bail out and wants to make it quick. God knows I dreaded routing the man from his own house, but it's done.'

They walked into the library, still empty of guests. The sound of laughter from the dining room.

'I managed to get two of the best nurses in Sligo. Cassie Fletcher is very competent, she cared for her old father for some years. He did the same thing—dried out at home at a late age—so she's familiar with the backside of Gehenna. She'll live in, with Eileen as relief. As to Eileen, she's quick to carry through, and good-hearted.'

Feeney went to the fire, though the night was warm. 'I'll do all in my power to keep her comfortable, Tim. The odds look impossible, but I'm going to believe it can work.'

'I'll believe it with you.'

'She's tough. Very tough. Maybe she can do it. God knows, I hope so. 'Tis dangerous business—the seizures, for one thing, if it comes to that. The tremoring has already begun, the rapid heart rate, the nausea. Then there's the hematoma—I don't think you knew. The swelling is massive, half the size of her leg.'

He'd made hospital rounds in Mitford for roughly twenty years; he was familiar with the hell of hematoma.

'What was her general condition before this happened?'

'Nutritionally deprived—the usual in this case. Dehydration. A compromised immune system which begs respiratory infection. So, she started low and this will drive her lower.'

'The detox—how does it usually progress?'

'Depending on the length and severity of the addiction, tremoring and nausea, then blinding headaches, heavy sweats, tactile hallucinations—usually itching, as if bugs were crawling on the skin. In the end stages, it all escalates to delirium tremens. Mother of God, we must pray against that.'

Ash lifted from the turf, vanished up the chimney like moths.

'Let's say it goes better than expected. How long to get clean?'

'Three, maybe four weeks. After that, she'll be completely wiped for a few months until we get her weight up.'

Liam was right about the Sisyphus business.

'All that said'—Feeney drew in his breath—'there's a bright side. It wasn't a broken hip, which requires surgery and begs the blood clot. And with two disabled arms and a leg, she has no recourse to the gin.

'I'm only twenty minutes away in an emergency, and of course I'll stop by Catharmore every evening. There's no one waiting for me at home but the old housekeeper, who slips in to watch my telly if I'm running late.'

'Flat-screen, I'm guessing.'

'Forty-two inches.' The doctor laughed, ironic, walked away from the fire. 'I must speak with Liam tonight about the seriousness of this. Not looking forward to it.'

Blow upon blow for Liam. For everyone, really.

'Seamus says she wants you up there in the morning?'

'Aye,' he said.

Feeney shook his hand. '*Bail ó Dhia ort*,' said Feeney. 'The blessing of God on you.'

He had no capacity for laughter and small talk. When the new crowd flooded into the library, he went back to the room.

'Evelyn Conor asked me up tomorrow at eleven.'

'That's good. Thank heaven.'

He emptied his pocket onto the dresser top, in view of Ben Bulben. 'How about a little after-dinner entertainment?'

'You've learned a poem.'

'I have not. I've merely planned to learn a poem. Let's see what Fintan is up to, poor devil.'

'I thought his vow to Caitlin very moving.'

'I agree. A few entries back, he referred to what he called *these mute pages*. Not so mute, I'd say.'

'Do you ever?'

'Ever what?'

'Long for someone else?'

'Good grief, woman, who would I long for?'

'Really?'

'Really.'

'Good,' she said. 'I would kill you.'

He switched on the avid bulb, found the bookmarks, opened the skim of a man's life.

9 November 1863

I have never felt such despair—The knife I thrust to the hilt in my own heart is no recompense for the two hearts I have torn asunder.

Tis little more than first light as I walk out this morning into a sullen rain & cross the yard to the carriage house. Keegan gives me a look as he hitches Adam to the traces. He does not speak—I know at once the nature of his surly mood. So closely have we worked together that I often ken his thoughts before he realizes them himself. Tis a blow to find he thinks so little of whatever character I may possess.

I do not want him helping her into the carriage—he does not deserve the privilege. I will drive to the rear door & help her up myself, for all that.

Lay a fire in the Surgery & bedchambers, I say to him.

He stands gawping at me.

Now, I say.

He gives me a fierce look—I could crack him with the whip for his bloody insolence.

I draw the carriage as close to the door as I am able & see Caitlin & Aoife waiting inside the hall. C's face is drawn with suffering. Aoife is wearing the thin dress she wore when she came to us. The Bride of the World stands further back, looking as contemptuous as her husband. I am judged & will be judged, by a household gone from sweet temper to sour suspicion.

There is nothing in her young face to betray her feelings, she who so naturally displays feeling of every agreeable kind. I harden my heart against the torment which we all feel so keenly, enough to break us if we but let it.

I stand down & offer my hand as any civilized being would do & she takes it & climbs barefoot into the carriage & I hoist up her stool & the one bag with her two frocks & the shoes from her father's last—she will not take more, not even the coat I had made for her in Dublin.

There are no useless parting words cried from the hall, no masking chatter.

We drive for some time without speaking—she clutches the stool in her lap, as for comfort.

I never touched you, I say.

You never did, no.

She is different today, even her dark hair is done up in a way I have not seen. I had all along thought her to be a lass, but she is a woman today with a woman's face set toward the eye of the storm.

I am wicked, I say.

You are not wicked, she says. You are good.

I feel the tears on my face.

My father will be angry with me for failing.

Twas I who failed. You must never think you failed.

Something I done . . . did, she says, I don't know what.

You did nothing wrong. You were of the greatest help to us. We could hardly have made it without you.

I thought of her lighting the lamps in the evening, the clear, clean bell of the globe shining, the flame finding its being in the trimmed wick.

I should like to go to school & become a Physician, she says.

I am astonished & pleased, but the Truth must be told.

A woman can't become a Physician, I say.

She turns her head & looks at me for the first time. Her green eyes blaze. That is wicked, she says.

Yes.

She is right, of course. There is so much I would tell her, but none of it will do.

I believe in you, I say at last. There is a terrible longing to speak her name & I know at that moment I will never speak it again.

Aoife, I say.

My God, my God, I cry, silent as a stone.


What's she done to put ye off, that back she comes as spoiled goods?

Aoife has gone inside & I am standing in a misting rain with O'Leary the Shoemaker, chickens pecking about our feet.

She has done nothing wrong, I say. She is a fine worker & considerate of all.

Was she a liar, then, or a thief? I'll give her a flaying she'll not forget.

Please understand—she has done nothing wrong. I nearly shout these words. She has been the best of helpers, even assisting us in the Surgery. This is a grave loss to our household.

O'Leary's wife stands in the doorway, a

beaten look about her. The sisters gather in
the yard, one holding a baby & shielding it
with her apron from the rain.

Then why in God's name are ye bringin'
her back to make a laughin' stock of the
O'Learys? His voice is rising, his face red as a
poker. Has your man Keegan been at her?

My God, no! For God's sake, we cared for
her like our own daughter, she comes back to
you better than she went for all she's learned
of housekeeping & proper English.

I despise this pompous remark, as if I
were trying to sell him an improved hair
comb.

Twas a gentleman's agreement we had, says
he. Twas a livin' for our family that ye had
her sarvice in your fine house. These days
there's naught but a tap here an' a heel there.
You claim she works hard & don't lie nor
steal, yet back she comes like a lame horse. Tis
only right ye declare th' reason for bringin'
her back—Name her offense, or God strike ye
blind!

There is no reason I can cite aloud to any
man, & especially an hysterical Irish farmer. I
hand him the envelope, heavy with coins. He
hesitates before he takes it, as if by restraint he

might gain pride in negotiating this
monstrous affair. He weighs the payload in his
hand, looking me in the eye.

There will be more where that came from,
I say, sick to death. I will look for her a place
hereabout.

There is no place hereabout but Balfour's &
I would not fob her off to a stump of maggots
such as that.

Indeed, I say. I shall look further abroad.

I turn to go, for the rain is getting up &
scattering chickens & sisters inside.

Could ye have a look at th' Missus before
ye take leave, then, doctor? He pronounces
the word doctor with violent distaste.

What's the trouble I say.

From th' last babby, he says, as angry as if I
had caused the wound to his wife.

I take my bag from the carriage &
drenched as any cur pass into the cabin where
those crowding the doorway move apart,
taciturn & dubious. Aoife is sitting by the
cold hearth on the little stool, sobbing, her
head in her hands.

Tis a strange thing I do. I stop on the way
home at Rose McFee.

Still damp as plaster, I remove my hat &
duck under her sill to the one room.

She is seated at the fire in one of her two
chairs & is smoking a pipe. I seen ye go by
with th' lass, she says.

Rose, I say. As God is my witness, I never
touched her.

Aye, she says. I believe ye.

I am judged, I say, for what I did not do
nor ever would do.

She gestures to the other chair at the
hearth & I sit.

Ye couldn't have kept her, then?

No.

The missus.

Yes. And myself frightened by something
wicked in me that I never knew before, I say.
I am enfeebled, as if my very blood were
being let into a bucket.

Rose, I say, what shall I do?

I am asking a toothless crone who cannot
read nor write to tell me how to go forward, I
am that weak & stupefied.

Keep doin' what ye've been doin'—healin'
th' sick & payin' y'r dues to God above an'
nobody else.

A small thing, her fire with its little
heart & heat, but nonetheless I am grateful.

30 November 1863

A stinging cold

C is at her dressing table in nightclothes &
a shawl—I sit on the bench at the foot of
her bed, wondering why I have come. Her
hairbrush cleaves streaks of gray mingled
with the old familiar chestnut. I have a
moment's quick desire to go to her & perform
the nightly liturgy of brushing, but I do
nothing.

If you should die & I am left
behind . . . she says, speaking to me in the
mirror.

My heart has the dull feeling at this.

Cathair Mohr would be left to Padraigin,
she says.

Yes, I say, again feeling regret at this
reckless decision & further regret for having
not rectified it in some way.

And I would be put out, she says.

Even two years ago, we had thought to live
forever. Not so, now. How much I have
learned.

Perhaps not, I think not—if you wished to
stay on.

If Padraigin were the master of Cathair
Mohr, she says, I would not wish to stay on.

You know you will have funds to keep

you, I say. You might take a flat in Dublin or
go to your sister in Roscommon.

The few times I have considered such a
future, I think of her in Roscommon, in her
older sister's cottage with its large garden &
many geese & a window seat where she might
read & be happy.

She lays the brush on the table & is quiet
for a time. I wish to put my arms about her &
protect her from such thoughts as these, but I
hold myself away.

She bows her head into her hands & covers
her face as if shutting out the world.

The boy, the lad, I say. He wants to
become a Surgeon.

She doesn't speak.

His father, I say, will drink himself to
death before it's over, according to Padraigin's
wife.

I am trying to work something out in my
mind, though I am not certain what. I get
up & walk about the room, uneasy, feeling the
weight of it all, all at once—the diminishment
of our American investments due to the War
in the States—the extremes of our practice in
a region so remote—the enormous effort of
everything, even to buying breeding stock

this morning. I have not been in some time to the Mass Rock, I have let the world come in upon me & now it is coming in upon Caitlin.

Christmas is nigh, I say. Shall we send Keegan for the lad?

She takes the brush in hand once more & looks at me in the mirror.

Send word to Padraigin, she says, that the rooms they used are under repair—we can take only Eunan. Tis true, for I am having the wallpaper put up in those rooms.

I say nothing of the probable expense, as she never spends a bob on anything, including herself.

We'll have a fine Christmas, I say, feigning enthusiasm. Roast geese & bacon & sausages of our own & the Port that came over from Uncle.

And garlands of holly, she says, for the stair rails. And a fire in the front hall & a Yule log.

She turns on the bench & fixes me in her gaze & then she smiles. I cannot reckon the last time I saw her smile. The air is suddenly quickened & my heart roused from its long stupor—the thought of Christmas becomes real & beautiful to me.

Your sister, I say, would she come?

Fintan! Oh, yes, I think she would. What a
wonderful idea. And your brother Michael—
would he come?

He doesn't get about, I say, without
Kathleen.

But we shall have your niece, too, of
course. How gay it will be!

The wallpaper, I say.

We shall delay it til spring.

And beds! I say, as we have none but
makeshift for those quarters.

She thinks & soon says, O'Hara the casket
maker!

Of course! O'Hara makes beds for the
dead & the living. I determine to see O'Hara
tomorrow & post a letter to Michael & one to
Padraigin to tell him Keegan is coming.

We must do something for the lad,
I say, something grand. A pony or such as
that, shall we?

She is laughing. Oh, yes, she says, Yes!
And Father Dominic, as well, we must have
him out for the Christmas feast.

I move quickly about the room to disguise
the trembling which comes from a terrible
gladness & desire. I step to the window &
look away to the lough bleached by a Winter
moon & know I can no longer bear to contain

such strong feeling. I go to her & lean down
& kiss her yielding mouth & sink to my knees
overcome with gratitude. I hold to her & we
weep like children with a joy never before
known to us.

Some time in the night, he dreamed of a
pony.

# Twenty-nine

'Cassie Fletcher,' she said, extending her hand.

'Tim Kav'na,' he said, taking it.

She eyed his collar. 'Father or rev'rend?'

'Father in the States, reverend here. Dr. Feeney says you're the one for the job.'

'I've done th' same for my da and a few others.'

He liked this bony, wryly attractive woman with the dry palm and fierce handshake.

'I hope you don't mind th' look of a hematoma,' she said. 'We must keep the covers off it.'

'I've seen a few.'

'She rested well enough last night, but the

pain is fierce even with th' meds. She's after seein' you but it musn't be long, Rev'rend.'

'I won't stay.'

'She's had a bad go, comin' home only yesterday from hospital an' all.'

'Of course.'

'Just a warnin'—the tremors have begun and th' nausea. There's worse ahead but we count our blessings today.'

She led him by Paddy's closed door, and into the darkened room.

The sight of her was jarring—the splint, the cast, the grossly swollen leg with its hellish purpling, the anguished plea in a face grave with shock.

The old Lab came to him and sniffed his pant leg.

'Mrs. Conor.' He wanted to touch her, it was instinctive, he always touched the suffering, but her injuries were many. He stooped and scratched Cuch behind the ear.

'Is it you, then, Rev'rend?' Her voice a vapor.

'It's Tim Kav'na, yes.' He pulled the chair close to the bed, sat down, saw the tremoring in her fingers where cast and splint gave way.

She did not look at him, but stared at the ceiling. 'I have one question and one only.'

'Yes, ma'am.'

'Can I do this?'

'You can do this,' he said. 'With God's help.'

'I do not seek nor expect help from God. Keep him out of it. Answer me. Can I do this?'

'As for keeping God out of it, you're asking the wrong person. With that in mind, however, my answer is yes. You can do this.'

'Are you lying to make me feel cozy, as they say?'

'I don't believe anything could make you feel cozy just now, least of all a lie.'

She flinched, said something in Irish, licked her dry lips. 'Tis a brutal punishment being unable to lift one's arms, unable to dress oneself. One must do one's business in a pan and shout for another to scratch one's nose.

'Nor is there anybody to comb my hair in a sensible fashion. Think about it, Reverend, and tell me how you would feel in such a case.'

'With so little to comb, Mrs. Conor, I'm hardly the one to ask.'

She closed her eyes against him. 'You're a difficult man.'

'You're a difficult woman, enormously stubborn, from all I've observed, and full of grit— just two of many reasons I believe you have what it takes to do this.'

She caught her breath. 'A scalding pain,' she said. 'My God.' Sweat shone on her face.

He stood to leave, whatever professional poise he had, shaken.

'Water,' she said.

A glass of water with its bent straw was on the bed table. His father, his mother, his Grandpa Yancey, his grandmother, all had sought the bent straw in their suffering. He held the straw to her lips, she sucked, and nodded it away.

'One glass of gin and 't would be over, this wretched nausea and trembling like an ould woman—they say it's the instant cure . . .'

Her unbound hair was dark against the pillow, the streak of silver more startling than he remembered. She was panting now, her words hard-won.

'. . . but I thought to combine all the torment into one living hell. One doesn't wait for sunshine and roses to do a hard thing, Reverend. I know how to suffer; I have suffered all my life. Life is but one long suffering.'

'Sometimes we grow too fond of our suffering,' he said. 'We count it too dear and it becomes exquisite, the holy of holies.'

'Answer me again.'

He met the pale ferocity of her gaze, measured his words. 'You can do this.'

Fletcher was waiting near the door. 'You're white as any sheet,' she said, raising an eyebrow.

'Scary business.'

'Oh, aye. Tell me about it. But that's nothin'. That's your comedy show you just had, compared to what we'll see this evenin'.'

'I wouldn't have your job.'

She raised the other eyebrow, grinned. 'Nor would I have yours, Rev'rend, believe me. Not with all th' antics your Church is up to in th' States.'

That was his laugh for the day.

Seamus was waiting in the kitchen.

'I spoke hard to her, Seamus.'

'Joseph an' Mary,' said Seamus, stung by this.

'I don't know why, exactly.'

'What did ye say, for all that?'

'I told her she was stubborn, enormously stubborn.'

'Aye, an' you told th' God's truth, it's just that your timin' was off.'

At Broughadoon, he changed clothes, ran along the lake path, but no time for the Mass rock expedition. Back at the lodge, he shared a late lunch with Cynthia, their bed a picnic blanket.

He gave her the full report from Catharmore. 'Your turn now,' he said. 'Tell me everything.'

'I've been thinking how we'll never have this time again, that it's come to us as a gift, though maybe we don't know how to open it.'

'I think we've opened it and we're unsure of the contents,' he said.

She laughed, spooned crème fraîche into her bowl of fruit.

'You're an amazing woman, Kav'na. But I worry about you. No tears, no lashing out at the unfairness of life. You're a better man than I am.'

'Oh, but I did go nuts, Timothy, the day you and Liam went to the lough I completely lost it, but there was no pleasure in it. Remember me, sweetheart? I'm the girl who tried to take her own life. Since then, life has looked pretty good—I've learned that, if nothing else. Besides, I'll probably never do this again, loll about like the queen of the Nile. I've surrendered to it; it is what it is. I can't even apologize anymore, to you or anyone else.'

'That's an achievement.'

'And I'm not sorry at all to miss days of popping in and out of hotels, packing and unpacking.'

'It's the long confinement I worry about. You're not the woman for it.'

'I have company all the time. Anna, Bella, and now Maureen, our honey in the rock, and Irish poets from the sixth century to Seamus Heaney—*Between my fingers and my thumb, the squat pen rests . . .*'

'That's everything you have to tell me?'

'And there's the wonderful view of the lough and the dear old beeches for company, and think of all the sleep I'm getting.'

'Yes, but is that everything?'

'As soon as we get home, I'm going to start another book.'

He took her hand and kissed it.

'That's my girl,' he said.

When he delivered the tray to the kitchen, he heard the fiddle. Close by, he thought, listening. In the lodge. Yes. The music was coming from Ibiza.

He went up to the library and rifled through a stack of magazines. A cover feature on the Irish rose garden. Worth a look. He wondered about his own roses in their double-dug beds at the yellow house, and the many he had planted at Lord's Chapel. What havoc had the beetles wrought? And the black spot? Had Mitford gotten enough rain?

'I don't need to know,' he said aloud.

'I beg your pardon?'

He turned around and looked behind him. It was the writer with the cloud of hair, hidden by the chair wing. He saw a lap with a book in it, her feet in the odd shoes.

'Sorry,' he said, embarrassed. 'I've been driven to talking to myself.'

'And what drove you there?' she asked.

'Ease and indolence. I've done next to nothing for days on end!'

'I should like very much to be driven somewhere, anywhere, by Ease and Indolence rather than Stress and Striving. I'm just off a book tour. A grueling business.'

'I'm sure. Mystery? Romance?'

'Both. Romance is, after all, a mystery.'

'I'll say.'

He wondered if he should get up and go around where they could talk face-to-face. But he rather liked looking at roses climbing a stone wall in Kerry while speaking with someone he couldn't see.

'Is that Tim, the clergyman?' The sound of pages turning.

'It is. And is that Lorna Doolin, Irish-American from Boston, born in Houston?'

'The very same.'

'Your niece is a wonder.'

'Honor student. Plays the harp. Raises corgis. Now busy cataloging the flora and fauna of Lough Arrow.'

'Good gracious!'

'You're from the South.'

'Mississippi. My wife is from Massachusetts.'

'Do you like being married to a Yankee?'

'I do,' he said. 'This particular Yankee, anyway.'

'I married a Yankee once.'

'Aha. Here to do some fishing?'

'Heavens, no. Here to escape the rigors of reading my reviews. They're mixed, to say the least. Are you a fisherman?'

'Never got the hang of it.'

'I must take my niece out tomorrow with a ghillie—she has the most insatiable curiosity. I, of course, shall be entirely out of my element. All I've ever done is muck about in words— except for two years of managing an inn in New Hampshire. If you ever wish to give your-self a bad back, irritable colon, and possibly a stroke, well, then, manage an inn. I'm off for a walk.'

He heard her close the book, lay it on the table. 'It's been lovely seeing you—in a manner of speaking.'

'Yes, yes, very pleasant.' He stood, hoping to shake her hand or something civil, but she was already across the room and entering the stair hall.

Catharmore's complaints were writ large on every face at Broughadoon—Anna, Liam, Maureen, Bella, William, all were quiet as they went about their tasks in the evening. Liam was sobered yet again.

In a move, he presumed, to restore jollity to the Broughadoon board, Anna seated all guests together at dinner: the three generations of Sweeneys, the author, the niece, and himself. But he was the sore thumb, unable to withdraw his thoughts from the family's concerns. He realized he didn't feel like a guest anymore. He left the table before dessert orders were taken, and went into the kitchen.

'May I give a hand?'

'Ye're an oul' dote!' said Maureen, as if she'd been expecting him. 'Ye could help with unloadin' th' dishwashers, as the next course gives us another load.'

Anna looked up from arranging the dessert tray. ''t would be a *féirin*,' she said.

No one was pushing him out, or requiring him to remain a guest. Yet every string was taut, he could feel it.

Liam jiggled something in a pan on the Aga. 'I'm finishin' the dining room paint job tomorrow, if you'd care to join me. Around noon, if you're about. An hour or so, an' it's done.'

'I'm in,' he said.

Out there was the world, in here was something better.

At two-thirty in the morning, the knock came. He knew without being told.

'I'll be right down.'

He dressed in the bathroom, and picked up his prayer book on the way to the door.

'Stay,' he said to Pud.

# Thirty

'I pray th' worst is over—for th' night, anyway.'

A barefoot Fletcher appeared in the hall, a wraith in a white nightgown. 'She's burned our ears off shouting at God, givin' him th' devil if I ever heard it. I was lookin' for lightning to strike th' place.'

'What can I do?'

'Eileen's with her, an' Seamus is up if you'd like tea. I'm telling you, Rev'rend, even with th' lorazepam, her mind is a steel trap, I've never seen its equal in an old lady.' The nurse drew her hands through her hair, looked at her night-dress, her bare feet. 'Excuse my getup; round here, we must hit th' floor runnin'.'

'Liam said I was wanted. Has she asked for me?'

'She's been askin' for you, yes, we hated to rout you at such an hour.'

'No rest for the wicked, as we say back home. Perfectly fine. Paddy?'

'Dr. Feeney packed him off drunk as a lord an' blubberin' like a babby. Some gosser from Jack Kennedy's came for him.'

'Blubbering because he didn't want to leave?'

'Oh, no, he wanted to leave, for all that, I don't know why he was blubberin'. Th' drink does that with some, you know.'

'Dublin?'

'That's th' plan.'

'Anything else going on?'

'Until a bit ago, it was weeping an' gnashin' of teeth like in th' book of Revelation—my uncle told me all about the end times, which he shouldn't have done as I was a nervous child. Talkin' out of her head, calling for her mum an' sisters enough to break your heart. And God above, th' screamin' she can do. It elevates th' pain, but she does it anyway, to see how much she can dish out to herself.'

'How are you getting on?'

'Even after what I went through with my

father, it still scares th' daylights out of me. 't is
like the devil himself gets loose. But I'm fine,
I'm keepin' up. Eileen goes on short hours
soon, her brother's in a bad way; I'll be th' one-
armed paper hanger for a time.'

'Is she sleeping?'

'She slept for a bit after wearin' herself out,
but she's awake now, has something to ask you
that's agitating her. If you don't mind, Rev'rend,
I'll just try an' catch a wink, as God knows I've
had none. There's Eileen if you need her, and
Seamus. Overlook th' smell, we got a bite
down her an' back it came an' more. We'll air
out tomorrow.'

A single lamp burning. Eileen in a chair by
the door, Cuch sleeping. He stepped into the
room.

'Eileen.'

'Yes, mum?'

'You may leave.'

The nurse left at once.

'Reverend.'

'Yes, Mrs. Conor. I'm here.' The desperate panting; her reddened fingers thick with
swelling.

'Call me Evelyn. Everything must be sim-
plified now.'

The ghastly leg uncovered. He pulled the chair up and leaned close, as if offering fire to a cold hearth.

'You can do this,' he said.

He was gripped by the look of her, as if she were going away to nothing, would be but an impression on the pillow the next time he came. And yet her will was there, he felt the iron of it.

'I have a question,' she said.

'I'm listening.'

'Something happened tonight.' Her finger movement rapid. 'After all the promises to myself that I could do this, I felt I couldn't bear it, after all. The agony was overcoming; I knew I was dying. I wanted to die. If I could be said ever to pray, then I prayed I would die.

'But I didn't wish to pass until I told God what monstrous evil he is and how he had fooled so many but not myself, not Evelyn Mc-Guiness, no, he could not mock me. I emptied myself of my last strength—with everything in me I obliterated him, I erased him from the heavens.'

Her quick breath stirring the sour air.

'There was nothing left then of either of us, I thought I had died. But I had not died, as you see. What I thought was death was a peace such as I've never felt or believed possible. It was completely strange to me, and cannot be explained. I knew it had nothing to do with God, for God was dead, I had killed him in retribution for the many killings he has laid upon me. The peace did not pass quickly, as I believed it might. I thought, if this is dying, then I am not afraid to die.'

'Don't die,' he said, simply.

'There's no reason to live. I only wished to live as proof I couldn't be made to die.'

'You must rest, Evelyn. You must give yourself time to heal.'

She licked her dry lips. 'I cannot rest.'

'Is the peace still with you?'

'No. I did not deserve it, and it left me.' Tears.

He sat, head down, feeling called out of himself, beyond his powers.

'Water,' he said, taking up the glass and bending the straw to her lips. She sucked.

'So sick,' she said, turning away.

He took a cotton-tipped stick from the jar and opened the lip balm and dressed the tip. 'Let me,' he said.

She opened her eyes to him, and he succored

her lips as he had done for his mother. She was too frail to wrack herself like this, it was suicidal.

He stepped to the door to call Eileen, remembering for some reason his mother's eyelids in death, how thin they seemed, and blue, like the wings of a moth. She had died at home, whispering that the garden gates were closed.

He turned and looked back and saw that she had gone to sleep, her mouth open in the awful gasping.

*Wait,* he wanted to say, *you had a question.* He went to her bed and fell to his knees and with his own last strength did what he could in the face of the impossible.

# Thirty-one

Without opening his eyes, he reached for his watch on the bed table, squinted at it. Nine o'clock. Unbelievable. He hadn't slept 'til nine o'clock since when? Ever. He felt robbed, somehow.

There she sat in a chair by the bed as he had done at Catharmore.

'Good grief, woman, why did you let me sleep the day away?'

'I was painting you, that's why.'

'Painting me?'

She thrust the damp portrait in front of him. He sat up, put on his glasses.

'Why did you paint me with my mouth open?'

'Because it *was* open, of course.'

'No fair.'

'It was only *slightly* open.'

'Slightly? It looks like Linville Caverns. You can practically see a stalactite.'

'I'm not after mouths and noses and eyes and ears, it's the *likeness* one strives to catch. This is a marvelous *likeness*, Timothy—admit it.'

'I hardly ever see myself in profile, so I can't vouch for it.'

'Oh, please,' she said, disgusted. 'I'm trying to *occupy* myself. You were the only person in the room.'

'We'll tack it to a fence post in the garden, to keep out the crows.'

'Wretch,' she said. 'What are you doing today?'

'I'll bring up breakfast if they'll still make it for us.'

'Maureen brought coffee at eight, you were sleeping like a bear cub. I can afford to miss a meal.'

'Or I could carry you down.' He didn't know how, but he would give it a shot. 'You need to get out of here.'

'True. But what can I do? Possibly two more days of elevating, then the moon boot and I can start the old hobble . . .'

'With great caution, Feeney said.'

'. . . on the crutches.'

'And then we'll soon be home.' A strange feeling as he said it. Weeks in Holly Springs and at Henry's bedside in Memphis, and nearly two weeks now in Ireland. Home seemed lost in a mist.

She gave him the Worried Look. 'Do you think it's good to be called out like that, in the middle of the night?'

'Of course it's good,' he snapped. 'Sorry. Yes. It's good.' *I'm all they have,* he wanted to say. 'You're still keen to finish the journal?'

'Definitely.'

He pulled a knit shirt from the armoire, laid it on the bed. 'Time's winged chariot is at our backs.'

He gulped the water on his bed table. 'I need coffee. And a bite of something. Juice, too; I need juice. Anything I can bring you?'

'Surprise me.'

'Done.'

'Your insulin.'

'Right. When I come back, we'll hit Fintan a good lick, then I'll help Liam with the paint job and have a run in the afternoon. What's going on with Bella?'

'She's very winsome, really, and bent, of

course, on persecuting herself over what she's hiding. I do love her, Timothy.'

'Remember that Feeney's stopping by to have a look at you this evening.' He had a look himself—the swelling seemed somewhat diminished. Enough, he thought, enough of this.

In the bathroom, he gave himself the shot, removed his trousers from the doorknob where he'd hung them at nearly four this morning.

'How was it at Catharmore?'

He tried to find a way of condensing it for her, for himself, but he had no words for how it was.

'Later,' he said.

Feeling strangely off-kilter as he went downstairs, he shook his head as if to clear it. Sleeping 'til nine. He was an orderly creature, liking things to go according to custom, to habit. He liked a crease in his jeans, so be it.

And the dream of Henry, of looking into a bathroom mirror while shaving and seeing Henry's face. It was his own reflection, he knew, yet it was Henry's face in dark contrast to the white shaving foam. So he, Timothy, was actually a black man? How had he kept this knowledge from himself these many years? What did it mean and how was he to go forward? Was he both Henry and himself in one, or had he become Henry altogether? He felt the fear rising in him, leaned closer to the mirror, looked into his brother's eyes. Why had no one mentioned this, made him see it? In the dream, something broke in him and he wept, and then the smell of coffee, and the notion that Peggy must be perking it on the stove.

Anna also had the Worried Look—it was going around.

'How did you rest?' she asked.

'Well enough,' he said.

'I'm sorry you were called out.'

'A hard night.'

'Yes.'

'Not for me, for her.'

*Will you go up?* he wanted to say. *Will you forgive her and go up to her?* But he said nothing.

Back in the room with the tray, sitting in his accustomed chair, he realized a certain contentment, after all. The coffee hot and strong, the juice sweet and cold, their breakfast modest and good. And at least for now, their room a refuge, not a confinement.

They read together the *Venite, exultemus Domino*, prayed for those at home and those in the two households of this place and time.

She took the journal into her lap, then, and read to him, both of them happy in whatever way they could summon.

8th Day of Advent 1862
Frigid

Adam & Ltl Dorrit getting their Winter corn & through C's insistence, each a blanket into the bargain

I must wonder to whom Uncle's generosity would incline. To the Union would be my thinking, & even Sukey, formerly a slave, would place her allegiance there. On those days when C & I wish to be serving in Philadel we look about us & know we have undertaken the right course.

Rose McFee's infant double-great-grandtr stillborn, though we did all we could. When I passed the long mirror this morning, I was astonished to glimpse my father looking back. I felt an instant's joy at seeing him, then realized the truth.

The lad arriving ten days hence— Michael & Kathleen the following week by train.

The Bride is set upon producing the finest Christmas Feast of her fortysome

years tho we have yesterday reduced her
allotment for Provisions. She gives me a
Warring look & says she has made do all
her life, twill be nothing new, & if she is
carried to the grave for the extra work
required to stretch this miserly sum, she
will do it nonetheless as a matter of
personal pride—end of sermon.

C said in November that Padraigin
would want money for the lending of his
sister-in-law's son. He would not put it
that way, C said, but would somehow
seize this opportunity which he has
regrettably done. Three-hundred pounds
he's asking, desperate was his word, for a
debt owing on his business.

If you do not send the money, C says, I
believe he will not send the lad.

I considered offering less but this
smacks of playing cheap with a human
soul. Indeed it is small payment for the
pleasurable company of a lad who daily
entertains my thoughts.

C insists that the wallpapering can wait.
The time has come when we cannot have
everything we wish whereas with Uncle
we might have had wallpaper & the lad's
visit, together. These days we must make

choices, a reasonable thing in this life
when so many must choose between
filling their bellies or the bellies of their
children, between meat or broth, between
one room or none.

9 December
A bitter evening with smoking turf due to
heavy winds
    My hand trembles to write that I have
been to the Mass Rock in a falling snow
& received what I believe to be a message
from God.
    I would describe the experience as a
warming sensation about the heart coupled
with a light head, during which I closed
my eyes & saw before me a commission of
just three words printed in thick letters on
a severely white paper. I have said nothing
to C & feel a terrible urgency to act upon
the commission. It may be that I am going
a little mad, I do not know—I am both
frightened & overjoyed.

A fair, temperate day, cannot keep track
of dates—perhaps 11 Dec
    Keegan, I say—we are sitting at the
door of the carriage house, each of us

peeling an apple with our pocket knife—
how are you taking to the Married life?

There is a long silence. With the point
of his knife he scratches his grizzled chin.

Well enough to get by, he says at last.

I say nothing. He is a talker & will say
more if I remain silent. But he does not
say more.

Only well enough to get by, is it?

She likes to commandeer things, he
says. Meself at th' top of th' list.

I thought that was what you found
appealing—that she would take charge,
keep you in tow.

He gives a bitter snicker.

And I believe you said she makes you
laugh.

Haw, he says. She's bloody sober as a
nun now we're tied. All work an' no play
now she has me in her pocket.

He cuts a piece of apple & stares off
into the woods, his jaw clenched.

He turns suddenly to me, on the boil
now. An' a monstrous pack rat, he says,
the like of which we'll never see again in
this earthly life. Last night when I went to
climb in my spot by th' wall, there sits a
dishtub of dinner plates broke in a

hundred pieces, which she'd turned up in Balfour's dump hole. Move th' bloody dishtub, I say, & let a man get his rightful sleep. There's nowhere else to put it, she says. And where will you put meself, if you don't mind me askin'? Hang yourself up on a horseshoe nail, she says.

With that, I have my opening. I can hardly believe such good fortune.

You'll soon have space in plenty, I say. I am moving my pharmacopoeia into your quarters on Wednesday morning at first light. Running up and down stairs to my books is a waste of valuable time—I'm having Jessie sweep out the cabin for you.

I say this mildly, as if we are talking pork prices.

He looks as if he hasn't heard aright.

Wednesday, I say. Early, of course, to get ahead of the patients.

Keegan is at once shocked by the suddenness of the announcement & fearing the outrage of his wife.

But she dotes on bein' in the big house, he says, his voice rising.

Of course.

Wouldn't like walkin' over in rain or

foul weather of any kind, or at night
when th' bastes are out.

He is throwing down the gauntlet now.

Oh, yes, there's that, I say, sanguine.

I refuse to remind him of the cabin's
many fine qualities—two spacious rooms,
the broad hearth, a chimney that draws
sweetly.

I stand & toss my apple core to a clutch
of chickens scratching about in winter
weeds. Well, then, I say, Wednesday
morning it is for moving my library
down. You'll need to be set up in your
new quarters by late Tuesday, with
everything taken away from here so Jessie
can sweep out.

He is aghast.

But I must go to Mullaghmore on
Thursday & back on Friday, he says, as
if such tasks in a row are too weighty
for him.

I walk across to the house, dismissing
his complaint. My knees are weak as pond
water. I have never been so forthright
with him, a problem born of cowardice. I
had just arrived here when we met &
befriended one another—he became an

intimate to whom I told much & from whom I learned a great deal about country ways. Then I hired him & money entered into it, switching matters to the business side & formenting unease between us.

I find C in the Surgery, making the table ready, pulling out the stool for young Mick Doolin who will be coming up the lane about now with his fierce young Collie. There is a fire on the hearth, the tea kettle singing.

Is it done?

I nod to her.

There, she says, I'm proud of you.

I feel at once a child & do so relish the feeling.

I hope we won't taste her displeasure in the Christmas pudding, she says.

She's too proud for that, I say, as if I know the truth which I do not.

She has the serious look on her face. The lad must have his pony, she declares. Brigid Collins tells me Willie has got himself a pony from Connemara, a mare but a year old & pulling a red cart.

The thought of this makes her smile.

Since our discussions of altered income,

I had planned to forgo the pony. Her goodness is a nourishment to me.

As Little Dorrit is now well-broke to the old carriage from O'Keefe, I shall send her to Mullaghmore with Keegan & ride Adam out to Sullivan the Mason on Thursday. Then we shall see about Willie Collins.

The date? God only knows
A pale sun, very cold

I could not help myself. I have bought both pony & cart from Willie, for an offer he could not resist.

I hadn't thought to sell her, he says, looking aggrieved.

Saying nothing, I hand him the envelope.

He breaks the seal, looks in, removes the money & counts through it.

Jesus, Joseph & Mary, he whispers.

I had given him enough to cover his expenses in seeking another like Brannagh—a name which he says means 'beauty with hair as dark as a raven.'

Sullivan the Mason hard at work with his helper Danny Moore & nearly done with the job—the bookcase ready for staining. I have said the room is for the storing of trunks and such.

Keegan & Bride gone to the Cabin, C & I feel the monolith resting on us these months is lifted off.

18 December

The lad has come!

He asked for her immediately he entered the hall & burst into tears when told that she went away to her family.

Why, he says, desolate, why did she go away? She liked it here very fine, she told me she did.

Tis her *family*, I say, as if that explained everything.

I thought you was her family, he says.

I do not know how to proceed with this. C takes him in hand & we go to the kitchen where a bale of sweets is arrayed upon a silver tray. Silver for a lad but eight years old!

Fiona stands arms akimbo & beaming down upon him as if from On High. No, we will not taste her displeasure in the pudding, for her Great Pleasure is standing here before us in his suit, the scant sleeve

revealing a thin arm as he reaches for a
floury scone.

After lunch, he slipped down to his job in
the dining room, where Liam did brushwork
around the French doors, and window frames,
and he rolled the wall opposite the painting.

Warm, humid; birdsong in the beech grove.

They didn't talk much, though he sensed
there was much to be said.

'The cost of around-the-clock nursing must
be affordable here,' he said to Liam, making
conversation.

'Some of the cost is paid by the state—the
better part of it's paid by Seamus. The oul' fellow he worked for in New York left a trust to
last Seamus his life. No staggering sum, but
something to keep him in old age. Paddy was
after it pretty hard in th' beginning, but Seamus got wise and put a stop to it.'

'A very fine fellow, your Seamus.'

'He says we're the only real family he ever
had, poor devil, as if 't was a family worth havin'.'
Liam caught his breath. 'Look, Rev'rend—
there's no way I can ever thank you.'

'Don't try. It isn't necessary.'

'We've never before put anything on a guest.'

'I don't feel put-upon. Going up to your mother—it's what I do.'

''t isn't as if we were your own parish.'

'Wherever I am, he supplies a parish.'

'I don't understand that, you know.'

'I hardly understand it myself. But it's okay. Let it be.'

'Corrigan called. He paid a visit to Slade in prison. Got nothing out of him. No surprise.'

'Will they continue the investigation?'

'Corrigan says they'll keep it open, but . . .' Liam shrugged.

He stood back, surveyed his work. Done.

Liam's mobile gave its odd ring. 'Conor. Yes. Standin' right here.' He passed the phone over. 'Th' nurse.'

'Fletcher?'

'What's left of me, Rev'rend.'

'How is she?'

'Sleeping since we saw you, and at it again all mornin' 'til a half hour ago. Seein' spiders on the wall, snakes in the drapes—all real enough to convince Eileen they were there, poor dote. Dr. Feeney's increasing her dosage of loraze-pam, you'd think she was a draft horse th' way we must pump it into her. But she's quiet now an' had a bite of oatmeal without givin' it back.'

'Good. Great.'

'Says to send up th' Protestant.'

He went to their room for his prayer book, realizing again how much he liked the feel of it in his hand, the wear along the spine.

William sat by the fire, anxious, a manila envelope on his lap.

'Will she make it, d'ye think, Rev'rend?'

'I don't know. She's brave and stubborn, William. Perhaps—with God's help.'

'Ye're askin' his help, are ye?

'Yes. Are you?

'He wouldn't be after hearin' from me.'

'Why so?'

'What have I done for him, or for anybody, to tell th' truth? 't is best to ask for nothin'.'

'Yet he gives us everything. For you, a wonderful home. People who love you. Good health.'

'If I was to get his attention, he might be reminded to take it all away.'

He laughed. 'Pray for her, William. I guarantee that God would like you to give him a shout.'

William thrust the envelope into his hand. 'Will you carry it up to her?'

'The portrait?'

''t is.'

'You're making a gift of it?'

'Ah, no, I'll need it back. I wanted her to

see . . .' William choked up, cleared his throat. 'I wanted her to see me oul' face . . . one more time.' He took out his handkerchief, wiped his eyes. 'My compliments to her, if you'd be so kind.'

'You want her to see that you're still a handsome man, is that it?'

'No, no, Rev'rend, you're slaggin' me now.'

He was going out to the Vauxhall when Liam came around from his work on the addition and spied the envelope.

'His portrait?'

'It is.'

'He's sending it up to Mother?'

'Yes.'

'God above, and him eighty-some. Does it never end?'

'She's in a bad way, Liam. Any chance you might go up?'

'Don't ask me to do it, Reverend. I don't want to tally th' many reasons, but she's been no mother to me.'

He nodded, walked away. Liam called after him.

'Rev'rend.'

'Yes?'

'Sorry to disappoint you.' Liam tried to say

something more, but could not. He turned and stepped quickly around the side of the lodge.

'Hold up, Rev'rend!'

William came toward him on the cane.

'Yes, sir.'

'I don't suppose I'd be welcome to ride up with ye.'

'That's outside my jurisdiction.'

'I wouldn't trouble her a'tall, wouldn't even see her. I'd sit quiet as any mouse in her reception hall, not sayin' a word.'

'What would be the point, do you think?'

'Just to be there, Rev'rend, just to be there.'

'She's in no shape for company, William.'

'No, no, I would wait in th' hall, which I've never laid eyes on these many years. You mustn't tell her I'm there, no, I wouldn't do that; 't would add to her troubles. Just let her see th' portrait, just hold it where she can look on it a bit, that's all I'm askin.'

Should he be party to mixing it up with the long darkness between Catharmore and Broughadoon? What could be gained by it? On the other hand, what could be lost?

# Thirty-two

'When I was here before, you had a question.'

In only a few hours, her cheeks had grown more hollow, her eyes more sunken.

'What was that peace . . . that visited me?' she whispered.

'I believe it was God.'

'We have so little time, Reverend, there's none available for the ridiculous.'

He said nothing. The old dog snored in his corner bed.

The hematoma was not on view today, but hidden beneath a kind of tent in the bed linen. Her fingers picked at the coverlet. 'If what you say is true, why would he do such a thing?'

'Because he loves you.'

'No one loves me, Reverend. I've made certain of it.'

'I beg to differ. Seamus loves you.'

'Seamus,' she said, dispassionate.

'Liam loves you.'

'There's no reason for him to love me, I failed him utterly as a mother. I withdrew from him and let his father enjoy his affections.'

'Right or wrong,' he said, 'I believe I can speak for Liam in saying he loves you. Not in the way we think of love, but in the way of blood to blood, bone to bone. My father was a broken man who treated me brokenly—the same way he treated my mother, and her housekeeper who bore his son. Yet in that bond of flesh which is more powerful than any pain, I loved him with a reckless love that was regularly wounded but never killed. God puts it there, this love we often don't want, that we war against—yet there it is, all the same.'

The room was being aired; behind the draperies, a breeze shifted the heavy fabric, pushed it out, sucked it back.

'Why do you come when I call?' she whispered. 'What am I to you?'

'One day you may call and I won't come. There will be an ocean between us. But call on

God and he will come. That's his job—if called, he shows up.

'As for what you are to me, I don't know, exactly. All I know is that you have a need and I'm appointed to fill it however I can. That's true for me since I was a boy. I have a question for you. Why do you call for me?'

'Because you have nothing to lose in coming and absolutely nothing to gain, Reverend.' Sweat shining on her face.

'Please call me Tim.'

'That's a modern foolishness. I despise modern foolishness.'

'You prefer a more classic or historic foolishness?'

'You're a difficult man.'

'You're a difficult woman. But I think we've touched on that before.'

The tremoring, her voice shaken. 'All hope of forgiving and being forgiven is lost.'

'I tell you this truth above all others, Evelyn—it's never too late.'

'The cleric is all about hope—a tiresome feature of your calling. It is entirely too late for me. I haven't the strength for anything more or even anything less. I am what I am in this wretched husk—an old woman with ills and torments to last the rest of my days.'

'Now you're being tiresome.'

A pale ferocity in her eyes. 'What do you mean?'

'Speaking always of your torments, your griefs, your many persecutions. The fact is, God visited you, he sought out your company, and you refuse to believe it.'

'How can I possibly believe such an absurd notion?'

'You make a decision to believe it. Unlike what you say of me, you have nothing to lose but everything to gain.'

'Do you know what happened to my mother and sisters?'

'I do.'

'I opened the door,' she said, weeping.

'You opened the door because you were going back to ask forgiveness, and to offer it. That's reason enough to open any door, anytime.'

'I banked the fire, I pulled the chairs to the hearth, I hung the laundry over the chairs. There was the spark to the dry cloth.'

'You were going back to ask forgiveness and to offer it. Please remember that.'

The draperies sucking in. A thin keening rising from her.

He bent toward her, praying, silent.

'I was the survivor. Not dead like them, but

alive and alone, and yes, beautiful—it was a curse, something my sisters hated me for. I was left to recall every day and night of my life the horror I had seen and the suffering I had caused.

'My God,' she said, panting. 'My God.'

He had an intense desire to touch her, to lay his hand on her forehead, but he held back.

'Tell me something,' he said.

'I have told you everything of consequence.'

'Tell me whether William is Liam's father.'

He said it gently, yet his heart pounded. He'd been in such territory before—the territory of the hot spot, the truth that people reserve until last or until never.

She turned her head on the pillow and faced him, ravaged now, beyond defenses. 'Why are you such a hard man?'

'I'm actually a pathetically soft man.'

'Is it important that you know this?' There was no bitterness, merely a question forwardly put.

'It is. Things have gotten tangled up; they've gotten people tangled up.'

'A web,' she said, panting. 'A snare. If you must know, William was the love of my life.'

He thought of the old man sitting in the reception hall, the inscription engraved on the window pane.

'I learned to hate him to the same degree I loved him. He was cruel and self-serving. He came home at last when Paddy was six, he thought he might have me again for his own. Nothing mattered to him—not my husband, not my son, not my fine house for which I had surrendered everything, not even my mother and two sisters whom I had lost for all time.

'I toyed with William then, as he had toyed with me. I led him on, let him think he might take me to himself, that I had no care for my husband or child or anything but his unspeakable ways, the big boxer who'd been to Scotland and had his face bashed in, the man of the hour, the bloody self-serving gamecock of the world.

'Aye, and he thought he had me, that I was all but done in the oven of his heathen lust. And then I took my husband's pheasant gun from the cabinet; 'twas a twelve-bore Purdey side-by-side from the twenties. The stock was carved Turkish walnut and Riley was very proud of it. I was the only person allowed to shoot it other than himself, and I was an exceedingly fine shot.'

He watched a certain color return to her face, noted something like a grimace that might be amusement.

'I took it to the beech wood where I was to meet William for the offering of my body, my flesh—the one prize he had not yet won. I was standing behind a bench Riley had put there, and I see William coming out of the wood, gawping at me like a bloody savage.

'I raise the gun, then, and fire off a shot, for I intend to kill him and let the vultures take care of the rest. Oh, if you could have seen . . .' She was suddenly laughing, a raw, hoarse, half-hindered laugh, as if it were wrenched from her like an infant when it won't be naturally born. On and on, her shoulders heaving, and then the coughing.

'All right,' he said. 'No more.' He put his hand on her head, felt the heat of her scalp with its coarse silk of hair.

'I would have killed him,' she said, plucking at the coverlet, 'but he ducked as I fired, then did what the spineless do. He ran.' She looked up at him. 'I despised him all the more for that. For all his taking it like a man in the ring, for all his standing up to whatever black torment the public demanded, he ran before the fury of a woman. What do you say, Reverend?'

'I say I would have run, too. Oh, yes.'

They both laughed now. Hard and long; it hurt his sides.

'Water,' she said, and he offered the straw, and she drank a little, and he opened the manila envelope and removed the portrait.

'I've been asked to show you this.'

She lay still against the pillows and examined it with a solemn gaze.

'The oul' gallute,' she said.

He laid it on the table.

'Who did that portrait?' she demanded.

'My wife.'

'Your *wife*?'

'She's an author and illustrator of children's books. She has a newfound gift for portraiture.'

'Show it to me again.'

He held it before her, feeling the odd beggar of pride in Cynthia's achievement.

'Your wife is very competent. Where is she?'

'At Broughadoon.'

'I would like her to paint me in exchange for a pearl ring.'

'I'll tell her of your offer.'

'The setting is white gold. I wish to be painted while I'm at my worst.'

'A very unusual request.'

'I wish to see what life has written on my

face. It will be for my own amusement. Perhaps there will be something left of the young bride in the portrait after Sargent. Riley loved my beauty, Reverend, all the while looking away from my misery, refusing to see it because it was not lovely, but deformed and carrying me away like someone caught in an undertow.

'Suffering was all I had and he wanted to deprive me of it, as anyone in his right mind would. He wanted my beauty to be everything, to be all, to be enough.

'But William would have let me have the sorrow; he was unafraid of it, for he had sorrow himself. Beauty would not have been enough for William; he would have wanted all that I had, all the pain, all that I was, and if we had married, perhaps I could have been healed, relieved in some way I can't know.'

The draperies stirring, afternoon light shimmering on the walls.

'What is your wife's name?'

'Cynthia. She's nursing a fractured ankle, but has wanted to see Catharmore.'

'Show it to me again,' she said.

She looked at it, expressionless.

'He's waiting in your front hall.'

'What do you mean?'

'Just to be near, he says, not wanting to trouble you.'

She tried to rise, felt a scalding pain, lay back. 'Tell him to get off my property at once or we shall call the Gards.'

In the kitchen, Seamus gave him a fervent back-slapping.

'Joseph and Mary! I've never heard the like. When has the woman laughed? I can't recall th' time, though I remember bein' much younger.'

Something was shaken off them; they were laughing—cracking up, as Dooley would say.

'I could kiss y'r bloody hand.'

'Don't be doing that,' he said, bursting into another fit of laughter. Both of them at it again, bending over, carrying on like two pagans.

'Great God!' said Seamus, wiping his face with a handkerchief.

'Yes, Seamus, yes. He is a great God.'

Sober now, the two of them, looking at each other. Tears in their eyes.

# Thirty-three

'Walk out with me, if you will,' he said to Liam.

'I'm cookin' tonight an' much to do . . .'

'We won't be long.'

They sat on the garden bench in the mild and seamless afternoon.

'William is not your father,' he said.

'What?'

'You can let it go.'

'How do you know this?'

'I asked your mother.'

'But she lies, my mother.'

'She wasn't lying about this. William isn't your father.'

Liam spoke in Irish, crossed himself, shaken.

'The visit when Paddy saw them together—there was no real intimacy between them. She led him to believe there would be, and they arranged a meeting. She brought along your dad's old Purdey and fired off a shot. She aimed to kill him, she said, but he dodged and ran.'

Liam stared at him in a kind of dazed wonder. 'He ran; she would have killed him.'

In the library, he glanced at the sepia anglers, wondered once more if one was Liam's father. No matter. Knowing who was not seemed solace enough.

In their room, he saw the look of despair on his wife's face. Too long, this sojurn, too long. He went to her and kissed her forehead.

'Good news,' he said. 'You have a portrait commission.'

She looked at him, wry and disbelieving.

'Evelyn Conor. She says she wants to be painted at her worst.'

'That's a new one.'

'Payment is a pearl ring in a white gold setting.'

'I love white gold,' she said, listless. His own melancholy was one thing; hers quite another. He could hardly look at it.

He told her about Evelyn seeing the portrait

of William and finding it well done; told her how they had laughed, and Seamus, too.

She showed no interest in his gazette. 'I can't pretend anymore,' she said. 'I cannot bear another minute of this dreadful thing sticking up in the air.' Tears. He was grateful.

'Feeney's coming tonight. Let's press him to move ahead to the boot if reasonable.'

She put her head in her hands, wept. 'Why?' she said.

His wife never asked why. She seemed always to know why without having to ask.

'I'll have dinner with you in the room tonight. We'll order champagne!' He was in the Pete O'Malley mode, desperate.

'Tea,' she said, blowing her nose.

He would fetch it at once.

'Earl Grey,' she said.

He should book Aengus Malone for the airport trip, reunite him with the hat on the antler. 'Put on your Darling Robe; I'll read to you when I get back.'

She looked wistful. 'I'm going to miss all the dead people we're reading about,' she said. 'They seem so very alive.'

O'Hara delivered this morning three
beds of good quality—fires laid.

The lad came to us with a pasty look &
has eaten little; Fiona desperate to
provoke his appetite.

We will not according to our early plan
delay the surprise of Brannagh until
Christmas Eve, for that leaves such little
time for the lad to enjoy the truth. Willie
Collins brought her over this morning
& away Eunan & I go in the red cart,
bundled against a piercing cold. I do not tell
him the pony is his, but plan to withhold
this surprise until after we finish our calls.

Is she a beauty, then, lad?'

Yis, he says.

Tis Ireland's only native breed, the
Connemara. They say Spanish horses
swam ashore from sinking ships & bred
with our mountain ponies. In Brannagh,
we have the best of horse & pony
together.

He is quiet as any mouse.

Easy keepers, the Connemara, I say.
Willie Collins tells me they needn't the
fancy diet to stay strong.

He does not look at me, nor at
Brannagh, but into the long distance. We
are silent for a bit—the wind is getting up.

Can we stop in to see her, he says at last.

We've no time, I say. We must keep to our appointed rounds. If a doctor says he's coming, he comes.

Now your Brannagh, I say . . . (I realize I have let the badger out of the bag & hurry along to distract him) . . . is a full fifteen hands high & can do anything at all from hunting to driving to carrying heavy loads, but—& this, lad, is a very fine feature—tis her grand intelligence & big heart she's famous for.

He has not heard me.

Eunan? I say.

Yis?

His eyes are bright, too bright, I think. I put my hand to his head & find it burning. Something tells me not to wait.

Tis your own pony we're driving, I say. And a merry Christmas to ye.

I hand the reins to him & he is unbelieving.

Take the reins, lad, & do as you've seen me do.

Brannagh stops in the lane.

Ah, now, she wants the taste of the whip. Give it to her on the flank like this.

I demonstrate the flick of the whip & say, Giddyap, ye little brute.

But I have given the lad too much at once—too much joy, perhaps, & too much to do with taking the reins & learning how to sting the lovely flank of his Brannagh.

20 December

The lad took only broth last night & that very little. We suspected a type of influenza. C put him to bed & said prayers over him. When I went in to wake him this morning he was not in his room. We commenced a search throughout the house including the upper floors, then out to the carriage house where we found pony & cart missing.

I saddle Adam & meet Fiona & Keegan on the path from the cabin. They have not seen him. I ride along the lake road but do not find him. I call in at several cabins but he has not been sighted. Then the Clooney lass says she watched pony & cart go by while emptying their chamber pot. She threw up her hand in greeting she says, but he did not appear to notice & was going at a trot.

As E would not know how to find the O'Leary cabin, I dismiss this train of

thought & continue my search. At a little
past noon I return home in a state of
frenzy & spy pony & cart coming up the
lane. Tis O'Leary the Shoemaker & the
lad delirious with fever.

We live in a country rightfully terrified
of the many fevers that court us. O'Leary
is furious & demands I keep the boy from
their door.

My God, he weighs nearly nothing, is
less heavy than my heart as I carry him in
to C.

21 Dec
Late evening
The lad very ill.

At her insistence, we move him into
C's chamber on a cot. We tremble to
name it, but given the symptoms, are
pressed to believe the worst—Typhoid
Fever. Tho it prevails in the autumn, it
may occur in any season & in epidemic
proportions.

We are treating it as such & burning
the soiled rags & bed linen. Though
possible to receive the poison by
inhalation, it is most frequently passed

through the urine, stool, & vomitus of the victim. I have mixed a solution of Chloride & lime in which the same must sit for an hour before being emptied into the Trench Keegan is digging. The two porcelain bed pans are scalded after each use & stand for an hour filled with the solution.

Fiona sensing danger & fearing for her life but willing to keep after the bed linens. As reason returns, we realize we cannot continue burning good linens, & will instead let them lie for some time in a strong antiseptic after which they must be boiled. Keegan to maintain a fire under the iron pot in the carriage yard.

We keep him well away from Jessie for the unborn infant's sake & from Keegan who goes among the neighbors. We have not spoken the name of this wracking Fever, but have nonetheless sworn our household to secrecy. Cleanliness is the sermon we repeatedly preach to Fiona.

Aconite our principal drug with Specific Echinacea, Jaborandi & others as useful—Hydrochloric Acid for the sores of tongue & lips. I am ever at the

pharmacopoeia for any wisdoms
unknown to us.

Jessie admitting she gave the lad
direction to O'Leary's cabin, not knowing
his intentions. He harnessed the pony
badly, yet well enough—I am struck by
his native intelligence & his strength to
perform such a task.

I have sent for Fr Dominic. Mother of
God, have Mercy upon this innocent lad.

As I write, the snow begins.


'Poor dear Eunan,' said his wife. 'Have you
ever found yourself praying for these people?'

'Can't say that I have.'

'Twice I've prayed for them before realizing
the truth.'

It was Maureen stopping by their half-open
door.

'Come in, come in!' he said.

'Lord love ye!' She limped to Cynthia and
gave her a kiss on both cheeks. 'I'd stick me own
foot in the air if 't would help ye get through
this. But ye're lovely in that green chair with
your blue eyes shinin' an' so talented with your
gift for makin' people feel special. I hear Herself
has asked ye to do up her portrait, an' if that

isn't th' cat's pajamas I don't know what is, an' her lookin' like a witch on a broom, poor soul . . .'

Maureen McKenna. Good medicine. His own spirits lifted.

22 Dec

Consummatum est.

Danny Moore & Sullivan the Mason have done a fine, quick job of it & gone home with jingling pockets after the snow began. Keegan has hung the door.

I had thought of having a quarantine room, but would not have acted so quickly without the three words on the white sheet which I took to be urgent. *Conceal a room*, it said in India ink.

Tis a tidy small room with but two cots & a table. To have a morsel of light from the outside is an advantage to both doctor & patient, but a disadvantage to Privacy. We think no one will easily spy the window for its small size well-hidden by trelliswork propped against the exterior wall. Nor will anyone suspect that along the hall from the Surgery &

behind the tall bookcase well-fitted
with volumes & concealed casters is a
door. What is done in that room shall be
coram Deo—in the presence of God
alone.

The lad in for a long siege, God help
us. Snow & Christmas together will
reduce the patient load thereby freeing
time to attend him. He must be sponged
each day with soda water & given milk
every three hours. C making a sherry
whey—one forth cup sherry to three
forth cup hot milk & stir to curds. She
strains & adds a little sugar & he seems
avid for it. I read that broths at this stage
aggravate the diarrhea.

He must be kept to bed & turned
regularly to prevent Sores. His fever high,
the pulse small & frequent, a sign that
heart action is weak & must beat faster to
make up the difference. It is to our
advantage that Fiona possesses an
unbridled liking for him—she is sleeping
with Keegan on a pallet in the kitchen,
and makes herself available when called.
Jessie weeping a good deal but carrying
forth her duties.

It snowed throughout the night & has

come down heavily all day. We do not
expect brother & niece, nor C's sister on
tomorrow's train which we would be
unable to meet in any case. I think of my
brother, badly stooped with arthritis,
unwrapping the twenty-year-old ham he
has put by for so long, & hanging it up
again in his storeroom. He had been
excited that we would all enjoy such a
treasure together. Tis tender as goats
butter, he had written to say.

By the time Fr Dominic reached us, the
snow had become too heavy for return
travel & thus he is unable to celebrate the
Holy Mass of Christmas in the parish
church. Not even the faithful remnant
would be getting about, he says. Fretful
over missing the first Christmas Day Mass
of his priesthood, he nonetheless remains
cheerful.

I shall be your Christmas Goose, he
says.

Keegan has shoveled a path to
the carriage house where we now keep
our fire in a pit beneath the wash pot.
He measures six feet & ten inches
fallen upon what will be our kitchen
garden.

Christmas Eve

Snow abated. A final measurement of
seven feet four inches altogether.

The lad very ill.

We do not succeed in lowering his
temperature, but seek to fortify the
heart so that it may stand against the
strain. On my knees, I recall what I
can of Mother's native wisdom. I am
at once given the memory of Lobelia,
much recommended for the oppressed
pulse & labored breathing.

Fr Dominic prays over the lad
untiringly—this evening he said
Mass & we received Holy Eucharist by
the kitchen hearth. All seemed to find the
greater heat & Christian fellowship
consoling. I believe we felt a moment of
happiness in wishing one another *Nollaig
shona dhuit!*

A child is born for us, a son given to
us . . . The darkness that covered the
earth has given way to the bright dawn of
your Word made flesh.


On his evening call, Feeney brought a moon
boot. A once-despised thing of no beauty

whatever, such a boot now seemed to possess a good-humored cachet.

'I had a suspicion,' said the doctor, 'that the time had come, and indeed it has. Well done!'

He turned away from the sight of his over-joyed wife, wiped his eyes.

# Thirty-four

Evelyn Conor appraised his wife, eyes narrowed. 'Crutches.'

'Yes. But we don't talk about it.'

'You're an attractive woman.'

'You're the one for that,' said Cynthia. 'The lovely portrait after Sargent . . .'

'The artist painted the truth. You must paint the truth.'

'I'd find no satisfaction in doing otherwise.'

'The ring is on the table. The white gold setting was designed by a jeweler in Belfast. The pearl is from the Pacific and good enough for evening. 'Tis all I have to offer.'

'I'd like to paint you for pleasure only, Mrs. Conor. I hardly wear jewelry.'

'Call me Evelyn. When profit is in it, one does one's best. You must take the ring.' The tremoring of the fingers, the sweat.

'Profit isn't interesting to me,' said Cynthia. 'You are.' Emptying the hamper, setting out the jar of water, the paints, the brushes. He sat quiet in the corner, the dunce.

I washed her poor face, Fletcher had said, and did up her hair but I'm no beauty parlor, for all that. She had a desperate tongue this morning and no wonder, with her diet nothin' but air.

'What do you want me to *do*, Missus Kav'na?' Impatient.

'Please call me Cynthia. You needn't do anything at all. I'm sketching a quick impression as an exercise, we'll see where it leads.' The ferrule making its music against the water jar. 'You have a splendid nose, Mrs. Conor. Where does such a nose come from?'

'Do you mean from which marauding horde? Africans, Vikings, Mongols—Huns, perhaps?'

'Exactly.'

'It comes from the fairies.' Her jaw set, eyes distant.

'The fairies! Have you seen one, then?'

'Of course I've seen one. I've seen many.'

'What do they look like?'

'No one who sees fairies tells what they look like. When someone tells what they look like, you may rest assured they have not seen fairies.'

His wife was smiling. Her cup of tea.

'May I ask where you were educated, Mrs. Conor? You have a grand way of expressing yourself.'

'I read my husband's library. It's unfortunate that the son who inherited his father's books does not read.'

'I imagine he has no strength left to read, Mrs. Conor, what with keeping his guests happy.'

A very civil remark, he thought.

'Are you a woman of faith, Missus Kav'na?'

'I am.'

'Your husband presses it upon people.'

'Does he? I've never noticed him pressing it—not very much, anyway.'

'Do you believe as he does?'

'I do.'

'Have you no mind of your own, then?'

Cynthia laughed. 'Too much a mind of my own, some say.'

He reached down to Cuch and gave a scratch behind the ears.

'How is your impression coming?' asked Evelyn.

'Very well but for the mouth.'

'How do you mean?'

'A certain . . . something there, I can't say what. Hard to grasp with the brush. Subtle.'

'My teeth are quite ruined. I take trouble to hide them.'

'You wish to be painted at your worst; you may as well grant the poor things freedom to be seen.'

'I'm an oul' hag, it's come to that.'

'A beautiful old hag, I think. God showed great favor when he cobbled you together.'

'It's been my undoing.'

'Yes, well, they do say beauty has its curses. I wouldn't know.'

'False modesty is unbecoming.'

'So be it,' said his wife. 'The silver streak in your hair—very handsome.'

'It came in after the death of my mother and sisters; I was but a girl.'

'There. That's all that can be done. Let's have a go at the real thing. Water?'

'Yes.'

The bent straw, the slightest raising of the head.

'May I see it?'

'I don't show the impression, it's for myself alone.' The tearing of the painted page from the sketchbook.

'You can be hard like your husband.'

The chime of the ferrule. 'Keep looking beyond me, as you're doing. Yes, he's a hard old thing.' She glanced over at him, sly as a ferret.

'What favor has God shown you?'

'Every favor,' said his wife.

'What do you mean?'

'Companionship in loneliness, peace amid chaos, hope against desperation. Among other things.'

'Why would he do that?'

'He loves me. Your eyes, yes, keep looking just there. He loves me desperately.'

'Desperately. A childish thing to say.'

'It's okay. I'm his child.'

'I don't understand you people.'

An actual giggle from his wife; the true music for him.

Panting, now. 'You've been good all your days, I suppose.'

'Good? *Me?* Hardly. I once tried to kill myself. It was the greatest impertinence of my life.

But he gave me beauty for ashes, Evelyn. He unbound me and opened my prison.'

'Why did he do that?'

'Because I asked him to. I cried out to him with everything in me, I gave my old self to him, and he gave me a new self in return.'

'Were you frightened to do such a thing?'

'Frightened to do it, frightened not to do it. Yes.'

'My heart is gall,' said Evelyn Conor. 'I realized that while lying here alone. I cannot imagine living with nothing to soften the blow of such knowledge, the loneliness of it. The drink was my friend. Do you understand that?'

'I do, yes,' said Cynthia. 'Completely.'

A long silence; his wife visibly moved. 'Friends can deceive us,' she said, 'even the best of them. God does not deceive.'

Evelyn gasped, closed her eyes against the pain.

'Do you want Fletcher?'

'No. Paint me.'

'I had thought he might be deceiving, that he might even be fierce and churlish. But I found him gentle. I couldn't have known that until I gave myself to him. I had gone to live in the country after failing to put an end to my misery, and it was there that it happened, that he came into my heart and spirit and changed everything. Of course, it had been happening all along, his coming to me and I to him, but I hadn't seen it. All my life, I'd felt a famishing void, the thing Pascal talked about. There is a God-shaped vacuum in the heart of every person, he said, and it can't be filled by any created thing. It can only be filled by God—made known through Jesus Christ.'

'You gave yourself to him, you say. All your control surrendered. I can't imagine it. If he gives us the free will everyone seems so excited about, why would you give it back? That alone is an impertinence.'

'Good question. What would you say to that, Timothy?'

'Do not ask your husband to speak for you.'

'Well, then, I gave it back not because I despised it but because I had no idea how to use it.'

'That doesn't make sense.'

Cynthia smiled. 'You're a difficult woman.'

'You flatter me.'

'You're doing a very hard thing here, and you're doing it alone. Fletcher, Seamus, Dr. Feeney—in this, no one else counts, really. You're doing it alone and proud of that, I suppose.'

'I've always been proud to do something

alone, without assistance from the weak and cowardly.'

'I found doing it alone too great for me to bear. It was disabling. I was Atlas with the world on my shoulders, I was Sisyphus—my heart the stone.'

'I cannot fathom that kind of talk. Leave off, now! Leave *off.*'

The buzz of a bee marked the runes of his prayer.

'Do you know what happened to my mother and sisters?'

'I do.'

'I have spent these many years trying to keep them alive. Thinking of what they would be doing, where they would be sleeping— sometimes in summer, Ailish slept on the roof. Would you sleep on a roof, Cynthia?'

'I would not!'

'So many crawlers in the thatch, I could never understand why she did it, she was peculiar, Ailish. Day after day and night after night, I have forced myself to think what they talked about and had for supper, about the dresses and aprons they wore—I have tried to remember the colors, the patterns in the cloth. I have tried to keep their smells alive—Aileen smelled of garden peas when the shell is opened, and Ail-ish, always of sweat, no matter how she washed off in the pond. My mother had a sour smell, she was a sour woman with sour thoughts.'

'And Tommy?'

'We adored him. Tommy smelled of tobacco and all the things men are to smell of, except in a young, bold, laughing way.' She was quiet for a time, then said, plaintive, 'It is very hard to keep the dead alive.'

Cynthia put down her brush. 'It's very wrong to keep the dead alive, for it keeps us from living truly. You must forgive yourself, Evelyn.'

'I cannot.'

'You must forgive God.'

'I cannot.'

'You cannot have peace without forgiveness.'

'I do not deserve peace.'

'It's what God wants us to have.'

'Does God ask me what I want him to have? I want him to have pity, to have mercy, and the common decency to give us a life without struggle and disgrace.'

Cynthia laughed. 'Oh, my. We can forget that last notion. He is formed, himself, of the greatest pity and mercy, but without struggle and even disgrace, how would we ever know him, run to him, seek his refuge? We would not.'

The panting again. 'I see no reason, any-more, to live beyond this agony. I had thought to be courageous, but courage doesn't matter now, not by half.'

Cynthia laid her hand on Evelyn's head, si-lent. Evelyn's tears, wet on her face.

There was a long stillness in the room. The tears he had witnessed in his life as a priest might plenish a river.

'Have you ever seen a rainbow over the lough, Evelyn?'

'Often.'

'I'm hoping to see a rainbow. Timothy hopes to see swans fly.'

'One hopes all sorts of things in this life.'

Fletcher at the door.

'There's duck broth for you, Missus.'

'Broth.' A long pause. Then, 'Give me some-thing I can get my teeth into,' she said, fierce.

The tearing of the sheet from the sketchbook. 'There now, it's done. I hope you like it.'

He knew Cynthia was anxious to please both Evelyn and herself.

'Shall I sign it?'

'Sign it, of course. They tell me you're famous.'

'Not terribly. Mostly with small children.'

'Small children,' said Evelyn, oddly wistful.

Cynthia showed the portrait to her subject, who studied it a long time. 'Yes,' she said at last. 'Yes. Take the ring.'

'Not yet. I'd like to paint you again, if I may, but we're leaving soon.'

'I find this taxing, but come tomorrow, then.'

'What time?'

'Call first. You'll want to make certain I'm not lunatic and raving, as I've heard them say.'

They left the bedroom at half-past twelve and went across the hall to the kitchen. He carried the hamper and the tablet of heavy paper with its cunning textures, and the flashlight Seamus was borrowing from Broughadoon. His wife was spent, but encouraged by the morning's work.

'There you are!' said Seamus, wracking his mustache with the comb.

'She liked it,' said Cynthia.

'God bless ye! I'm hopin' she'll take a soft egg with toast now.' The erstwhile butler of Catharmore was beaming, a schoolboy.

'She's a wonderful, frightening, courageous woman—it will be good to have another chance tomorrow.'

'Strong tea,' said Seamus, pouring. 'And

quiche, just out of the oven. Real men are no longer afraid to eat it, isn't that so, Rev'rend?'

'Absolutely.'

'Sit up to the counter, then, an' tuck in. I've made fries for us.'

'Fries!' said Cynthia. 'I love fries. And you're good to take us to the basement afterward.'

'We'll go out th' back with no steps, and down th' bank with its easy grade to th' lower quarters.'

'We're wanting to see Dr. O'Donnell's surgery,' she said, 'and where he kept his medical library, and of course the concealed room, as he calls it, which he set aside for quarantine. You really must read the journal, Seamus, it's all about this place and the terrors of the old days.'

Seamus served the plates. 'I don't know of a concealed room, an' God knows, we've terrors enough *these* days.'

They laughed, and blessed the food and asked God's peace upon all life within the borders of Catharmore and Broughadoon, and Fletcher called for the egg and toast, and they felt the small triumph, and a certain peace.

Then, out the back way and down the slope to a badly neglected basement door, swollen

with age and damp. He carried the Broughadoon flashlight; Seamus carried a ring heavy
with keys.

'Since th' painting went missin', we've been
keen to lock up.' The rasp of the latch; Seamus
tugged at the door, tugged again—it opened to
the smell of all basements situated near water.

'Not a pretty sight,' said Seamus. 'Keep your
eyes skinned an' watch your step.'

Cynthia peered into the chiaroscuro of
moldering plaster and limestone. 'This is the
only door to the basement?'

''t is.' Seamus switched on the overhead bulb.

'Then the patients would have come into
the waiting room here . . .' She stepped inside.
'But what a very small room. What do you
think, Timothy? Could Edema and Goiter and
all the rest have squeezed in here?'

'Owners change; walls get knocked down,
new ones put up.'

'I think this may be it, it feels right,' she said.
A narrow window, the sill crusted with dead
flies; walls blackened by damp.

'That door should open to the surgery,' she
said.

Seamus moved ahead and opened it, and
ha! the old fireplace—still there after so many

years, and the two windows 'always kept open in summer.'

'Here would be the examining table,' she said, 'with the little stool beneath, and there would be the table where he kept the skull that Aoife tricked out with the nurse's cap.'

His wife was entranced, jubilant, the cheapest of dates.

A stash of windows with broken panes, an open box of men's dress shoes gone green, wooden crates, a headboard with peeling veneer. Heaven knows what bacillus festered here. He covered his nose with his handkerchief, a wimp in the face of venture and discovery, while she explored cracks in the plaster, the cold hearth, the wasted hole of the fireplace.

They moved along to a room with windows protected by iron bars. He helped her navigate the uneven floor tiles.

'The bars?' he asked Seamus.

'To keep thieves out of th' coal, they say. There was where th' chute came down.' Seamus pointed to what was undeniably a pile of coal. ''t was here when we arrived fifteen years ago; we may be near to a time of needin' it.'

'So Paddy did no remodeling to the basement?'

'None at all, save for th' heating system an' new plumbin'. You're seein' these quarters with their *original fabric,* as th' historians say—overhead beams, original; limestone floors, original; walls an' damp, original.'

They were passing along a narrow hall, lighted by a single bulb that swayed from the pull of the chain. Shadows danced over the stone.

'O'Donnell hid the door to the room with a bookcase,' she said. 'I can't imagine a rolling bookcase would still be sitting around down here. But the room was along a hall, he said. Is this the only hall?'

'Ah, no, there's a bloody warren of halls an' rooms, all kept locked in those days. This room for th' cider an' that for th' potatoes, this for th' laundry tubs, that for th' general storage of pecularities.'

'Such as?' she said.

'Such as a human skull with yellow teeth, an' a wicker wheelchair with a sheep bell attached. Then there's th' mannequin used for sewin' ladies' clothes—which you don't want to come on in th' dark.'

'Have you ever seen a bookcase down here?'

'Not that I recall.'

'So it's a matter of finding the right door,'

she said. 'It was a small room with a window, holding just two cots and a table. Dr. O'Donnell and his wife were very proud of the quarantine room—we're just reading about it.'

Seamus stopped at a door long ago brushed with blue paint. 'This was Mr. Conor's storage for his fishing tack. He didn't leave it at Broughadoon out of season, they say, for there'd been a theft or two.' Seamus tugged at the door, scraping it along the flagstone. 'But there's no window in here, nor any bulb, either, you must go in with a torch to see your hand in front of your face.'

The flashlight shone on piles of waders, boots, rods, vests hanging on nails. There was the distinct, though faint, smell of fish.

They moved along to other doors. Behind one, a toilet for servants, dark as a cave. Behind another, shelves of moldering books, accordion files, accounting ledgers. He was the only one to spot whatever fleet, dark thing fled the nest of literature and commerce.

'Now, here's one with a window!' said Seamus. ''t is where th' boys' childhood things are stored.'

In the grainy light from a small window, a small room filled with two bicycles, bedraggled; a wooden wagon without wheels; bunk beds piled with twin mattresses; fishing gear; a basketball net on a bent ring; a large box labeled TRAIN; a hat rack with ball caps embalmed in dust. Leaning against the beds, a stack of window louvers, many slats missing, and at their rear, a glint of something that wasn't a louver. He stepped in and shone the light on it, and Seamus was quick to move the louvers, one by one, away from the ornate gold frame.

In the beam of the flashlight, they saw the fisherman in the boat, and the mountains beyond, and the small cottage with its plume of smoke, and the swan on the morning lake.

# Thirty-five

Anna had brought in an extra chair, opened the windows to an August breeze.

He'd told Anna they had important news, yet dropping a bomb into a tea party in Ibiza wasn't his cup of Earl Grey.

Cynthia took lemon, a cube of sugar, stirred, set down her spoon. 'The Barret,' she said to Anna, 'is at Catharmore.'

'Catharmore?'

'We saw it today in the basement, in a storage room.'

'But that means . . . Paddy.'

'We thought you should tell Liam,' he said. 'You'll know best how to handle such news.'

'In a storage room?'

'Where the boys' childhood things are kept,' said Cynthia. 'Among a stack of louvers.'

'Any harm done to it?'

'None we could see.'

'The Garda,' said Anna. 'The uproar it will bring. Dear God.'

'Yes,' he said.

'I can't believe it.' Anna shook her head, took a deep breath. 'It's hard to consider the good news for thinking how Liam will feel. This black betrayal will cap it all. Does Seamus know?'

'He does,' he said. 'He'll mention it to no one. It will be a hard thing for Mrs. Conor.' The upheaval of a police investigation, inevitable. The news of one son stealing from another, inevitable. The extra drain on Evelyn Conor's diminished physical resources, inevitable.

'I'm sorry for her,' said Anna. 'I want you to know that. I'm not completely coldhearted.' She looked at her hands in her lap. 'I must think of how to tell Liam—he seems happier just now. I can hardly keep up with all that comes at us—'t is a battering ram at our door.'

He thought of Fintan O'Donnell and the fruit spoons; how the doctor had quietly removed them from the thief's possession and returned them to his own, with no word spoken. This would be different.

'I've heard fiddle music a couple of times,' he said, 'as if it were coming from this room.'

'Yes. I share it now with Bella. Things feel better, if only a little. Thank you both for your kindness, your patience with her, with all of us.'

'Thank you for your patience with us,' he said.

'Soon you'll be leaving. It seems you've been with us a very long time.'

He couldn't help smiling. 'We *have* been with you a very long time.'

'I shall hate to see you go.'

'We will hate to go,' said Cynthia.

'If you change your mind, you can have your room through next week.'

'Thanks,' he said. 'We must get home to our son.'

He wanted to tell Anna that William was not Liam's father, should she have any lingering question. But Liam had talked to him in confidence, and the need to relieve Anna was not his concern.

He stopped with Cynthia in the library and looked around—at the fine bookcases and worn rug, the chairs with their silent history of sitters from every realm, the fireplace with its eternal flame. 'I'll never forget this room.' He put his arm around her. 'Did you mean it about hating to go?'

She looked at him, thoughtful. 'Yes.' They hoped to be ready when Feeney gave the word.

'Has Pud seen the suitcases?'

'He has.'

They had no energies left to chat up the Sweeneys and the author and niece at the social hour, nor any *joie de vivre* for dinner downstairs. They took it in their room, withered as weeds.

She put on the declining robe; he donned pajamas and, raising a glass of fairly decent port, opened the journal to their bookmarks and read aloud.

January 1863

After bitter days of solitude & sickness at Cathair Mohr, the snow melts fast & we have seen three patients. I wonder at the low number; they are uneasy & tell me there are rumours abroad.

I ride out on Adam, dodging the worst of the mud.

Inside her door, I remove my heavy coat & hang it on a peg. Her red hen perching on the other chair gives me a menacing look.

I pull up a stool. What are they saying, Rose?

They're sayin' ye've a lad sick with Cholera at your place.

Who is saying it?

O'Leary got th' word passin', he didn't call it th' Cholera to me, but 't was turned into Cholera by th' time it went round. They say Balfour is comin' to your door with such as th' Health Board.

I had thought the rumour started when Keegan went four days ago to Mullaghmore to pronounce the lad too ill with food poisoning to travel, & met Padraigin coming this way saying the lad's mother is in Hospital. The poor woman suffers the same evil symptoms we are wrestling with here but Keegan swears he stuck to his story of food poison.

How is th' lad? she says.

Frail as any feather, we do all we can. Tis the typhoid fever, but you must swear to say nothing.

She dips her chin, affirming her honor to me.

Tis passed to another through feces or urine or vomit, I say, & no need to worry for he is quarantined & I come to ye clean.

She puffs her pipe, nods. I am pleased to see a makeshift pie sits warming on her hob.

And you, Rose? Are ye well in this wether?

Aye, but for th' Rheumatics.

She holds up her hands, displays her gnarly fingers.

Keep them warm, I say. Is there anything ye need?

Mutton, she replies.

Ye'll have it, I say.

I go to the peg & pull on my heavy coat.

Bring him here when he's stout again, she says. I'll boil 'im an egg from Cliona.

Stout again! My heart leaps. I salute her.

*Bail ó Dhia ort*, I say with my little Irish.

*Bail ó Dhia is Muire dhuit*, she says.

Cliona has not moved from her perch.

I return home, brooding with an unnamed anxiety. There is Balfour's untidy carriage, fair covered with mud. Balfour & two men—both English—are

coming down the steps of the front
portico, Keegan stands on the top step,
arms folded, looking sour. Caitlin stands
in the open doorway, a statue of marble in
her white nurse's apron. I do not
dismount.

We have searched your house, sir, says
Balfour, the Great Boar Hog in Trousers.

I say nothing.

We were informed you have Contagion
here, says one of the men.

I see by C's expression that they have
not discovered the lad.

I trust you are pleased with your
findings, I say.

I rein Adam about, mud flying. At the
carriage house, I find I am trembling as if
with the ague.

It happened that Jessie had been
sweeping out the upper floor & looked
down to see Balfour's carriage in the lane.
She alarmed the house so that Keegan &
C got the lad well-wrapped & down the
stairs to the quarantine room in good
time.

Jessie cleared the table by his bed,
chucked it all into a pillow casing & hid it
in the laundry. C stuffed his wee dab of

clothes behind her bureau. Fiona's sour humour came to marvelous use—she met the men in the hall & forced them to remove their muddy boots!—this action giving Keegan & C time to roll the bookcase away & get the lad into the room.

As she tells me this, C is trembling as I had done.

We put him on the cot, she says, & covered him with the blankets. I asked him not to cry out whatever he did and he did not. They searched the house— what terrifying & wicked little men they were, & yet so very stupid-seeming in their sock feet. If men were robbed of boots with their dangerous heels, wars would cease.

She clings to me. We must keep the lad there, she says, for they will be back, I can feel it.

What did you tell them, I say.

Twas a poor job, but the best I could muster. I said a relative of his had come for the boy & we know nothing of his circumstances. I said he had recovered from what appeared to be food poisoning & was well & able when he left us.

They asked about Padraigin & the rest?

Yes.

What did you tell them?

The truth, she said. That they live in Mullaghmore, but I am not certain where.

I go down to him carrying a slab of heated stone wrapped in a scrap of linen. In the cold room, my breath is vapor. I am brought low by the smallness of him beneath the blankets & the heat of his head in this punishing fever.

I place the wrapped stone beneath the covers at the foot of the cot & pull the little stool from under the table & sit by him.

Lad, I say.

He opens his eyes to me. I see the tribulation of the world in but eight years of living.

You are safe, I say. You will be strong again. You will make a fine Surgeon.

I am babbling like an idjit, tears streaming. I turn my face from him & make this promise aloud in the desolate room—With God's help, we shall see a nasty thing fixed back to a good thing.

Day following, January

I have set up my own cot by the fire in
the Surgery & am in & out to him
frequently, managing the pan, turning
him, applying the ice if need be. All
possible clues to his presence in the house
are now with him in the room. I look at
once for the little vapor from his breath, a
small flag that signals good news. All the
writings on this subject have been
delved—we are advised to keep him abed
so that no Energy is wasted in tottering
about. He is patient & kind, without the
urgent desire of the young for his sickness
to leave off—he simply endures. My
mother Bessy would so relish giving him
comfort. Mother, I sometimes say aloud,
as if she were near.

We are blessed of God with a day
unseaonsably warm. I open the small
window for ventilation—Keegan has
obscured it from any outside view.

14 January

Some improvement. Fever lingering as
it does in such a case. Taking beef broth.
C with him frequently. Fr Dominic here
overnight to help us & discuss plans to

build a new parish church, yet some years away. C & I make decision to give beyond our current means.

15 January

Balfour & his thugs have come again & gone away cheated.

I am not convinced they are Health Board for they are ignorant in manner & smelled strongly of whiskey—perhaps personal associates of Balfour out to have a malicious bit of fun & turn us over to authorities.

I think how near we have come to disaster, had it not been for the three words formed with a thick nib. I am Noah who was asked to build the ark & when it was done, flood waters rushed in upon the Land.

Date?

Whipping winds two days running

I will not write here again until the lad is out of danger. It requires all our forces to tend him and the Surgery combined, for there are many patients now and a number of deaths into the bargain. I found a few holly berries in the cellar, dropped from the garlands we had made for Christmas—I remembered that Christmas passed us by as in a dream. All that is left of it is our faithful Goose, who comes again and again to pray us through these unholy times.

15 Feb

Unseasonably warm & wet

A month has gone since writing here & I am awkward as any intern. I come to these pages to report—nay, to shout *IMPROVEMENT!*

C & I stood yesterday at our chamber window after a downpour & beheld a most unusual sight—a rainbow above the bright shingle of the lough—in February!—& twas a double.

He will be well again, she says, taking my arm.

I slept in the room with him last night & when I awoke this morning, yes, by God, he was improved! Not hale, not hearty, but improved.

Aoife? he says. Has she come?

I open the window a crack & put on my shoes.

Brannagh is waiting to take you about

in the sunshine, I say. And fat as any pig from his winter corn.

I cannot tell him of his poor mother who died in hospital the tenth day of this month with the fever. The doctors thinking it was the milk delivered in a can washed with polluted water. The contagion did not spread to Padraigin & family for they get milk delivery from another man & there had been no contact of late between households. This we learn in a letter received from P, demanding the lad be returned to him. I delay posting an answer.

He wants money, says C.

He shall not have it.

He is likely claiming himself as legal guardian, she says.

I have written my Solicitor about a number of pressing issues, not least of which is the man to manage this demesne. Even with little outdoor work to be done in winter, this small holding seems a gaping maw of thousands of acres demanding attention.

We have today moved the lad back to his old room & shall keep the turf fire going round the clock. Fiona cooking as for the Roman legions. He is but a lad, I say, stern as a cleric. She is stirring a pot of rice that would feed Mesopotamia.

She removes the spoon, slams the lid on. With a bit of cream & molasses, she says, he'll be eatin' th' lot of it, mark my word.

God knows he did eat a small bowlful & I had a portion, myself.

I choose not to worry any longer about hiding the lad; we will not live in fear of fools.

I tell C—If Balfour comes sniffing about, I shall kill him.

Remember he has a child, she says, & a wife to look after.

Well then, I say, I shall but maim him for the rest of his days.

19 February 1864
A cold snap

At two this morning, I delivered Jessie of a healthy boy—nearly nine pounds! He was squalling in the little room behind the scullery as I had breakfast in the kitchen. In winter we do not take meals in the dining quarters for the perishing cold.

A lusty boy, I can say that—name of
Brian, after his father whom Jessie expects
each day to turn up, hat in hand, & take
her away.

And where would Away be? I ask.

The Land of Plenty, sir, she says with a
most cheerful smile.

And where might the Land of Plenty
be found?

Why, Boston, sir, she says, & makes a
small curtsy.

I tell C we should pack up our jumble &
get away quickly to such a Land!

I ask the Lad if he wishes to remain
with us & of course he does. Against my
better judgement, I sent Keegan to
Mullaghmore with an envelope, enough
to put P off until we can manage the best
solution.

14 March

We have taken the lad—riding upon
my shoulders—to the Mass Rock &
shown him the date 1774 engraved upon
it & the cross beneath. The lilies we
planted have sent up their green shoots,
the wood is fragrant with smells of earth
& leaf mold.

We do not expose this holy shrine
to fools. Who can know what destruction
may come upon us yet? In our prayers
we remember those run to ground like
fox, those for whose severed heads the
English were keen to pay a shilling
apiece.

The Lad gains strength & eats with
increasing appetite, though he tires easily
& must have a long rest following the
mid-day meal. I will take him tomorrow
in the cart, wrapped like a mummy as
Keegan the Wether Predictor calls for Dry
& Colder.

Have not seen hide nor hair of Balfour &
his minions—rumour has it that
Palmerston again enchants him with big
doings at his Monstrous Pile.

The glad news from Dublin that P has
no legal charge over the Lad. We are
seeking his Father—whereabouts
currently unknown.

30 April 1864

Uprooting Fiona from her kitchen
pallet is kin to removing a large oak from
the field, one must hoick it & burn the

stump. Back they go to the Cabin, she in bad humour. Our new man arrives on Thursday with family of four. We will lodge them in the carriage house as it contains a fireplace for whatever Groom I thought we might employ. Keegan fractious. God save us from Squabble & ill temper which spread in a household like Measles.

Having a lad about is a consuming piece of business. I have put him to work two or three hours each morning as his stamina permits. He is fascinated by the common Goiter as I once was & curious about the removal of digits & limbs. The subject of Coughing is another interest & anything to do with skin disease. He studies a rash as some look at a map of the world & its many Wonders. He now has access to my microscope & is keen to examine anything at all, including maggots found in a rotten log.

The sobering matter of Last Will & Testament will be properly finalized Monday next.

Twill be the fixing of a nasty thing back to a good thing.

He closed the journal. They were quiet, pondering.

'We can't finish it,' he said. 'Maybe another round before bedtime or first thing tomorrow, but we can't make it through.'

'I hate to leave it—what will become of all these lives opened to us?'

'Would be good to have a paperback edition to tuck in your hamper.'

'Without his journal,' she said, 'we wouldn't have found the painting. Hats off to Fintan.'

'How far away are you from starting to pack?'

'Far, far away. Have you called Aengus?'

'Blast,' he said. 'I forgot. First thing tomorrow.'

'How about now? He'll be mowing verges tomorrow.'

'I'll go down to the kitchen. Have you seen his card?'

'On the dresser with the cuff links you brought.'

But no cuffs to go with them—yet another item he'd left behind in Mitford.

'What do you think will happen?' she asked. 'Do you think Liam would let Paddy be prosecuted?'

'I don't know.' He didn't like thinking about

it. 'We've done all we can.' He would be curious about fingerprints, if any.

'I'm painting Evelyn tomorrow morning. If she's able,' she said, going off to the bathroom. 'And I'd like to paint Anna and Liam before we go, but this doesn't seem the best time.'

'How is it?' he called after her.

'How is what?'

'You know.'

'Great,' she said.

They had agreed not to use the *a*-word ever again.

He was edgy, scattered, as he dressed to go down to the phone. He could feel himself pulling away from Broughadoon like moss scraped from a log. It was discomfiting, the same way he'd felt when he left home to come here. He was no traveler; this would be his last jaunt for some while.

In the kitchen, he squinted at the various phone numbers on Aengus Malone's card, and punched in the one not penciled out.

'Hallo!' A woman, irritable.

'Aengus Malone, please.'

'Who's callin' Aengus?'

'Tim Kav'na from th' States. He drove us to Lough Arrow some time ago.'

'Aengus is out to 'is dance class.'

'His dance class!'

'Learnin' th' oul-style step dancin' for th' competition.'

'Will you have him call me? It's important.'

'He'll be in late.'

'Will he be mowing tomorrow?'

'Mowin'?'

'The verges.'

'He's left off mowin' verges,' she said.

'Well, then.'

'I'll take your number.'

No telling what time the call would come, disturbing the household. Call a taxi, he thought, or whatever people call around here.

'Ah, but you're in luck, now, here comes th' poor devil lookin' like he was flogged by a rooster. Aengus, it's your customer from th' States.'

'Hallo!'

'Aengus! Tim Kav'na here. You left your hat at Lough Arrow.'

'Aye,' he said. 'Is it you, then, Rev'rend?'

'It is. How are you?'

'I've a ragin' thirst, if ye must know; I've been dancin' like a jackhammer for two bleedin' hours.'

'I hear there's a competition.'

'Aye, an' I'm needin' my hat for good luck.'

He gave Aengus date, time, and airline.

'Strandhill, is it'

'Dublin. We're skipping Strandhill this go-round. We'll see more of Ireland going down to Dublin!'

'I'll send me cousin, Albert.'

'We can't get th' top dog?'

'Tis th' day of my competition; I'll be nervous as any cat, an' shinin' me hard shoes.'

'How will you make it without your hat?'

'I'll do as I've done these last weeks an' ask help from above. Send me oul' hat off with Albert.'

'Will do. What time will he fetch us?'

'Six-thirty A.M., sharp. He'll load everything in, ye needn't turn a hand. How's th' missus?'

'Good, good. Sorry to miss you.'

'Aye, an' same here. I don't suppose ye lift prayers for such as dancin' competitions.'

'May he make you able to do your best, Aengus.'

'I thank ye for that, Rev'rend, an' for your business with Malone Transport. Good luck to ye, an' come again.'

He forgot to ask what the prize might be, or what work had come around since the mowing job.

He passed Bella coming downstairs with their dinner tray. She lowered her eyes.

'Good evening Bella.'

No reply.

'Bella dislikes me intensely,' he told Cynthia. 'I just passed her on the stair, she wouldn't speak.'

'It's the collar, sweetheart. I think it causes her to feel a kind of shame.'

The collar definitely had its downside: it provoked shame in some, anxiety in others. On the upside, it also provoked its due share of consolation. In any case, he seldom took it off—let the chips fall where they may.

*Albert at 6:30*, he wrote in the calendar of his notebook. Why did he write this down? He'd had zero appointments these last weeks; maybe *Albert at 6:30* was a small way to prepare for reality, for going home to his own mowing.

While Cynthia occupied the bathroom, he pondered his unease. Dooley and Lace, unfinished. Evelyn, Liam, Paddy, unfinished. Bella totally unfinished. The whole Barret business, unfinished. He despised the unfinished, and yet all of life was continually under construction and he was continually at odds with that plan.

He closed his eyes, breathed deep. Prayed.

She came steaming into the room from the shower.

'We can't go home, Timothy.'

She often spoke what he was timid even to think. 'We'll miss seeing Dooley off to school,' he said.

'He's young; she's old.'

'Of course, we'd have him only one day before he takes off to Georgia, but we'll see him at fall break for a week. Dooley, Sammy, Kenny, all the boys together, right next door.'

'A week of my pizza and your hamburgers,' she said.

'Not to mention my barbecue and your fries.'

'Ruinous, but lovely. I shall need this long rest to face the onslaught.'

'Do you feel it's fair to claim medical reasons?'

'We've been here an eon,' she said, 'and owing to medical reasons, I've hardly left the premises.'

<Dear Emma,

Not flying out of Dublin as scheduled. Medical reasons. Advise Puny no pick-up needed. Pls get open-end ticket deal.

As ever>

Thank heaven Walter didn't answer his cell phone and he could leave a message. No Guess what, no You'll never believe this, he was beyond that.

'Walter, it's Tim. We won't meet you at the airport as planned, we're going to take a few days to see the sights. If you need my apologies, you have them in spades. Peace and plenty and love to Katherine.' He should feel guilty, but didn't—they would laugh about this in their dotage.

He left a message canceling Albert, relieved to skip a chin-wag with Mrs. Malone.

'Anna,' he said, 'what is Dublin's finest hotel?'

Cynthia was in bed when he came back to the room, Pud trailing, no shoe.

'An odd thing,' she said. 'For the first time, I feel like we're on vacation.'

He stepped out of his loafers; Pud leaped onto the duvet. 'Why is that?'

'Because the ticket will be open-ended,' she said. 'I love open-ended.'

# Thirty-six

<You are out from under the gillotine—for a penalty of $500 you can book another flight when you get your act together. Thanx for worrying me to death with 'medical reasons,' whatever that means. I am exhausted from hours spent hanging on the phone listening to elevator music while Snickers pooped on my best rug because I did not let him out on time. Thank the Lord it was firm.

As ever>

He ran with Pud along the shore; looked for a swan—got bingo, saw four; wondered if Liam knew yet, prayed for him and for Paddy; wondered if Anna would tell Bella, and then again, why not tell everyone? The beans would have to be spilled sooner or later, making their rounds to Jack Kennedy and beyond. He sweated profusely in the close morning, wiped his face and head with the bandanna; stopped to look at a merganser, at the neon of green in its feathers; composed the email to Dooley: *Hey, buddy, we have decided to capitalize on our time/travel investment and extend our stay here by a few days. Sorry we won't be there to see you off—we look forward to fall break with you and brothers next door. Will call later. Some things must be finished before they can be done. We love you.* No. He would say *We cherish you.* Maybe people didn't say *cherish* to twenty-one-year-old men, but he would say it.

Back at the lodge, he rang Fletcher.

''Twas a hard night, Rev'rend, with th' hematoma and havin' but one side to turn her on. An' Dr. Feeney wasn't pleased with her urine production, so he puts her on th' IV which keeps us on th' hop. She's quite exhausted, the old dear, an' I'm ruined into th' bargain, for Eileen's away.'

'Her spirits?'

'Th' same. But you can't help but love 'er for all that.'

'Does she want to be painted today?'

'She does, but it's her hair she's fretting over. She's very particular about her hair.'

'She wants to be painted at her worst, she says.'

'Aye, but she doesn't mean it where her hair's concerned. I've no idea what to do with it, as I can hardly manage my own poor thatch, an' Seamus, I think he would try it if he could, he says 't would help her feel herself.'

'When do you think my wife should come?'

'She's napping now, and I must get a wink if I can. Let her have her bite of lunch, an' come after. She wants you, too, Rev'rend, if you don't mind. She says you can sit in th' corner like last time; she likes you near, I think.'

It was a small, odd pleasure he felt.

Cynthia was at the chicken run, sketching the flock with pen and ink. 'Isn't this divine? I've wanted for weeks to do it.'

'We can get chickens for you at home. The town allows hens, but no roosters.'

'Who would want hens without roosters?'

'If its eggs you're after, you don't need roosters.'

'It's the whole business I'm after—all the feathers and crowing and the lovely hens pecking.'

'We go up after lunch,' he said. 'A hard night, but she asks that we come. She's worried about her hair. Anything you could do?'

'No, darling, as you're aware, I've no skills in that department. I'm fretted about my *own* hair; 'tis a hay bale.'

He derived scant satisfaction from having next to none to worry about.

He went to Anna in the kitchen. 'May I use the phone for a quick call to Sligo?' His phone charges would, at the end, be accounted to his credit card.

'Of course,' she said. She was trying to pull up a scrap for him.

'And would you give me the name of a car rental company?'

'You'll be seeing the sights, then?'

'Finally.'

'I know it's humble, but we'd love you to take the Vauxhall. Unless you're going a distance.'

'No, not planning to do that. Just want to get around and enjoy this area.'

'Do take the Vauxhall, then, if you would. We would like that. Please.'

'Very generous, Anna. Will do, then. We're grateful. May I ask if you've told him?'

'This afternoon, I think—he's working the sheep today. I don't know; it's very hard. I dread telling him before dinner, but then I don't want to tell him at the end of a hard day, for he'll be sleepless. The sentence for such a thing—who knows how many years it might be? I wish we could just bring the painting here and hang it in its rightful place and leave things alone.'

'Would Liam be willing to do that?'

'No. He will be cut to the quick and wanting justice done.'

With no idea of the effect it would trigger, he needed to push through to another of her apprehensions.

'I have something to ask. Forgive me if I ask too much. Cynthia is painting Evelyn again today after lunch. Would you come with us and do up her hair for the portrait?'

She gazed out the window, through the scrim of curtain, and didn't reply.

'I've asked too much,' he said.

'No.' She turned and gave him a steady look. 'You haven't. It's always been coming to this. 't is the right time, isn't it?'

'I believe so, yes.'

'The Sweeneys are bringing family for dinner, and the author and niece were going to be in Sligo for a play this evening, but changed their minds.' She bit her lip. 'Nonetheless, I will do it. But Reverend . . .'

Her hands trembled; she clasped them together.

'I'm frightened.'

He wanted to console her, to say he thought it could be a good thing, but he thanked her and said nothing more.

He helped his wife into the Vauxhall and took her to lunch at Jack Kennedy's. It was the 21 Club, the Paris Ritz; she was dazzled.

'Tomorrow,' he said, 'a holy well. And Innisfree, if you'd like. There's an old fellow there with a boat to take us over—if we can find him at home.'

They ordered things they shouldn't order, including fries. His penance, a Diet Coke; hers, a salad with vinegar and a mite of oil. There was a certain ease in the low murmur of the room, the occasional burst of laughter.

Jack Kennedy gave him the glad hand. 'So you've stopped by with your lovely daughter, Rev'rend. Introduce us, if you please.'

On leaving, two elderly checker players doffed their caps to her.

'I love this,' she said, sitting on the stool beside him, the sun at their backs.

'What don't you love, Kav'na?'

'Needless rules and regulations, foxglove
seeding itself in our rose beds, age spots.' She
showed him the back of her hand, the small
blemishes.

'Freckles,' he said.

He always said that; it was a tradition.

At Broughadoon, they got their jumble
together—Cynthia's hamper, his prayer book,
Anna's packet of hairpins. 'She loses them all
over the place,' Anna said.

'Ye're goin' up to her, then?' asked William.

'Shall we deliver your compliments?'

William looked aggrieved. ''t would be good
to go with ye.'

He laughed. 'No way. Too much ruckus with
her calling down the Garda on our heads. I'm
not getting in the middle of that.'

'Ye owe me a checkers game, Rev'rend, I
hope ye remember.'

'I remember. Consider it done.'

'An' Anna girl,' said William, 'behave yourself—the oul' woman's in a desperate way.'

They went up in the Vauxhall. Seamus surprised at the sight of Anna; the two of them
awkward in this setting.

'Fletcher?' he asked Seamus.

'Nodding off in th' kitchen a bit. She's kept on th' hop.'

'Mrs. Conor?'

'Sleeping when I looked in five minutes ago.'

Anna waited in the hall as he went in with Cynthia.

Evelyn Conor was sleeping, yes, but something wasn't right.

He saw at once the bluish shadow around her mouth, the blue of her nail beds, the compromised breathing.

'Get Fletcher!'

*Don't do this*, he said to her without speaking. *Don't do this.*

# Thirty-seven

'My God, I could kill myself.'

'It happens,' he said. A trite remark in view of circumstances, but it served. 'No Eileen and too little sleep. Don't punish yourself.'

Fletcher was clearly agonized. 'She could have died. Joseph and Mary, I've never done such as that before.'

'The way she came back was miraculous. Biblical!' He knew what it meant to be gob-smacked.

'The Narcan. Dr. Feeney left it just in case. He's a very shrewd man, not every doctor thinks ahead like that. So yes, it happens, it definitely happens, an' I'm tellin' you, Rev'rend, I'm not th' only one who ever gave an overdose.'

'She came awake almost instantly.' He was still marveling.

'That's how it works with that drug, even the point-four milligrams I gave. But some bounce into a pain crisis, she could have come awake in pain she couldn't bear—it can go either way.'

'And see there, Fletcher, now she's having her hair done.'

They sat on stools at the kitchen island. Seamus set out a pot of tea and two mugs, poured for them.

'Thank God I'm not a drinkin' woman,' said Fletcher. ''t would be a double whiskey I'm havin'.'

He reflected on what happened when Anna walked into Evelyn's room, holding the packet of hairpins as if a sacrament. She stood by the bed, looking down at Evelyn. Evelyn looked up. No one spoke. A certain ease came into the room then—as if something once taken up was laid down.

Seamus wiped his eyes, blew his nose. ''t is a bloody roller coaster around here,' he said, laughing a bit.

'She's asking for you, Reverend.' Anna at

the kitchen door, her face revealing the answer to his question, but he asked anyway.

'How did it go?'

Anna smiling. It was manna.

He went to her, embraced her, and stood away, grateful.

'She says she's too weary to be painted today. She wants Seamus to show Cynthia the music box Mr. Riley gave her. Could you step to the hall a moment?'

They stood by the window with the etched inscription.

'I thought, what if she should die, Reverend, and we never know the truth? And so I asked her who Liam's father was, I asked very kindly, I was putting her hair up, and she said, Why do you ask such a wicked thing? And I said, Because you once told me it was Mr. Riley's business partner. She seemed stricken and said, I told you that? And I said yes, and she said she'd been black-hearted to speak such a hurtful lie and that, no, 't was Mr. Riley who was Liam's father. She swore it to me, and I believe her— she seemed very shamed. She asked me if I had suffered over it and I said yes, and she took my hand and held it a moment. It was . . . affecting, Reverend.'

'You told her that Liam never knew?'

'Yes. She was grateful.' Anna drew herself up. 'I don't wish to weep,' she said, smiling a little, 'for I may not be able to stop.'

He went in and took his chair by the bed.

'*Bail ó Dhia ort,*' he said. He had copied it out of the journal this morning, asked Anna how to pronounce it, for the Irish is not phonetic.

She turned her head and peered at him. '*Bail ó Dhia is Muire dhuit.*'

'You're looking very beautiful,' he said. 'If you don't mind my saying so.' The pearl ring lay on the table.

'Where did such a sentiment come from?'

'From my heart,' he said. 'The truth without varnish.'

A tinge of color in her cheeks. 'I'm too weary to be painted today. I regret having troubled you.'

'No trouble at all.'

'I hear you're staying on for a time. Perhaps it can be done another day.'

'Of course. We were afraid for you, Evelyn. You stood on the brink.'

'I've stood on the brink all my life. I should like to be standing elsewhere for the days left to me—in a green *pairc*, perhaps, with a view of Ben Bulben.'

She lay quiet, looking at the ceiling.

'I wish the peace to come back,' she said.

'He himself is peace. He comes if we invite him, and stays, if we ask. It's ourselves who wander away.'

'Why do we wander away?'

'It's the old free-will business—we're charmed by the self, by our own pointless self-seeking.'

'What does he want from us?'

'He wants us to ask him into our lives, to give everything over to him, once for all.'

'I can't imagine.'

'I couldn't, either. I heard it preached and talked about all my life. I exegeted Romans and memorized vast amounts of scripture before I was twelve years old, but somehow it went in one ear and out the other—I got the bone, but not the marrow. Long after becoming a priest, I remained terrified of surrendering anything, much less everything. And then one day, I did.'

'Why?'

'Because I could no longer bear the separation from him.'

She licked her dry lips. 'You said there would be nothing to lose.'

'And everything to gain.'

'I don't wish to be humiliated.'

'By God?' He took the lid from the balm and moistened the swab.

'By anyone, and especially God.'

'God does not humiliate the righteous. He may fire us in the kiln to make us vessels, crush us like grapes so we become wine—but he never humiliates. That is the game of little people.'

'I have always depended on my own resources.'

'God gives us everything, including resources. But without him in our lives, even our resources fail.' He applied the balm.

'Tell me again why the peace comes—and then goes away.'

'His job is to stick with us, no matter what, and it's our job to stay close to him. Draw nigh to me, he says, and I will draw nigh to you. When we wander away, all we need to do is cry out to him, and he draws us back—into his peace, his love, his grace. He doesn't wander, we do.'

'Why must it come to this? Why must our lives be shackled to some so-called being who can't even be seen?'

'But he can be seen. We see him in each other every day. I see him in you.'

She closed her eyes. A long breath from her, as if she'd been holding it back.

'I've hurt many people,' she said.

'Despair can be passed like a wafer to everyone around us, especially to those close to us. Into the bloodstream it goes, and down along the family line. Then comes the clot that stops someone's heart, that puts a welcome end to it for them, but not for the others. You were not the direct cause of that terrible death, Evelyn.'

'Such an emptiness,' she said.

'You may have come across Blaise Pascal in your husband's library. He said, There's a God-shaped vacuum in the heart of every person, and it can't be filled by any created thing. It can only be filled by God, made known through Jesus Christ.'

'I don't wish to go on . . . without the peace.'

'Would you like Tad to come?'

'Tad is with his brother, leave him be. You are all we have.'

It was his own surrender he saw in her.

They were on the porch with Seamus and the dogs when a vehicle of uncertain vintage roared up the drive.

'Paddy!' said Seamus, reaching for his comb.

The driver braked, left the motor running, stepped out, and removed a large suitcase, then another, from the trunk. Paddy stood down from the car, glanced up at the assembly.

'Seamus! Give a hand here.'

Paddy was blowing as he reached the porch. He removed dark glasses, eyed the Broughadoon trio. 'Are you celebrating her recovery or is she still screaming bloody murder?'

His jaw felt slightly locked. 'Some better, we think.'

Paddy glanced at Anna without greeting. 'I'm intent on wrapping up my novel, I suppose you've heard I'm writing one. 'Tis impossible to find proper solitude in Dublin with its blather and nonsense.'

He would have introduced his wife, but Paddy passed quickly into the entrance hall, a sharp smell of aftershave in his wake.

Seamus made it to the porch, thumped down the heavy bags. 'Joseph and Mary,' he said, aghast.

# Thirty-eight

*Dear Henry,*

*You must not think I forgot my promise to write regularly—the guilt of not doing so is felt each day. Further, I left my cell phone with its internat'l calling plan in Mitford and am dependent upon the business phone here, which is why I didn't call back after speaking with Sister's eldest. He says your last doctor's visit was good. Thankful to hear you are growing stronger, though yet fatigued. I have a foolish worry that you will forget and eat a 'thin-skinned' fruit, as you were cautioned not to do!*

*In any case, we remain in the fishing lodge at Lough Arrow, and circumstances have been in flux, to say the least.*

*Cynthia had an ankle incident yet again, but is on way to recovery.*

*We have made the acquaintance of an Irish woman who, until this afternoon's unleashing of her heart to God, reminded me of our father. (An amazing story which I will tell you later.) Dad is unforgettable for many reasons; I am today moved by a great tenderness for him. As I once said, you got his good looks—something to be pretty happy about.*

*Then there are the two brothers and their long antagonism—now it appears that Paddy, the elder, who inherited the manor house and a hundred acres, has stolen the painting (mentioned in my last letter) from Liam, the younger, who through a twist of circumstance inherited but a few pictures and books. Pardon the tangled density of that sentence.*

*I Googled such a theft in the US and learned it is a felony. If Irish law is similar to ours, Paddy could serve a sentence of up to twenty years if convicted.*

*Liam will learn this evening from his wife, Anna, that the painting has been found in Paddy's cellar, making Paddy the prime suspect. Anna, who remembers her convent studies of volcanoes, predicts a large eruption by her husband, 'with a Plinian column several miles high.' Actually, Liam is a sensitive soul with many of the most charming Irish*

*characteristics including melancholy and ebullience in
somewhat equal measure. I have taken him to heart,
as we have the entire household.*

*For these reasons and more, there have been a
few tears around here, some my own.*

*Would you pray for this family as they move
through unprecedented change and, I hope, healing?
And will you pray for Dooley as he returns to school
for another year on his journey to becoming a vet?*

*Thanks to the vagaries of C's ankle, we have
been largely housebound, but tomorrow will visit
Tobernalt, a holy well not far from Lough Arrow,
then on to WB Yeats's Innisfree. We are at last
being Tourists From the States.*

*I will sign off now and call on arrival home. I
know the fatigue was anticipated, but I hope not too
much to keep you out of your cantaloupe patch in
the cool of the morning. You, Peggy and Sister
faithfully in our prayers. C sends fondest love,
as do I.*

*Dhia dhuit, my brother*

He signed the letter, folded it, glanced at his
wife, who was looking out the window.

'What are you thinking?'

'Thinking I'd hate to be an innkeeper,' she
said. 'I could do everything but keep up ap-
pearances.'

'How do you mean?'

'I mean I could do the laundry and cooking—all that, if I had to—but the smiling and being charming to guests through thick and thin? No way. Poor Liam. Poor Anna. And what about Paddy? What if he should go down to check on the painting and really hide it, so it's never seen again?'

'My guess is, Liam will get Corrigan out here pronto. You know Corrigan will want to speak with us.'

'And Evelyn. They'll want to question her, too. I hate that.' She sat in her chair, tapped her foot. 'We weren't supposed to go home, of course.'

'Maybe we weren't supposed to mess about in people's basements, either. An innocent bit of sightseeing that opened Pandora's box.'

'Darling,' she said, 'around here, Pandora's box *stays* open.'

A knock at the door. Liam.

'Can you step away?'

'I can.'

Boiling this time, none of the ashen, anguished look following previous domestic cataclysms. They went along the hall and down the stairs and turned into a dark passageway with a door at the end. Liam opened the door to a large room filled with light and the smell of sawn wood.

Liam closed the door behind them, furious.

'If I go up, I'll kill him. No weapons.' Liam held out his hands, palms lifted. 'Just these, Rev'rend, that's how I'd do it. I got in th' Rover, but Anna pulled me out an' I know she's right. I can't murder my own brother, be Cain to Abel. And so I shake myself and try to be grateful th' Barret's turned up, then it comes over me again, this fierce craving to throttle him, an' I knew I needed help.'

'When is Corrigan coming?'

'Half an hour. Before th' dinner rush begins in th' kitchen.'

'You don't have time to murder your brother.'

'God above.' Liam sat on a sawhorse. 'Th' Sweeneys bringin' family tonight. Twenty for dinner.'

'Eighteen for dinner. I'm taking Cynthia to Jack Kennedy's.'

At five o'clock they were sprawled fully dressed on the bed when Maureen gave a knock.

'Can ye come to th' kitchen, then, th' both of ye? Th' detective with th' big eyebrows is here with his man takin' notes, an' two Gards in th' car.'

'We're coming,' he said.

'There's no stoppin' a goin' wheel, is it, Rev'rend? If 't isn't one thing, 't is grown into twenty.'

William, Anna, Liam, Bella at the kitchen table with Corrigan. Maureen took a seat by the door.

Corrigan gave a curt nod toward empty chairs at the table. 'Reverend, Missus Kav'na, sit there, please. I believe you're rescheduling your return to the States, Reverend?'

'My wife's ankle . . .'

Corrigan's eyes nearly disappearing beneath his brows. 'A deal of trouble, that ankle.'

'I'll say,' said Cynthia.

'You were with Seamus Doyle when the painting was discovered?'

'Yes,' he said.

'Would you tell us how you came on it?'

'We wanted to see the concealed room,' said his wife. 'And so—'

'The concealed room, Reverend?'

'It was written about in a journal kept by the doctor who built Catharmore in 1862. It was his quarantine room.'

'And did you locate it?'

'Yes. Seamus was taking us around to the rooms we wanted to see—'

'There were other rooms you wished to see?'

'Yes. The surgery and the waiting room.'

'Because we'd been reading about them,' said Cynthia.

'How did you come upon the painting, Reverend?'

'We found what we believed was the quarantine room, as it fit the description in the doctor's journal. Currently it's a storage room for the Conor boys' childhood paraphernalia. Having been a boy myself, I was curious to see what they'd held on to over the years. There was a stack of louvers leaning against a bunk bed—the louvers caught my eye because they were out of context.'

'Storage rooms typically lack context.'

'Indeed. Then I saw something in the stack that didn't look like a louver, so we put the flashlight on it. It appeared to be a gilt frame. Actually, I didn't immediately think of the Barret, I was surprised to see such a thing stored in a damp basement. Then it dawned. Seamus pulled the louvers away, and there was the Barret.'

Liam's face drawn. Bella hunched, head lowered.

Corrigan pushed away from the table, undid the single button of his tweed jacket. 'Did you have physical contact with the frame or the canvas?'

'We did not.'

'Did you replace the louvers?'

'We did.'

'Who did?'

'Seamus.'

'Did you have permission from the owner to look at the premises?'

'The owner was away at the time.'

'Who gave you permission?'

'Paddy Conor is said to be proud of the place and doesn't mind showing it now and then. Mrs. Conor knew we were looking about; in fact, we were there at her request.'

'We'd like to take this journal to the station. Where would we find it?'

'In our room,' said his wife.

'In plain view?'

'Yes.'

'Describe the journal, Reverend Kav'na.'

'Large. Leather-bound. On the table between the wing chairs.' He didn't like the idea of the journal leaving their room.

'But we're *reading* it,' said Cynthia.

'To your knowledge, was anyone else reading it these last weeks?'

'Nobody reads it.' Liam, snappish. ''t is long-winded as any politician, an' faded ink into th' bargain.'

'Reverend?' said Corrigan.

'I'm guessing it hasn't been read by anyone else in some time. Also, it's been in our room for a week or two, not certain how long.'

Corrigan spoke to the Gard taking notes. 'Second floor, second door on the right, and bring it down.'

'What are you up to, then?' Liam asked Corrigan.

William thumped his cane. 'A good question!'

'I'm going up with the Gards and have Seamus Doyle show us through the cellar, for one thing.'

'Sir,' said William, 'there's a very sick oul' woman up there. I'd like to ask ye not to trouble her.'

'She must be troubled, Mr. Donavan, as must anyone else in the household at this time. Mr. Conor, I'd like you to come along.'

'No way can I come up. We've eighteen for dinner this evenin' an' goin' on six-thirty, by my watch. No, no.'

'We'll need a statement from you.'

'My statement is that this whole bloody thing is a bloody torment, and I look forward to seein' it bloody done with. That's my statement.'

'We'll ask you to come to the station tomorrow. Noon sharp. We'll be taking the painting with us for evidence, dusting for fingerprints, building a case. You say your brother knows nothing of the discovery?'

'He doesn't know,' said Liam. 'What could be th' sentence for such as this?'

'Ten years, and possibly a fine into the bargain. Please come with us, Reverend. As you were the one to discover the painting, you may be helpful.'

His wife had that look. 'Detective Corrigan, you can't possibly make use of the journal while you're at Catharmore. Please be kind enough to leave it here and collect it when you're done up the hill.'

Corrigan gave her a cold stare.

'I'm *reading* it, sir.'

Corrigan stood, buttoned his jacket. No cigar.

# Thirty-nine

He stared at his face in the bathroom mirror.

Bags under his eyes. A five o'clock shadow gone wild. No wonder Corrigan eyed him as if he were a common criminal. While banging around in the Catharmore cellar an hour ago, he reached up to scratch his chin and was dismayed to find he hadn't shaved. What day was this, anyway, and what had he done with it?

To reckon whether his brain was still operative, he ticked off the list.

Up early this morning and a run by the lake.

Jack Kennedy's for lunch.

Catharmore and the alarming overdose scenario.

Evelyn's peaceful surrender, the simplicity of it; he would not forget the ease of both their spirits, and the benediction he felt.

He slathered on the shaving cream, ran hot water over the razor head.

Then he had written Henry and put it in the post box and gone with Liam to the unfinished guest room for a bit of hysteria, then off to the kitchen for a round with the detective, and then up to Catharmore for another plague of questions. All this followed by Paddy being put under arrest and taken away with the painting. Evelyn had been briefly questioned by Corrigan, with only Feeney in the room; at news of Paddy's arrest, she had turned her face to the wall, stoical. As for Fletcher, Feeney was stern but forgiving, and bringing on a replacement for Eileen.

He felt the circumstances of the day in his bones; he was sautéed, baked, broiled, fried. Seven-thirty. In a half hour, dinner at Jack Kennedy's. God help him.

The razor had made a clean sweep of the left jaw when he heard someone knocking; heard Cynthia say, Come in.

Then he heard Bella say Paddy didn't do it, and then the sobbing, which went on for some time. He shaved the other side, wiped his face, stood frozen as a mullet, listening.

'Come,' said his wife, her voice nearly inaudible. 'Come and tell me everything.'

'Jack was usin' me. He never meant to take me to Dublin to see Da, and New York was but a black lie, a bit of chat he might give any bird on the street. And th' way he never met me in the lane as he said he would, and me waitin' so many hours in th' night, and for all that, I was still after doin' something for him, something terrible.'

More sobbing.

'Th' cupboard business, like I said, was for credit cards an' cash, an' a fine watch to show his mates in Dublin. But the cupboard went wrong and he was angry about it, as if I'd let him down somehow. I was glad it went wrong, for I hadn't wanted to be part of it, yet I couldn't say no to him.

'And so he'd seen th' painting an' thought it very grand, and I went on and on about its great worth, you see. Hundreds of euro it's worth, I said, and he said he was sorry about not takin' me to New York an' all that, and if I'd stake him to another chance, on his word he would take me an' we smoked a j together to seal th' promise.'

'You did drugs with him?'

'Only th' j an' only th' once. He withheld

everything from me, including his charmin' affections, but he was ever promisin' more to come. 't would be grand, he said.

'I told him I was doin' th' concert for guests an' he said would I keep them entertained an' out of th' dining room. Five minutes was all he needed, he said, but ten would be better, for he'd be liftin' th' painting off th' wall and must then get round th' house and into th' lane. He said I'd see th' painting again, in th' form of fancy gear an' nice pubs, an' th' bling I'd be flashin' as he danced me round Dublin on his arm.'

Sobbing.

'He had only a bicycle, you see, no van or car to put anything in, but he said he'd get a mate with a van an' they'd carry it away. An' so the painting disappeared as planned, and then th' terrible uproar with th' Gards, an' Liam an' Mum so broken by it, an' even Mamó sufferin'. I saw it only as a painting, I didn't know about th' insurance an' all that; I didn't know it meant so much to Liam and everyone here. I thought they loved it because 't was pricey, but they loved it for its beauty, Liam said, an' 't was nearly all he had from his oul' da.

'How did you feel about that?'

'Sorry, very sorry to cause so much hurt,

and frightened that I'd be linked to it, that Jack would be caught and confess.'

'And then?'

'I was to meet Jack th' evenin' after th' fair and we would go away, but then he went and sliced that poor bloke nearly to bits. 't was horrible to know I would have run away with someone after killin' a man, an' th' whole thing so vicious. I knew deep inside he was a bad lot, Jack. I knew it, but I wanted to get away from Broughadoon for all that.'

'Did he take the painting to Catharmore?'

'I don't know. I only know he'd done work in Paddy's cellar an' after that, came and went as he pleased, for th' door was never locked. He sometimes slept there, he said, when his rent was late, and no one knew it—he was on th' pig's back, he said, to be goin' in an' out of such a grand place an' no one the wiser. He never mentioned Paddy, I don't think th' painting was anything at all to do with Paddy. I think Jack couldn't get a van or whatever he needed, an' had no other place to put it 'til he could carry it away to Dublin. He had a mucker there, he said, who would fence it in London.'

'Why no fingerprints on the cupboard or in the dining room?'

'Gloves. Jack said he always wore gloves when stealin' from th' rich to give to th' poor, which was himself.'

'You must tell all this to your family, Bella, and then to the Garda.'

'They say an accomplice gets th' same punishment as th' one doin' th' crime. I don't want th' terrible desperation of prison. My da knows blokes released from prison; 't is a nasty life. I couldn't do it, Cynthia, I couldn't, please God.'

'They will love you through this—your mother, Liam, Maureen, William. They will love you through it.'

'No one really loves me, not even my da.' Weeping. 'I don't deserve love, not from anyone.'

'God loves us whether we deserve it or not. He's loving you right now as you release your sorrow to me.'

'I can't believe that.'

'There's something my husband often quotes: Love is an endless act of forgiveness. Over and over again, we need forgiveness from others, just as we need to forgive others—over and over again.'

A long silence.

'Confession makes us clean again, Bella—it reconciles us to God. Forgiveness does the same. And God will forgive you, Bella, just as everyone here will forgive you. All you have to do is ask. I promise.'

'I knew I was doin' wrong and hurting others yet I did it anyway, an' sometimes I felt really smug over bein' cruel. I can't ask God to forgive that.'

'I'll ask him for you, then.'

There was a stillness in the room, then his wife praying. He crossed himself and prayed, also. Where two or more are gathered together.

'What I came up to say is your husband needs to call Dooley Barlowe. I spoke with Dooley on th' phone, he said he liked th' funny way I talk an' I told him he has a funny way of speakin' himself.'

Cynthia laughed.

'An' so I came up to give you the message, and when I opened th' door, I couldn't hold it in any longer, it came pourin' out.'

'I've just read something about seeing a nasty thing fixed back to a good thing. You will see this fixed back, Bella.'

'I don't want to see Paddy sent away for what he had no part in. He can be a dreadful man, Paddy, but he's always been kind to me. He took me fishin' many times when I was little, an' always liked my music.'

'When will you tell your family?'

'I mustn't say anything 'til dinner is over. We'll be slammed tonight with eighteen on us, an' it must be very special. I wish you didn't have to go to Jack Kennedy's.'

'We'll be back.'

'His meatloaf is gross, his chops are cremated.'

'I'll remember that.'

'If you could be with me when I tell them . . .'

'Of course. Yes. I'll be with you.'

'Even your husband, who seems to settle Liam down.'

'We'll do it. I'm proud of you, Bella. You're living up to your name.'

'I couldn't go on like I was goin'.'

'You're growing up.'

He heard the door close and went into the room and put his arms around his wife. They held each other, wordless, looking beyond the window to the lough, as Fintan and Caitlin had done when they saw the rainbow.

# Forty

'Hey, Dad.'

'Hey, buddy.'

'Thanks for callin' back. I wanted to tell you I'm not done.'

'Great. Terrific!'

The kitchen crew going hammer and tong.

'Bet you're done, though. You've been gone a long time for a guy who doesn't like to travel.'

'Right. But I'm not done, either. We'll be a few days yet, I'll let you know.'

'She apologized.'

'Wonderful.'

'Said she was sorry she called me a rich puke of shallow character.'

Classic Lace Turner. Self-educated largely

through the services of a rural bookmobile, now an honor student at the University of Virginia. Impeccable grammar, colorful way of putting things.

'Are you a rich puke of shallow character?'

'I don't think so.'

'Trust me, she doesn't think so, either. How about you?'

'What do you mean?'

'Did you apologize?'

'For what?'

'Come on. Whatever you said or did to make her punch you.'

'Yes, sir.'

'May I ask what it was all about?'

'I wasn't going to tell you, because it makes you crazy. But since you're asking—we had a date, I was late.'

A cloud of steam over the stove top; Bella hoicking a roast from the oven.

'How late?'

'There was this friend who came by, I never get to see him—'

'How late?'

'An hour.'

'First time?'

'I wish. I've been late a lot, and she hates it; I mean, really hates it. But hey, Dad, love is three-sixty-five, twenty-four/seven. Why get upset about a few minutes?'

They'd had the Punctuality Talk many times over. It was a thorn. 'That sounds good, but . . .'

'But what?'

'Love shows up on time.'

The dreaded phone silence.

'Well, look, son, they're busy here. Know that we love you. Catch you later, gotta go.'

That was Dooley's sign-off protocol—he'd never used it before. He wasn't sure how he felt about it.

He was thinking of Evelyn Conor as he went upstairs. He felt he should be there, but Feeney had sent him home. 'You have a date with your wife,' Feeney said. 'Best to keep it.' Anyway, off to Tobernalt and Innisfree tomorrow and no chance to visit Catharmore. This wasn't feeling right.

Jack Kennedy's was loud, crowded, upbeat. They sat at the bar.

'You're plenty beautiful,' he said.

'Thanks. I love it when you talk like that.'

'Proud of you.'

'Proud of you back. Bella says skip the meatloaf.'

'What'll it be, Missus Kav'na? I hope you're not a teetotaler like th' rev'rend here.'

'Ah, no,' she said, 'not a'tall. I'll have th' po-teen, if you'd be so kind.'

Jack Kennedy amused. 'Th' poteen, is it? An' which kind would it be?'

'Which kind do you *have,* Mr. Kennedy?'

'I can pour you th' fightin' kind, th' lovin' kind, or th' cryin' kind.'

'I'll take th' cryin' kind, for we're leavin' soon an' I'll be sad t' go.'

Jack marveling.

'Just kidding,' said Cynthia. 'Make it a gin-ger ale, straight up.'

Laughter all around.

'I can't take her anywhere,' he said.

She sipped her drink.

'What are you thinking?' he asked.

'How bad could the meatloaf *be,* Timothy? Because now I'm hungry for meatloaf.'

The Vauxhall crunched onto the Brougha-doon gravel at nine-thirty. Laughter floated out to them.

'Merriment,' she said. ''t is a lovely sound.'

'We'll be having our own merriment soon enough.' At fall break, four boys, mostly grown, each a dazzle to their adoring younger sister. Picnics in Baxter Park. Grilling in the back yard. And Barnabas looking for a handout. Oh, yes.

'Let's sit on the bench,' she said. 'It's been ages.'

'Good. But let's go through the lodge. Too much gravel to navigate.'

Pud raced out, tail wagging. No shoe. Maybe he should get serious and help the little guy find his shoe. He leaned down, gave Pud a scratch.

'Did you take his shoe again?'

'I did not,' she said. 'Scout's honor.'

'Rev'rend! Missus!' William by the fire in his blue jacket, a pocket handkerchief, a tie they hadn't seen.

'It's Mr. Yeats himself!' said Cynthia.

'You're slaggin' me, now.'

'Not a bit. You look wonderful.'

William's cheeks coloring, eyes bright. 'Thank ye, thank ye. Sit down an' take a load off your foot, Missus. Y'r Pud was at th' door since ye went out, not lookin' left or right.'

They sat on the sofa. He patted the vacant cushion; Pud leaped onto it.

'So, William, how about a checkers game tomorrow evening?'

'Will do. Seamus is stayin' close to home for a little. I'll try to go easy on ye.'

'Very kind of you.'

'Are ye goin' up Catharmore tomorrow?'

'Not tomorrow. We're off to Tobernalt.'

'It's good ye're seein' th' sights now. Did Jack Kennedy treat ye right?'

'He did.'

'When ye do go up, might I come along?'

'Now, William.'

'Takes th' Gards a while to make it over to us, we'd be well away by then.'

'Sorry. Against the rules.'

'I'll be no trouble a'tall; she'll never know I'm about.' William leaned forward. 'I'll sit in th' portico. If she knows I'm about, 't will be because ye told her.'

'And if she asks me, I'll have to tell the truth. She'll have both our heads.'

'I'll sit on th' front steps, so.'

Right up there with the midges.

'Can't do it, William.'

More laughter from the dining room. 'Having a bit of fun, the Sweeneys.'

'Aye. Sweeneys like their bit of fun,' said William, looking glum.

'It might be a while,' he said to Cynthia. A while for the Sweeneys to uproot and go to their slumber, for the kitchen to settle down and hear what Bella had to say. He felt the urgent pull to Catharmore. 'Half an hour,' he said. 'Would that be okay?'

She knew what was on his mind. 'Take your time. I'll just have a chin-wag with William.'

'I'll tell ye about th' bloody Black an' Tan that came along our road when I was in th' cradle, how my grandfather did his bit for Ireland.' William drew out his handkerchief, gave a honk. 'An' where are ye off to, Rev'rend?'

'Mesopotamia,' said Cynthia.

Fletcher met him in the hall. 'She's completely done in. Dr. Feeney left a few minutes ago.'

'Won't stay long. Just wanted to be here. How are the wrists healing?'

'Th' splint can come off soon, we'll be doing OT, get those joints movin'. We think th' break is fine, she'll need th' cast at least another four weeks. 'Tis th' hematoma that's th' worst of it; my heart's breakin' for her, Rev'rend.'

'Make that two of us.'

The lamp burning in the corner, Cuch looking up as he came in, the air close. He sat, elbows on knees, head in hand.

'Is it you?' she whispered.

'It is.'

A long silence; minutes must have passed. He

thought she may be sleeping, then she turned her head and looked at him.

'I lost the peace. You said that would happen if we wander.'

The Enemy ever prowling to and fro. 'It was fear that pulled you away—Paddy, and all that happened today,' he said.

'What will we do? How will we all go on without each other, the way things were?'

'The way things were didn't work.'

'Yes, but they were familiar. At Cathair Mohr, we care for each other after our own fashion.'

'I understand.'

'Do you really understand, Reverend, or is that what you were trained to say?'

'It's how my own family cared for each other. I do understand.'

He couldn't tell her what Bella hadn't yet confessed to Liam and Anna, that wasn't his precinct. What if they learned Paddy had hired Slade to do it? Anything could happen.

'Let's work on the fear,' he said, 'on running back to his peace.'

'Work on leavin' off the drink, work on being courageous, work on defeating the pain. Work, work, work, Reverend, and now I must work to reclaim what I thought had been given for all time.'

'Faith is radical and often difficult. It's the narrow footpath, not the broad wagon road. Have you asked him to draw you back and take the fear away?'

'He should be good enough to do it without being asked. He's God, after all.'

'Here we go, then. Hold on to your hat.'

He touched her forehead, prayed for her—for the fear to be released, for peace to flow in.

In the long silence, her even breathing. 'What shall I do without you?'

'You'll do just fine without me. You have the one who's always available—for peace, mercy, grace, forgiveness—you name it. And of course there's Fletcher as long as she's needed, and Seamus and Liam and Anna and Tad and Feeney . . .'

'Anna, perhaps, but not Liam. I was unfair to her, but I've been especially unfair to Liam. How does one know, Reverend, what a mother is supposed to be if one has had no mothering? I suppose mothering comes from a place of deep feeling, but after the fire, that place was locked away.'

'Ask Liam to forgive you.'

'Paddy,' she said, her thoughts elsewhere. 'I tried to help him—with everything—but in all the wrong ways, I see.'

'Ask Paddy to forgive you.'

She gave him a fierce look. 'If I do all you say, Reverend, I shall be a hundred years old before I catch up.'

He laughed. Then laughed some more.

She smiled a little. 'Bloody Protestant,' she said.

The Sweeneys were still at it, but they'd spilled out to the garden, into an August night lit by fireflies and the glowing tips of cigarettes. Voices murmuring now, with the occasional bursts of laughter, little explosions of some long-held happiness or hope.

They sat in the dining room and had a decaf, watched a light moving on the lake. The kitchen was cleaning up.

'Can you make it?' he asked. 'It's been a long day.'

'Weeks were crammed into this day. But yes, I can make it if you can.'

High-five with his deacon.

'I hate that they took our journal,' she said.

It did seem their own; no one else had been interested. 'But we left off at a good place, I think.'

'The lad improved, their marriage spared, Balfour off his back.'

'The pony,' he said. 'Don't forget the pony.'

She laughed. 'Shall we drive by Balfour's place tomorrow? Anna says it's on our way home.'

'Let's do it.'

She looked toward the kitchen door. 'Bella will be in a state. To have to work all evening with that on her heart . . .'

The kitchen door swinging open, and Bella coming to them, grave. 'Are you doing . . . you know, what you should be doing?'

Cynthia embraced Bella. 'Not at this precise moment, but yes, ever since you told me. God is with you and it will be good; it's going to be good.'

'If th' Sweeneys ever leave,' said Bella.

The Sweeneys' guests were indeed leaving. They crowded into the lodge, saying their good nights to Liam and Anna and tossing fags into the fire and slapping each other on the back and speaking a bit of Irish into the bargain. The scent of wine and cologne mingled on the air, then out the door they went, crunching into the car park, as the remaining Sweeneys hied themselves to bed.

''t was a hard evening,' said Bella. 'Everyone is all-in, even Mamó, who never gets all-in.' She was trembling.

He had never seen such trembling as had

been roused at Broughadoon and Catharmore—
his own included.

'You're brave,' said Cynthia. 'Your family
will be, also.'

'I'm tryin' to be brave like Liam's oul' mum.'

There! he thought with sudden pleasure.
There's one for Evelyn Conor. And definitely
one for Bella Flaherty.

He slept hard and woke fresh, as if he'd
journeyed in himself to an unknown spring of
curative power, and drunk of it through the
night.

They lolled in bed. 'When do you think we
should go home?' he asked. 'We'll need to allow
a little time for Emma to get the tickets hammered out.'

'When we see what Corrigan thinks of all
this, I suppose. I can't dwell on the thought of
Bella getting a sentence. I cannot imagine it, I
will not.'

He dressed and went down for her coffee and
took it up, then went down again to drink his
in the garden and pick up the fag ends, make
himself useful. He checked his watch. They
needed to get going by ten, Anna said.

Liam came out in jeans, a cotton shirt, barefoot. There was the smile, almost.

He rolled out the corny proverb with the kernel of truth in it: 'The oul' silver lining.'

'Righto,' said Liam. And there was the full smile he hadn't seen in a coon's age.

'Bella was brave to tell us. She dodged a bullet with Slade, he would have mucked her life up for good.'

'Paddy's innocence will help your mother.'

'Paddy, for God's sake! I hope it teaches him a lesson, to spend time in th' slammer.'

'Did they release him?'

'They're holdin' him 'til we take Bella in for a statement. He deserves a bloody fortnight in th' can, just on general principles.'

He laughed. Liam laughed. Laughing was good.

'Any fingerprinting done yet?'

'They didn't find Paddy's, an' Seamus's were only around th' light switch an' furnace box. They'll keep working.'

'You'll put in a good word for Bella.'

'No question,' said Liam. 'Beg if we have to. I think she's turned a corner, we mustn't let it count for nothing.'

'Amen. And is there, by any chance, what we call a chain of title for Catharmore? Would Paddy have it?'

'I have Da's papers, they came with his library. He was pretty meticulous about records. Endless fishing logs, correspondence with his solicitor, that sort of thing. Why?'

'Curious. Reading the journal has us interested in how things fell out for O'Donnell and his crowd.'

'Can't do it now but I'll give a look. We have a loft room where all that's stored. I need to get up there anyway, for the provenance on the painting. Da made quite a thing of it, several pages on Barret, Sr., that I haven't read in years. A must-do.'

'How's Anna this morning?'

'Grand. Having breakfast with Bella in Ibiza, then we're off to th' Garda station.'

'Ah, Ibiza.'

'I'm takin' Anna to th' real place, Rev'rend.' Liam grinning. 'For two weeks. Don't say a word to a soul, especially Maureen, she'll shout it from th' rooftop.'

'Scout's honor. When would this happen?'

'As soon as we see how things come around.'

'You mean with Bella?'

'And with Mother.'

'Who will mind the store?'

'God above, I've no idea. If I waited 'til that was sorted out, we'd never leave th' car park.

It's only fourteen years we've talked about it. I'm lookin' in Riverstown for someone cheerful to manage th' place.'

'Thumbs up,' he said. 'What's that sound?'

Wings threshing the air overhead. He looked and saw the great white bird flying above the beeches, then another, and another; heard their snorting cry and the sound of their terrible wings, like a contraption designed by da Vinci.

''t is th' swans goin' over,' said Liam. 'They fly about now and again—to exercise their wings, it's said. Clamorous wings, Mr. Yeats said.'

Another and another, their orange beaks and black masks against the blue sky . . .

He was five years old, his mouth open in a gape, heart pounding. Back up the stairs, then, and out of breath with the morning gazette:

He'd seen swans flying, he said. You can hear their wings working. They *creak*.

The Conors would beg the judge or whoever they had to beg for the best decision for Bella.

Liam had laughed—out loud.

And here was the cover story, the best of the breaking news:

Liam was taking Anna to Ibiza as soon as things settled down and they could find someone cheerful to manage the place.

'Don't look at me,' said his wife.

The old boatman was nowhere to be found, though a small boat was drawn into the reeds.

Out of the car with the art hamper, stumbling about to find a stone to sit on, and the ensuing sketches of *A Boat in Reeds at Innisfree*.

'Very small,' he said of the island. 'Clearly no human habitation on it, and too densely wooded to walk about, anyway.'

'Yes, but on the other hand, midnight's all a glimmer there, noon is a purple glow, and evening is full of the linnet's wings.'

'You have a point,' he said.

A warm day, the midges out in great number. They found Tobernalt at once serene and celebratory. Visitors were inclined to leave ribbons, beads, trinkets of all sorts hanging from every bush and tree. Coins slept like fish at the bottom of a clear pool, people spoke in whispers or not at all. And all the while, the cool, natural spring burbling up in the heart of the ancient forest as it had done long before St. Patrick first arrived as a slave boy.

They prayed for those at home, both here and abroad, for safe travel whenever that might be, and for God's richest blessing upon the Eire and its people. Though against everything in his nature, not to mention the Scout's oath to leave things better than they were found, he wanted to offer something, too—something beautiful, from the heart, not bought over a counter.

She went through the hamper to no avail. He went through his pockets and found the Connemara Black with its feather from the crest of a golden pheasant, dark fur from a seal, and beard hackle from a blue jay.

He held it in the palm of his hand and she put on her glasses and looked at it again. 'So delicate and beautiful. Are you sure you want to leave it?'

He couldn't say why, exactly, but he did. She sketched it—for posterity, she said—and he hung it on the smallest of twigs and thought it handsome there.

Balfour's pile was a shock of sorts, though Cynthia had known for some time what had happened.

'A terrible fire,' she said, 'on Christmas Eve of 1873. No one died, but it spread to the stables and . . .'

And there was the ruin of it, dark against the afternoon sky.

'All flesh is grass,' she said, 'and architecture, too.'

'Do you want to sketch it?'

'No.'

'What did Fintan have to say about it?'

'That it grieved him for the Balfours, and for the lovely horses.'

'When you read ahead of me that time, what did you learn about Eunan, what became of him?'

'I don't know,' she said. 'I only read about the fire and how people hereabout picked through the embers and found food stored in the cellar still edible.'

He took Cynthia to their room and went down to find Liam, who was repairing the hinge on a shutter.

'Thomas Jefferson said, It's wonderful what may be done if we're always doing.'

'Just foostering about,' said Liam. 'Dinner is easy tonight. Poached salmon, a few roast potatoes. How was your day?'

'Good in every part. How did it go at the Garda station?'

'They haven't released Paddy, they're pursuing his tie to Slade. A Gard had a chat with Jack Kennedy, who remembered that Slade and Paddy had knocked back a few together.'

'When was that?'

'During the time Slade worked at Broughadoon.'

'What do you think?'

'Paddy admits he had a drink with Slade, who was already there when he came in. A total of thirty minutes, he says, and Jack Kennedy agrees. Paddy says they talked about the economy, nothin' more. Paddy says he has no idea how th' painting got in th' cellar—his fingerprints aren't on it, that's one bit out of th' way. I don't know, Rev'rend. As low as Paddy can be, I'd rather think he had nothin' to do with it, though there are times I'd like to see him rot somewhere.' Liam looked down, kicked at the gravel. 'But he's my brother, for God's sake.'

'How did Bella do?'

'She was wonderful. Really sharp and clear. Terrific.'

'What do you think is next?'

'Corrigan was very touched by her confession, it seems. He has a daughter her age. We don't know. He says keep her close by, they'll get back to us.'

'What's your gut on it?'

'No way to know. She has no record, she's clean. That helps.'

'Your mother?'

'Anna went up with a jar of her famous chicken soup. Says Mother took a little an' it didn't come back.'

'Good,' he said. 'I'd best go to the room and get myself ready for the big game tonight.'

'William's not th' best player you'll ever come against, it's th' *craic* he's after.'

'*Craic?*'

'Th' fun, th' blather.'

He was ready for fun and blather.

'Oh, Rev'rend.' Liam trotting after him as he started up the stairs.

'I forgot to tell you I got into Da's papers. Amazing what's up there, your bit wasn't hard to find. If you've got a minute . . .'

They met for a half hour in the library, where he took a hurried scramble of notes.

All previous gazettes would pale.

# Forty-one

He'd just been down to speak with Anna, couldn't find her, left a note on the kitchen work-table, and came back up, blowing like a mule.

A knock.

Lord knows he was afraid to open the door around here.

Anna with a hesitant look. 'The nurse called, Reverend. She's asking for you . . .'

'Ah.'

'. . . and for Da, as well.'

He heard Cynthia say something she hardly ever said. 'Wow.'

'I'll be right along. Does William know?'

'He does, he's dressing. He's—how shall we

say?—a basket case.' She smiled. 'I saw your note asking about flowers—you mustn't go to a florist, absolutely not. You may cut from the garden in the morning—best to wait 'til the dew is off—and take anything you like. I'll have a trug on the bench, and clippers.'

'Many thanks.'

'They'll stay quite fresh; Ballyrush is no distance a'tall.'

'That will be good.'

'Thank you for going up with Da,' she said. 'I wanted to tell you she apologized to me.'

'Wonderful.' Beyond wonderful. He thought Anna a beautiful woman, ever at a loss to conceal her feelings.

'I believe she will do the same with Liam; it's just that she feels great shame about her treatment of him, and 't is harder.'

'Can he forgive her, do you think?'

'I pray so.'

He closed the door and turned to his deacon.

'We need to get out of here,' he said. 'It's time.'

'Yes. Whatever comes, they'll work it out. We can't stay 'til everything is worked out, we'd be here 'til the trumpet sounds.'

'Precisely.'

'Why are we cutting flowers in the morning?'

'Can't say. It's a surprise.'

'I love—'

'I know.'

'So.' She took a deep breath, exhaled.

'So how about this? Dear Emma, We're done. Get us out of here ASAP. Your humble and grateful servant forevermore.'

'I would not say humble to Emma Newland, and definitely not forevermore.'

'But it'll be a pain, don't you think, to get business class this time of year?'

'For us it would be a pain. For Emma, 't is her soul's delight. She loves going up against large corporations of all kinds, not to mention the occasional government agency.'

In the kitchen, he checked his watch for the date.

<Dear Emma, get us out of here Saturday
a.m. and order the lg. vase my Amex.

Your grateful servant>

'I forgot,' said his wife when he came back to the room for his collar and prayer book. 'Don't say servant, either. Definitely not. She will take it literally for the rest of your life.'

'Too late,' he said.

He met Maureen in the hall with her laundry basket, gave her a kiss on both cheeks. 'A miracle, her askin' our William up. Miracles still happen, don't they, Rev'rend?'

'All the time,' he said.

William gabbing, retying his tie, puffing up his pocket handkerchief as they rattled up the hill.

'Looks like you're preaching somewhere,' he said.

William's hands trembled. 'She'll be th' one preachin'.'

Ireland definitely won the trophy for trembling, he reckoned, and yet another for lachrymose. A shelf full of trophies he'd give the old Eire.

William looked done-in. 'I'll be fair game for ye tonight, Rev'rend.'

'We can do it another time.'

'I'll take a rain check, then, if ye don't mind.'

Seamus answered their knock.

'How is she?'

'I'm afraid to say it.'

'Say it anyway.'

'She's better. Aye. Some better.'

He crossed himself. William did the same.

'Still a lot of pain,' said Fletcher. 'Some tremoring, some nausea—and the depression, poor love, is terrible. But she's got th' quick wit comin' back, Dr. Feeney says, and a bit of appetite. She might really make it, Rev'rend, I believe she will, 't will be a Guinness record! On the other hand, I remember hearin' of an' oul' gent who got sober at ninety but it killed him for all that—he only lived a year or two.'

'That'll work,' he said.

William hanging on to his cane for dear life.

'How shall we go in, Fletcher? One at a time?'

'She wants you both together.'

'Joseph, Mary, an' all th' saints,' said William.

He thought he could hardly bear again the sight of the splint, the cast; the entrapment of both arms at once.

'*Dhia dhuit*, Evelyn.'

'*Dhia is Muire dhuit*, Reverend.'

'Where would you like us to sit?'

'Please sit in the corner. Ask Mr. Donavan to sit by me.'

William fairly collapsed into the armchair. He took his place in the corner; Cuch got up, stretched, came and lay at his feet.

Evelyn's hair dark against the pillow. She turned her head and studied William.

'Ye oul' bandit,' she said.

'Did ye see my portrait th' Missus Kav'na done?'

No, no, William, back off that, for Pete's sake.

'I thought you might use it, sir, to keep the crows from your broad beans.'

William retrenching, clearing his throat, diving in. 'I'd like to say I forgive ye for tryin' to kill me, Evie.'

'You, th' bloody savage runnin' off to disgrace an innocent girl you promised to marry—and you forgive me?'

'Now, Evie . . .'

'And no more callin' me Evie, as if you deserved to put tongue to my private name.'

''t was meself give you that private name, remember?'

'I remember nothing of the sort.'

William rethinking, giving his handkerchief a honk. 'Well, then, to go on, if ye'd be so kind—I forgive ye for marryin' th' oul' man an' bearin' his children an' not mine.'

'A fine husband you would have made, Willie Donavan, with naught to warm y'r bones but a ravin' lunatic pride in th' number of lives you maimed and squandered.'

'I never killed a man, Evie, an' maimed but a few.'

As far as they were concerned, he had vanished into the paper on the walls.

'I forgive ye for th' thankless manner ye showed when you were hard up an' I bought Broughadoon,' said William. 'An' that's all th' forgivin' I can give ye.'

'Has it occurred to you even once in that thick skull of yours to ask forgiveness of me? Had you no wrongdoing toward me?'

'Well, then, if it's come to that . . .' William gathered his forces. 'Forgive me for bein' a brute an' lettin' ye down!'

Evelyn speaking Irish. Heated.

'I don't understand a word ye say in the oul' tongue. I'm a modern man, Evie, a *modern* man. Ye'd be better off to say a kind word in dacent English, if ye don't mind. 't would be an improvement to your health.'

Way to go, William.

A long release of breath from Evelyn. 'Reverend.'

'Yes?'

'Bring me the Purdey.'

'Oh, very sly ye are, with your blinkin' wit. Still th' sleeveen, I see, an' you a woman up in years.' William stood, huffed.

'Sit down, ye oul' gossoon.'

'Why should I sit an' be treated like an eejit when I've come with forgiveness of every kind, th' same man who bought your hundred acres an' a pile of rubble an' made it lovely so as to give ye a dacent neighbor?' William's breath short. 'An' why did ye ask us up in th' first place, as if we had nothin' more to do than take th' lashin' of your desperate tongue?'

'Sit down,' she said.

William sat.

'Thank you for forgiving me, William.' The tremoring. 'As you might imagine, I asked you up for a purpose.'

'I'd be keen to hear th' purpose.'

'I forgive you, William.'

William waited. 'That's all ye have to say?'

'That should be enough.'

'I'd thank ye to put a bit of shine on 't, if ye wouldn't mind. Is it th' matter of bein' a brute an' lettin' ye down which you're for-givin'? Ye could try bein' more . . .'—William chose his word—'*specific.*'

'Well, then. I forgive your brutish ways and selfish pride, William Donavan. I forgive your indifference to human suffering, your cunning deceptions, your careless betrayal, and until now, your refusal to admit any wrongdoing whatever.'

He was quiet for a moment. 'An' I forgive you, Evelyn McGuiness, of each an' every one of th' same, thank ye.'

They rattled down the lane after a cup of tea with Seamus.

'That's a mean oul' woman,' said William with some pride.

'Aye,' he said.

He was having a quick look at *The Independent* when Liam came into the library.

'I'd like to know how it went, but it's O'Malley on th' phone—another bit for th' lovelorn columns. Wanted your contact in th' States; he's thrilled to find you're still about.' Liam handed over his mobile. 'Step out, you'll get better reception.'

Out into birdsong and a mild breeze whipping up. 'Pete!'

'Tim, you lucky dog—still soakin' up th' best of th' west at ol' Broughadoon!'

'Leaving soon.'

'How's Cynthia?'

'Ankle improved. We're seeing a few sights.'

'Great. Just wanted you to know she's still here.'

'Aha. How's it going?'

'I'm afraid to say.'

'Say anyway.'

'Looks like she's in for th' long haul.'

'You must be doing something right, O'Malley.'

'I'm tryin', Tim. Keep your fingers crossed.'

'That does no good a'tall, I hate to tell you.'

'Do th' other, then, and thanks—thanks a lot. You an' Cynthia try to get back next year, okay? I'll bring Linda.'

'Linda *and* Roscoe, and we might have a deal. What do you think did the trick? I might launch a scientific study.'

'All th' stuff you said, plus . . .'

'Plus?'

'Leavin' tomorrow for two weeks in Ibiza.'

'Keep up the good work,' he said. 'And Pete?'

'Yo!'

'Remember to listen when she talks.'

'That's the bloody hard part,' said Pete.

He gave Pete his home number, returned the phone to Liam.

'Looks like we're in th' marriage counseling business,' said Liam. 'How did it go up th' hill?'

'I suppose you could call it a miracle and be done with it. Or maybe an uneasy truce. They forgave each other, after a fashion.'

'I never know what to say for all you do.'

'I didn't do it.'

'We'll call it a miracle, then, an' be done,' said Liam.

'Any developments?'

'God above, my head's thick as plaster. Corrigan called. He wants us at the station tomorrow to make things official. Bella's clear.'

'Thank heaven.'

'No previous record; she fell in with a bad sort, made some bad decisions, then had the guts to come clean about it, Corrigan says. He wants her to stay close for six months, and write a letter of apology to her mother an' me. One to th' Gards, too, who blew out time an' money.'

'A very fair man, to say the least. Does Cynthia know?'

'She does. Bella's with her now. They had Slade's fingerprints from the Tubbercurry arrest, matched 'em with prints on th' louvers, th' light switch, all over th' cellar. And here's another gobsmacker. Lorna Doolin, the book writer, wants th' Broughadoon job while we're away. She managed a four-star inn in New Hampshire an' can make a fry into th' bargain. Bella's after takin' over dinner, an' we think she'd be grand. What do you say, Rev'rend?'

What could he say? 'Wow.'

'But we have to shake a leg an' go before th' niece's school opens. Lorna's in training as we speak, 't will be fodder for her next mystery, she says.'

'She just missed the mystery!'

'We didn't want to be away if things, you know, don't go well with . . . up th' hill. I asked Feeney—he said such a chance won't come round again, he thinks we should go.'

'Anna knows the plan, then?'

'She's blown away.' Liam rocked on the balls of his feet, eyes blue. 'Me, too. Any advice for the oul' second honeymoon crowd?'

'Oh, just the usual. Be sure to listen when she talks.'

'That's tough,' said Liam.

'I know,' he said.

<Dear Fr Tim,

<e-ticket, Biz Class, 11:00 a.m. Saturday, Dublin, non-stop Atlanta, express to Hky., details below.

<Pray for Harold's test on limp nodes.

<This will come as a shock but I am retiring. Don't worry you can still be my servant, ha ha. Call when home.

<Vase ordered.

<Love,

<Emma>

He met Bella coming from their room. He realized that until now he had never seen her smile.

'Good work,' he said.

'Thank you.'

He wanted to give her a hug, but he'd done that last night.

'*Dhia Dhuit*, Bella.'

'*Dhia is Muire dhuit*, Rev'rend.'

He didn't show Cynthia the email.

'We have this evening and tomorrow. Then up and away at six-thirty Wednesday morning. I'll call Aengus.'

'Busy, busy.'

He headed downstairs. By rough calculation, this was his thirteenth time on the stairs today. Like the rest of the common horde, they'd need a holiday to rest up from their vacation.

# Forty-two

Their last hurrah.

'The full Irish!' Cynthia told Emily.

'Make it two,' he said.

Lorna Doolin was at the Aga this morning; she and Emily served them with a certain bravado.

'Perhaps a mite long under the broiler, your tomatoes,' said Lorna, using the short *a*.

'That's how we like them,' said his agreeable wife.

Emily poured their coffee. 'I read your books when I was a child,' she said.

'And how long ago was that?'

'Ages ago,' said Emily. 'I found them really well done.'

'Well, thanks very much. And you, Lorna, I hear you're doing this two-week stint as research for a book.'

'Hoping to refresh my lapsing memory of the innkeeping business. I've always wanted to set a murder mystery in a guest lodge.'

'Nothing too bloody, I hope,' said his wife.

'Aunt Lorna loves blood and gore,' said Emily.

'Nonsense; I don't like it in the least. It's my readers who love blood and gore. Back to the States, then?'

'First thing tomorrow.'

'Will you want your fry?'

'We must be out by six-thirty. Just coffee and fruit, thanks.'

'I'll have it on the sideboard at a quarter 'til six.'

'We wish you well in your new occupation,' said Cynthia.

'I'll relish it for precisely two weeks and not a moment longer.'

'Running a guest lodge can be very taxing,' said Emily.

They were off in the Vauxhall, the contents

of the trug nearly overcoming the smell of motor oil and aging leather.

'I thought Lorna looked confident in her hair cloud and borrowed clogs.'

'Um,' he said.

'Whatever happened to child labor laws?'

'Um,' he said.

She gave him a look, itching for a clue.

'You'll get nothing from me, Kav'na.'

It was a morning the poets might easily call glimmering; their last morning of a full day in Ireland. In their time here, they'd seen very little, though somehow he felt they'd seen everything. It had been Blake's ocean in a drop of water, a broad beach in a grain of sand.

'St. Patrick's Church, circa 1886,' he said as they pulled into the car park at Ballyrush. 'Aughanagh Parish, Diocese of Elphin.'

'Tad's church?'

'Yes.'

An arched eyebrow, a knowing look.

'You think you've guessed?'

'I think so.'

'We'll see about that,' he said.

He took the trug; helped her navigate the grassy maze among Rooneys and Rileys, Mitchells and Moores, McKinneys and McConnells.

They took their time gazing at inscriptions,

she ever on the hunt for one to top his all-time favorite from St. John's in the Grove: *Demure at last.*

'Should be along here, I think." He had a bit of chill up his spine. 'Yes. Right here.'

She adjusted her glasses, leaned close to the old stone. 'Cormac Padraigin Fintan O'Donnell, MD.' She looked at him, beaming, then read on. 'Born County Sligo October 28, 1810, departed this life December 12, 1887. Passed into the Care of the Great Physician.'

He held the trug. She took cosmos and rosemary and verbena and wrapped the stems with a vine and laid the offering on the green mound.

He made the sign of the cross. 'For the many good works of Dr. Fintan O'Donnell, for his people and for Ireland—Lord, we give you thanks and praise.'

'Amen,' she said.

She moved to the mound beside Fintan's. 'Caitlin Alanna McKenna O'Donnell, Departed this life May 15, 1888. Healer, Protector, Devoted Wife and Mother, Generous Friend.'

She looked at him. 'Mother?'

He extended the trug. 'Save a few back.'

She took rosemary and verbena and wrapped the stems and laid the offering on the green mound and made the sign of the cross and prayed. 'For the tireless and loving generosity of Caitlin O'Donnell in a time of trial for her people—Lord, we give you thanks and praise.'

'Amen,' he said.

He walked a few steps. She joined him, silent.

'This one,' he said.

She leaned to the stone and its crust of lichen. 'Eunan . . . *Eunan*! The lad!' And there came what really watered Ireland.

'Keep reading.'

'Eunan Michael O'*Donnell*! MD.'

'There are Dooleys everywhere,' he said. 'Even in Ireland, in the old fled days.'

'Did you bring a handkerchief?'

He dug it out and there it went, not to be recovered.

She was taking the remaining stems . . .

'Save some back,' he said.

She placed the flowers on the grave; he made the sign of the cross and prayed. 'For the joy that Eunan O'Donnell brought Fintan and Caitlin, and for the opportunity you afforded Eunan to be of service to others—Lord, we give you thanks and praise.'

'Amen.' She shook her head, marveling.

'Eunan! Doctor Eunan O'Donnell. This is the best.'

'Let's sit here a minute,' he said. They took the trug and walked to the nearby bench, and sat in the deep shade of an old chestnut. The heat of the day was quickly coming on.

'Thank you for doing this, sweetheart. How did you know?'

'I have my sources,' he said. 'The stones are pretty revealing in themselves, but here goes. When Fintan died in 1887, the estate passed to their heir and adopted son, Eunan, who trained at Trinity College and became a surgeon in Sligo. Eunan and his family lived at Catharmore until his death in 1921, when it passed to Eunan's eldest son, Fintan. This Fintan and his family owned it 'til Riley Conor bought it in the 1940s. Pretty derelict by that time. Anyway, turns out Eunan was quite the family man—fathered nine children.'

'Nine! How scary and good. And how wonderful it must have been to hear children laughing in that house. Who did he marry?'

At Eunan's grave, he read aloud the inscription on the adjoining stone. 'Aoife Caireann O'Leary O'Donnell.'

'Aoife!'

'A,' he said, feeling pretty happy about it himself.

'He married A! Hooray for them! An older woman!'

'By eight years.'

'And nine children!'

'Read on,' he said, wiping his eyes on his bare arm.

'Healer, Protector, Devoted Wife of Eunan, Loving Mother of Fintan Michael, Caitlin Cathleen, Kevin Barry, Ciara Aileen . . .' She read to the end. 'This is the best,' she said again. 'This is the best.'

He held the trug. She collected the remaining flowers, wrapped the stems with vine, placed them on the grave.

'You pray,' he said.

She made the sign of the cross. 'For Aoife's earnest spirit of truth, Lord, her kind heart, and her desire for the good of others, we give you thanks and praise.'

'Amen,' he said.

They stood on the grassy path for a time, holding hands, silent.

'One more,' he said.

Count fourteen stones, turn right, look left, according to Riley Conor's notes.

'You read,' he said.

'Michael Andrew Keegan of Cathair Mohr, County Sligo, died 1891. Faithful to the end.'

The Bride of the World was nowhere to be found.

At Broughadoon, they carried up the bit of lunch left for them on the worktable, and made a feeble effort to begin packing.

Cynthia gazed out the window, which was her way to jump-start the odious chore. He sighed and walked around in a state of confusion, which was his way to begin.

It was Bella at the door; Dooley was on the phone.

He felt embarrassed to have someone ever on the trot with his phone affairs. No doubt Broughadoon would be glad to see them go.

'Has he always talked that way?' Bella asked as they went along the stairs.

'Which way?'

'That sort of different, really funny way,' she said in her own different, really funny way.

He laughed. 'Always.'

'Hey, Dad.'

'Hey, yourself! What are you doing up at this hour?'

'Callin' from th' hall, couldn't sleep.'

'Anything wrong?'

'Hey, look, Dad, Lace and I are meeting you and Cynthia at the airport on Saturday.'

'I was going to give you a call. How did you know we're coming?'

'Emma called, said you'd want me to know.'

'You're driving all the way from Georgia to meet us at the airport?'

'Lace will be home for the weekend.'

'Ah. Well. Can't wait to see you. Thanks.'

'I'm, like . . . thinking of giving her a ring.'

This train was moving. 'You're sure about that?'

'I'm sure. But not . . . you know, an engagement ring.

'Right. A little early for that.'

'And not exactly a friendship ring, either. Any ideas?'

'I gave Cynthia your Grandmother Madelaine's rings, so can't say I know much about buying jewelry. However, I do know this: If you're going to give a ring, give a ring. Call Tiffany.'

'When we talked before you left, you said a little money can be a dangerous thing, I should be careful at all times.'

'In a case like this, picking the right jeweler is being careful.'

He savored the good news, but savored this nearly as much: Dooley Barlowe actually remembered something his old dad had said.

'What about them apples?' he asked Pud.

This small gazette popped out the blue in her eyes.

'A ring!'

'He's just thinking about it, he said. And not, you know, an engagement ring or anything.'

'Right. A little early for that.'

'But not exactly a friendship ring, either.'

She laughed.

Déjà vu all over again.

There was the Darling Robe slung across her open suitcase. He reckoned he would never see the end of it; she would be buried with it, as Tut with his ostrich fan.

Best to make a feeble start at his own packing.

He pulled his three-suiter from beneath the bed, stood looking at it, mindless; moved to the chest of drawers and stared at whatever lay on the surface: three American dimes, six euros, two gold cuff links, a receipt from Jack Kennedy's, her earrings, the strand of pearls, one brown sock, seven views of Ben Bulben.

He walked into the bathroom, stared at himself in the mirror, fumbled through his shaving kit, went back to the room, gazed out the window. Sunlight striking the water. Sighed, went to the cupboard to pull out his extra pair of shoes, except there was only one shoe, not a pair. He flipped up the skirts of their wing chairs and looked beneath; hunkered down and peered under the bed.

'Have you seen my other shoe?' he asked when Cynthia came back to the room with a mug of tea.

'Would this be it?'

She stood aside, and Pud trotted in, shoe in mouth.

'He was in the hall with it, chewing like a puppy.' She seemed pleased. 'Well, I mean, think of his *age*, Timothy, and still *chewing.*'

'Good grief.' He made a lunge for the shoe; Pud escaped under the bed, shoe in tow.

'Don't take it from him, darling.'

'But it's my *shoe.*'

'Yes, but it's more than a shoe to him.'

'I found his old shoe,' he said. 'I *gave* it to him, he doesn't *need* this shoe.'

The raised eyebrow.

'They're my good loafers,' he said, standing firm.

'How long have you had them?'

He threw up his hands. 'Twenty years. Twenty-five, I don't know.'

'Have you gotten your money's worth?'

He remembered his good hat blowing off in a field as he drove with the top down from Holly Springs to Memphis—he had decided not to stop and retrieve it, it was only a hat, after all.

And of course this was only a shoe, and come to think of it, he might feel a bit of pride that his old-boy loafer from Mitford had replaced the prim pump from Cavan.

He yanked up the bed skirt. '*Okay*,' he said to Pud. '*Okay*,' he said to his wife.

'Chewing a shoe,' she mused. 'Very relaxing, I should think.' She opened her side of the cupboard, stared at the contents.

'The robe,' he said, not looking in that direction. 'You're taking it home?'

'I was actually thinking of burning it.'

'Great!'

She turned her gaze on him. 'And scattering the ashes over the lough.'

'You're a drama queen, Kav'na.'

'I was just kidding about burning it.'

'I'm sure.'

'So nice and soft, the Darling Robe—soft as the wings of a moth.'

He rolled his eyes, opened what he had used as a sock drawer.

'Twenty-three years of blissful consolation, that robe . . . far too lovely to throw away, and such a deep, handy pocket—room enough for an entire sandwich—wrapped, of course. When we were living at the rectory and I worked at the yellow house, I often popped through the hedge in it, with a turkey and cheese on rye.'

The everlasting Ode to the Robe. He had lost the battle, and nothing was worth war.

'In any case, Timothy, I'm leaving it as cleaning rags for Maureen.'

She let this gazette sink in.

'And regardless of what you may think, she's thrilled and so am I. And here's the best part— a bit of something I love will be left at Broughadoon, which Maureen says will bring us back.'

'God's *blessin'* on ye!' he hollered. High-five and hallelujah.

'Would it not be a beautiful thing now if we were just coming instead of going?'

'Surely you jest.'

'I rather like being in this family.'

He stuffed his socks in a side compartment of the suitcase.

'After all,' she said, 'I never really had a family. All I saw was pushing and pulling between two people. In this case, it's pushing and pulling among lots of people.'

'I'll say.'

'Seamus is certainly glad to have this family, warts and all.'

'Righto.' Taking his shirts off the hangers.

'Look at Miss Sadie—unmarried, and all those years thinking she had no family, and right down the street, Olivia Davenport, her very own grand-niece, who thought *she* had no family. And you wanting a brother and waiting seventy years to get one. And thinking you'd never have children but then a boy shows up on your doorstep . . .'

He folded a knit shirt; she thumped into the green chair.

'It just seems that families can be very hard to come by.'

'Granted,' he said.

'And now that I've come by this one, I'll miss them.'

'There's the telephone and email and pen and paper.'

'Not the same.'

He folded another shirt. 'We can't be moving here, you know.'

'I know,' she said. 'Because then I would miss Mitford, and want to move there.'

She had gone into the bathroom when the knock came.

Liam with his hands behind his back, serious as an altar boy.

He couldn't take another catastrophe.

'For Cynthia,' Liam said, presenting a fistful of flowers. 'For puttin' up with th' Conors. There's a vase under th' sink.'

'We thank you, Liam. Very much. Any plan yet for Ibiza?'

The blue eyes, the big grin. 'Day after to-morrow.'

It was a high-five kind of day.

'Dinner will be early an' quick this evening, six-thirty. After, we'd like you and Cynthia to come with us to Cathair Mohr—if you don't mind.'

'We don't mind a bit, glad to be asked.'

'Lorna an' th' niece are off seein' castles, so no guests at th' table this evenin'. 't is a wee holiday for us, then ten cyclists comin' to take up th' slack th' day we leave.'

'Great news.'

'Tad's back a bit early; he'll join us on th' hill. Feeney's with us for dinner, says bring your prayer book, we're ecumenical this evenin'.'

He knocked on the bathroom door. 'Did you hear that? We have an invitation to Cathar-more this evening. Dinner here at six-thirty. Be there or be square.'

She came into the room and held out her hands for the flowers, happy.

'I don't know what's going on,' he said, 'but I think it's going to be good.' He had to do something with the energy that surged in from out of the blue. He picked her up, flowers and all, and swung her around a time or two like in the movies. It just felt right.

# Forty-three

'Paddy's home,' Feeney said over dinner. 'Looks like he's cleared of any suspicion.'

Liam pushing his plate away. 'Who does she want to come up?'

'She says matters are settled with Willie Donavan, she'd like to see only family and the Kav'nas and myself. And Seamus, she says, Seamus is family.'

'Am I family?' Bella asked Anna.

Liam put his arm around Bella. 'For better or for worse, kiddo.'

Tad was vested in the violet chasuble over white alb. They met in Catharmore's front hall, greeting one another after the manner of warm acquaintances.

'She says she's turned her life over to God; that you came often and prayed with her.'

'I think she was eager for you to be home.'

'I hadn't planned to come back so soon. The Holy Spirit literally yanked me home by the collar.'

'What may I do?'

'Whatever you like—pray, read a Psalm, just be here. I'd like to keep it simple, let the Spirit move. She's set on making her confession to the whole family—can't say I ever witnessed such an event.'

'She seems entirely ready to be sober, to let God have control.'

'The family are grateful, Tim, as am I. Thanks for everything.'

He grinned. 'I was all they had.'

The others lining up in the rear hall.

'I never got to the hard part with her,' he said. 'Forgiving herself.'

'Twill take time.'

They all nodded to Fletcher as she left the bedroom. Carrying a stethoscope, Feeney entered first, then Anna, Bella, Liam, Cynthia, himself, Seamus, Paddy, and Tad. Feeney stood at Evelyn's left, Tad at her right. The others formed a half circle around the bed, save for Paddy, who stood by the door, his back stiff to the wall.

Evelyn's breathing was even, her eyes closed— she might have been sleeping. The early evening light came in to them; he saw a rose in a vase on her table.

Tad made the sign of the cross. 'In the name of the Father, and of the Son, and of the Holy Spirit.' Without opening her eyes, Evelyn signed the cross with the forefinger of her right hand.

'May God, who has enlightened every heart, help us to know our sins and trust in his mercy. Amen.'

'Amen.'

Evelyn opened her eyes, looked around the room.

'I made my last confession to a Roman priest and Almighty God before I was married sixty-five years ago. I confess that immediately afterward, I waged a cruel self-determination against my husband's love of God and Church. Riley Conor was a good man, but I had taught myself to despise what was good.'

Her forefinger tapping the coverlet.

'I confess to you, Liam, my son, that you came into this world a motherless child. I have missed

the many years of knowing the kind and curious lad you were and the kind and earnest man
you've become.'

Liam broken by this, his hand over his face,
Anna's arm around him.

'I confess to you, Anna, that I was jealous of
your beauty, your thoughtful ways, and your
steadfast love of my son.'

Liam to his knees at the foot of the bed,
Anna to hers.

The room and all in it, frozen but for tears—
the loosing of regret.

'I confess to you, Bella, that I have neglected
you and bitterly judged you and your father. I
know nothing of your musical gift, which is
said to be from God. I know nothing of how
you think or what you might wish to become
in this sundered world. I pray God will allow
me time to remedy this grave oversight.'

Bella's head bowed, kneeling by her mother.

'Paddy, I confess to you that I have treated
you harshly by coddling you softly. I have
warred against your brilliant mind, and con-
signed to you the bitter role of ne'er-do-well
who cannot please me except by providing the
drink.'

Paddy's head against the wall, eyes closed,
his face wet with tears.

'I have lived a lie with all of you, even you, Seamus, whom I have treated always as a servant and not as a kind and generous man who cares for our family more dearly than we have been able to do.'

The panting. 'Water, please,' she said. Feeney took up the pitcher and poured and gave her the bent straw.

'Father O'Reilly, I confess to charging you never to speak of God to me, and though you never spoke of him, you revealed him in faithful concern for my well-being, and in honoring your promise to my departed husband. James Feeney, I confess the sin of looking without feeling upon the death of your wife, and for selfishly keeping you at a trot due to my unholy love of the drink.

'If God gives me breath, I will do all in my power to right these wrongs, and many which we've no time nor strength to name. And more than anything I would ask this of God—so newly known to me, and yet so long familiar—that I will be forgiven by him and by each of you, for these and other sins of which I truly repent.'

He and Cynthia went to their knees, as did Seamus and Feeney. Paddy stood by the door.

'God, the Father of mercies,' said Tad, 'through

the death and resurrection of his Son, has reconciled the world to himself and sent the Holy Spirit among us for the forgiveness of sins. Through the ministry of the Church, may God give you pardon and peace.

'Evelyn Aednat McGuiness Conor . . .' Tad made the sign of the cross over the penitent. 'I absolve you from your sins in the name of the Father, and of the Son, and of the Holy Spirit.'

Evelyn panting with exhaustion; Feeney stooping to her with the stethoscope. Paddy weeping yet, crucified.

The wafer, then, and the cup.

There was a bit of a fire in the front hall, where he sat with James Feeney.

'I'll be here every evening 'til things turn around,' said Feeney. 'On evenings when I'm late coming, I'll be in a meeting in a church basement near the clinic. At those times when I've something to share with the assembled, I open by saying, My name is James, and I'm an alcoholic.'

'How long sober?'

'Eleven years.'

'The other evening, you said I should keep my promise to take Cynthia to dinner. It seemed important to you.'

'It's the little things we fall behind in, we

think they can wait. I thought I'd get around to spending more time with my wife, but my work and th' drink took all my time. Then she died. And then I got sober. I cheated her, Tim.'

'Do you forgive yourself?'

'Still working on it, really, but getting there. The meetings are a lifeline for me, plain and simple.'

'Many a church basement has such a high calling,' he said.

'I hope I'm not wrong in encouraging Liam and Anna to get away. I've been on the edge about Evelyn—God knows I don't know whether she can make it. I think she can, but there are no guarantees. At the same time, if anybody ever needed a break, it's those two. And along comes th' woman with that great thatch of hair and it does look a Godsend.'

'What happened tonight seems the important thing in the end.'

'I agree. Yet it scared me to death for her. The rigor of it.'

'Vital signs?'

'Good, thank God. Thanks for all you've done, Tim.'

'And you, James. Thank you. Is she good to go, the Missus Kav'na?'

'Good to go. Keep an eye on her. Have her see her doctor as soon as you get home.'

'Will do.'

'I wanted you to know we'll get an AA meeting out to Evelyn each week.'

'How will she take to that?'

'She'll come around to it. She needs the company of others. We all do. Perhaps even Paddy will join us.'

The knot in his throat. 'You're a good man, James.'

'You'll come again, the two of you?'

'We'd like that, yes.'

He had an itch to speak to Paddy, to make contact, but Paddy wasn't about.

He went to the kitchen and had a bawl with Seamus and a laugh with Tad. Then they went home to Broughadoon and he settled their tab with Liam and knocked back a whiskey with William, who'd been badly beaten at checkers by Emily.

Their bags were down before six o'clock the next morning. Aengus arrived at six-ten. With a couple of exceptions, they were leaving with precisely what they'd brought. There had been no crazed shopping trips, no remorses, and a few euros left for their driver, who collected his hat straight off and confessed to coming in third in the dance competition.

After making a last check of their room, they stood looking out the window to the lough.

'Sorry you missed your rainbow,' he said.

'I got to see another type of covenant. Much better.'

'I hope you're not so jaded by surprise that you can't handle one more.'

'Never too jaded by surprise, darling.'

'We're not going home,' he said.

She gave him a fierce look. She was ready to go home; he had stepped in it with his bloody surprises.

'Three nights in Dublin's finest hotel,' he said, pedaling. 'In the center of the best pubs in Ireland. A room right next to the elevator. A nice car anytime we want it.' No way could he cancel another reservation. 'The high life, Kav'na, the *high* life.'

'And shops, I suppose.'

'Shops, shops, and more shops, Anna says. We must take something home to Puny and the twins, after all.'

She smiled. The sun came out in the room. 'And Sammy and Kenny and Pooh and Jessie,' she said.

'Absolutely. And we mustn't forget Louella.'

'We can't forget Louella. And Lace and Dooley, of course.'

'Of course. And Marge, who's half Irish, and Hal.'

He was flying.

The luggage was going into the boot when they heard the crunch of gravel. Paddy had walked down with Seamus and the Labs to see them off. Liam and Anna came out, and there was Bella, looking dazed with sleep, and soft, somehow, and Pud—good Lord, Pud with his old loafer, he took out his handkerchief—and William, who wasn't fond of rising before ten, here he was dressed to the nines, and Lorna and Emily in their aprons and clogs, and then Maureen, the Sunshine of Broughadoon. He kissed her on both wet cheeks and she asked if he'd got his handkerchiefs and he said he had.

He shook hands with Paddy, but no words were exchanged. There was another sort of connection, brief but somehow fluent.

They had gathered like an inn staff seen in a travel brochure, yet something more—very much more—he, saying *Dhia dhuit* because it was all he could think to say, and they saying *Dhia is Muire dhuit,* and Come again please God, and Aengus passing out a new business card citing himself as president of Malone Transport.

Then they climbed into the car and Aengus closed the doors and turned the key in the ignition, and they were waving through the rear window as the Volvo coughed its way into the lane.

There was the long bed of the lough, still sleeping in its rising mist, and the low mountains beyond seeming close enough to touch. He handed his wife the other handkerchief, and though they were watering Ireland to beat the band, he realized he was happy in some oddly excruciating way.

*Thanking:*

Joe McGowan; Tommy Gillen; Trina Vargo; Stella Mew; Cassie Swift Farrelly; Diane L. Wright; Reverend Anita Kerr; Peadar Niall Little; the Very Reverend James Ronayne, PP; John McGuinness; Andrew Higgins Wyndham; Sara Lee Barnes; Edith Currin and her lovely neighbor, Kathleen Farrelly; the managing staff of Newport House, Newport, County Mayo; Simon O'Hara of Coopershill, Riverstown, County Sligo; Paddy and Julia Foyle, Quay House, Clifden, County Galway (ask for the Napoleon Room); Cromleach Lodge and Country House Hotel, Castlebaldwin, County Sligo; Fiach O'Toole of the Garda Technical Bureau, Sligo Town; Gard Faillon; Gard Riley; the Reverend Father Dennis McAuliffe; Aoife Kavanagh, Irish Georgian Society; Mike Thacker for help in many particulars; John Diven; Karin Wittenborg, University Librarian, UVA; Paula Newcomb, friend and bridge guru; Hunter Smith; Roger Birle; Andrew

O'Shaughnessy; Chief Timothy Longo, Charlottesville City Police; Jerry and Rosalind Richardson; our U.S. ambassador to Ireland, Dan Rooney; the American Connemara Pony Society; Jessica Waldman, Questroyal Fine Art; John E. Bishop; Polly Andrews; Roualeyn Cumming-Bruce; Don and Janemarie King; Bruce and Jim Murray; Peter Sweeney; the Reverend Monsignor Chester Michael; Albert and Donna Ernest; Ashley and Steve Allen; Phyllis and Frank Joseph; the Reverend Monsignor Francis Gaeta; Barry Dean Setzer; Brenda Furman; Candace Freeland; Virginia St. Claire; R. David Craig; Randy Setzer.

Dr. Thomas R. Spitzer, Director, Bone Marrow Transplant Program, Massachusetts General Hospital; David Krese, DDS; David M. Heilbronner, MD; Joann M. Bodurtha MD, MPH; Barbara Post, MD.

Tim Short, MD; Polly Beckwith Hawkes, FNP; the Very Reverend Arfon Williams, Dean of the Cathedral Church of St. Mary the Virgin & St. John the Baptist, Sligo.

Special thanks to my editor and valued friend, Carolyn Carlson, who walked with me on the pilgrimage of this work.

*Remembering:*

Matthew and Charity Wilson, my paternal ancestors, who in 1745 emigrated from County Tyrone to Philadelphia, later settling North Carolina's Catawba Valley

Bessie Bocock Carter (1929–2008), an unforgettable model of wit and gentility, whose maternal line issued from Ballyshannon, County Donegal

Jerry Burns (1941–2010), friend and former editor of *The Blowing Rocket,* who published *At Home in Mitford* serially before its publication in book form

Vacation.

The very word has been foreign to Episcopal priest Tim Kavanagh, who has traveled across the Pond but twice. As an unreformed workaholic, he's used every excuse out there to stay put and tend his erstwhile flock in the village of Mitford.

Now retired, he's making good on an old promise to show his wife, Cynthia, the land of his Irish ancestors. Arriving at a Lough Arrow guest lodge in the midst of a torrential downpour, he soon counts this trip the reason he's loath to leave home.

An intruder startles Cynthia, resulting in painful damage to her recently fractured ankle. A valuable and cherished painting vanishes without a trace. And the shocking wound at the center of a bitterly estranged Irish family is exposed.

As three generations struggle to find deliverance from the crucifying power of secrets, Tim and Cynthia discover a journal written more than a century ago by a Philadelphia-trained Irish physician. Who knew that faded ink could be the key to unlocking a crime and revealing the truth? Or that a country parson from the States would be chosen to enter the devouring conflict between Broughadoon and Cathair Mohr?

Set against the music of Irish song and storytelling, *In the Company of Others* reminds us of our desperate need to be heard and the reconciliation that comes with confession.

**JAN KARON** is the author of the *New York Times* bestselling *Home to Holly Springs*, the first Father Tim novel, as well as the *New York Times* bestselling nine Mitford novels.

VISIT MITFORDBOOKS.COM  VISIT WWW.VPBOOKCLUB.COM

JACKET DESIGN: ROSEANNE J. SERRA
JACKET PHOTOGRAPH ILLUSTRATION: SHASTI O'LEARY SOUDANT
JACKET IMAGE OF WOMAN WALKING © MICHAEL TREVILLION/TREVILLION IMAGES
AUTHOR PHOTOGRAPH © MARK TUCKER PHOTOGRAPHY

A member of Penguin Group (USA) Inc.
375 Hudson Street, New York, N.Y. 10014
**VIKING** www.penguin.com          Printed in U.S.A.

ISBN 978-0-670-02233-5

U.S. $27.95
CAN $35.00

1010

52795

9 780670 022335

EAN